Praise for Nisha Sharma

"Nisha Sharma's *Dating Dr. Dil* is what would happen if you put all my favorite romantic comedy tropes into a blender: a frothy, snarky, hilarious treat with a gooey, heartwarming center. The perfect addition to any rom-com lover's shelf."

—Emily Henry, #1 *New York Times* bestselling author of *People We Meet on Vacation*

"Bursting with character, spicy tension, and laughs, *Dating Dr. Dil* is the enemies-to-lovers dream book!"

—Tessa Bailey, *New York Times* bestselling author of *It Happened One Summer*

"Hilarious, swoony, and oh so sexy. . . . *Dating Dr. Dil* will steal your heart. Take it from me, seeing a man utterly ruined by love has never been more satisfying!"

—Adriana Herrera, *USA Today* bestselling author

"Nisha Sharma always delights."

—Meg Cabot, *New York Times* bestselling author, on *Radha & Jai's Recipe for Romance*

"If you're ready for powerful heroines, modern alphas, and I-need-a-cold-shower levels of sizzling chemistry, look no further, because the Singhs are here to melt your e-reader."

—Sierra Simone, *USA Today* bestselling author, on *The Legal Affair*

"Nisha Sharma launches her Singh Family Trilogy with this tale of sexy boardroom dealings and untapped family secrets. . . . The sizzle of the bedroom scenes is matched by the intrigue of the boardroom, drawing you into the mystery at the novel's center as well as Hem and Mina's crackling chemistry."

—*Entertainment Weekly* on *The Takeover Effect*

DATING
DR. DIL

DATING DR. DIL

A NOVEL

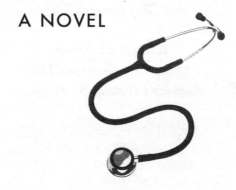

NISHA SHARMA

AVON

An Imprint of HarperCollins*Publishers*

DATING DR. DIL. Copyright © 2022 by Nisha Seesan. All rights reserved. Printed by CPI Group (UK) Ltd, Croydon. No part of this book may be used or reproduced in any manner whatsoever without written permission except in the case of brief quotations embodied in critical articles and reviews. For information, address HarperCollins Publishers, 195 Broadway, New York, NY 10007.

HarperCollins books may be purchased for educational, business, or sales promotional use. For information, please email the Special Markets Department at SPsales@harpercollins.com.

FIRST EDITION

Designed by Diahann Sturge

Stethoscope illustration © Volosovich Igor / Shutterstock.
Little House illustration © Janka Kute / Shutterstock
Old newspaper background © Here / Shutterstock

Library of Congress Cataloging-in-Publication Data has been applied for.

ISBN 978-0-06-300110-7

22 23 24 25 26   CPI   14

For the women who have been told to lower their standards.
I hope you never do.

There's small choice in rotten apples.
                    —Shakespeare, *The Taming of the Shrew*

Every apple has a little bit of bruising. It's up to you to add lemon juice and masala, so you can't taste the difference. The key is to get yourself some fruit.
                    —Mrs. W. S. Gupta, *Indians Abroad News*

DATING
DR. DIL

CHAPTER ONE

Kareena

5:45 A.M.

KAREENA: You are the reigning queen of rice! "Make your own biryani" bar? I mean it's genius. As your lawyer, I'm telling you that you have to trust me on this. You'll get the loan.

NINA: Are you sure? I'm so nervous!

KAREENA: I'm sure. I'll meet you at the bank later today.

NINA: I'm so glad I hired you and Women Who Work! You're really going to make my restaurant expansion dream a reality.

NINA: Sorry the bank had to schedule this on your thirtieth birthday, though. I can't believe you're general counsel of an incredible company at such a young age!

NINA: I mean, I was married, had my firstborn and my restaurant by thirty, but that's different. I WANTED a husband and family.

KAREENA: See you in a couple hours, Nina.

Kareena tore the eye mask off her forehead and straightened her Taylor Swift concert sleep shirt. She had secured her dream job at a company that developed women-owned businesses in the tristate area before her thirtieth birthday. But of course, one text from a client and her boss energy dissipated like mist. She tossed her phone on the rumpled bedspread and rubbed her hands over her face.

She was thirty and single.

No, no, thirty and *successful*.

Thirty and financially independent.

Thirty and . . . still lived with her dad and grandmother.

And single. Very, very single.

Without even a maintenance man to grease the plumbing.

If she had a time machine, she would've gone back to her last relationship in law school and said: *Sweetie, giving up dating until you achieve your career goals may not be the best idea. Especially if you're searching for a happily ever after with a man. It becomes way too easy to be alone.*

Kareena felt like her family, her aunties—hell, the entire New Jersey South Asian population—had been preparing her for being thirty and single, but did she listen? Nope. More importantly, did she really have to be reminded first thing in the morning?

Like T-Swizz said. Damn. It was only seven A.M.

"I should've taken today off," she mumbled as she crawled out of bed and walked toward the adjoining bathroom.

Even as she showered and mentally reviewed her schedule for the day, the misogynist adages she'd heard whispered at cultural gatherings echoed through her head.

If you're single at thirty, you have to lower your standards. If you're single at thirty, your prospects for a happily ever after are diminished.

If you're single at thirty, you are perceived as difficult, and no one will want to marry you.

Her father had never made her feel that way growing up since he had a love marriage versus arranged marriage himself. But now that her younger sister was engaged, it was like ghosts of ancestors past had taken over his body, and he had suddenly become a traditionalist.

"Beta, the oldest daughter should be at least engaged before the youngest gets married. You should date more. Or we can find you matches. Rishtas. Maybe someone will want to marry a woman so independent at your age."

His arguments, which were normally tepid, were becoming more and more frequent. It didn't help that her grandmother, Dadi, who Kareena also had a tendency to fight with on a regular basis, sided with Dad.

Dadi's arguments, however, were now paired with subtle passive-aggressive acts like cutting out a picture of Kareena's head and pasting it on the body of a bride that she tore from *Indian Matrimony Vogue Magazine*, which was then left tucked in a holy book in the temple room.

Kareena stood in front of her bathroom mirror, cringing at the memory.

Well, she was finally going to make everyone happy.

She was going to start dating again. She was ready. The list of qualities she wanted in her perfect man was ready to go. It had been waiting neglected in her notes app for far too long.

After she finished her makeup, she put on a white button-down collared shirt and a cobalt-blue sweater vest. She dropped a cute pair of floral heels in her tote bag that she'd wear when she finally got to the office.

Exactly forty-five minutes after she texted her client back, Kareena scanned her bedroom to make sure she didn't forget anything. It was the bedroom she had returned to after college. The same one her mother designed for her when her parents built the house. She had the same standing mirror, open closet, and desk shoved in one corner, with meticulously arranged framed photos with Bobbi and Veera and her law school *Bluebook*. The only major upgrade was the TV and stereo.

"Hopefully my morning will improve with food," she mumbled as she picked up her bag. It was time for birthday paranthas. The stuffed spicy flatbread was exactly what she needed to course-correct her day.

She opened her door, and instead of hearing the sizzling sounds of ghee in a hot pan, there was only silence. The delicious aroma of spices was missing. Usually, the smell of birthday paranthas permeated the house. Maybe Dadi was waiting for her?

Kareena paused in front of the framed photo of her mother that took up most of the freshly painted hallway wall. The large portrait had a string of fake marigolds tucked into the top corners, so it draped like a necklace over Neelam Mann. Her eyes were full of love, and she looked so happy.

"Miss you every day, Mom," Kareena whispered. She pressed her fingertips to her lips and to the base of the picture. "I feel you every time I take care of our house and work on your car. My car now."

After saying a quick thank-you prayer in the temple room next door, Kareena lugged her tote bag downstairs, and through the narrow hallway to the kitchen in the back of the house.

"Hello, I'm here— Oh. Um, what's going on?"

Instead of seeing Dadi in the kitchen hovering near the stove,

Kareena's grandmother and father were sitting at the dining table with bowls of cereal. Over a dozen glittery gold letter boxes sat between them. Dadi was on her large tablet, while her father was reading something on his cell phone. Neither of them spared her a glance.

"You guys are having cereal?" Kareena asked.

Dadi sat back in her velour maroon tracksuit. Her freshly dyed black hair was wet from her shower and combed back in a short severe style accentuating the happy lines around her mouth and eyes. "If you want something, you can make it yourself. I taught you how."

"Okay, but . . . well, aren't we celebrating?" Kareena responded in the same mix of Hindi, English, and Punjabi her grandmother used.

Dadi's eyebrows furrowed. Then with a look of surprise, she motioned to the gold boxes with her chai cup. "Oh this? Your sister wants us to look at invitations. She plans on personally delivering these gold boxes with scrolls in them to all her guests. You may have to help her. Her wedding is less than a year away, you know."

"Oh, I know," Kareena said. She'd known since the day her sister announced her engagement. It was right after Kareena had shared the news that she accepted a position at Women Who Work as their general counsel, which wasn't received with nearly as much excitement.

"Why are you standing like that over there?" her father asked. He sounded irritated, which was no different than how he normally sounded to her lately.

Kareena dropped her tote bag and pressed a hand to the ache in her chest. "This is a joke, right? You two couldn't have . . . I mean, I know I've been working late, and I haven't seen you for the last few days, but there is no way that you don't remember. It happens *every* year."

When her father and grandmother looked at each other, then at her, Kareena knew.

They'd forgotten.

She hadn't woken up particularly happy about her birthday, but damn it, she was really looking forward to those paranthas. And maybe even a moment that was about her. A moment that didn't revolve around her sister or her sister's wedding, or her sister's YouTube channel.

Kareena should've been angry, but after so many disappointments recently, this was expected.

"Happy thirtieth to me," she mumbled.

Her father and grandmother must've heard her because their eyes went wide.

"J-just kidding!" Dadi said, and bolted from the table. She hobbled forward, arms out for a hug. "Happy birthday, my bachcha! How could I forget my May grandbaby?" She squeezed Kareena around the waist.

Kareena patted her grandmother on the back. "It's fine, Dadi."

She met her father's eyes as he rose from his seat. He was dressed for work in khakis with a phone clip on his belt. "You don't want to celebrate today anyway," he said as he rounded the table to give her a hug. "Thirty is your first infertility milestone."

"And to think, I wanted to spend my morning with you both. Well, if there are no paranthas, I'm going to catch an earlier train into the city."

"No, no sit!" Dadi said motioning to the table. "Your sister wanted gobi paranthas today during lunch while we reviewed her wedding invitations. I'll just make them now for you."

Kareena didn't miss the double standard that existed for her sister when it came to food. "You know I hate cauliflower paranthas. Leave it, Dadi. It's fine." Damn it, what did she have to do to get that kind of treatment from people she loved?

Oh, that's right. She had to get married.

Her grandmother was already taking out the Corelle cups and plates with the cornflower blue floral design on the edges from the cabinets Kareena refaced the month before. Then came the ceramic yogurt container with homemade dahi, the mango pickle, a Tupperware container of dough, and a matching container with dry durum wheat flour.

"It's already prepared," Dadi said. "Just sit, it'll take me two minutes to make."

"Dadi, it's fine." Kareena really hated cauliflower paranthas. It was like putting garam masala on farts.

"You shouldn't be shouting at Dadi," her sister said. Bindu strode in from the mudroom with her cascade of perfect curls. They flowed around her like the loose fabric of her maxi dress. Her hooped nose ring sparkled, and her bangles clicked as she dropped a gift bag to the floor.

"Happy thirtieth birthday, big sister!"

Holy crap, her younger sister actually remembered her birthday. Kareena had to admit it was a nice surprise that she showed up at all, since Bindu spent more time with her fiancé now than anyone else.

Kareena opened her arms for a hug. Like a musical fairy, Bindu gracefully returned the gesture. That's when Kareena smelled something . . . earthy.

"Seriously, wake and bake, Bindu?" she whispered against her sister's ear.

Bindu's eyes sparkled. "Better morning sex," she whispered

back. "But don't worry, I Ubered here." She held out the birthday bag. "Happy birthday," she said loud enough for Dadi and Dad to hear. "Now why are you fighting this time?"

Kareena motioned to her father and grandmother. "They forgot my birthday."

Bindu gasped. "Seriously?"

"Have some breakfast," Dadi said, motioning with a rolling pin. "You too, Bindu."

"I'll sit. Hey, is that gobi paranthas? I thought you were going to make that for me later."

"It's for birthday paranthas!" Dadi said. Her voice had a false pep in it that no one was buying.

"Well, I guess that's okay then," Bindu said, pouting. "I'm teaching a calc class at a sister campus later today, so I should eat something heavy now to last me. Oh! I actually came here to talk to you, Daddy."

And there it was, Kareena thought. The real reason why her sister got out of bed and spent her precious time coming over to the house so early. Because she wanted something from her father. Since he was always in a better mood in the mornings, Bindu could get her family obligations out of the way and also talk to Dad at the same time.

"What is it, princess?" he said in Hindi.

Bindu flipped her long hair over one shoulder and pressed her palms together, already pleading her case. "I was thinking about having an engagement party in early September. The wedding isn't until next year, and we should really celebrate with friends and family. We can make it a big, festive event that will coincide with Loken's family's trip from Italy. Catering, DJ, open bar, all of it."

"Engagement party?" Dadi called out. She swung her spatula

around like a conductor. "Yes! What a wonderful way to celebrate Loken's family visit."

"That should be fine," Kareena's father replied, leaning back in his chair. "But I'm not paying for it."

"*Daddy.*"

"Beta, I told you that I have a set amount of money for both you and your sister. You get it as a down payment on a house, or you get it for the wedding. You've used every last cent of your share for this extravagant Italian desi wedding. And with two caterers! Because god forbid their vegetarian food is cooked with the same utensils that are used for the nonveg meals."

"Dad," Kareena chided. "Be respectful."

He waved a hand in her direction. "I have nothing against veg food, but I don't need anyone else making me feel bad about my goat meat."

"Excuse me, but this is about me," Bindu said, pouting. "It's embarrassing Loken has to chip in, but I guess we'll have to do it."

"How is it embarrassing?" Kareena asked. She took Dadi's chai cup and took a sip. "Your fiancé is from the richest Gujarati family in Italy. I'm sure that he can afford to cover something."

"Not your business, big sister," Bindu shot back. "Oh! Daddy, one more thing. If we do this engagement party in September, it's not going to interfere with your retirement plan to move to Florida, right?"

Kareena spewed chai all over the table. "What?"

"Bindu, she doesn't know yet." Her father pinched the bridge of his nose and let out a heartfelt annoyed sigh.

This had to be a joke. "You're retiring? In *Florida?*"

Kareena waited for a response, but the kitchen was pin-drop silent.

"Are you . . . are you selling the house?"

"Kareena . . ."

"Oh my god." The words were raw in Kareena's throat, like bile had burned her and she was struggling to speak.

Her family looked at one another, down at their plates, at the floor, anywhere but directly at her. Dadi turned her back and fixated on the stove.

"Please tell me you aren't going to sell Mom's house," Kareena exploded. It was a living, breathing entity that held all her favorite memories. And somewhere, between fixing pipes, changing wallpaper, adding her shed in the backyard, and replacing window treatments, the house had become hers, too.

"Dadi and Dad said you were going to be emotional about it," Bindu replied as she picked up a napkin to clean some of the chai spray that landed on the table in front of her. "And you are kind of proving them right, Kareena."

Kareena pushed back from the table, her brain racing to try to compute what was happening. "This is Mom's home. It's her dream home. She designed and built it from the ground up! *We* built it from the ground up." Kareena had even helped repair doorknobs and light fixtures in an effort to keep her mother's vision and passion alive. "Dad, why am I only finding out about this now? Why does Bindu know about it before me?"

"Beta," her father said gently. He folded his hands in front of his empty cereal bowl. "I know how close you were to your mom and how much this house means to you, too. How you thought maybe one day you'd live here. But I think it's time we all moved on. I can sell it, and then take the money and buy myself a retirement home. Your sister is moving out soon, your grandmother is thinking about moving back to India—"

"Dadi is going back to *India*?"

"Your father has worked hard almost all his life," Dadi said as she prepared a parantha. She pinched dough and rolled it into a small ball before flattening it with a slap of her palm. "It's time for him to enjoy himself. And for me to go back home."

"Dadi, you've been here for eighteen years," Kareena said. "This is your home. And Dad, this house meant a lot to you, too. I refuse to believe that you're going to sell it without talking about it with me!"

"I don't know why you're surprised," Bindu said. She scrolled on her phone as if nothing of importance was being discussed at the table. "He's been hinting about this forever. Mom isn't here anymore. He can do whatever he wants with the house. It doesn't automatically belong to you just because you painted a few walls."

Kareena pressed a palm to her breaking heart. Did no one else care their home was going to be sold off? Or at the very minimum, did no one else see how wrong it was for them to cut her so cleanly out of a major decision? She'd been the one taking care of it all while her father worked and her sister did god knows what on YouTube and her grandmother went to card parties in the afternoons.

"Your mom loved this house," her father said quietly. "But it's important for all of us to move on. And we, your sister and grandmother and I, all agree. The only reason why it hasn't fallen apart yet is because of you, but you have to move on, too."

"Sit down and drink some water," Dadi said. "You're wheezing again."

This was getting nowhere and fast. Kareena turned back to Bindu. "You're completely okay with losing our mom's home, Bindu? For real?"

Bindu shrugged. "It's just a house. Loken and I are thinking about getting a place closer to the college so it's easier for us to get to work."

Kareena pressed her palms against the table and leaned in toward her father. "Dad, you've always known that I wanted this house!"

"Which is why I didn't ask you." His eyes looked sad like they always did when he thought about Kareena's mom. "You have our old car. You can focus all your attention on fixing that, rather than trying to renovate a family home as well."

"Fine, then I'll buy it from you. Just like I bought the car from you before you tried to sell that off as well." She had savings. Her entire financial plan would go to hell, but she'd move things around if she had to. She had to at least try.

Her father leaned back and let out a laugh. He patted his round belly as if she'd told a joke instead of offering to save her childhood home. "There is no way you could afford the down payment on this house for what I'm listing it for. Especially not now with your job that pays you so little compared to what you used to be making."

His words were like a dozen tiny cuts. Dream job or not, she wasn't earning enough for parental approval, apparently. But that didn't matter right now. She had to figure out how to stop this madness. She had to stall as long as possible.

"When are you retiring?" Kareena asked.

He raised an eyebrow in her direction. "December. I'm listing it end of September." He named a figure that had her eyes go wide. Damn New Jersey housing market.

September was not nearly enough time to save for a large down payment. Kareena looked at Bindu, then at her grandmother who was eyeing her from the kitchen. Then she homed in on the gold letter boxes on the table. The answer seemed both absurd and perfect at the same time.

"The wedding money," Kareena blurted out. "You said you had

wedding money set aside for me. Why don't you give that to me now to use as a down payment for the house?"

"No way," her father said. "That money is only available to you once you're engaged. Which I've been trying to encourage you to do for the last six months."

The only people in the world who ever made her want to throw things were her family. "I don't understand why you won't just work with me here! If that money is earmarked for me, anyway, then think of it as a birthday present. You know, for the birthday you forgot?"

Her father gave her an exasperated look, as if she was the one being completely unreasonable here. "I started saving that money because your mother and I wanted to give you and your sister a wedding gift. We didn't have anything when we started our lives together, and our hope was to give you a nest egg for when you begin your future."

"News flash! I'm *thirty*. My future has already begun. I don't need to be married to have one."

"Call it tradition," he said mildly. "These are the rules. I'm not changing them. If you want the money, then you have to find your jeevansathi first."

Jeevansathi. Soul mate. Kareena wanted one in her life so badly, but actually finding her match was time consuming, and painful. That was one of the reasons why she'd pushed it off for so long.

"What an excellent idea!" Dadi said, waving a spatula in the air. "Beta, I can always reopen your Indian dating profile. You know, you can find someone in time for your sister's engagement party. Loken's family won't worry that there is something wrong with us then because the oldest daughter is still single."

Kareena had to take even breaths just so she wouldn't strangle anyone. This is what she hated the most about her family. It was as if they never listened to her, and she ended up screaming at them at the top of her lungs just to get them to pay attention. "I'm not getting engaged or married just because my younger sister is getting married! That's such an archaic practice and I expected better from both of you. And, Dadi, your matchmaking skills aren't exactly great."

She still had nightmares from the date in law school.

"Beta, it was *one* bad match, and his prison sentence was only six months. It's not like he killed someone. Just some bad checks, no?"

"Oh, that makes it so much better." Kareena waved a hand at all three individuals staring at her. "I want a freaking love marriage. Hearts, flowers, the works. Someone who understands me and doesn't make me lose my ever-loving mind."

"I think you know that people don't like your abrasive personality," Bindu said. "That's why you'd rather listen to Taylor Swift under a weighted blanket and drink chai while reading romance novels than go out and meet people."

"Hey, asshole, I've been *working*," Kareena snapped.

"Language, Kareena!" her father and grandmother shouted at the same time.

"Whatever. I was planning on dipping my toes back into the dating world to search for Mr. Perfect. If that's what it takes to get the money for the house, then fine. I'll get married. But it will be a love marriage." Her skin itched at the very idea, like her food allergy was acting up, but desperate times.

Dadi snorted. "Even I know that it's not as easy as you think it will be," she said in Hindi. "Bindu is right about your attitude, beta. And things are different for you kids now. Everyone is so picky."

"And attitude or not, love sometimes takes time," Kareena's

father added. "I know you've always wanted this house, but I have to do what's best for me, too."

Out of everything she expected to happen on her thirtieth birthday, this was definitely not it. Her mother was in every beam, every stud, every original nail that built the home, and Kareena couldn't lose it. Because once it was gone, it wouldn't just be her mother. It would be a part of her soul, too.

"It'll be fine," Dadi said in Hindi as she crossed the kitchen to put the stack of paranthas in the center of the table. "Now. Why don't you eat? I'll drive you to the station."

"The car!" Kareena burst out. She'd completely forgotten. "Where am I going to keep it?"

"Maybe you can sell that junker for parts," Bindu murmured as she scrolled through her phone. "It's so old."

Kareena didn't even bother rewarding her sister with a response. Her car was rare enough that if she did sell it, she'd probably make enough to supplement the savings she'd had for the house. But the special restoration project on her 1988 BMW E30 M3 was her pride and joy. It was a symbol of how far she'd come since she lost her mom.

"Now enough of this talk," Dadi said. "Sit and have some food so you can calm down before going to work."

Kareena had completely lost her appetite. She picked up her tote bag and slung it over one shoulder. "I have to go."

"Wait!" Bindu said. She ran over to the bag she'd carried in with her and held it up for Kareena. "Two things. First, I'm taking Dadi's car to an interview tomorrow. It's with a local TV show. They're talking about dating, and I need someone to drive me so I can prep my notes and makeup and things like that on the way. Will you do it?"

"Uh, yeah, sure. Whatever." She would have agreed to anything at that moment to make her escape.

"Great! Second, I got you a gift."

"Bindu, I'm really in a terrible place right now. I'll open it when I get home tonight."

"No, open it now!" Bindu said. "It'll make you feel better. I promise."

Kareena eyed the bag. The last time her sister had brought her a gift, it was homemade brownies that made her so paranoid, she had to have her friends spend the night to convince her that aliens with Mumbai accents weren't going to abduct her in her sleep and take her to an ice planet.

"Thank you," she mumbled as she opened the bag and pushed aside the tissue paper. She was praying for a wad of cash but that was doubtful.

It took Kareena a moment to realize what was inside. The white box was labeled *Asian Sensation* and pictured a large, tan colored, U-shaped vibrator. It was a modern design that didn't look like a penis. Quote bubbles read "waterproof" and "rechargeable."

"Bindu, please tell me this is not a—"

"Yup!" Bindu said. She tossed her hair back and let out a screeching laugh. "You're always so uptight, so I knew this would be the perfect gift."

"What? What is it?" Dadi asked. She hurried over from the table.

"You know," Kareena said as she pushed the tissue paper back in place to cover the brown sex toy. "One day I may find this hilarious. Today is not that day."

Bindu doubled over, wheezing.

Without a second thought, Kareena passed it to her grandmother. "Why don't you take this, Dadi? Bindu knows it's not my style. Bindu, you're going to tell her what it is, right?"

Bindu's face went sheet white.

Kareena shoved her glasses up her nose and turned to leave the kitchen. "I hope all of you realize how truly shitty you all are acting right now."

Her father's expression turned thunderous. Her grandmother looked appalled at her language, and her sister was still pale now that Dadi was holding the vibrator gift.

Kareena strolled out of the house and started walking toward the train station before anyone could say another word to her. "Happy thirtieth birthday to me," she said in a tear-soaked voice. "Happy fucking thirtieth birthday to me."

Dear Readers,

It's important to remember that your single children are born in a generation that is different from yours. To start, you must first learn why your children are against marriage. It is then your responsibility to convince them that they are wrong.

Mrs. W. S. Gupta
Columnist
Avon, NJ

CHAPTER 2

Kareena

Aunty WhatsApp Group

> **FARAH AUNTY:** Happy birthday, darling!

> **FALGUNI AUNTY:** Happy birthday, sweetheart. Your mother would be so proud of you and all you accomplished.

> **MONA AUNTY:** I have money for you, beta!

> **SONALI AUNTY:** ::religious birthday meme::

> **SONALI AUNTY:** ::religious birthday meme::

> **SONALI AUNTY:** ::religious birthday meme::

"I have no idea what I'm going to do," Kareena said as she took another sip of her drink. "You guys know how important that house is to me. To my mom."

"Here, let me call for another cocktail," Veera said. Kareena watched as her friend gracefully lifted a hand and grabbed a server's attention.

Phataka Grill, the brand-new restaurant right in the middle of

Jersey City, was a charming throwback to an old-fashioned Indian canteen. Bollywood movie posters hung haphazardly on exposed brick walls, and the chairs were painted bright colors with aluminum backing. Sexy seventies Bollywood remixes were barely audible over the sound of conversation from packed tables. It was the perfect place to get inebriated.

"Thanks," Kareena said as freshly made drinks were placed in front of them. "I need this. And you two."

"I still think that you should've let me throw you a party to help get your mind off things," Bobbi said, swirling her lychee martini. "We could've rented a limo to take us into the city where we would sweat our asses off dancing at a club, then hook up with sexy men we regret in the morning. Oh! And cupcakes. Cupcakes after dancing and hookups."

"I'm just not in the mood, guys."

"The last time we went was what, five years ago?" Bobbi asked. "Right before your dating moratorium. God, does your waxer find cobwebs in your coochie?"

Kareena threw a napkin at her best friend. "Oh, shut up. You work more than I do, and I don't see you getting regular checks for your *jalebi.*"

Their server arrived with plates piled high with biryani, butter chicken, veggie tandoori platters, and naan. "Here you go, ladies," he said, his New Delhi accent as thick as his full head of curling black hair. "Let me know if you need more drinks."

Kareena began piling food on her plate after the server left. Hopefully it tasted as good as it looked. She was starving since she hadn't gotten a chance to eat all day. That along with her restless sleep meant she was eternally irritated.

Bobbi leaned across the table, her cleavage on display. "You would've had such a kick-ass thirtieth that your mom would be calling in from her next life to join in, and then give you advice on how to keep the house."

Kareena snorted. "I doubt that. Besides, most of our mutuals wouldn't show up. Everyone we know is either in a long-term relationship, engaged, newly married, or popping out children. Do you think they want to celebrate a single friend turning thirty? Their calendars are filled with cake tastings or mommy playdates. If they do, by some miracle, have an opening in their schedule, they'll end up judging me and saying things like 'you'll know when you find the right one,' or 'you're so lucky to be single without responsibilities.'"

Veera squeezed Kareena's arm. "Don't be like that. I'm sure everyone would've come to support you. Thirty is a big deal."

"But only because we make it that way," Kareena said.

Her best friends, the same ones she'd met during freshman orientation at Rutgers, the only other Punjabi girls in her seminar classes, watched her, patiently waiting for her to adjust her glasses, step up on her proverbial soapbox, and explain.

"At thirty, people have all these expectations of how many life milestones I should've achieved, but how can I do any of those things when I don't have enough money to buy my mother's home, my car is still in a shed in my backyard, and trying to find true love makes me nauseous? Even though that's what I want. And in the past few months, that's all I've been able to think about."

Veera and Bobbi glanced at each other then back at Kareena.

"What do you mean?" Veera asked. "You've been thinking about true love? Like . . . dating?"

Kareena nodded. "I have the job I want. Now it's time to get the family I want."

"Girl, sometimes, life doesn't go according to your spreadsheets and timelines," Bobbi said. "Finding love may take some time."

"Which I don't have," Kareena said.

"Wait, you said your dad has the money, right?" Veera asked. "Are you going to . . ."

"Try to find a guy in time to get engaged and ask for my dad's wedding gift to pay off the house?" Kareena downed the rest of her drink. "That's the idea." She'd been thinking about it all day. Even if she put less than 20 percent down for the mortgage, she wouldn't be able to afford the house. It was in a prime location and way out of her price range. Getting married was the only option she had.

"I thought you wanted hearts, flowers, and romance," Veera said. "Please tell me you're not giving that up."

Kareena shook her head. "I'm making one promise to myself in this whole mess. I have to fall in love with this person before I commit to marry him. I want heart eyes, and racing pulse. Romantic gestures, and conversations about forever. I want all of it. He'll be my jeevansathi even though our falling-in-love journey will be a little shorter than expected."

"Jeevansathi," Veera said. Her expression became dreamy, and she clasped her hands together. "That word is so romantic isn't it? Life partner. For someone who puts up quite a shield, it won't be easy, Kareena."

"Like a needle in a fucking haystack," Bobbi added bitterly.

"Oh, I know. My dad hinted at the same thing. And there is a good chance I won't win. But I have to try. For my mom." *And for myself,* Kareena thought. The house meant so much to her, but it would be meaningless if she had an arranged marriage that was built on compromise only. She didn't want her life partner to be practical. She wanted him to be . . . well, she had a list.

"Where are you going to find these guys?" Veera asked. She grabbed a naan and began tearing it into small pieces.

"I think online is my only choice, to be honest."

"Online can work, but consider other dating options," Veera said. "People treat online dating profiles like they're shopping on Amazon Prime, and it can burn you out emotionally."

"Did you know Indians are doing singles cruises now?" Bobbi said with a grin. "And the *moms* go with their kids."

"Yeah, I'm not going to do that," Kareena said. "I have a short list of websites, and if I can't find someone that way, then I may try a professional matchmaker or something."

Bobbi and Veera glanced at each other.

"What?" Kareena snapped.

"Honey," Veera said softly. "There may be one option you haven't thought about."

"The devil works hard, but desi aunties work harder," Bobbi said.

Kareena volleyed between her best friends, and she saw the truth written all over their faces. The thought was so ludicrous that she almost bolted from her chair. "Absolutely fucking not!" she burst out. "The aunties are like loose cannons. Involving them would be *disastrous*. Besides, I want true love, not a clinically arranged match."

"Your aunties are fierce," Bobbi said. "They are your mom's best friends and if anything, they'll be as picky as, if not worse than, you. They know that they'll have to find someone who is your true love."

"They bring along so much drama!" Kareena's brain played back a kaleidoscope of memories. There was Mona Aunty, who dressed up like she was going to a movie premiere every day. She always had gold rings on her fingers and a perfect blowout. Then there was Sonali Aunty who was the most religious of the group. She often used her beliefs as an excuse to say the most ridiculous things. Falguni Aunty was constantly feeding everyone. She'd show up in kurta tops and Crocs and say that everything was going to be okay. And last there was Farah Aunty, the retired software engineer from IBM who knew a little too much about internet stalking.

Together they were dangerous. Kareena remembered the time Farah Aunty burst into her school to verbally destroy her English teacher who refused to pronounce her name correctly. And when Mona Aunty took her to get her first Brazilian and insisted on being within earshot to make sure the waxer was doing a good job. Kareena still had nightmares about Sonali Aunty's religious studies sessions, and Falguni Aunty's cooking classes.

"Your aunties will be able to sniff out a man with your quali-fications within weeks, which gives you time to date and get to know him," Bobbi said. "And they know how much a love mar-riage means to you."

"They're *exhausting*."

"No, they're progressive," Veera said. "They'll help you keep your mom's house. They had memories with your mom, too."

Their server arrived just in time with chai shots in authentic clay kulhars with heaping bowls of ice cream. He took away some of the empty plates and left as quickly as he came.

Kareena reached for one of the kulhars and tossed it back. She couldn't even taste the alcohol at this point with all the nervous anxiety rushing through her bloodstream.

There was so much that could go wrong if she involved the aunties. The worst being that she disappointed them. No. That wasn't it. The worst would be if her person rejected her.

Because then the aunties would kill that person and she'd be bailing them all out of jail.

Kareena pushed her plate out of the way and banged her forehead against the table in front of her. "I want to start slowly. I think I'll just do the online dating first. Just for a week or two. And then, maybe, I'll ask them for their help if that doesn't work."

"You need a monetary gift," Veera said. "There is literally no other way you can get this house in such a short time frame. As your financial advisor, believe me. I know. But is this really how you want to go about getting it?"

"I'm open to other suggestions." Kareena reached out for another shot.

"The aunties it is," Bobbi said. "They are better than the NSA. They could get in touch with every eligible bachelor from here to the West Coast. And probably in Canada, too."

Their words were a painful truth that Kareena hated hearing but knew was correct. "Fine, I'll think about it."

A chime interrupted them, and Bobbi reached in her bag to get her phone. She looked at her screen and gasped. "Son of a bitch."

"What happened?" Kareena asked.

Bobbi grabbed her drink and chugged it before she turned to Kareena. "My cousin is doing a wedding in Parsippany, and she needs me to come out there to help her. Apparently the Bollywood dancers they'd hired to perform at the sangeet are a bunch of strippers who *dance* to Bollywood. They started taking their clothes off, and the grandfather had a heart attack."

No wonder Bobbi wasn't pressed to find a man, Kareena thought. Her life was so full of drama and weddings that she practically lived out the stress between couples every day.

"Okay, let me get the check and we can all go," Kareena said.

Bobbi was already on her feet, waving at her to stay seated. "I already put my card on file. Just sign for it when you're done. Have another few drinks on me."

"How are you going to get out there?" Veera asked. "Train or car?"

"Whatever I can get," Bobbi replied.

Veera stood. "My car is parked around the corner. I can take you. I'm still completely sober. Kareena, are you up for a drive?"

"I can't," Kareena said. "I'm in the opposite direction. You two go. I'll be fine on my own."

Veera leaned down and hugged her. "Come back to Jersey City tomorrow then. We'll watch movies and get really drunk on boxed wine."

Kareena hugged her back. "I'll let you know. I want to put in shelves in the laundry room tomorrow and I still have to work on the car."

Bobbi hugged her next, then whispered in her ear, "Maybe you should reconsider having that fun hookup at the bar tonight to celebrate your thirtieth. You can start looking for your forever life partner in the morning."

Kareena snorted. "Yeah, like that's going to happen. The hookup, I mean. Text me details about the strippers."

"I'll take pictures."

After her friends left in a flurry of chatter and energy, she was left alone at the circular table with empty dishes and half-finished glasses spread out in front of her.

"A fitting ending for the day," she said. It had truly been shitty between her forgotten birthday and the news of her father's retirement. Despite her friends' advice, she was going home alone. Finding a hookup sounded exhausting.

She checked the time and realized that her train wouldn't leave for another forty-five minutes. Kareena grabbed her bag and headed over to the crowded bar at the center of the restaurant. She'd have one drink by herself and go home and try to get some sleep. Then in the morning, she'd think about what she had to do to save her mother's house.

After waiting for a few minutes, she found a spot between a group of older desi men and a couple on a date. She raised her hand to get the bartender's attention, and after he acknowledged her with a brief tilt of his chin, Kareena turned around to people-watch until she could put in her drink order. That's when she saw the man sitting at a table across the room.

Well, shit.

CHAPTER THREE

Prem

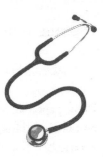

MOM: Today is the three-year anniversary of Gori's death, Prem. It's been too long. Being single is for white people. You need to stop it.

PREM: How many times have we talked about this? You can't SAY things like that.

MOM: Well, I don't care what other idiots say. I know it's true for my baby. You've mourned Gori long enough. It's time to get married.

PREM: I'm focusing on building my clinic.

MOM: Yes, I know, when you could be a surgeon and married by now. Prem, if you get engaged this year so I can plan a wedding next year, I'll pay you.

PREM: What?? Are you serious?

MOM: Yes.

PREM: . . . How much?

MOM: A lot.

Prem gaped at the most recent text he received from his mother and pocketed his phone. "My mother just offered to pay me to get married."

"It's the way of the modern arranged match," Bunty said. Benjamin Padda, childhood best friend, restaurateur, and chef, motioned for one of his staff and held up two fingers. "I know my mother is breathing down my neck, too. No matter how much we succeed, some cultural beliefs last forever."

"Isn't that the truth," Prem muttered. He never understood how his parents could be so desperate to get him married. He was a product of a relationship based on hormones and an intense emotional reaction from the midbrain. His parents claimed they had a "love marriage" when they rarely showed any sort of affection toward each other. Which only proved that emotions fade, and with that, all common sense.

It didn't seem to matter how Prem got married, just that he would. The promise of a great wedding, grandkids, and yes, seeing their son settled was probably why his mom was pushing old stereotypes.

There was also the aggressive need to see him move on from Gori. It appeared that his mother was convinced Prem had grieved enough.

"Thanks for treating me today, man," Prem said. "I appreciate it."

"I couldn't bear to see you sulk by yourself," Bunty replied. He held up his tumbler in toast. "To Gori. May her next life be filled with love from a man better than you."

Prem gave him the finger, then tipped back his glass. Over the rim, a flash of sweater vest, rectangular glasses, and pouty lips had him pausing.

Then he promptly choked.

Well, shit.

"What? What is it?" Bunty asked.

Prem could see her intensely beautiful face clearly from a short distance.

Wow.

Her shoulders were slumped, and that full curved mouth was set in a glossy pout. She'd piled that thick black hair on top of her head in a messy ponytail, and the glasses did nothing to hide her large brown eyes. Her prim and proper outfit was somehow sensual as her sweater vest clung to the swell of her breasts.

"What? What are you staring at?"

Prem cleared his throat and pounded a fist against his chest. "Uh, nothing." Prem's interest turned to amusement when the sexy librarian looked right at him. Her eyes widened. *Hello, there. Yeah, same here.*

Bunty turned back in his seat and rolled his shoulders as if he was trying to find a comfortable position in his suit coat. He was probably going to fidget all night, Prem mused. The guy was six four and almost three hundred pounds of muscle. In all the years he'd worked as a restaurateur, investor, and chef, he'd never been comfortable in a suit, no matter how great it fit.

"Do you want to send a drink over or something or are you going to continue to eye-fuck each other?"

"That's so crude, man."

"I call it like it is. But seriously, I'll tell my bartender to get her something. It'll be super undercover."

He finally glanced back at Bunty. "I know this is your restaurant. You don't have to flex."

"That's all I got," Bunty said ruefully. "That, or I'm the son of Naan King, the frozen Naan empire, and being an award-winning chef suits me better."

Prem grinned. Bunty would always be the Naan prince to him. Ever since they were kids in SoCal, his best friend would wear his title like a straitjacket instead of a letterman's coat.

Bunty picked up his whiskey tumbler and swirled the amber liquid. "Listen, if you're interested in a woman, which you haven't been for three years, at least go talk to her."

Prem glanced at the sexy librarian one more time. She was trying to pretend that he wasn't there and nursed what looked like a mojito from one hand while scrolling on her phone with the other. Someone was going to approach her soon. He had no doubt about it.

"I can't," he finally said to Bunty. "I have a meeting with a potential investor after my talk show tomorrow, which means I have to go home early and prep."

"Don't you usually do your talk shows on Sundays?" Bunty asked.

"Usually, but I'm interviewing this high-maintenance influencer from the area, and she asked that we change the date and time of the taping because she's planning her wedding or something. The producers wanted me to accommodate because she has a pretty big following."

"That's annoying as shit. I can see why you have to prep for her, but don't worry about prepping for your investor pitch. You've been working at this for years now."

"I'm too close to take chances," Prem said. "The office that I want to buy is finally on the market."

"Oh yeah? You get your name on the list?"

"I did." Prem thought about the perfect location for his health clinic in downtown Jersey City. The accessibility routes. The parking that was almost unheard of in that location. "I have to have the full deposit ready to go in four months to close on it, though."

"Do you have a lot left to raise?"

"Not much after the bank, you and Deepak, my own funds, and Gregory at LTD Financial." Prem named a figure that had Bunty nodding.

"I wish I could give you more, but I'm tied up until I can finish my expansion plans on the East Coast."

"Don't even worry about it," Prem said. "You and Deepak have already invested enough. Like I said. I'm close. After years of planning, my center can finally open its doors."

It was almost surreal to say those words. He'd been focused on his goal for three years, ever since Gori's death.

Because of her death.

He was already connecting with his network of physicians to bring in specialists who were as passionate as he was about caring for the South Asian immigrant community. Word was getting out, and the support was immense.

All thanks to *The Dr. Dil Show*. He hated being a TV personality for a local South Asian television network, but he'd done it purely for the exposure and the connections. What started out as a ten-minute spotlight turned into a half-hour live talk show where Prem discussed hot topics affecting the South Asian community with guest speakers. Thankfully, the show set up the speakers and the topics, and all he had to do was approve of each agenda, stick to the script, and show up on time, but the impact on his professional career was huge.

He'd never be the surgeon his parents wanted him to be, but he was going to make a difference. And he'd be happy.

"What are you going to do with your mom?" Bunty asked. "Between your job at that cardiology center, and your TV show, you are already strapped for time."

Prem gave him the finger. "Don't start on me."

"I'm just stating the obvious," Bunty said with a laugh. "The cardiologist who believes that love isn't a necessary emotion for a partnership."

"It's backed by science, asshole. That's what made Gori and me a great match before she died. That's why a large percentage of South Asian immigrants today actually pursue an arranged match like their immigrant parents."

"Are you sure it's not because our parents raised a bunch of anxious overachievers?" Bunty asked.

"*Practical* overachievers. Look, people who think that love can sustain a relationship believe in a toxic emotion that doesn't last. Love makes people depressed, insecure, and sometimes isolated, which affects heart health, as well as the midbrain and frontal cortex. It's like a chocolate craving that releases dopamine. Too much is bad for the body, and bad for our emotions."

Bunty grunted. "Fuck you, chocolate is never bad."

"My point is love has absolutely nothing to do with a happy relationship. Communication, mutual respect, physical intimacy. Complementary goals and ambitions."

Prem looked over at the bar and locked eyes with Sexy Librarian again. She was trying superhard to ignore him, and the feeling was mutual.

Bunty laughed. "Dude, I can't sit here and watch you with a woman for another hour. Get yourself together and go talk to her. I'm sure you remember how. I'm going to go check on my kitchen." With those parting words, he stood, and crossed the restaurant toward the double doors in the back.

Sexy Librarian watched Bunty go, and then she glanced in Prem's direction before looking down at her phone again.

What the hell, he thought as he stood. He could review his notes for his show later. His pulse beat just a little faster than normal as he wove through tables and approached the bar. Bunty was right when he said that it had been a long time since he'd approached a woman. But like his mother reminded him, Gori had been gone for a while. He'd barely allowed himself the time and space for relationships since. Not to say that this would be anything serious, but what was the harm in trying?

Prem grinned when the sexy sweater vest librarian woman looked up and did a double take at his approach. She turned left to right, eyes widening.

"Hi," he said when he stood inches away from her. "I'm Prem."

"H-hi," she said. "I'm, uh . . . Rina."

They stared at each other for a moment longer before she motioned to his drink.

"Want another drink?"

He looked down at his club soda. "Sure," he said. One was his limit when he was on call, and he hadn't reached that point yet. "I'd love to buy you one as well."

She looked at her glass that was two-thirds filled, and then, in a move that both shocked and delighted him, chugged the rest of it and placed the empty glass on the bar top. "Yeah," she said after swallowing. "I'd like that."

Prem motioned to the bartender, then leaned in close. Sandalwood and vanilla. The heady combination was intoxicating. "Rina, what do you do?"

"I . . . help women build businesses," she said vaguely.

I'm going to want to know more than that, Rina. I'll want to know everything about you.

"Do you enjoy it?"

Her eyebrows winged in surprise. "Yeah, I do. It's my dream job. What about you? What do you do?"

"I . . ." *Don't say doctor,* he thought. Sometimes, Indian women either avoided single Indian doctors like the plague, or immediately saw diamond rings. As pompous as that generalization sounded, he didn't want to take the chance in ending this conversation too soon. "I fix broken hearts," he finally said, then flashed her his most charming smile. "And I'm very, *very* good at my job."

She leaned in closer, and even though he towered over her in her heels, she was close enough that Prem could swear the noise around them drowned out.

"Tell me more," she said. "Can you fix someone like me?"

He lifted a hand, waited to see her eyes darken with interest, then brushed a wavy lock of hair off her face. Her shiver was like an electric bolt to his chest. "Absolutely," he said.

CHAPTER FOUR

Kareena

Three Hours Later . . .

"I want to touch you," he whispered against her neck.

Kareena felt like her bones were melting as his big hands ran over her back and under her sweater vest. She should be appalled at herself for following a stranger into a back room, but Prem didn't feel like a stranger. He felt . . . perfect. After hours of nonstop conversation, she felt like she knew him better than her best friends. And that he knew all the secret parts of her.

She gasped when his lips traced the line of her neck and his teeth sunk in the curve before her shoulder.

"Oh god," she whispered, clawing into his shirt. She was actually doing this. For the first time in her thirty years, she was making out with a stranger at a bar, and it felt empowering. Delicious. Hot as hell. Why didn't she ever try this before?

Probably because she'd never met the right guy.

She groaned when his mouth returned to hers, and he commanded her lips like a general commanded an army.

"More," she whispered into the kiss when he pressed her firmly against the wall of the dark office. "More."

His hand fumbled before gripping the hem of her sweater vest. She saw a flash of his determined expression before the sweater vest came up and over her face.

"Ouch!" she yelped. The fabric of her vest caught on her earring and a sharp pain immediately had her pulling back. Her arms were straight up in the air, and because the vest was snug, she was wrapped up like a spring roll. A wave of embarrassment hosed over her desire.

"Oh my god," he said. "What is it? Are you hurt?"

There was another painful tug, and she winced. "I wore earrings today for the first time in a while, and I think one is caught on my clothes." Of course, something like this could only happen to her. She sputtered when she got a mouthful of high-quality knit fabric again.

"Here, let me—"

There was a distinctive cell phone ringtone, and then a muffled curse. Before Kareena could ask him what the holdup was, she heard sound of footsteps then the office door opening and closing.

"Uh . . . Prem? Hello? Are you . . . are you there? Oh my god."

Twelve Hours Later . . .

Aunty WhatsApp Group

MONA AUNTY: Darling, your grandmother told us about your father's retirement.

FARAH AUNTY: If we had the money, we would give it to you for the house for sure.

SONALI AUNTY: We'll do pooja for you.

FALGUNI AUNTY: Now is an excellent time to get married! For the money, of course. We can help you.

KAREENA: Uh, thanks, aunties, but I think I'm going to search on my own first.

FALGUNI AUNTY: Well, at least send us your information so we can put together a biodata. Your height, occupation, allergies, blood type, interests, and preferences. Just in case.

KAREENA: Okay, maybe after I recover from this hangover.

MONA AUNTY: Pedialyte, darling. Drink some Pedialyte and eat roti with ghee. You'll be fine.

KAREENA: . . . I'm not getting out of this matchmaking scheme you're all thinking about, am I?

SONALI AUNTY: Nope.

MONA AUNTY: Nope.

FALGUNI AUNTY: Nope.

FARAH AUNTY: Nope.

KAREENA: Damn it.

Kareena pressed the cold bottle of Pedialyte to her forehead.

"You're supposed to drink it, not hold it," Bindu hissed. "You look absolutely ridiculous."

Kareena glanced up at the bustling Jersey City TV studio. It

was smaller than she expected it to be and filled with South Asian
camerapersons, assistants, producers, and directors all bumping
into one another. To think this was what her math professor-
turned-content-creator sister wanted to do on a Saturday after-
noon.

It could've been more interesting if she wasn't nursing the
worst headache.

"Can't you at least *pretend* to look sober?" Bindu whispered.
"The makeup helps, but people can hear you groaning."

"Shut up, Bindu."

Kareena closed her eyes and leaned her elbows on her knees.
It was as if she turned thirty and she couldn't handle her alcohol
anymore. She wanted to stretch out and get a hold of the pin-
pricks behind her eyeballs but the aluminum benches she was told
to sit on were not conducive for relaxing.

"Kareena—"

"Bindu, if you're about to lecture me, stop right now. You're
lucky I drove you out here as a favor, when I would rather be at
home, in my shed in the backyard, nursing my hangover."

Bindu's nose crinkled. "Why would you want to be in your
shed?"

"Because after hours of feeling like shit, and the aunties blow-
ing up my phone, all I want to do is hide, rebuild my rear axle,
install it on the frame, and then change all the outlets in the
house."

"You're so weird." Bindu smiled as one of the producers walked
by, talking into her headset. "How are you going to find a man in
four months, even with the aunties' help, if you're going to spend
all your time covered in grease or working?"

*I found one last night, even though he was a total douche and left
me stranded.*

"Stop pushing my buttons," Kareena said, and gingerly uncapped her Pedialyte for another gulp. "God, this is disgusting."

Bindu sniffed and made a gagging sound. "Reeks, too. Well, it serves you right. Especially after you put me in that position with your birthday gift."

Kareena glared at her sister. "You deserve it for trying to embarrass me first."

"I thought it would be funny."

"Well, it wasn't. Especially after Dad told me he was getting rid of Mom's *house*."

Bindu rolled her eyes. "I don't get why you're so obsessed with the house."

"To each her own."

Even though Bindu had been young when their mom died, she was more like their father anyway. She didn't see the house as their mother's legacy. As Kareena's legacy.

Kareena waited for someone with a long back wire to walk past them. "How long is this going to take? I want to go home."

"An hour tops." Bindu checked the time on her phone, then reached into her purse and pulled out a tripod. She began deftly unfolding it, until it stood about five feet tall. She pulled out her cell phone and attached it to the clip at the top. "There. Now while you help me livestream on my channel today, hopefully you'll learn something about dating and finding your true love."

"What is that supposed to mean?"

Bindu smirked at her. "I mean you need all the help you can get—"

"You keep insulting me, you can forget getting my help ever again."

Bindu held up her hands in surrender. "All I'm saying is that you're going to need to take some advice if you want to find love like Mom and Dad had."

Kareena looked down at her maroon sweater vest and adjusted her glasses. "And who exactly am I supposed to take advice from?"

"Dr. Dil, of course. And me."

Before she could ask who Dr. Dil was, a woman with dark kohl-lined eyes, a hoop nose ring, and audio equipment in one hand stopped in front of Bindu. "Bindu Mann, right? From the YouTube channel *Mann Your Business*?"

"Yes, that's me!"

"Cute name. I need to mike you up. Once you're ready to go, then you'll wait here. Dr. Verma will call you."

"Great!" Bindu stood and let the woman clip the receiver to her waist and explain how the mic system worked.

"It's still okay to livestream my segment on my YouTube channel, right?"

"Of course. When Dr. Verma calls you to the stage, you can just step up onto the platform from here, and your uh . . ."

"Assistant," Bindu said. "She'll be here to record, yes."

"Great. We're starting in less than a minute, and you're the first guest, so stay ready." The woman eyed Kareena's Pedialyte bottle and turned to leave.

"Assistant?" Kareena said. She'd be more offended if her head didn't ache so much.

"Every major influencer has one," Bindu said as she sat back down. "I didn't want to seem like an amateur. Just go along with it." She waved a hand in dismissal, and her row of bangles clanged musically.

"Whatever," Kareena said. She couldn't wait for this to be over so she could go home. Her stomach roiled, and she groaned again.

The overhead lights dimmed, and various members of the cast began calling out time, and camera positions. The circular platform in the center of the studio lit up, focusing on two red high-back chairs angled toward each other. The screen behind the chairs said *The Dr. Dil Show: Focusing on the Holistic Health of the Heart*.

"What garbage show are you making me sit through?" Kareena mumbled.

Bindu shushed her. "I'm starting to record on my phone. Now watch and be quiet." She repositioned her cell in the tripod and tapped a few buttons on the screen. The red record button appeared in the corner.

A woman's voice filtered through the speakers with a heavily Mumbai-accented voice. "Welcome to the Jersey City South Asians News Network and a very special Saturday episode of *The Dr. Dil Show!*"

Fake applause ricocheted through the studio speakers.

"Please welcome Dr. Prem Verma, our very own Dr. Dil!"

Prem?

Kareena's shoulders went ramrod straight when Dr. Dil appeared from behind the set backdrop.

Oh no.

She could've sworn she heard doom music as she took him all in. Dr. Dil was tall, lean, and broad chested. His suit fit him like a glove, and when he adjusted the cuffs of his sleeve, she had to remember to breathe.

And damn, that jaw. That really fantastic angular jaw.

That *familiar* jaw that she had kissed and touched just the night before.

Her failed hookup from the restaurant, Prem Verma, was

Dr. Dil. What's worse, this confirmed that he was an official desi fuckboy.

Desi fuckboy. Definition: a gorgeous brown snack of a man with a dream body, a pedigree that would make a traditional aunty sell her soul for a marriage rishta, and the ability to use charm and influence to make her regret all her life decisions. Like leaving a crowded bar with him so they could make out in someone's office.

"This is the worst thing that has ever happened to me," Kareena whispered.

"It's just for an hour," Bindu said. She leaned back and scanned Kareena's face. "Are you okay? You look like you're going to be sick."

"I just may," she whispered. With all the Indians in the state of New Jersey, why did she have to run into the same one for a second time in one weekend?

Kareena's pulse jumped when he turned to her direction. She knew the moment he spotted her. Prem's eyes widened like saucers, and his mouth fell open.

Yeah, I'm as surprised as you are. This wouldn't have happened if you told me that you were actually a talk-show host.

She looked down at the Pedialyte in her hand and immediately tucked it between her ankles. This man could not know that she spent the rest of her night drinking because of him. She had her pride.

Despite the humiliation he put her through, the embarrassment that would plague her forever, Kareena was not going to look like a coward. He was the one who screwed up and left her in an awkward position! What gentleman did something like that?

The studio's fake applause quieted to a whisper. Then, Dr. Dil opened his mouth, and his voice sparked a trail of goose bumps up her spine to the back of her neck. She could still feel the imprint of his palm where he'd held her for a kiss.

Then he turned away from her in a smooth move that felt so dismissive her mouth fell open in shock.

"Thank you, everyone, for tuning in for another episode of *The Dr. Dil Show*. I'm your host, Dr. Prem Verma, a cardiologist here in Jersey City. And as many of our Hindi-speaking South Asian viewers know, *prem* means love, *dil* means heart, and this show is about the holistic health of the heart."

Holy cow, when Prem had told her that he fixed broken hearts, Kareena thought that was a line! The bastard meant it in the literal sense! Who did that? Who made funny, adorable puns about their jobs just to seduce women?

"Last week we spent quite a bit of time discussing coronary artery disease and the Stanford study pointing to a higher mortality rate in the South Asian community."

He looked straight at Kareena again.

She crossed her arms over her chest and glared.

"Today, however, we're switching gears to a heart health topic that, oddly enough, doesn't get a lot of attention from cardiologists. Romance. Part of heart health, especially for younger generations, is romance. That's why I'm thrilled to welcome Bindu Mann, popular lifestyle influencer and YouTube channel host of *Mann Your Business*, to our show."

He held out a hand and motioned for Bindu to join him onstage. "Bindu?"

Kareena watched her sister stand, tilt her chin up, and stride across the floor in her fitted skirt and blouse, before ascending the stage at the entry point one of the producers pointed to. Bindu turned to the camera and flashed her brilliant white smile, before she held out a hand and shook Dr. Dil's. "Thank you for having me," she said.

They took seats across from each other on the stage and when they were finally settled, Dr. Dil spoke first. "Now, Bindu, when you and I spoke on the phone, you mentioned that you were recently engaged. Congratulations."

"Thank you," she said, and flashed her princess cut diamond ring. "We're excited."

"If you don't mind me asking, was it an arranged marriage or a love marriage?"

"Do you believe in love and romance, Rina?" Prem traced a figure eight on the inside of her wrist. The delicate caress had her shivering.

"Of course," she said breathlessly. "Hearts, stars, flowers. I want all of it in my life. What about you?"

His gaze had dropped to her mouth. "I believe there are some things stronger than love."

Where was this man going with this? Were these questions preplanned, or was he referencing their conversation? To be honest, asking about love marriages and arranged marriages was smart. Kareena knew that very few cultures differentiated their marriages the same way—people either had a match arranged for them where they agreed based on compatibility, or they dated and fell in love like Western culture. Bindu, of course was—

"Love marriage," she said. "In addition to creating lifestyle content for my YouTube channel, I'm a math professor. My fiancé, Loken, is a Gujarati-Italian I met when he started working as a visiting professor at my college."

"That's great for you, Bindu."

Kareena's back straightened. There was something about his tone that she did *not* like.

Prem glanced at Kareena again, then asked her sister, "Now, Bindu, what if I said that your chances of a successful marriage are more about you two working in the same vicinity than it is about your feelings for each other?"

Bindu nodded, then flipped her long curls over her shoulder. "I'd say that it definitely doesn't hurt that we work at the same institution. That was one of the biggest problems I had when I was single. I could never find the time to meet with someone who was far away. My free time was limited as an entrepreneur and a professor with a full course load."

"Exactly." Dr. Dil leaned back in his chair as if Bindu just said something to validate a point he had yet to make. "Your proximity means convenience. It means your adjustment from single to a couple doesn't create an imbalance in your life. Now, if your decisions were purely based on love, you may chance long distance, which would create heartache, stress, depression, and anxiety. You may push off other responsibilities to make time for travel.

"That is why today, we're going to talk about how love is actually dangerous for heart health. Because love, ladies and gentlemen, is an illusion that does not sustain long-term partnerships."

I BELIEVE THERE is something stronger than love.

KAREENA LET OUT an audible gasp. She knew that she was loud enough for the entire studio to turn and face her, including her wide-eyed sister and the host. She couldn't care less. This man was a fraud! Or he was very good at seduction. Either way, he lied by omission just to get in her pants. She almost broke her dating moratorium for a man with a talk show.

A talk show titled *Dr. Heart* with a host whose name translated to *love*.

He was Dr. Heart, the cardiologist who didn't believe in his namesake.

"Bindu," Dr. Dil said, glancing at Kareena again, "let's use your love story as a case study."

Nope, this is not okay, Kareena thought. Her hand shot up in the air. If anyone was answering his questions, it was going to be her, the woman he tried to seduce then left in a compromising position.

The studio was collectively looking in her direction now, but she was on a mission to defraud this man. He continued to glance at her. His forehead looked dewy under the lights.

Yeah, you should be sweating.

Bindu cleared her throat. "I'd be happy to talk about my love story, Dr. Dil."

Prem adjusted his tie, and the collar of his shirt. "Uh, great. When you met your fiancé, did you spend time together before falling in love? Or did you feel like it was instantaneous?"

"I'd like to think it was instantaneous, but we were friends for a semester."

"Let's look at your health before Loken and after. Did you feel like you were eating better, sleeping more, more productive, before or after you fell in love?"

Bindu let out a musical laugh, and Kareena knew that her sister was purposely trying to draw everyone's attention in the room to herself. Kareena sat at the edge of her seat with her hand still in the air.

"I was definitely sleeping more and way more productive before Loken and I confessed our feelings for each other," Bindu replied.

"And that's because our health takes a back burner when we get distracted by love. However, a relationship based on compatibility as the foundation will lead to a healthier lifestyle. Love, on the other hand, specifically the long-term effects of love, is linked to an increase in heart disease."

Kareena made a strangled sound. She'd been fleeced! The way Prem spoke to her the night before made her think that he was on the same page when it came to love. Her reality was looking worse and worse. She almost had sex with this man in the back office of an Indian restaurant.

"What we need in our lives is less emotion in establishing relationships," Dr. Dil continued. "Love doesn't have be a factor at all."

"But I do believe it's a nice side benefit," Bindu said with a laugh. "I mean, isn't attraction one of the first things that brings people together?"

"Feelings of lust and attraction are collectively the illusion of 'love,' but that can fade with time. In a recent study, researchers concluded that trust, communication, and compatible lifestyle are the top traits that couples look for in a suitable match, not love. The concept of love actually encourages individuals to take advantage of each other."

Kareena was practically on her feet now. The producer motioned for Dr. Dil to cut.

Dr. Dil glanced at Kareena one more time, then smiled into the camera. "Let's revisit this conversation after a short commercial break. Stick around, everyone. We're just getting started."

The cameras cut, and the studio went dead silent.

Kareena stepped over a cable wire and moved toward the stage.

"You hypocrite!" she shouted. "After everything you told me yesterday, I thought you were one of the good guys, but it was all just an act, wasn't it?"

Prem glanced at his crew then back at her before getting to his feet. "Maybe we should talk in my dressing room."

"No way." Kareena's head rang, and she lowered her voice to control the throbbing in her temples. "We know what happened the last time I was alone with you."

Sounds of grumbling rose from the crew. Someone whispered, "Oh my god."

"Wait, you two *know* each other?" Bindu asked.

"Yes," Prem responded.

"No," Kareena said at the same time.

Prem held up his hands in surrender. "I think there has been a bit of a misunderstanding about what happened, Rina—"

"Her name is Kareena," Bindu interjected.

Prem glanced at her sister over his shoulder before turning back to Kareena. "Oh?"

"I was protecting myself," Kareena replied. "Obviously not well enough."

Dr. Dil stepped off the platform stage to stand next to her. He was as tall as she remembered and made her feel dainty standing next to his broad-shouldered, six-feet-plus height. Damn it, he smelled great again, too. Even in her hungover pissed-off state, she wanted to crawl all over him.

"I WOULD LOVE to drive you home, but since I'm on call, I can't leave Jersey City," he said. "But would you be comfortable coming over to my place?"

Kareena remembered her last hookup and the guy's porn studio camera set up in the bedroom. She couldn't risk it again until she got to know Prem better. "Maybe we could just find a quieter spot away from the bar?"

Prem nodded. "You know what? My friend Benjamin actually owns this place. He has couches in his office in the back where we can sit . . . and get to know each other better. Is that okay with you?"

That sounded great, Kareena thought. She didn't care that she was going to be in a stranger's office. She just wanted more time with Prem.

"Lead the way," she said.

"I GOT AN SOS call." Prem interrupted her train of thought. He looked back at his producers and then at Kareena. "I came back to find you after I hung up, but you were already gone."

"Because I was in a private office stuck with my sweater vest over my head," she hissed.

Prem leaned in until their noses were practically touching. "I'm sorry about that. I was an idiot, but that doesn't make me a liar."

"But you are," she said, louder now. She took a step back for distance and clarity. "You are on a network targeting older South Asians, telling a bunch of aunties that marriages based on compatibility, not love, are the only ones that can work, while you're duping younger generations into thinking their feelings are misleading. You're gaslighting people by using Bindu Mann as an example. Hell, you duped me last night, too! Do your viewers know that you use romance to get your way in your personal life?"

His eyes widened and his mouth gaped like a fish. "We didn't talk about love at all! And this has nothing to do with arranged versus love marriages," he snapped.

She waved at his long, tapered torso. "You told me that you

fix broken hearts, and that you believe in something greater than love, while you're onstage here saying that love is bad for heart health."

The crew gasped again.

"You are a *fraud*, Dr. Dil," Kareena said.

"Oh no," Bindu whispered.

"There are *real* doctors who actually have done extensive studies on love."

Dr. Dil's shoulder's straightened, and he moved closer until they were practically chest to breast. Her nipples tightened into peaks, and she swayed on her feet. Damn it, it was as if her body recognized him.

"Do you have any idea how ludicrous you sound right now?" Prem replied. "You are visiting *my* show, interrupting *my* team, just because you disagree with a point I'm making? Oh wait, I know what this is. You're the type of bitter old single woman who blames her lack of a love life on people who view relationships practically. Is that why you were out last night? Hoping for lightning to strike?"

"There are countless relationships that are based on love that last the test of time," Kareena said evenly. "Don't you have people in your life that love you? I bet there is a woman who left—"

The heat in his expression iced over from one blink to the next. He stepped back and motioned for the producers. "I'm sorry about yesterday, *Rina*, but like I said, I had an emergency call. And thank god, because we would've had more regrets than we do now." He turned to the nearest person with a headset. "Can we please get security to take this woman out of the studio? Some of us have work to do. Work based on fucking *science*. Bindu, if she's with you, you can go with her, or stay."

"Running away just like you did last time," Kareena said. She motioned for her sister to follow her out, but Bindu was already shaking her head.

"I'm so sorry about her unprofessionalism, Dr. Verma."

"*Bindu.*" The knife that Dr. Dil had shoved into her chest was only twisted and pushed in harder by her sister's insensitivity. Bindu turned her back on Kareena and walked onto the stage.

Kareena looked around, and for the first time since she opened her mouth, she felt embarrassment from the whole experience. It was like a double dose of shame and humiliation, and both at the hands of this desi fuckboy.

"Fine, then!" she snapped, holding her chin up by sheer determination. "But just remember that you benefit from the parts of our culture that are oppressive. Which is why you hit on women and promise love and romance, when in actuality, you're just another asshole."

She stormed over to her seat to pick up her clutch and her Pedialyte. As she turned away from the pitying, horrified expressions of everyone in the studio, rage began to consume her.

How dare he? How dare everyone?

She uncapped her Pedialyte and in a moment of spontaneity, tossed it at Dr. Dil like a grenade.

A collective shriek filled the room.

"And that's for ruining my sweater vest, fuckboy!"

Dr. Prem Verma, a cardiologist and host of the TV talk show *The Dr. Dil Show* on Jersey City's South Asians News Network, found himself in a very public argument during a commercial break last weekend when a woman named Kareena accused him of making promises of love and romance in his personal life while also preaching unorthodox views on love marriages. Dr. Verma is a health-care advocate for the South Asian community working toward building a clinic supporting South Asians in Jersey City. However, many residents in the area aren't too pleased with the altercation aired on the *Mann Your Business* YouTube channel by his guest, Bindu Mann.

CHAPTER FIVE

Prem

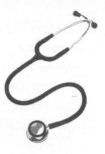

Prem rubbed at the tension in his temples as he collapsed on the edge of his bed to unlace his shoes. It took him a few minutes before he was able to get back up and stack them in his closet. His suit coat went next, along with his tie and slacks. Whatever needed to be dry-cleaned was put in a separate wicker basket, which he'd have to remember to drop off on Saturday.

He'd never looked forward to something so mundane as dry cleaning before.

After dressing in athletic shorts and a Columbia T-shirt, he walked through his apartment to the kitchen. He immediately headed toward the corner cabinet, where he took out the ibuprofen bottle and swallowed three pills dry.

Regretting his life choices, Prem called out to his smart home device. "Google, play Dudes' Night playlist."

"Playing Dudes' Night," Google replied.

Taylor Swift's album *Reputation* slipped through his wall speakers, filling the open space up through the exposed beams and ducts.

After one of the worst weeks he'd had since Gori's death, a night with his friends was exactly what the doctor ordered. He'd been twisted up inside for so long that this was hopefully going to be the release he needed.

"SOMETIMES I THINK that we, as the first ones born in the U.S., feel so much pressure to excel because our parents don't know if their intercontinental move was successful until we are successful," Kareena said. "We are the reward to their sacrifice."

Prem nodded, fascinated by the way the dim lights at the bar flickered over her face. "I think that's why we're so forgiving when they push us, too."

"Do your parents push you toward their dreams, or are you doing what you want, Prem Verma?"

"Soon," he said. "Hopefully, I will be soon."

PREM BRISTLED WITH anger all over again. How could he have a life-altering conversation with a woman, a woman who he felt so connected to for the first time in . . . well, in ever, who would turn out to be the same person to throw a bottle of Pedialyte at him the next day at his studio?

Granted, he was the idiot who left her in a precarious situation, but still.

Prem put a couple highball glasses and a bottle of whiskey in the middle of his round dining room table. Three mats went next, along with plates he'd ordered off an Instagram ad at three in the morning the year before.

After grabbing a huge stack of old textbooks from the kitchen island and placing them on one of the chairs in front of one of the mats, he logged into his laptop. The familiar ding of a video chat request popped up on the screen. He rolled his eyes before accepting the call from his mother.

An older Punjabi woman with coiffed hair and thin lips painted in red filled his monitor. "Hi, Mama."

"Mama ka bachcha," she snapped. She was using her doctor voice, the same one that she pulled out when she was really upset. "Do you know how many times your father and I have tried to call you this week?"

He'd stopped counting after sixteen. "I'm sorry, I've been busy."

"My son, a cardiologist, went viral on a TV show. It's all over the WhatsApp groups!"

Great. The Aunty WhatsApp groups. The fastest way now to disseminate gossip and false information. The last time he'd checked the family chat, his physician parents were telling his cousin that drinking turmeric milk every day would increase his sperm count.

"It's not like I intended it to happen, Mama."

"You know, if you had just taken that job at Einstein Medical and become a surgeon like your little twat of a cousin—"

"Oh my god, we've had this conversation. You can't say that word in the U.S. Stop watching *Bollywood Wives*. I thought you were going to try to do something productive during your early retirement instead of learning inappropriate curse words."

"I am being productive! I'm trying to find a wife for my stubborn son, but he's busy making a fool out of himself. You know what young girls call you now? Fuckboy."

Prem had to school his features. His mother would come straight through the screen and smack the shit out of him if he rolled his eyes at her. "You know what? You can't say that word, either. And stop comparing me to that t—that jerk. Also, this is entirely your fault."

"My fault?" She pressed a hand to her chest. "How is this my fault? Indian children always are blaming their parents."

"Mom, you texted me the family emergency SOS code!" He burst out. "I left Rina, that girl who was in the video with me, without any explanation or excuse because I thought there was a true emergency."

"It was an emergency," she said, with belligerence. She pursed her lips and leaned in closer to the camera. "Your cousin is getting *married*. Before you! Your aunt will never let me live this down."

Prem pressed his fingertips to his forehead. He couldn't get the image of Kareena's arms up in the air, her sweater vest stuck covering her face, as he bolted out of the office with his heart pounding.

He tugged, and she went rigid in his arms. "Ouch!"

"Oh my god," he said, hands pausing at her waist. He looked at the outline of her face through the fabric of her sweater vest. "What is it? Are you hurt?"

"I wore earrings today for the first time in a while, and I think one is caught on my clothes." There was a strain of amusement in her voice.

He was going to die of mortification right there. He was like a sixteen-year-old trying to take off a girl's clothes for the first time.

"Here let me—"

His phone buzzed, and the ring was specific to the SOS family line.

He stepped back and glanced at the screen. He thought he could feel his heart stop. Flashbacks of the day he found out about Gori cascaded through his mind. "I'm so sorry, I have to go," he said, and bolted out the door.

"Prem!" his mother snapped. "Are you even listening to me?"

"Yes, Mama," he said. Prem had thought that someone else had died.

He knew now that SOS call was fate intervening and saving him from ending up with a woman who was the devil incarnate.

"Mom, I have to go."

She practically pressed her papery cheek against the screen. "Prem Verma, don't you dare hang up on your mother! We have things to talk about."

Prem sighed. "What, Mama?"

"My offer to pay you to get married."

He really couldn't talk about money when he was hurting for it. He might do something rash and make a deal with his mother. "I told you. Health center first, then you can send me as many rishtas you want. As many biodata documents with matching résumés that you can get your hands on."

"I'll find you someone prettier than that girl, too," his mother said.

I doubt that, he thought. Kareena may be his nemesis, but he wasn't going to lie and say she was anything but the most beautiful woman he'd ever seen.

"Thez," she continued. "I bet she's thez."

Prem winced. He knew that older Indian aunties called younger desi women *thez* as an insult. As if being street-smart was a bad thing. "Mom, do you want another lesson on stereotypes?"

"Oh, chup kar. Your grandmother used to call me that, too, but of course, that was just because she didn't like me. Beta, what was the point of becoming a handsome doctor if you're not going to attract the best life partner by your credentials alone? You don't even need a personality to be married once you have an M.D. Look at your father."

"*Mom*." Prem pinched the bridge of his nose and let out a deep breath. "You aren't helping my situation at all."

Her expression softened. "I'm sorry, beta. It's just I never want to see my children take the long hard road."

He thought about his conversation with Kareena again and cursed himself for the amount of times her face appeared in his head. "It's my choice. I really have to go now."

"Fine. Go eat something."

"Yes, Mom. Bye." He hung up and adjusted the computer so it was positioned on top of the stack of books with the screen at eye level to where he'd be sitting for dinner.

Then he let out a frustrated groan.

The only person he'd met in his life who was worse than his mother was Kareena. His mother made his life difficult, but Kareena Mann had straight up ruined it.

Which in turn meant he had to deal with his mother.

He recalled his week like a bad highlight reel. His meeting after the show from hell was a dud, and then he received a call from Gregory at LTD Financial, his largest investor, who pulled out after seeing the viral video. That meant Prem had four months to come up with a lot more money than he expected. The funds he needed were now well beyond what he'd hoped to raise. Then, his producers had been sending him scripts all week about a new love segment in an effort to capitalize on his viral fame.

His laptop pinged with an incoming call, and Prem sat up to answer it. Always the punctual one, Benjamin Padda's name popped up on the screen, then his face appeared moments later. Prem's best friend grinned at him.

"Oh hey, it's that doctor who went viral for getting fucked on a TV show for South Asian aunties. Did you know there are memes out there of your clueless face while you're getting roasted?"

"Up yours," Prem said. "Not only has this been a shit week, but

I also just got off a call with my mother who is *not* happy. I really could use some compassion right now."

Bunty snorted. "Then why did you agree to dudes' night? If you think I'm bad, wait until Deeps shows up. He's worse."

"Don't I know it. Normally he sends a text or two during the week, but I haven't heard from him at all. Radio silence."

The doorbell rang.

"Speak of the devil himself," Bunty said.

Prem braced himself before he went to open the door. On the other side, Deepak Datta, best friend since Columbia, wearing a suit and a Rolex that cost more than Prem's mortgage, shoved a large reusable shopping bag in Prem's arms.

"You're one dumb motherfucker."

Okay, he was pissed.

"Yeah, it was bad—"

"And what did I tell you about social media?" Deepak said as he toed off his loafers. "When I connected you with my network head, what did I tell you about using your online presence?"

"Uh, that Twitter is toxic?"

"It's your fucking *brand*, Prem! Social media is part of your brand. You should've done damage control." Deepak strolled into the apartment, tossed his jacket over one of the chairs, and reached for a whiskey glass. After raking a finger through his hair, which fell back perfectly in place, he said, "Why didn't you make a statement on how important emotional connections are? Something to make you look less like an idiot. What up, Bunty?"

Bunty toasted his webcam. "Cheers, brother. Ignore me, I'm here for a show."

"If you wanted me to make a statement, why didn't you tell me?" Prem said as he locked the door. He carried the bag to the dining table, smelling the contents along the way. "As the owner of the network, isn't that your job?"

Deepak poured a shot and tossed it back. "I'm the owner of a network, not your personal manager, Prem. As it is, I'm buying the Chinese food. That should be enough."

"Don't even start with me." Prem began taking out white cartons and set them between the three place mats. "I had to check out that acne cyst on your balls last year because you refused to see a doctor. I'm still collecting my appointment fee."

"Lucky," Bunty said. He held up a carton. "Not about the ball zit. About the free food. I always have to pay for my own."

Prem poured some lo mein onto his plate. "Can we focus, please? Because of one woman who went absolutely ballistic—"

"—that you left in my office," Bunty interrupted. "I saw that security camera footage. You need help, dude."

Prem scrubbed his hands over his face. "I'm glad we didn't actually hook up then. But gentlemen, because of this woman, I've now lost my biggest donor. What's worse, the location that I want needs the money by September. What the hell am I supposed to do?"

Bunty motioned to the screen with a similar set of chopsticks. "Hold up. How bad is this? Like, can this blow over?"

"Hell no," Deepak and Prem said simultaneously.

"He's officially known as a desi fuckboy now," Deepak said. "Bindu's YouTube video hit three million views and was picked up by mainstream local news."

And because Rina, or Kareena, actually threw a bottle of Pedialyte at him. He had to smell like starchy baby vomit for the rest of the show.

Damn it, that suit was toast.

Like her beautiful blue sweater vest.

"Can you pass the hot sauce?" Deepak asked.

"Is that all you can say?" Prem pushed the packets of hot sauce over. "I'm drowning here."

Deepak picked up a clump of noodles. "In this situation, the only advice I have for you is to show your new viewers that you aren't a heartless bastard. You have to produce a woman at your side who is going to make the haters doubt this Kareena woman's character assassination."

"You want me to get a *girlfriend*? This is not a daytime Indian serial soap opera."

Deepak nodded. "But it's your only option. And you need to move fast."

"Do you think it'll reverse some of the damage that Rina did to my reputation?"

"Kareena," his friends said in unison.

"Shut up, assholes."

"Look, this is the only way I can see this working," Deepak said, stabbing into a baby corn. "We all know empty apologies aren't enough. If you don't find a girlfriend, you may never convince your donor to come back."

"If Gregory at LTD Financial doesn't want to give you money at the end of this fiasco, you can use the same fake girlfriend to convince your mom to give you cash," Bunty said. "She was willing to shell out money for you to get married. A lot of it."

"That's actually a solid plan," Deepak said. He motioned to Prem with his chopsticks. "Your mom would be too distracted with the opportunity to plan a potential wedding that she wouldn't know whether you were faking it until it was too late. Two birds with one stone: you get your reputation back, and you get the money you need."

"No," Prem said. He shoved his plate aside and grabbed the whiskey bottle. His heart sped up just enough for him to register the anxiety reaction he was having to the idea of being tied to another woman. Another woman who was fragile and breakable. Nope. That was a terrible idea.

Rina's face flashed in his mind, and he began to sweat.

"I think you have both lost your minds," he said over their voices and threw back the whiskey. "Who comes up with stuff like this anyway? No thank you. And besides. Getting hitched is *not* easy."

His friends began tossing ideas back and forth, the worst one being online dating, specifically Indian online dating apps, since there was a better chance that an Indian woman was going to understand his motives.

Before Prem could shut down the conversation, his phone buzzed on the counter. He grabbed it, frowning at the unknown number.

> **UNKNOWN:** Hi, this is Bindu Mann, from *Mann Your Business*. The show producer gave me your number. I hope that's okay. Please call me.

"What the hell?"

"What is it?" Deepak asked. "A patient?"

"It's Bindu Mann, the woman I interviewed for the show. After Rina stormed out, Bindu was a nervous mess for the rest of the segment. She completed the interview, then left in a rush. But now, she wants me to call her."

"Why?" Bunty and Deepak blurted out together.

"I have no clue."

"Then you should call her to find out," Deepak said.

"Maybe it's to apologize," Prem mused. But did he want to get on the phone to hear her chipper voice grating in his ears saying sorry a dozen times? He looked at his phone, then his friends.

They stared at him expectantly.

"What, you want me to do it now?"

"Yes!" they snapped at him.

"Fine, fine." He pressed on her number and put the call on speakerphone.

"Hi, Dr. Verma?" the familiar voice answered.

"Hi, yes. It's me. I mean, it's Dr. Verma. You asked me to call you?"

"Sorry, I know this is weird," she said in her overly peppy voice. "But I wanted to invite you over to my house for chai. This week preferably. Would you by any chance be able to drive out to the Edison area?"

"Wait a second," he said, and pinched the bridge of his nose. This had to be a prank call. "You want to invite me . . . to your house . . . for chai?"

She let out a small sigh, like he was wasting her time, instead of the other way around. "I know you're super busy, but I owe you one after what my sister did to you on the show."

"Your *sister*?" he said, jaw dropping. Rina was Kareena Mann, Bindu Mann's sister?

Bindu giggled. "I know, we couldn't be more different."

Not in the slightest, Prem agreed. Bindu was petite and willowy, with long flowing hair. Meanwhile, her sister had thick black waves, big eyes behind sexy black framed glasses, and the fire in her stare. Damn it, he was salivating over the thought of the enemy.

"I think it's best if we all forget this ever happened," Prem finally replied. *I'm going to hold this against Kareena Mann for the rest of my life.* "But thanks for calling, I guess."

"Wait! I promise you it'll be worth your while. I know how you can 'recover from the show'! It's the least I can do for you. But I'd rather not tell you on the phone."

Prem had no idea what she could possibly recommend to salvage *Dr. Dil*, but she'd definitely piqued his interest. He looked up at his friends, who nodded. "I'm listening," he finally said.

"Great! I saw all the comments, I know that you are trying to build a community health center. All you have to do is come for chai. We'll talk about my plan, and I know you won't regret it. I'll text you the address. Thank you for giving me this chance, Prem! Dr. Verma!" With that she hung up.

"What do you think she has planned?" Bunty said on the computer screen, mouth full of stir-fry vegetables.

"I have no idea. But I also don't have options." Deepak's solution was fake dating. Bindu's plan could potentially be something better. Prem looked down at his phone again then back at his friends. "I think I'm going to Edison."

CHAPTER SIX

Prem

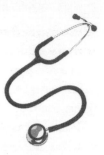

> **GREGORY LTD FINANCIAL:** I don't know if I can trust you. I'm sorry, my decision still stands.

> **PREM:** I'm going to keep trying to change your mind. This health center is really important for my community, Greg.

> **GREGORY LTD FINANCIAL:** I believe you, but you're asking for a large investment, and with the way that your community currently perceives you, I don't think you can be trusted.

> **PREM:** Then I'll have to gain back their trust and yours.

An impending sense of doom haunted Prem as he walked up the front stone path of a beautiful white colonial with black shutters and a small front porch. His curiosity was the driving force behind his agreement to the meeting, but now that he was here, he wasn't so sure this was a good idea.

He paused at the base of the porch steps and scanned the neighboring yards. He always figured that maybe one day when he was married and settled, he'd find a place like this in the suburbs that was close enough to the city, but also had a nice yard.

Later though. After he finished his health center.

He raised a fist to knock on the freshly painted front door. "Here goes nothing," he mumbled.

What did Bindu want? Why did he have to come over for chai to talk about her video? Was she going to shoot a follow-up or something and claim that the first video was a setup? Would that even work? Was he going to see Kareena Mann again?

He hoped he did. Then he could strangle her. "Here goes nothing," he mumbled.

Prem pulled at his neckline in the early June heat, and seconds later Bindu opened the door and stood framed in light.

"Hi! You made it. You came from work?"

He looked down at his scrubs. "Yes, I did."

"Great! Come on in."

Prem peeked in the door. It looked like a normal house. "Uh, can't you just tell me why I'm here first?"

"Nope!" She grabbed his arm and pulled him through the entryway.

Years of conditioning in a desi household had him toeing off his Chucks. Bindu held on to his arm the whole time, assuming correctly that he was a flight risk. "Bindu, this is really strange. I appreciate you doing the show and everything, but I don't know how else you can help this situation."

"You'll see."

There was something about her tone that had him glancing around. That's when he noticed there were quite a few sandals in the foyer. Ladies' sandals.

He then smelled something delicious.

Prem froze. "Wait, Bindu are there . . . aunties here?"

There was a brief moment of panic on her face before her grip on his arm became viselike and she dragged him into the kitchen. Damn it, he should've known it was a trap. Smelling ghee, curry leaves, and cumin seeds with a hint of rose incense was always the indicator of aunties present.

The scent grew bolder as Bindu dragged him down the hallway into the kitchen.

Before he could call out "Stranger danger," he was faced with five older women sitting in a semicircle in a kitchenette. A table covered in snacks was pushed against a wall, and the only empty seat was in the middle of the semicircle facing the firing squad.

Aunties were literally Prem's worst nightmare. The older married Indian women in his community were ruthless. It didn't matter if they were East Coast aunties, West Coast aunties, aunties in Australia, or aunties in India. He was a tall, single, thirty-five-year-old desi dude with an M.D. His parents were doctors, and he even had his own talk show. It sounded pretentious, but he was aunty catnip, and he barely made it out of social gatherings unscarred.

"Everyone, meet Dr. Prem Verma," Bindu said. She practically shoved him into the chair.

His training kicked in before he could get up and make a run for it. "Uh, namaste," he said, folding his hands together.

The aunties smiled at him in approval.

"Hello, beta," the oldest woman present said. She was wearing a maroon velour tracksuit, thick socks, and Adidas house chappals that smacked against the tile floor as she got up to retrieve a plate of samosas from the table. She shoved it in front of his face. "I am Kareena and Bindu's grandmother, but you can call me Dadi. Would you like a samosa?"

"Oh no, thank you, Aunty—"

"Dadi."

"Uh, no, thank you, *Dadi*. I'm fine—"

"Now, now—you must eat."

She had a manic expression on her face, so Prem took the samosa. Damn it, he should've taken advantage of that coupon from Deepak's lawyer and drafted his will.

A woman wearing matching slacks and a blouse with a slew of diamond and gold jewelry on her fingers and wrists spoke next. "Darling, my name is Mona Aunty, and all of us are very close to the Mann family. We helped raise Bindu and Kareena when their mother died."

Every person in the room nodded.

Another aunty, this one with a kurta top and mom jeggings, spoke next. "I'm Sonali Aunty, and we have the best idea for how to save your reputation after your show last weekend. Because log kya kehenge if this continues?"

"Log kya—what will they say? Aunty, I think they're already talking."

They all nodded, and their expressions ranged from amusement to concern. What the hell was happening here? This was just too weird. Everything felt like a setup, but he didn't quite know what the end game was yet.

"Now you just have to keep an open mind," a third aunty said. This one had dark kohl-lined eyes and a streak of red powder in her hairline. "I'm Falguni Aunty, beta. Bindu, where is your sister?"

Prem's stomach dropped to his gut. "Sister? Like . . . like Kareena?"

Everyone nodded.

Before Prem could get up and leave, the front door opened and a familiar voice echoed from down the hall. "Bindu, what is it? I'm busy."

"Just get in here!" Bindu shouted back.

Prem was on his feet when Kareena entered the kitchen, dressed in pink overalls, with grease smudged across her cheek. She was pushing up her glasses with the back of her hand. He hated that despite everything she'd done to his career, and his chances at raising enough money for his center, he still found her breathlessly attractive. He cleared his throat to cover the wheeze.

"Are the aunties here?" Kareena said. "I just saw all the cars in the driveaway. Also, who bought the Audi? That's such a pretentious—"

She froze at the kitchen entrance, her eyes going wide. Prem pointed a finger at her just as she did the same in return.

"What is she doing here?"

"What is he doing here?"

They spoke in tandem, and Prem had no idea how to process the twin feelings of lust and unadulterated rage clouding his brain. Despite the presence of aunties in the room, he really wanted to bend her over and spank her. Hard. And then leave her even if she wanted more.

"I live here!" Kareena yelled back. "You need to get out."

"I invited him," Bindu interjected.

"Then *uninvite* him. How could you?"

"I don't understand why you're so angry," Prem snapped. "I'm the one whose reputation is literally in shambles because you came to my show and hurled accusations."

Her gaze narrowed on his as if to say, *We had a connection that one night and then you pulled my sweater over my head and left.*

"You know what you did, asshole."

"Listen, Rina—"

"It's Kareena!"

"—Instead of letting me explain, you interrupted me in my place of business, hurled false accusations at me, started screaming like a churreyl, then assaulted me with Pedialyte!"

"Did you seriously just call me a witch?" she shrieked.

Prem leaned forward, shoving a finger in her direction. "And I'll do it again because you sure as hell aren't sweet and charming like you pretended to be when we first met. Or do you go to bars pretending to be chill until you can trap someone into believing in your warped vision of true love?"

Every woman in the kitchen gasped in horror.

"Don't sound so shocked that I was at a bar," Kareena snapped at her aunties. She pointed at each and every one of them. "I've heard you all talk about how you used to troll for men in Mumbai and Delhi. None of you all are as innocent as you're pretending to be."

"Not me," Dadi said, patting a hand to her chest. "I was always appropriate, and Kareena, I expected the same of you."

"Yeah, Aunty, tell her," Prem said.

Kareena whirled on him. "I'm seriously going to kill you!"

"Why so hostile?" he taunted. "Is it because you finally realized that I'm right? That love is a bullshit excuse that women like you use when no one wants them?"

"That's it, you're dead." Kareena lunged for him, and Prem dodged her. She jumped over a chair and chased him around the kitchen island. The aunties all stumbled out of their seats, shouting. Not like Prem could hear them. He was busy trying to save his package from blunt force trauma at the hands of a she-demon.

"If you hit me, I'll hit you back," he shouted from behind Falguni Aunty with Crocs. The woman let out a hysterical laugh.

"So much for being a gentleman," Kareena said, and hurled what looked like a round ladoo at him. He dodged it and watched as it slammed against the wall and slid to the floor.

"Stop throwing things!" Dadi shouted.

"She started it," Prem shouted back. When he reached the snack table and grabbed another samosa from one of the trays so that he held one in each hand.

"This is for the damn Pedialyte!" he shouted and chucked them at her. A fried triangle hit her square in the forehead and smashed flat like a pancake.

"Ouch!"

"Not the bloody samosas!" Sonali Aunty yelled from behind him.

He lunged to the left, then faked right, and went left again. Kareena grabbed a potato tikki and hurled it. Before he could dodge the flying disc, it hit him in the arm.

"You deserve to burn in hell, Dr. Phil!" she shouted.

"I thought the show was called *Dr. Dil*," Dadi said over the chaos.

"She's saying it wrong on purpose," Bindu replied.

Kareena's voice cracked as she shouted, "You're setting women back *decades*. Using emotions to get in their pants but then claiming that love is an illusion, so you don't have to commit to anyone. Aunties are going to think that everyone should go back to only having arranged marriages. Marriage should be about finding your perfect life partner!"

"Life partners?" He let out a humorless laugh. "*Jeevansathis?* You have got to be kidding me. Because of you, I'm going to dedicate every episode for the rest of the season to how people like you are delusional."

She gasped, jaw gaping as she stood behind her aunties. "You wouldn't *dare*."

"Watch me."

Before Kareena could grab Prem, the fourth aunty, who had remained undisturbed throughout the chaos, stuck two fingers in her mouth and let out a whistle sharp enough to rupture eardrums.

Everyone paused.

"Sit down," she said.

"No, thank you," Prem said. He'd had enough of this nonsense. "I'm leaving before I—"

"Sit down!" she roared.

He followed the authoritative order like he'd been conditioned to since childhood and sat in the closest available chair. Kareena reacted in the same way, and now he was stuck next to the woman who smelled faintly of motor oil and hints of sandalwood and vanilla.

Sandalwood and vanilla. His hands fisted at the sensory memory.

The aunty looked pleased with herself as she clasped her hands in front of her. "Now. I'm the last to introduce myself. I'm Farah Aunty, Prem, and I think it's better if we start in the beginning."

"That would be helpful," Prem murmured. He was going to need to get a drink after this just to cope.

"You see," Farah Aunty started. "Because Kareena is like a second daughter to us, we care about her well-being."

Every single woman in the room nodded. Kareena still looked mutinous sitting next to him, but she didn't argue. Interesting.

"This house was designed by Kareena's mother when the Manns moved to New Jersey," Falguni Aunty began. "But Kareena's father is retiring, and he needs money for his retirement so he's selling the house. For Kareena to keep this house, she has to buy it from her father."

"But Kareena doesn't have the money, so she has to get engaged so she can get the money set aside for her to use as the down payment," Mona Aunty said.

Huh. She'd told him that night she was trying to buy her mother's house, but the rest was interesting.

Kareena gasped. "Seriously? Why are we giving this man ammunition?" The last remaining samosa potato and pea that was stuck to her forehead fell off, and she brushed it aside.

"Oh hush," Sonali Aunty said. She turned back to Prem. "Beta, her mother was one of our dearest friends, and we're just as attached to the memories in this home that will hopefully go to Kareena."

"Good luck with that," Prem snorted.

"Hey!" Kareena snapped. She leaned forward into his space, and he could see the thick sweep of black lashes behind her glasses. "It didn't take me too long to get you wrapped around my finger, did it?"

She was absolutely correct, but before he could defend himself, Bindu held up her hands in a T-shape. "Neither of you are married or seeing anyone. The aunties did background checks."

"Background checks?" Prem asked. "How did you . . . I mean, I didn't give you any of my personal information."

Farah Aunty stood from her chair, brushed off her shoulders, and then stepped closer until she could whisper in his face, "I have your home address, genealogy history, the balance on your credit card, and your Social Security number, beta. As well as the name of your pet beta fish when you were six. Don't test us."

Damn, that was scary.

"The bottom line is that Kareena needs a man," she continued. "Which is why we asked Bindu to help us bring you here."

Prem scanned all the expectant faces in front of him and realized exactly where this was going. Damn, he knew this was a setup. If there were aunties and single people in a room together, there was bound to be some sort of matchmaking. "You're joking if you think that this *woman* and I would be a good match," Prem said. He'd believed it at one time, but not anymore. "I mean, we both dodged a bullet when I got a call and had to leave our—"

"Date," she interjected.

"*Date.*"

Bindu rushed on, her wrists covered in gold bangles clinking as she wrung her fingers together. "The aunties sent out Kareena's biodata in their network, and literally no one wants to date her. She'll have to marry someone who isn't desi at this rate."

"What are you talking about?" Kareena asked. She turned to her aunties. "I didn't give you my biodata."

Every last one of them looked guilty. Farah Aunty said, "Darling, we just wanted to help. We wanted it to be like a birthday present for you."

"We got the platinum subscription plan ready for Shaadi.com," Mona Aunty said, referring to the popular arranged marriage dating website. "But no matches yet according to the criteria we chose. We also used my coupon for a session with the matchmaker pandit in Jackson Heights, Queens, who was supposed to give advice on your future match. It was twenty minutes, and all he said was that you'd meet your match this year, so not very helpful."

Falguni Aunty cleared her throat. "And to be honest, beta, we reached out to our personal network, and all the other aunties didn't want their sons near you. They were afraid that you'd be too . . ."

"Difficult," they said in unison.

"God save me from desi aunties and desi men," Kareena grumbled. She propped her elbows on her knees to rest her chin on her fists.

"Prem, your reputation is, frankly, not that great, either," Bindu said. "This is not just affecting my sister."

"Because you livestreamed our argument!"

"I forgot it was still recording." Bindu tossed her long wavy hair over her shoulder. "But I'm not mad about it. Viewership is up. I know this sucks for you, so I'm helping the aunties. Because you two only have each other now."

"Bindu," Kareena snapped.

"The best marriages start this way," Farah Aunty. "Don't you watch Bollywood movies? You two have so much *fire*. Everyone saw it. Our proposition is that you two get to know each other. Just see if there is anything more."

Prem would've believed the aunties a week ago when he had the best conversation of his life with a woman named Rina at a bar. Now, any attraction between them didn't matter. He was almost 100 percent positive of that. This was a disaster waiting to happen. "Mrs. Gupta said this can work," Dadi added.

"Who is Mrs. Gupta?" Prem asked. "Another aunty?"

"Close enough," Kareena said. "She's a gossip columnist who gives dating advice for *Indians Abroad*."

"She wrote that a woman with intelligence and beauty, with fire, needs a partner who has the same amount of intelligence and handsomeness." Dadi motioned to Kareena and Prem. "See? She's right."

Kareena covered her face with her hands. "Oh my god, I'm

not a charity case. This has gone way too far. I can't believe you would even think something like this would ever happen!" She got to her feet. "I love all of you, but I could never love a man like him—"

"Sit down," they all said in unison. Judging by their placid expressions, it wasn't the first time they'd told Kareena to be quiet, either.

Sonali Aunty called his name. "You need money for your center, right? How wonderful would it be if you could regain your investors by presenting your family?"

"Have you been talking to my friend Deepak?"

"And Kareena's father won't give her the money to pay for the house unless she is engaged. She has four months, too."

"Aunty!" Kareena snapped. "Stop trying to guilt people into going out with me! That's so humiliating."

Prem ignored Kareena's outburst and volleyed his gaze back and forth between the aunties.

If they both need money, maybe there was an opportunity for partnership after all. But not in the way the aunties were thinking. He was too practical to believe that anything romantic between him and Kareena would work now. But they *could* make a business agreement.

"You have to be married by September?" he asked.

"She has to get *engaged*," Mona Aunty said. "That's the only way her dad will give her the money for her house."

This could work. It was a long shot, but maybe this insane plan had a chance.

Like Sonali Aunty and Deepak suggested, if he was able to repair his public reputation, then maybe, just maybe, he'd get his donor back. And if that didn't pan out, there was always his mother. But he'd have to be engaged in either situation.

He looked over at Kareena's profile while she argued with her sister. She was still as gorgeous as the first time he saw her. Could both of them remember how things were when they first met?

Good lord, what was he even thinking? Prem rubbed the back of his neck and tuned out the conversation around him. There were way too many things that could go wrong, but like Bindu said, they only had each other as an option.

"Prem?" Bindu said, interrupting his thought process. "So?"

"Bindu, you can't just pimp me out!"

Prem nudged Kareena in the arm, interrupting her indignation. Frankly, since this whole experience was like *The Twilight Zone*, what was the harm in shooting his shot?

"You talked about your mother's house when we first met. How much does it mean to you? Like really mean to you?"

Kareena's eyebrows furrowed for a moment, before her jaw dropped. "Please tell me you're *not* considering this."

"I mean, they have a point," he started. "Maybe we just need to hit the restart button and go back to when we first met. You want this house, I want my reputation fixed, and although this setup is a little . . . unorthodox, we could give it a try."

"Absolutely not."

"You still have to have some sort of feelings for me."

It bothered Prem more than he cared to admit when Kareena shook her head, then turned to argue with her aunties.

"You have lost your damn minds," she shouted and got to her feet. "I refuse to lower my standards and be with a man who could never love me back. Mom wouldn't want that for me, and neither should any of you." She pointed at all the women in the room. "I'd rather be alone and heartbroken then be with a man who could never love me."

She whirled and stormed out of the house. A second later, the front door slammed shut.

"That went well," Falguni Aunty said. "Is it time to eat the samosas?"

"You know what?" Prem said, grinning. "I think I'll have one now."

Indians Abroad News

Dear Readers,

It's important to encourage your children to diversify their candidate pool. In addition to using their networks, there are a slew of online sites available, including ones specifically designed for arranged marriages. For those of you who follow me on my website, subscribe to my newsletter to receive a free spreadsheet of all online dating sites with a high percentage of South Asian profiles.

Mrs. W. S. Gupta
Columnist
Avon, NJ

CHAPTER 7

Kareena

MONA AUNTY: What happened between you and Prem? Are you ever going to tell us?

KAREENA: Not that again.

SONALI AUNTY: Every couple has conflict, beta. I'll pray for you both.

FALGUNI AUNTY: If Prem isn't going to work out for you, then we'll keep trying with the biodatas to see if we can find someone else for you to date. And with the online websites.

KAREENA: I appreciate the help. I can manage the online websites myself.

MONA AUNTY: Okay, beta. Here is the login for the accounts we've already set up. Just make sure to send us any of the dirty pictures that you get so we can inspect them as well.

KAREENA: AUNTY!

KAREENA: I have a good feeling about this. The aunties set up online dating profiles for me without me asking for help. They sent me logins and everything. I started talking to a guy already and he wants to go out for coffee. That's a good sign, right?

BOBBI: The fact that he didn't waste five months of your life sexting through a hookup app? Yeah, definitely a good sign. But then again, you are a smoke show.

KAREENA: Good. What color sweater vest do I wear?

BOBBI: Ahh, there you go, being the smoke show that you are.

VEERA: Ignore her. Wear whatever you want. It's a rule that first blind dates no longer require our best outfits.

KAREENA: Black sweater vest it is. I don't anticipate there being a hookup problem this time.

BOBBI: Ooh, bringing out the big guns.

KAREENA: Don't be an ass, otherwise no date debriefing for you.

BOBBI: Nooooo. Okay, I'll stop.

Kareena stepped out of the car that she'd taken from the train station to the local coffee shop where she was supposed to meet her first date. She'd been a wreck for the last six hours, thinking about every possible way to cancel. It had been her first date in so long—first official first date, anyway—and she had completely forgotten all the rules. Was it normal to want to cancel and go home to read? And damn it, she really had to figure out how to control the sweating.

But she had to face the music at some point. Disregarding her timeline, and all the nonsense in her life that was happening at the moment, thirty was supposed to be the year that she focused on her personal life. This was all part of her life plan.

And she needed to try if she was going to have a fighting chance at her happily ever after.

Positive thoughts. Good energy.

She straightened her black sweater vest, turned her phone on silent to avoid any impending work calls that might come in, and walked into the trendy little shop to half-filled tables and the smell of freshly roasted coffee beans. There were chalkboard walls and a menu that included chai and claimed that it was "organic" and "authentic." A bulletin board hung on the wall next to the entrance with a flyer for Thursday night poetry open mics.

The air smelled of vanilla and spice.

Hopefully just being in this place didn't trigger an allergic re-action. She'd forgotten her EpiPen at home. Admittedly, that was stupid when she was going to a coffee shop, but she'd just have to be careful.

"Half caf soy chai tea with sweet foam for Courtney!" the barista yelled at the end of the counter.

Kareena checked her phone and scanned the faces of the people in line. Dave obviously wasn't here yet. Or he was significantly older than he claimed to be, and she was being catfished.

A few people turned to stare at her, including one of the baristas behind the counter. Should she order? Should she sit down? Did people recognize her from the stupid viral clip on *The Dr. Dil Show*?

She'd wait outside so she didn't look like the woman standing around waiting for her blind date. Kareena turned and ran straight into a brick-wall chest.

"Oh, I'm so sorry. I didn't mean to . . . oh no."

Dr. Prem Verma, dressed in his hospital blue scrubs, grinned at her. "In all the coffee shops in all of New Jersey. Hello, Rina."

She backed away, pressing a hand to her racing heart. "This can't be happening." He was so much taller than she remembered. She was five-seven, an easy five-nine with heels, and she still had to look up at him. "I've died and gone to hell."

"Nope, you're just in New Jersey."

"You cannot be here," Kareena hissed. She scanned the coffee shop, praying that no one was watching. "Go away before I pelt you with another drink."

Instead of wariness, she saw a glint of challenge in his eyes. "Why so panicked? Is your date here yet?"

She froze. "How do you know I'm on a date?"

"Your sister found out from your grandmother and then told me."

Kareena had to stop telling Dadi where she was going. That woman couldn't keep a secret if her life depended on it.

She stepped in closer to his chest and drilled a finger between his impossibly hard pecs. "I don't know what you're trying to accomplish by being here today, but you need to leave. I don't have time to deal with desi fuckboys."

Prem's broad shoulders straightened. "First, I am *not* a desi fuckboy. I may look gorgeous and have a medical degree, but I also have a sensitive side. Second, if you just give me a few minutes, then you don't have to worry about your date at all."

"Showing up is disrespecting my wishes, and that's exactly what a desi fuckboy would do."

"Something about you makes me think that you find a little disrespect sexy."

Her cheeks warmed. "I fell for your cheesy jokes once, I'm not going to do it again."

"Come on, you know you liked it," he said. Prem winked this time.

Kareena pressed her finger harder against his pecs. Man, there was zero body fat there.

"What makes you think I'd ever want to waste another moment with you? Now if you'll excuse me. I'm searching for true *love*."

He gripped her finger, then pressed her hand flat against his chest. His skin was like hot fire under her palm. Prem then leaned in until their noses practically brushed. "It looks like your date isn't here yet. Why don't you sit and have a cup of coffee with me? We'll call a temporary truce. We can talk about how our situations could be mutually beneficial."

"I'd rather murder puppies," she said, and pulled away from him. Her skin tingled.

Before she could step aside and exit the coffee shop, a man who looked like Dave's profile pictures entered through the double doors behind Dr. Dil. He glanced at Prem, then at Kareena. His button-down shirt and slim-fit pants were in direct contrast to Prem's scrubs. Like his pictures, he was clean-shaven with a trim haircut and a kind smile.

"Hi, Dave?"

He held out a hand to shake. "Yes, that's me. I'm sorry, am I interrupting?"

"No, not at all." Kareena ignored Prem's rude muffled laugh and took Dave's hand for the shake. She appreciated the handshake. There was no pressure, even though Dr. Dil obviously didn't approve. "Just running into a . . . a total stranger."

"Oh. Uh, okay? Should we find a seat?"

"Yeah, that works for me." Kareena gave Prem one last dirty look and followed Dave across the coffee shop. She felt the prickle of Prem's stare at the back of her neck and had to bite her lip to stop herself from shivering. Damn hormones. That's all it was. There was nothing at all redeeming about Dr. Prem Verma, and the ache when she looked at him was probably a residual effect of prolonged abstinence.

Dave motioned to two armchairs facing each other next to the fireplace. It was a quiet corner, and casual enough that they didn't have to worry about being too close to Dr. Dil.

"I can get drinks," Dave asked after Kareena sat down. "What would you like?"

"A medium latte, please, with no foam. And definitely no cinnamon. Not even on top."

He grinned at her, flashing straight white teeth. "For a second I was thinking you were going to give me a super complicated order. Half caf soy whatever. I was ready for it, too."

Kareena smiled. "Medium latte, no foam, no cinnamon is as adventurous as I get."

He nodded. "Yeah, now that you mention it, you look like a straight black coffee kind of person with that plain latte for special occasions."

"Uh, I don't—"

"I'm right, aren't I? Dave said. He pointed a finger-gun at her. "I have made it a game to guess my date's drink based on what I think their personality will be like. I'll be right back." Dave turned without another word and walked toward the counter.

Kareena whipped out her phone from her small bag.

KAREENA: Do I look boring?

BOBBI: What?

VEERA: No, of course not. Why? Aren't you supposed to be on your date right now?

KAREENA: I'm on my date. Dave. Hedge fund guy. Really nice teeth. He just said that I looked like the type to order black coffee, and then plain lattes with no foam for special occasions.

BOBBI: Did you tell him you freeze bottles of peppermint coffee creamer so when it's the off-season, you always have it?

VEERA: Or that you only order lattes to avoid an allergic reaction?

KAREENA: I didn't tell him any of those things! Ugh, I'm so off my game as it is. DR. DIL IS HERE.

BOBBI: What?

VEERA: What??

> **KAREENA:** I'll tell you later. For now, I'm counting this as a red flag. I need a way to weed out dates without wasting time. Three red flags you're out.

She glanced up, and Prem was looking right at her from a small table across the café. He'd gotten what looked like iced black coffee, and smirked in that I-know-I-look-good way that drove her insane. No, she was not going to be attracted to someone who put her in this predicament in the first place.

Kareena put her phone away right as Dave returned with two large cups in hand.

"The mediums looked pretty puny, so I got you a large one. I hope that's okay."

"Oh, uh. Thanks."

She took the cup from him and glanced around to see Prem sitting at one of the bistro tables directly in her line of sight. As if he knew that she was watching, he saluted her with his cup and went back to scrolling on his phone.

"I hope it's not too much caffeine for you late at night," Dave said. "I'm a night owl, so it doesn't bother me. I didn't even think about it."

"Law school was where I lost my sensitivity to caffeine," Kareena said with a smile. "I appreciate it." She cupped her hands around her drink and sat straighter, remembering that she shouldn't hunch during these things. Some magazine article once told her that hunching gave off signals of low confidence.

And Prem was still . . . there.

After a moment of staring at the floor, Kareena realized that they were dangerously close to creating an awkward silence.

"I appreciate that you didn't want to spend a month texting," she started. "I'm back online after a while and that's the one thing that I was dreading the most."

"Oh no. At our age, we have no time to play games, am I right?"

"Right," Kareena said. Wait, was he calling her old? "Uh, are you local?"

Dave spread his knees and leaned back against his chair. "No, but my parents still live here in Edison. I'm trying to get them out of New Jersey, though. Maybe Delaware. The property taxes in this area are just too difficult to manage, especially since my father is going to retire next year. It's such a burden, you know?"

"I know," Kareena said. "I'm a Jersey girl through and through, though."

"Yeah?" he said. "I can see that."

Now what in the hell did that mean?

"Where do you live?" Kareena asked.

"I'm in Guttenberg. Awesome apartment. Right across the river. I even have a little balcony. I do scotch tastings on my balcony with some of my friends. It's classy."

That sounds like the most boring thing in the world, Kareena thought. Was that in his profile? No, his profile basically said he liked movies and hanging out with friends.

"Sounds like a lot of fun."

"Oh, it is," he said. "In fact, my roommate and I are thinking of going into business together and starting our own premium liquor brand."

"Roommate?" Kareena couldn't tell quite yet if that was a red flag. At their age, tons of people still had roommates. The tristate area was expensive, after all. But he'd said he lived alone when they texted.

Dave leaned back in his armchair, legs spread. "She's working in publishing, but she has the best tongue for tasting ever. Tasting scotch, I mean." He laughed at his own joke. "She's never tasted anything else of mine, if you know what I mean."

Kareena looked up at Prem who was now watching her like a TV show. He had to have heard Dave's comment. Judging by the smug smile on his face, he was enjoying every minute of it. There was nothing for him to be smug about, though. She'd give Dave the benefit of the doubt that he had a platonic, healthy relationship with his co-ed roommate. They probably only shared utilities and a common area . . . right?

"I know what you're thinking," Dave said with a laugh.

"You do?"

"I do. How do my Indian parents let me live with a straight, single woman? Well, I'll be honest. They don't know. They think my roommate is a guy. But I'm not worried. What they don't know won't hurt them."

"Oh," she said.

She looked at this too-cocky, legs-spread-wide finance guy who lied to his parents about his roommate, who lied to her, and realized that he wasn't attractive at all.

Kareena wanted to speak to the manager. She wanted to return this model. It was not the right fit for her.

As Dave continued to ramble about the justifications for lying to his parents, Kareena couldn't help but wonder why she second-guessed herself, when she was usually so decisive. She needed to sharpen her intuition if she was going to start dating again like this.

Kareena began mentally drafting her text message to her friends in her head. She took a sip of her drink and was instantly hit with a ton of milky air.

"There's a lot of foam on this," she said, interrupting Dave's monologue.

"Oh," Dave said. "Yeah." He grinned at her like she'd just discovered his brilliance. "Foam is totally the best part of the drink."

"I am not a foam fan," she said. "I'm just going to have them scoop it out. One second, I'll be right back."

"Wow," he said, his smile slipping from his face. "Okay, well, what if you try it again? Maybe it'll change your mind? It really is the most delicious part of a latte, feel me?"

There was absolutely nothing delicious about foam, she thought. It was literally air. And she really wanted to tell him how much she absolutely did not want to feel him at all.

"Come on! Try it again."

Because she knew that Prem was watching, she lifted the cup to her mouth and drank deeply hoping that some of the milk would come through the froth.

The hot liquid practically scalded her tongue, and it definitely didn't taste like a plain latte. It had been so long since she'd had cinnamon that it took her a moment to identify it. By then, she'd already swallowed a huge gulp. Kareena put the cup down as far away from her as she could.

"Is there cinnamon in that?" she blurted out.

He nodded, his white teeth flashing again like shiny pieces of Dentyne gum. "Yes! It's the flavor syrup. I know you said no cinnamon, but what normal person doesn't like cinnamon? I knew if you tried it again, you'd change your mind. Flavor can change your life, Kareena. I hope you don't mind."

"I do mind," she said. "I absolutely do mind."

His eyebrows furrowed. "Because of some concentrated cinnamon syrup? I didn't think you'd be that kind of person."

She had no idea what that meant, nor did she exactly care.

"When a person tells you what they want, don't ever think that you know better." *Achoo!*

"Oh. Uh, bless you."

Achoo!

And here came the itchiness, she thought. She pushed up the sleeves of her button-down and saw small red bumps forming on her arms. Damn it, she'd jinxed herself by forgetting her EpiPen and Benadryl. The last time she had to use either was a decade ago, so she had no idea how she was going to react now. A little bit of cinnamon in Indian food gave her some rashes, but the concentrated stuff? It could send her into anaphylaxis.

"Whoa, uh, your face is looking a little red, and that's something with our skin tone."

"I'm allergic to cinnamon."

"Shit."

Before she could get out of her chair, Prem was crouching next to her. "Where is your EpiPen?" he said.

"I don't have it on me. *Achoo!*"

"You came to a coffee shop with an allergy to cinnamon and forgot your EpiPen? That's great."

He remembered.

"Open up," he snapped.

"What?"

He held her head in his palms. "Open your damn mouth, Kareena."

There was something in his tone that had her snapping to attention. Prem used his cell-phone light to check her throat.

Seconds later, he was pulling her to her feet. "Come on. Where is your car?"

"I don't have one here," she said. *Achoo!*

Kareena barely had a second to grab her bag before she was pulled across the café and through the front door. She registered Dave's shocked expression as Prem dragged her to his pretentious

Audi A7 toward the back of the lot. He shoved her in the passenger seat, ran around the front, and got behind the wheel.

"I need you to tell me if you start to have a hard time breathing. We don't want anaphylaxis."

"What will you do, celebrate? *Achoo!* God, I'm so itchy. I told him I didn't want cinnamon!"

"He didn't seem like the kind of guy who cared," Prem said as he sped out of the parking lot. "Any allergies to latex or other medication?"

"No."

"I think I remember you saying that the last time you had an episode was years ago."

"Yeah," she said. "Wow, we talked about a lot that night."

The harsh lines around his mouth softened. "Symptoms? Tongue swelling? Throat swelling?"

"Throat feels like it's itching but that could be panic," she said. *Please, for the love of god, don't pass out in front of Dr. D.*

"Deep breaths. Do you have your insurance card on you?"

"Yeah," Kareena said. Her throat was starting to feel a little itchy. She gripped the seat belt she'd struggled to put on. Who would've thought that she'd be speeding through Edison toward the hospital with Prem Verma?

The itchiness was insane. She hated every moment of it. Curse cinnamon!

"You need to always carry your EpiPen with you," he said. "Especially if you're going to a café. What if the barista was the one who made a mistake? And I don't understand why you don't have a car. You should always have a ride when you're going on dates. It's about *safety*."

"*Achoo!* It was a cinnamon concentrate. A syrup. And I'm still restoring my car. The one I told you about. *Achoo!*"

"The BMW 1988 E30, right? Did I tell you that my father was all about the BMWs when he immigrated to the U.S.?"

"You did. *Achoo!* First sign of success, I guess." She wheezed. Her eyes began to tear, and her chest tightened. She wheezed.

"In through your nose," he said softly. "A panic episode isn't going to help you. We're almost there."

He twisted a few dials on his dashboard and the sound of a phone ringing poured out of the car speakers. "RWJ."

"This is Dr. Prem Verma from Jersey City Cardiology Center." He rattled off a few numbers. "I'm bringing in a patient through the ER entrance. She was at a café. Allergic reaction to cinnamon. In danger of anaphylaxis."

When he hung up, Kareena brushed a tear off her cheek. Her skin was on fire now. "Don't text my family."

His head jerked in her direction. "What? Why not?"

"They'll make this whole thing worse for me," she gasped.

His small sporty car jumped the curb as he took a sharp turn into the RWJ campus entrance. He barely slowed down enough to drive over the speed bumps and came to a screeching halt in front of the ER doors.

Kareena was helped out of the car a second later. Everything went hazy, but when she felt Prem's hand on hers, she had one clear moment where their eyes locked.

"I got you," he said. "I'm here."

Dear Readers,

If your children have found their chosen matches, they must not only declare their intentions to each other first, they must also share their declaration with you, their guardians, as soon as possible. The poorest service is paid in a thank-you, and that will not cover the cost of your wedding venue.

Mrs. W. S. Gupta
Columnist
Avon, NJ

CHAPTER EIGHT

Prem

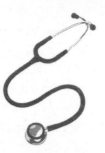

When Bindu texted Prem to let him know that Kareena was going out on a date, Prem spent a long time thinking about whether or not partnering with her would actually solve the problem at hand. But after a week of getting zero responses from other investors and fielding negative publicity, he knew that he had to at least try to talk to Kareena again. Showing up at her date probably wasn't the smartest way to get time alone with her, but then again, if he hadn't been there, she would've definitely gone into anaphylaxis.

He propped his feet up on the edge of her hospital bed and tossed back a handful of mixed nuts he'd scored from the vending machine. He debated caffeine since he never did get to finish the drink he'd ordered at the café, but hospital coffee was way too disgusting.

"You don't have to wait with me, you know," Kareena said looking up from her cell phone at his loud crunching. She had dark bags under her eyes now, and her hair fell in thick waves around her shoulders. Some of her exposed skin was still splotchy and red. "I appreciate you bringing me in, but I'm perfectly fine."

"I can take you home when we're done," he said. "Since you don't want your family to know that you're here."

She shook her head. "It's better if I take a car service. Or I'll ask one of my friends to come down and take me. I don't want to have to explain myself if my family sees you."

Prem shrugged. He could understand that sentiment. He'd had similar thoughts when he and Gori discussed living on their own. "Well, at least now we can talk," he said as he shook out more mixed nuts from his snack pack.

"Ugh, really?"

"I think it's time, don't you?"

"Not particularly. Hopefully, I won't be here much longer."

Her nurse had left a few moments ago after a barrage of testing and visits from various professionals. Now they were waiting for her results to come back before determining whether or not she would be discharged. She was hooked up to an IV, and pumped full of epinephrine and steroids, but they'd stopped the reaction in more than enough time that they didn't feel like they needed more than that.

"When was the last time you saw an allergist?"

Kareena, with her glasses perched on top of her head, lying back against the upright hospital bed, glared at him. "A while ago, and no, I'm not going to see one tonight. I think I've had enough needles, thank you very much. Is that what you wanted to talk about? Prem, my reaction stopped like ten minutes after they gave me the shots. The itching, the throat swelling . . . what? Why are you grinning like that?"

"You said my name," he blurted out. "You haven't since we first met." It felt . . . sexy? No, that wasn't it. Intimate. It was an intimate experience hearing his name from Kareena's mouth.

"Don't worry, I'll be referring to you as Dr. Phil shortly." She crossed her arms after motioning to the discarded sweater vest at the foot of her bed. "I don't understand why they had to cut my sweater vest. Did you tell them to do that? You have it out for my sweater vests, don't you?"

Prem rolled his eyes. "They cut it because you were wearing

too many layers. By the time they realized you were passing out because of a panic attack, not because your airways had closed, it was already too late. And no, I didn't tell them to cut your sweater vests. I'm partial to them. That's one of the first things I noticed about you."

The ruefulness in her expression faded, and she grew solemn. Fiddling with her phone, she said, "Did you hit on me because you thought I was easy? At the bar."

"What? Where did that come from?"

"Never mind, forget I asked."

"No," he said. Prem reached out and touched Kareena's hand, so she'd look over at him. "No. I was there with my friend that night, but he didn't want to sit with me because I kept looking over at you. So, he left, and I figured what the hell?"

"But you definitely regretted it when we started making out," she replied. "That's why you faked your emergency call."

"I didn't fake it," he said. And because he knew the time for lying was long past, he added, "My family has an SOS ring tone. That way my parents, my aunts, my uncles, all of whom are physicians or professors, know to drop everything, including their patients, because there is something wrong."

Kareena's eyes widened. "Pineapple," she said.

"Excuse me?"

"Pineapple. That's our SOS text with our dad so he knows it's an emergency and has to stop in the middle of seeing patients. I'm assuming while I was tied up with my sweater vest, that phone ping was your Pineapple."

"Exactly," he said with an exhale of relief. "I really was going to come back."

She shook her head. "I think it was meant to be. Dr. Dil's philosophy really doesn't jibe with mine," she added ruefully.

Prem knew that she was right, even though he hated it. He could never give her what she wanted. In all his years on earth, he'd never told anyone that he loved them. Hell, he hadn't even told his parents his feelings for them. The words always seemed so trivial, and he wasn't going to start using them now. He couldn't start now.

He held out the half-eaten bag of nuts, and after glancing down at it, and back at his face, she took the packet, shook out a small palmful, and handed the bag back.

"I started the show three years ago as a way to raise money," Prem said. "My friend owns the network as part of his portfolio of shows. He heard from management they needed someone to fill a spot, and I thought it would be a good way to get the message out to as many people as possible about community health. It started as a small audience, but just enough to plant the seeds for my community health center."

Kareena's eyebrow arched. "The South Asian community health center you're trying to build downtown?"

Prem nodded. "That's the one."

"THIS HEALTH CENTER. It means everything to me."
 "Why?" Kareena asked.
 "Because. It's important."
 "Ahh," Kareena said. "Maybe one day you'll tell me the whole story."
 He grinned. "Yeah, I hope so."

"I LOST . . . I lost someone who meant a lot to me," he said. "She had a tumor, and it killed her because she wasn't getting the medical treatment she needed. I was busy finishing up my cardiology fellowship and I had some part to blame in not helping her get in front of the right specialists."

Kareena slipped her glasses back onto her face and pushed them up the bridge of her nose. "But she did see doctors, right? What did they say? What was their excuse? I hope you held them accountable." She waited for him to answer with those big brown eyes framed by long, thick dark lashes.

"Her family didn't want to make waves."

"Bullshit," she said.

How could she still look so beautiful with smudges under her eyes and exhaustion etched in the lines of her face? But she still burned brilliantly. Gori would've liked her.

"Are you going to let me tell my story or not?"

She tossed back the remaining nuts she had. After chewing and swallowing, she said, "Okay, Dr. Prem Verma. I'll listen, but please tell me it has nothing to do with my aunties."

He grinned. "It has something to do with your aunties."

"Damn it, Prem—"

"Hear me out. The building I want for my community health center is available, but I have to put in the deposit by September. I was close. So close to having the funds for it all. But after our argument, my largest donor backed out. If I can work on my reputation, there is a chance I can get him back."

"And how are you going to do that?"

"It's a long shot, and to be honest, it sounds ridiculous, but I'm going to prove to him that I believe in everything I say on the show," he said. "A stable relationship demonstrates that commitment and communication work. It'll last long enough for me to get the money I need."

Understanding blanketed her face, her mouth gaping open. "Seriously?"

"Seriously," he said. "And if I can't convince my biggest donor into recommitting to my center, then I'm going to leverage the relationship with my mother. I know you understand since you're in the same position with your dad."

Kareena was already shaking her head, strands of her dark hair falling around her face. "I get what you're trying to do, but no one who knows us is going to believe us. Not to mention, this is cheating. I want my mom's house, but I'm also trying to find someone I can spend my life with. My parents had a love marriage, and if my mother were alive, I know that she'd want that for me, too. Otherwise, it feels like betrayal if I inherit the house through deceit."

"And you think the cinnamon idiot from today could be your true love?"

She wrinkled her nose and shook her head. "Obviously not."

"Did your aunties set you up? If so, he's a terrible rishta."

"They paid for my online dating accounts. That's where I found Dave. I am currently on the platinum plan on three different desi dating sites."

He'd just tossed back another handful of nuts and almost choked. "God, that's miserable."

"How would you know? You're a tall, desi dude with an M.D. The minute you got your degree, you became organic grass-fed filet mignon in a case of Costco-brand chuck roast."

"The irony of comparing a Hindu to beef is not lost on me," Prem said, amused.

The corner of Kareena's mouth twitched. "Meanwhile, the more educated I get, the older I get, the faster people think my expiration date approaches. At least that's what my aunties believe. So online dating is my only option."

He dropped his feet to the floor and leaned in closer to her now. "Kareena, I know that you want a love story like your mom had, no matter how much I think love is a—"

"Don't fucking start with me, Dr. Phil," she said.

Prem held up a hand in surrender. "Rina, honey, what are you going to do if you can't find someone in four months?"

Kareena quieted, and the seriousness in her expression had him pushing on.

"We know we have chemistry."

"Prem—"

"We do," he said. He wasn't going to lie to both of them about that. Even now when he brushed his hand against hers, he felt a current straight up his arm. "And we also know that forever isn't possible for us when we believe in different things. I *can't* give you the love you want. All I'm asking you for is right now. A couple of dates, a couple of pictures, a big engagement announcement. In the end we both get the cash, then call it quits."

"Why me?" Kareena blurted out. She motioned to her calamine-smeared face with fingers covered in peanut salt. "Your credentials are every Indian family's wet dream. I'm sure you can find anyone that you can stand to be around."

"It'll take too long to find someone who won't get the wrong idea," he said quickly. "Since you know the truth about me, we aren't going to have any problems."

"Prem . . ."

He touched her hand and turned it over to brush the softness on the inside of her wrist. "Rina, give us a shot."

"Can I ask you a question?"

He brushed a curl off her face; she looked startled but didn't jerk away from his touch. He'd done that once before, almost like it was an instinctual need for him to be close.

"Ask," he said, his voice husky.

"Why *don't* you believe in true love?"

Prem let out a sigh, but leaned into her space, so it was just the two of them. Nothing else. No one else. "Rina, love is an emotion that can literally damage the heart, and it isn't sustainable for long-term relationships. An emotional connection? That's fleeting. Relying on body chemistry means you're relying on something fickle."

"Body chemistry," she said slowly. "That's what we have."

"Rina—"

"Kareena."

"I like calling you Rina," he said with a smile. "It reminds me of the woman who chugged her drink just so she could have one with me."

She smiled, and it reached her eyes this time. "Distracting me isn't going to work. You may think love is an illusion, but it's real. I saw it when my parents slow danced in the kitchen on Sunday mornings. Love was the stupid car my father bought for my mother that I have to keep in the shed because he gets really sad when he sees it. It's the echoes of laughter I remember every time I come down the stairs in the house my mother and father built together."

"Do you really want that much emotion in your life?" Prem asked quietly.

"Absolutely."

He groaned when the realization hit him like a smack in the face. "Oh god, you're one of those girls who has a secret list of things that make you think you're in *love*, don't you?" Kareena grinned at him, and her entire face lit up like sunlight.

Even though he'd known her for such a short amount of time, that smile could completely short-circuit his nervous system. Prem's heart pounded in overtime, and for a moment, he forgot about what they were talking about. Her happiness was blinding.

"I've had a lot of time in my dating moratorium to think about what I want," she said, completely oblivious to his reaction.

"Until you find Mr. Right, pretend to date me for a few months, then we can announce a pretend engagement. After the new year, we'll break things off. No one will see it coming. Even your aunties won't find out. This way you don't have to settle for someone who is less than your perfect man."

Kareena didn't say anything for a minute, but Prem could see the wheels turning. Finally, she crossed her arms over her chest, a stubborn line set across her mouth.

"I want to keep dating other people for a few more months before I give you my answer. You'll have to be my Plan B."

"What? No way." The idea of her flirting, having drinks, or spending time with anyone else was completely unacceptable. He wanted to keep all of her laughs to himself.

"That's a deal breaker, Prem," she said. "I need you to think about this for one second from my perspective. If I say yes to you, and we start fake whatever it is we're going to do, then *everyone* is going to know. All the people who watched our video? They'll want the update. Mrs. W. S. Gupta may write an article about it. Your family in California will find out."

"That's the point," he said, thinking of his investors. "We want *everyone* to know."

"They're also going to find out when we break up. And do you know what's going to happen after that? They'll turn on me. Because hello! We live in a shit world where it's always the woman's fault."

"I don't think—"

Kareena held up a finger, her eyes widened with a look that only an Indian woman who demanded attention could give. "Don't even think about trying to lie to me on this one," she said.

"My reputation is going to be completely fucked. And I may have the house, which is something I desperately want, but the chance of me finding a person to love after that is going to be infinitely harder. So, while I have the time, as short a time frame as it might be, I don't want to get engaged to you, or pretend to marry you just yet. I want to try to find the real deal before I risk my entire future. Otherwise, I'll be stuck trying to find a man from California."

"Hey, I'm from California."

"My point exactly. You still smell like narcissism and avocados."

"Cute," he said.

But Kareena wasn't wrong about her stakes. At the end of the day, the stakes were a lot higher for her than for him, and he'd be an asshole if he didn't respect that, didn't understand the power dynamics that still existed for Indian women.

Prem reached out and linked his fingers with hers, enjoying the pleasant jolt that coursed up his arm. He rubbed the pad of his thumb over her knuckles. "It's just we have so little time . . ."

Kareena pulled away, her hand trembling ever so slightly. "I don't want to put all my ovaries in one basket," she said dryly.

Prem shook his head. "Okay, but you've made your point. And when it comes down to it, I'll take the fall as much as I can to protect you as much as I can. But I do want to say something on my next show."

"Tell your audience that we've met and talked. That we've come to a mutual understanding that you're wrong."

"Ha ha," he said. Her mutinous expression made it clear that she wasn't going to budge.

"Fine," he said. "We'll play it your way. Try to date other people before you come back to me. But that doesn't mean I'm going to wait around for you to make up your mind. Give me your phone."

She stuck her tongue out at him but handed over her cell. He quickly called himself, and then handed back the device. "Please don't block me; otherwise, I'll have to involve the aunties again."

Kareena groaned. "Keep them out of this. At least for now. I don't want them to make this situation more complicated for me."

"At least your aunties aren't vicious," he said. He thought about the women at home who were best friends with his mother. They were more of the traditional, stereotypical aunty archetype. They judged, and gossiped, and upheld old colonialist and patriarchal views, and then pinched cheeks and pretended that what they said was to help others. Meanwhile, Kareena's aunties were a bit more . . . progressive.

"My aunties are meddlers," she said. "Seriously, if you want me to consider your plan, then you have to keep them out of this."

Prem gripped the bedrails and leaned in until their noses were practically touching. He could hear the hitch in Kareena's breath, and he liked to think that despite her animosity, there was something about him that affected her the same way he was affected by her presence.

"I will keep the aunties out of this for a little while longer, but once we get close to our deadline, all bets are off. I have a lot of money riding on our engagement, and I need it to build my health center. I will play dirty if I have to."

Her eyes narrowed into slits. "Are you seriously threatening me?"

"Not at all, Rina."

The glass pane door of their ER cubicle opened, and the curtain whipped back. An older woman with a helmet of white hair, wearing a pink pair of scrubs, entered. "Kareena Mann?"

Kareena nodded.

The woman turned to Prem. "Dr. Verma, I didn't realize that you were still here."

He stood and crumpled the empty plastic mixed nuts bag. "I was just leaving. Kareena? I'll talk to you later. Text me if you need anything."

"I won't."

"I will be seeing you soon."

"You don't have to sound so smug about it," she mumbled.

Prem stared at her for a moment longer, then he motioned for the nurse to follow him out of the room.

She gave him a wary look and ignored Kareena's protest as they stepped behind the curtain and glass pane. When they were out of hearing distance, the nurse said his name like a question.

"Mrs. Baker," he said to the nurse. "Kareena and I are . . . close."

The nurse's eyes went wide. Prem could only imagine that she'd be bursting at the seams, ready to tell the rest of the staff at the station that he was in a relationship.

"Yes, sir. We'll take very good care of it."

"I know you will. Can you recommend to her physician that they add to her aftercare notes that she's in need of a full physical and an allergy test? She's going to complain, but I want to make sure that this doesn't happen to her again."

"You got it," the nurse said, and turned to walk back into the room.

Prem waited a few moments longer until he heard Kareena's shriek of indignation. He grinned and strolled away whistling. This was going to be more fun than he'd thought.

CHAPTER NINE

Kareena

DHRUV: Hey, gorgeous. Thanks for accepting my profile.

KAREENA: You're welcome!

DHRUV: Are you into golden showers?

KAREENA: *BLOCK*

USER 875387: I want to eat you

KAREENA: *BLOCK*

PARTH: Nic pic, u wan franndship????? 🍆

KAREENA: *BLOCK*

EDWARD: Hey, how's it going?

KAREENA: Hey. I never met a desi person named Edward before! Nice to meet you.

EDWARD: :-D Oh, I changed my name. Women let me bite them like a vampire more with my current name than with the name I was born with.

KAREENA: *BLOCK*

VINNY: Hi, hello. I am seeking a wife.

KAREENA: *BLOCK*

JASPREET: Hey, aren't you the girl who is supposedly dating Dr. Dil from that show?

KAREENA: *BLOCK*

PREM-DR. PHIL: Hey, you want to go out this Saturday?

KAREENA: Not particularly.

PREM-DR. PHIL: Do you have a date with someone else?

KAREENA: No, not yet but keeping my options open.

PREM-DR. PHIL: I think we need to get to know each other better for when we announce that we're together.

KAREENA: I think we know each other fine.

> **PREM-DR. PHIL:** Okay, then we need to meet for a picture. I have to post at least one social media picture since I talked about you on my show.

> **KAREENA:** That sounds like a you-problem.

> **PREM-DR. PHIL:** Fine. Don't say I didn't warn you.

Kareena wrenched the bolt a little too hard and nicked her finger. "Ouch," she hissed. There was just enough light underneath the carriage of her car that she was able to pull off her glove to check to see if she was bleeding. Thankfully, it was just a red welt.

She dropped her head back against the hot pink creeper seat and closed her eyes. The early June weather made her car shed a sauna of epic proportions, but it was quiet and peaceful, which was exactly what she needed. Between work and dating and avoiding her sister's rage-filled engagement party requests, she was exhausted.

Thankfully, Kareena's new job, her dream job, was a place filled with wonderful women who supported her after *The Dr. Dil Show* continued to go viral, so work, in addition to her car, had become a place of solace from the madness.

Behind her desk at her office, or here in the backyard shed, she could finally think about Prem's offer in peace.

Partnering with Dr. Dil meant she'd have to deal with the aftereffects of an even more public breakup later. She didn't know if she'd be able to recover from that. But at the same time, it made sense to join forces because neither of them had very many options.

Although it may be her only option since online dating was coming up empty-handed. The aunties refused to help any more than they already had, because they were convinced that Prem was perfect for her.

Like always, Kareena was on her own. And to be fair, the house meant more to her than it did to anyone else.

"Do you just lie under there or do you actually get work done?"

Kareena jerked and almost hit her head on the undercarriage of the car. "Son of a bitch!"

"Are you hurt?" Prem's voice was sharp now. She felt him grip her bare ankle and roll her out from her position.

She squinted at the light and looked up at his sharply defined cheekbones highlighted by the sunlight coming in through the open shed doors.

"What are you doing here?" she blurted out.

"Where are you hurt?" he asked, crouching down at her side. Good god, his crotch was practically at eye level. Luckily he wasn't in those thin scrubs this time around. Those jeans were still pretty fitted, though.

"I'm not hurt," she finally replied and sat up on her pink creeper. He was too close, too overwhelming whenever he crowded her space.

When he didn't say anything after a moment, she looked up and met his stare.

"You're just as beautiful in engine grease as you are in a sweater vest," he said quietly.

Her heart thudded hard in her chest, and she could feel her brain malfunction even as she pulled back. "Why are you here?"

He got to his feet, his warm hands grasping hers and pulling her up. Their bodies brushed, and Kareena jerked again, a tingle shooting up her spine.

"You haven't been responding to my texts," he finally said. "Since I'm done prepping for my show tomorrow and I'm not on call tonight, I decided to come out and see you myself. Wow, this is the E30 you're working on, huh? I can't remember if you told me. Was this your father's car?"

She narrowed her eyes at him as he walked slowly around her car touching *everything*. "Dad bought it for my mom from a guy who barely drove it. After Mom died, Dad was too sad to drive it anymore, so I bought it off him before he could sell it to someone else."

Prem ran his fingers through his thick black hair. One stubborn lock slid back into place across his forehead. "It's nice. Looks like it needs a lot of work, though."

"I told you."

"CARS? THAT'S PROBABLY the hottest thing I've ever heard," he said.

Kareena shrugged. "I think my obsession was born out of necessity."

"Because your car means family to you, right?"

"Yes. And the memory of someone I've lost."

"I can't tell you how much I understand that," he replied.

PREM CROUCHED TO inspect a tire. "I know you said you finished the engine last year, but what are you working on right now?"

"I just have to replace the dash instruments, and then the rest of the work needs to be completed in a shop. Upholstery. New mirrors and windows. Refitting with interior trim. Body work." Kareena hated that she couldn't do all the work at home, but some skills required years of apprenticeship to get just right. Not to mention tools.

"Is this why you've been busy?"

"And because we don't have anything else to say to each other."

"We were able to communicate pretty well when we first met."

Kareena put the wrench she'd been holding on the makeshift bench covered in a grease-stained towel. "I've read a lot of romance novels, and do you know what happens at the end of every single one that has a fake relationship in it? Someone finds out. And then the whole thing blows up. Except, we won't have a happily ever after. Why? Because we're too damn different, Prem. What? Why are you looking at me like that?"

He was grinning, hands tucked in his back pockets, as he rocked back on his heels. "Nothing, it's just you sound really cute when you're freaking out."

She adjusted her glasses, praying that the heat in her cheeks wasn't noticeable. "Stop trying to distract me with flirting. You have to keep your distance until I have no other options. Use this time to find other investors."

"Rina, there are no other investors," he said. He motioned to her shed, then outside her double doors at the house. "Four months will go by before we know it. The sooner we accept that, the faster we can secure the money we need. I told you. I'll protect you when we walk away from each other."

"Let me do it my way first," she said. The thought of pretending to be in love with him made her nauseous. Especially since everyone would know that he didn't believe in love and couldn't possibly feel the same way. "I just started looking . . ."

"Swiping right on dating apps isn't going to work when you're on a deadline." He shoved his hands in his pocket. "You'll barely be out of the 'talking phase.'"

"Excuse me?"

His smug expression rubbed her raw even as his long, tapered fingers brushed gently over the hood of her car. "You know, where you just message back and forth until one of you says something completely ridiculous, and you end up ghosting each other. Since your last date I'm assuming that's what you're doing, too, right?"

Kareena scowled at him. Damn him for being right. She was currently having mind-numbing conversations with four different people, and trying to figure out if any of them were worth an in-person coffee meeting.

"Come back in three and a half months, Prem. I'm busy right now," she finally said. "I've said it before and I'm going to say it again. You are my Plan B."

Prem turned to her, and the corner of his mouth curved up, as if he knew all her secrets.

Calm down, bitch. He ain't for you.

"Do you really think the aunties are going to believe you when you show up with me by your side two weeks before your sister's engagement party? Will your *dad* believe you?"

She scowled at him. He had a point. Everyone was going to think she'd lost her mind.

Kareena very well might before the end of this.

She began lining up the rest of her tools on a felt mat after wiping them down with the towel. Without turning to him, she said, "I'm not saying yes, but how do you propose we make this look like we've been dating for months?"

"Get dressed in something other than your Mechanic Indian Barbie outfit, and I'll take you out to lunch. We'll take pictures and talk about logistics. Or we can pick up where we left off last time."

She whirled on him. That *had* to be a joke. "I think you need to stop bringing up my birthday mishap."

Prem slowly shook his head, his eyes darkening. "If you're asking me to forget my one night with you, no matter how short it was, then you're out of your mind."

She stopped, every part of her frozen with confusion. "Prem . . ."

"Come on. Get dressed. I'll buy."

Kareena thought about it for a moment longer. "Fine," she said. "But I want Indian food."

"Punjabi Express?"

Her jaw dropped. "You remembered?"

He rolled his eyes, as if her surprise was a ridiculous reaction. "Of course. Now hurry up. Let's get out of here before your grandmother and sister come out to find us."

Kareena grabbed her phone. "Speaking of my family, you don't want to go through the house unless you plan on spending time helping Bindu plan her engagement party. I can meet you out front by your car."

"Good idea."

She swore she felt Prem's fingertips graze the base of her back as they cut across the yard in two separate directions. But then again, it could've been the early June heat playing tricks on her.

Either way, she had to be on her toes for the next couple hours. If she was going to spend it in Prem's company, she couldn't let her guard down. He was the type of man who pushed until he got what he wanted, and there was no way she would ever roll over for a partner, especially someone like Prem Verma.

Dear Readers,

If you are arranging with the matches for the first time, encourage them not to eat. Food is often a distractor and an opportunity for one candidate to judge the other. A classic cup of chai is always preferred.

Mrs. W. S. Gupta
Columnist
Avon, NJ

CHAPTER TEN

Prem

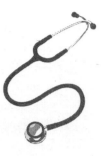

It took less time than Prem figured it would for Kareena to surprise him again. Fifteen minutes, in fact. The car ride from her house to Punjabi Express was filled with the same easy conversation he'd discovered with her when they met the bar. Their sentences connected one after the other as if they were not only on the same page, but in the same paragraph, creating the same story together. "I'm starving," she said as they entered the small strip mall restaurant. Prem hummed in agreement. He pressed his fingertips at the base of her spine, and even though she stiffened under his touch, she didn't pull away.

"Should we order first?" Kareena paused in front of one of the empty booths. "Or should one of us sit to hold the table?"

"You sit," he said. "I'll get us something to drink to start off with. Mango lassi?"

She looked up at him, startled.

Yup, I remember.

She pushed her glasses up the bridge of her nose. "Sure, that would be great. I can pay for my own, though."

"Rina, honey, sit down," Prem said, and stifled a laugh at her mutinous expression. He crossed the restaurant but paused before reaching the counter so he could turn back and watch Kareena slide into the booth. She immediately began scrolling on her phone. Who was she talking to? Was she still hell-bent on finding another guy to hang out with for the rest of the weekend?

"Excuse me?" the uncle behind the counter said. "What is it you want, sir?"

"Uh, two mango lassis, please. To start."

The man rang him up and slid the cups and straws across the table.

Kareena was still scrolling on her phone when he returned with their drinks.

"Can you please refrain from having conversations with other men while we're together?" Prem said. The idea of her talking with someone else still rubbed him the wrong way, especially when it was obvious that she had options while his only choice was her.

Kareena rolled her eyes, even as she put her phone down, and shoved a straw into the opening at the top of her cup. "I'm checking my work email."

"On the weekend?"

"You're working, too, aren't you?" she said, pointing to the phone he'd placed at his elbow. "You're on call. I'm just answering client emails."

"Touché, Rina. Touché."

"It's *Kareena*, and I have no idea what you're talking about."

"I prefer Rina."

Kareena's expression grew pensive as she drank. "Do your parents get it? What you're trying to accomplish?" she asked.

Prem snorted before he could stop himself. "Not at all. They want me to become like my perfect cousin, a surgeon who is happily engaged and planning a big-ass wedding. They think I'm pissing away my education."

Kareena nodded. "My father says he's happy I found my calling and my passion, but I know he's irritated I took a pay cut. He recently threw it in my face that I would've been able to afford the house on my own if I had stayed at a top law firm."

"I don't see you thriving in a place like that."

She shook her head. "I wouldn't. I didn't. I worked at a big firm until I made the switch, and I've never been happier with my decision. But I can't really blame our parents for feeling the way they do. Their roots were torn clear out of the soil in India, and they had to work hard to plant them again in the U.S. Then, to ensure that the whole family tree remained stable, they tried to usher us into stable jobs."

Prem leaned in across the table until they were inches apart. "Their purpose doesn't excuse their actions, Rina."

"No, but it helps shape my actions," she replied.

Before Prem could say anything else, a plate of pani puri artfully arranged on a tray floated past their table. The snack food was one of his favorites. The fried shells were crispy and the shape of an oversized golf ball. He loved cracking a hole into the shell, then stuffing it with seasoned potatoes, chickpeas, diced red onions, chutney, and spicy water.

"Oh my god," Kareena said, her voice as reverent as he felt.

Prem was already salivating. "Yeah, I'm thinking the same thing."

The server gave the pani puri to a couple across the room, and Prem watched as they each picked up a shell, cracked it with a quick firm tap of the thumb, added the fillings, and immediately popped it in their mouths.

"OKAY, FAVORITE SNACK food," Prem asked.

Rina's eyes brightened. "Pani puri," she said, without hesitation.

"Excellent choice. They're just a fun food."

*Rina's expression became dreamy. "I remember visiting India with
my parents when I was a kid. We'd go to see my grandmother and walk
down to the local market where there was a pani puri cart. The man
would tap the shell and fill it between one blink and the next. Then
scoop in the water, put it in the dried leaf shaped like a cup, and hand
it to me. My sister and I were so young, but we'd try to compete to see
who could eat the most pani puris."*

THE MEMORY OF their conversation had Prem smiling. He motioned to the tray. "That's a lot for two people."

Kareena scoffed. "Hardly. With my years of practice? I could
probably polish that off myself."

It delighted him that she remembered their conversation. "You
could probably eat half of one," Prem said. "But definitely not the
whole thing."

Kareena adjusted her glasses. "I'll have you know that I am the
best pani puri eater in our family. But I doubt that's something a
health-conscious doctor like yourself would understand."

Prem's eyebrow twitched. "*Excuse* me, Rina. I bet you I could
eat double the pani puris that you eat and not even blink an eye."

"I doubt that. We both know that you're all talk."

An idea formed in his head, one that even had his Charlie
twitching in his pants. An image of Kareena stuffing . . . well,
something in her mouth—

He shook his head. "Challenge accepted, Rina."

Prem marched to the counter. The staff behind the register
raised an eyebrow.

"I'd like two of those giant pani puri trays, please," he said as
he pointed to the one at the nearby table.

"Two?" The man balked and pulled at his red collared shirt.

"That is a plate for four, sir. One tray can maybe be consumed by two people as a whole meal."

"Two trays," Prem repeated. The man's eyes remained saucer sized as he punched the keys in his register and ran Prem's platinum credit card.

"We're about to have ourselves a little pani puri eating contest," Prem said when he returned to the table.

Her eyes sparkled. "What, just so I could prove you wrong?"

"To see if you know yourself better than I already do," Prem responded. "Competition stops when someone has enough."

"You know I was on the debate team," Kareena said. "I was the reason why our team made it to nationals. I play to win."

"Then this should be fun, since I was on the varsity tennis team, and we *won* nationals."

They grabbed napkins and paper plates and pushed two tables together so they both had enough space. Prem knew he had made a mistake when a server arrived carrying two giant trays of pani puri shells. The hollowed shells looked like a tower of deliciously browned golf balls. They were followed by another server carrying a jug of spiced water, and a smaller tray of toppings. They carefully put everything in front of Kareena and Prem, then backed away. Holy hell, Prem thought. They were both going to spike their blood pressure.

"You're out of your mind," Kareena said with amusement.

"If feeding you this tower of perfection is going to convince you that I'm serious about our partnership, then bring it on."

Prem was very aware that everyone was watching them now. He picked up the empty bowls and filled them with spiced water. It smelled like tamarind and mint with a hint of spicy chili. He poured the second bowl for Kareena.

"Are you ready?" Kareena asked.

Prem passed her a shell and took one for himself. "Yeah, ready as I'll ever be."

Prem felt for the thinnest spot on the shell, then tapped it hard with his thumb. The tiny hole formed, just large enough to pour in his toppings.

He grabbed one of the spoons and began to fill. The key to winning this competition was an even distribution of toppings and water.

Before he filled the shell with water, he held it up to Kareena. "To second chances," he said. "And convincing you that I'm always right."

She flashed him a saucy grin, then tapped her shell against his. "To renewed friendships. And proving you wrong."

"Ready?" he asked.

"Set," she replied.

"Go!"

Prem dunked his shell in his water just like his mother taught him when he was a kid at chaat food parties. Kareena mimicked his actions. Once her shell was filled to the rim, he shoved the entire thing into his mouth.

Favor *explosion*. The salty, savory water, the tangy spiciness of the chutney, and the soft neutral flavors of the chickpeas and potatoes were like heaven.

He closed his eyes and moaned, then popped them open again when Kareena tossed a napkin at his head.

"You have water all over your face," she said with a laugh. "Are you already calling it quits after one?"

"Not on your life, Rina, honey," he said. Prem immediately filled a second shell and shoved it in his mouth.

By the fifth pani puri, they were starting to attract a crowd.

By the dozenth, the owner of the restaurant pulled out a small dry erase board and started counting for them.

When they reached two dozen, Prem's stomach was cramping, and he felt like he was about to have water gushing out of his eyeballs. But he refused to give up just yet. This was about his honor now.

As Prem pushed another through his lips, he watched Kareena do the same. Her eyes teared up, and she bit down on the shell.

He barely managed to swallow one more and knew that the nausea was a bad sign. The satiety reflux triggered a long time ago and was now prompting vomit if he had any more. Prem had to stop. He collapsed back against his seat.

"I'm out," he croaked. Someone dabbed a napkin to his forehead.

The crowd that had assembled around him booed.

Prem watched as Kareena's fingers trembled. She grabbed one of the last remaining shells on the tray and cracked it easily. It took her a few seconds to scrape the last of the fillings out of their bowls and fill the shell. And her forehead was dewy.

"This is the winning pani puri," the owner whispered. "If you eat this, you are the champion."

Kareena tilted her bowl to pour the rest of her water into the shell, then shoved it into her mouth.

She chewed, then swallowed.

The restaurant waited. No one made a sound.

Kareena got shakily to her feet, then raised both fists in the air. "I win!"

The room erupted in cheers and applause.

Uncles patted her on the back, aunties cheered her on by whistling. The owner handed her a gift card to the restaurant for fifty dollars and thanked her for such a great impromptu show.

Prem knew he was grinning ear to ear. He couldn't help it. She had so much joy on her face. It was the kind of expression that turned her from sexy into stunning. It was also the expression that told him this woman was going to get exactly what she wanted.

Kareena dabbed her face with a napkin and tossed it on the table. "Thank you for a . . . fun non-date, Dr. Prem Verma."

Prem slowly got to his feet. He leaned over the table, across empty dishes and plates, and ignoring her wide-eyed expression, as well as the gasps from those still watching, he pressed a kiss to the corner of her mouth. He tasted the salty tang of the pani puri water and felt her soft skin. "Next time we're going out on a real date."

When her cheeks flushed, he knew that he'd gotten her.

That's right, he thought. *Match point.*

CHAPTER ELEVEN

Kareena

USER 567900: Hey there

KAREENA: Hey

USER 567900: You look familiar. Do you do porn?

KAREENA: *BLOCK*

TREVOR: Hey. I like your profile!

KAREENA: Thanks! I like yours.

TREVOR: Awesome. Wanna fuck?

KAREENA: *BLOCK*

GURU: Hey

KAREENA: Hey

GURU: What's good?

KAREENA: Uh, nothing. Just getting off work now.

KAREENA: Hello?

KAREENA: You know what? Fair enough. I've ghosted people, too.

GURU: *BLOCK*

SATYAM: Hey. How's it going?

KAREENA: Not bad. How are you?

SATYAM: I'm great. I mean, other than being online.

KAREENA: Oh, I know what you mean.

SATYAM: So would it be weird if I gave your number to my mom?

SATYAM: She wants to make sure you're legit and from a good family

SATYAM: She also thinks that "looking for true love"' is cliché on your profile. And that you need to lower your standards a bit, and that I may also be too good for you. Also, she thinks you look familiar.

KAREENA: *BLOCK*

PREM: Hey, how goes wedding dress shopping?

KAREENA: Fine. I'm swiping on dating profiles while I'm waiting, so it's productive.

PREM: I told you, you should just go out with me. You already know that I can keep up with you in a pani puri battle.

KAREENA: But can you give me what I need?

PREM: Did you know that romantic love wasn't even a factor in marriages until the late eighteenth century? And not just for South Asians.

KAREENA: I'll take that as a no.

PREM: I can buy you time for your house. Isn't that what you want?

Kareena read Prem's last text message over again. She had no idea what she was supposed to say to him or what she was supposed to do.

He'd texted a couple times since their pani puri–eating competition, and every time his name appeared on her phone screen, her mouth tingled in memory.

"Who was that?" Bobbi asked. She sat back against the plush seat of the velvet couch, her cell phone in one hand and a flute of champagne in another.

"Prem."

"Ahh," Bobbi said.

Kareena glared at her. "Ahh. What does 'Ahh' mean? You don't make sound effects and faces like that without a double meaning."

Bobbi shrugged. "It means 'Ahh.'" She put her phone and champagne down on the large glass coffee table in front of them. "It's just that you've been spending a lot of time talking to Prem when you guys were screaming at each other in a viral video a month ago. And before that, you were texting us, cursing him, because he lied to you at a bar to get in your pants, then left you horny in a stranger's office. By the way, I wish you'd taken a look around that office. I've been trying to get Benjamin Padda's attention for ages."

"Sorry, I was in a bit of a rush," Kareena said dryly. "And I don't carry grudges." Just memories of Prem's kiss.

He'd purposely planted one on the *corner of her mouth*. That was like expert level on the romance hero skill scale. That was a type of kiss meant to throw her off her game and remind her what it was like to make out with him. She'd been slightly intoxicated the night they'd met, so when he corner-of-the-mouth kissed her, it brought back a flood of memories that went from hazy to crystalline.

One thing was for certain. The man could make a woman weak with his mouth.

She couldn't tell Bobbi or Veera about it yet. Not until she had more information. Otherwise, they would be hounding her for weeks to find out what was going on.

"Kareena, you do more than carry grudges," Bobbi continued, oblivious to Kareena's train of thought. "You have a list and keep receipts. True Taurus energy through and through. But Prem is no longer on your hate list, is he?"

Kareena shook her head. "We called a truce, and then I beat

him in a pani puri–eating competition." It was kind of hard to stay mad at someone who made her laugh when she knew she was being exasperating, and had the guts to kiss her in an Indian restaurant. Every aunty and uncle in the place was watching.

Bobbi sipped her champagne. "This is the guy who thinks love is an illusion. The one who believes that love marriages aren't sustainable because they're built on emotion. He's also the same guy who needs something from you, because to Dr. Dil, relationships are transactional. Don't forget that."

"Bobbi, I don't need your help analyzing my relationship with Prem. I need your help figuring out why I'm not getting any other matches online. Is it because I'm in Edison? What if I change my location to something like Boston for a few weeks? Do you think I'll have better luck up north? I always liked a man in flannel."

"I think men are men wherever you go. You're looking for a needle in a haystack, honey. Welcome back to the world of heterosexual dating. Any word from the aunties?"

Kareena shook her head. "I think they're so set on matching me with Dr. Dil that they aren't being super aggressive with their search."

"They picked a good one," Bobbi said. "Despite the argument between you two, there is definitely chemistry there." She fanned herself with her free hand.

"Thanks for the help," Kareena muttered. "I have a little over three months left here, and I do not need you to agree with the aunties."

"Hey, I'm planning your sister's wedding and engagement party at a discount," Bobbi replied. "I have no time to help. Be nice to me."

"Ugh, don't talk to me about this stupid engagement party." A Labor Day weekend event that was the definitive end to her chance of finding her perfect man. Her jeevansathi. And once her time was finished, her father was going to sell the house. He'd already brought an agent to come out and assess the property, and Bindu had sent out invites to two hundred people.

"How are things at home?" Bobbi asked, as if reading Kareena's mind.

"Bindu comes home every day with her massive binder, and another reason why she and Loken are fighting about the wedding, and the guest list," Kareena said. "Do you think they'd be willing to push the engagement party back?"

"I doubt that," Bindu said, picking her nails. "What does Prem think about it?"

There was something about the way Bobbi said it that had Kareena twisting in her seat. "Oh no," Kareena said while she tugged Bobbi's purple ponytail. "Is this the real reason why you don't want to help? Because you think Prem is a-a match? You can get out of your auntie-brain and back into your Bobbi brain."

Bobbi swirled her champagne flute. "All I'm saying is that a woman is a fool if she can't resist a man. Your lack of resistance is showing, Kareena Mann. The question is, are you willing to be the fool?"

Kareena wanted to argue, wanted to prove to Bobbi that nothing but a cordial platonic friendship was forming between them. But that text message. And that kiss.

Even her Taylor Swift nighttime playlist couldn't put her to sleep. Her usual insomnia was now infinitely worse.

"You don't know what you're talking about, Bobbi."

"And I think you're treading in dangerous territory, friend."

The sound of a door chime rang across the small Indian bridal boutique, and Kareena turned to see Loken enter.

She'd only met him a handful of times, but he'd always been

quiet, sweet, and attentive to Bindu. He had a chiseled jaw that made him a stone-cut, marble-faced beauty. His black hair was gelled away from his face, and he wore a three-piece suit every day, just like Kareena preferred a sweater vest every day.

He carried two small bouquets of summer flowers in his hands.

"Hey, it's the groom!" Bobbi cheered. She held up her champagne flute. "Don't Italian Gujaratis have a thing where you're not supposed to see the wedding dress before the big day?"

Loken approached the couch, his happy smile contagious. "I wanted to be surprised, but you know Bindu. She makes her own traditions." His thick Italian accent had always charmed Kareena. Who would've thought there were desis in Verona?

"Kareena, you look beautiful today."

He leaned down to give her a kiss on either cheek, then turned to do the same to Bobbi. "Where is my bride to be?"

"She's changing into another dress," Kareena said. "She only comes out if she likes it, so it may take some time. You got her two bouquets?"

Loken shook his head. "One of these is for the gorgeous sister of my bride." He presented her with the bouquet like he was gifting her a diamond set. "Thank you for taking such good care of Bindu all these years."

Kareena could feel herself tearing up as she accepted the flowers. They were so pretty, and sweet. "Bindu took care of herself," she said quietly. "I'm so happy for you two."

Loken beamed at her. "Now we must have you just as happy, no?"

Bobbi muttered softly, "Oh, boy."

"I'm trying, Loken. Do you have any friends who want to get engaged by your sagai?"

"My darling future sister-in-law," he said, rocking back on his heels. "If that were the case, I doubt they would be single, no?"

"Now you sound like Prem," she mused. What was it with these dudes who thought her true love didn't exist?

"What do you think? Loken! You're here!"

Kareena twisted in her seat and promptly dropped her bouquet in her lap. "Oh, Bindu."

Her sister looked stunning. She wore a white fitted mermaid-style gown that had a loose draping across the front and a waterfall of sheer fabric over one shoulder.

"It's a concept sari!" Bindu said, holding her arms out, and doing a slow spin. "A combination of a gown and a sari in one. I'm kind of obsessed. What do you think?"

Her face was glowing, Kareena thought. It looked like pure happiness. "I think you look incredible."

"Really? Loken? What about you?"

Kareena looked over at her sister's groom, and he also had tears in his eyes. "I think," he said, then cleared his throat. "I am the luckiest man alive."

Bindu clapped her hands, and bounced, her long waves flowing over her shoulder. The attendant reached out and adjusted her train. "There is an opportunity for custom embroidery at the hem of your shoulder draping," she said.

"Loken, I know you liked the idea of me wearing white and red like your mom and aunts did when they got married, but I hope this is a decent compromise."

"I think it's lovely," he said.

"Really? Then, I am going to have the numbers 831 embroidered in the trim. What do you think?"

"831? Don't you want something a little bit more . . . personal?"

"What could be more personal than 831?" Her voice sharpened. "Do you not know what it means?"

"Of course, I know what it means. You've told me, darling,

but maybe your mother's name or something since this is *your* dress."

"You want no part of it?"

They began to bicker, much like they'd been doing since Bindu first pulled out her giant wedding binder. Even as Loken crossed the room and held out the bouquet of flowers, Bindu snapped at him like an angry chihuahua.

"831?" Bobbi whispered. "What the hell is that?"

"Cyber definition for 'I love you.' Eight is the total number of letters in the phrase. Three is the total number of words in the phrase, and I still can't figure out what the 1 stands for, but I'm sure Bindu can give you a whole summary on it. She's been obsessed with 831 since she was a kid, and our mom bought her a book on codes. It was one of the first codes she cracked."

"I'll pass," Bobbi said. She stood, brushing her hands down her fitted pants. Bobbi called out over the commotion, "Do you want to look at anything else, Bindu?"

Bindu stopped midsentence, her hands on her hips, and turned to Bobbi. Her smile beamed. "No, I love this. I think it's perfect for the religious ceremony. I'm going to wear something more Punjabi for the reception. Right, Loken?"

Loken ran his fingers through his now-mussed hair. "Right, my love."

The dude seriously looked like he'd just gone through a hurricane, Kareena thought. Her sister was so explosive.

"I'm going to go work out the pricing for the dress, and the delivery timeline," Bobbi added. "If your ceremonies are happening in the spring, we want to make sure that the dress comes in time." She sashayed off, phone in hand.

"She's the best, isn't she?" Bindu said to Kareena. "Thank you for having awesome friends who can plan my wedding."

"You're welcome."

Bindu kissed Loken on the cheek again and stepped back. "Loken, we'll argue about this later. Kareena, can you come and help me get out of this thing?"

"Don't you have to get measured?"

"Each one is custom stitched," the attendant said. "This is just a floor model. We took some measurements with her in the sari-gown, but now we're going to take body measurements."

Kareena didn't even pretend to understand what everyone was saying. She stood, ready to follow Bindu into the back room when her phone buzzed again.

This time it was a selfie from Prem. He stood with an arm around a skeleton. The skeleton had a piece of paper stuck to its chest that read:

KAREENA, I'M YOUR PERFECT DUMMY.

> **KAREENA:** Damn, I guess you've found my perfect man.

> **PREM:** I'll introduce you next week. I'll be in the city.
> Want to go out?

> **KAREENA:** You mean, like, intentionally meeting up?

> **PREM:** We need to be seen together, and also get to
> know each other.

> **KAREENA:** You were serious?

> **PREM:** Why wouldn't I be?

> **KAREENA:** Fine. I'll let you know.

Her stomach was still a riot of butterflies when she left her phone, flowers, and bag on the couch for Loken to watch and followed Bindu into the back room.

Kareena knew that Prem was interested in money for his clinic, just like she wanted funds for her mother's home. But she couldn't help but think that what they were doing was cheating the soul mate search. And liking Prem, enjoying the time they spent together, despite how their relationship started, was only going to complicate things later on for her. Because one thing was clear: he would never give her what she needed.

She stepped inside Bindu's changing room, her head spinning with the truth.

"Can you help me unpin?" Bindu asked. She'd stepped on top of a pedestal and pointed to her shoulder.

"Sure." Kareena started to remove pins from the draping. "This looks great on you. You really do look beautiful, Bindu."

"I wanted to ask you something," Bindu said quietly, her expression drawn. "I don't want you to get mad."

Kareena met Bindu's eyes in the mirror. "What is it? Did you do something?"

"No." There was a ghost of a smile. "Not yet. Loken asked me to move in with him after the engagement party. He thinks that Dad and Dadi would be more receptive once the sagai is over. I want to do it. I want to move in with him. His place is pretty nice. His family helped him buy it. I'll have my own room for filming and creating content and I'll be closer to the school on the days that I have to teach. Plus I'll be with him."

Kareena's stomach twisted, tightening just a little bit as she processed her sister's words. "Go for it. You already spend half the nights out of the week with him, anyway. I'm happy for you. Loken is great."

"Really? You wouldn't be upset that I'm leaving Mom's house?"

Kareena shook her head. She briskly began folding the fabric just like she remembered her mother doing after they came home from Indian Association parties, and like her grandmother did after Diwali celebrations. "My choices are my own. You are free to live your life how you want it, Bindu. You don't have to follow what I do."

"But you're my older sister," she said, her bottom lip quivering. "I know you're annoying as fuck, you drive me insane, and you've threatened to pester me in my married life, but I want you to be happy with my choices, too."

Only Bindu could say such a backhanded compliment with a smile on her face. "I *am* happy with your choices," Kareena said. She cupped Bindu's face, being mindful of the artfully applied bronzer on her cheekbones. "Hey, what is this really about? Most of the time you're jumping down my throat or trying to mess with me."

Bindu nodded, then sniffled. "The last time someone left the house was—"

Ah.

"Mom. I know." Kareena's throat burned at the reminder. Her grief was old, but sometimes it was so strong, it brought tears to her eyes. It was always swift, and sudden. Whenever she or Bindu experienced firsts, Kareena felt her mother's loss like the sharp shards of glass in her throat, choking her.

"Bindu," she said, clearing her throat, pushing down the sudden onset of grief, "you're getting married. And honestly, if I can't find a man, then the house might be gone soon, too. Focus on your wedding. And on Loken."

"Maybe with my leaving you can convert my room into an office like you've always wanted? With the floating bookshelves for your romance novels. I don't know how long it'll take for Dad to sell, and—"

"Stop," Kareena interjected. "Don't worry about me. You need to stay calm; otherwise, you'll break out."

Bindu sniffed. "No way am I getting acne," she said. "My photos have to look perfect."

"And they will," Kareena said.

Bindu, in her concept sari halfway off one shoulder, pressed her sniffling snot against Kareena's sweater vest.

"Love you, didi."

"Love you, too, Bindu."

CHAPTER TWELVE

Prem

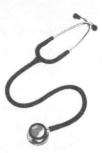

MOM: Your father is being a pain in my ass again.

PREM: This is why you can't trust emotions to make decisions about marriage. I can send you the study from France about midbrain activity if you want.

MOM: I was a doctor before I retired, my baby baboon. I know those studies better than you. Don't try me.

PREM: Wow, baby baboon? My phone translates terribly from Hindi to English. What is it, Mom?

MOM: I want you to come visit. So we can talk about your future in person. I saw your show, and how you're now friends with this woman who embarrassed you. What is going on?

PREM: I'll tell you when I figure it out.

PREM: Hey, bring sensible walking shoes for our date tomorrow.

RINA: Can you stop calling it that? We're just getting to know each other in case we have to mobilize your RIDICULOUS plan.

PREM: Just bring the shoes, Rina. And don't be late.

RINA: ⊗ ✂ ☹

PREM: You know what? I can't even be mad at that. That's clever.

Prem had not been able to stop fantasizing about Kareena Mann. He'd reached for his phone more times than he cared to admit, hoping for a text, or even a simple emoji. He knew that the only reason why he was so preoccupied was because so much of his future was dependent on her. His fractured focus had nothing to do with her wit, or her silky-smooth voice, or the memory of her thick hair running through his fingers.

He thought he'd be prepared when he saw her again. All those sexy thoughts were locked up tight in the back of his mind. But then he noticed those three-inch heels and all those thoughts came rushing back. Even though the lobby of the Metropolitan Museum of Art was full of noise and laughing families, Prem felt like he could distinctly make out the echo of those shoes hitting the tiled floor.

He admired the rest of her fantastic package as she cut through families and groups of people. Despite the summer June heat, Rina wore black pants, a cap sleeve button-down, and a thin black sweater vest over it. Her hair was in a high ponytail, and she had small gold hoops in her ears.

"What are we doing at the Met?" she said in greeting.

"Hi, Rina, great to see you again. You look . . . wow."

She rolled her eyes. "Prem, I wear the same thing all the time, so people take me more seriously."

"I'm taking you seriously," he said. "But even though I love the outfit, you didn't pay attention to the homework. I told you to bring walking shoes."

"These are my walking shoes." She blinked wide-eyed behind her frames and Prem realized that she wasn't joking.

"I hope you mean that," he said. He plucked her bag off her shoulder. It had quite a bit of weight to it. "You're going to have to ditch this. I don't want you to slow me down."

She snatched her bag back. "Slow you down?"

He checked the time on his phone. "Damn, it looks like you're going to have to carry this for the next couple hours. I have a feeling we're going to lose."

"What are you even talking about?"

Without preamble, he linked her hand with his, and despite the small jolt that radiated from their palm-to-palm touch, he didn't pull away. Prem led Kareena through the lobby, where he handed over the two special admission tickets he'd purchased before her arrival, and turned left through the Greek statue hall.

"Prem, where are we going?"

"You'll see."

At the end of the hall was a large open space with bench seats. A woman stood in front of a sketch of the original Met Museum and held up a clipboard, calling everyone to attention. Her hair was fire-engine red, and she was wearing coveralls that reminded him of the *Ghostbusters* jumpsuits with large black combat boots and hot pink laces.

"There has been a murder in the museum!" she shouted in a Broadway voice.

There was a wave of hushed whispers across the crowd gathered in front of her.

"What in the hell?"

"Shh, she's about to give the instructions," Prem said. He leaned in to whisper it in her ear and delighted in the rise of goose bumps along her neck that stretched under the crisp collar of her shirt. "This is important."

The woman took a deep breath, and she practically bristled with indignation. "An art curator was found *dead* in the Asian artifacts wing with a centuries-old dagger stabbed through his heart. There are four suspects, and it is up to you to find out who the killer is. Please hand in your tickets and get your information pamphlet and pencils. You have two hours, and you must stay together to win together. If you decide to leave prior to finding the killer, you will not be issued a refund."

"Oh my god," Kareena said, her voice reverent. She gripped Prem's bicep, crushing the fabric of his polo shirt. "Is this . . . is this a murder mystery scavenger hunt at the *Metropolitan Museum of Art*?"

He grinned. "Cool, huh? I remember you saying that you liked murder mystery theater. I thought this might be a fun date idea."

"Absolutely," she said. She bounced on her heeled toes and clapped her hands like a dolphin. "Oh my god. I wonder what kind of dagger it is. Do you think we get to see some of the closed exhibits for investigation purposes? Oh wait, what are your strengths? We should compare notes."

Prem learned something in that moment as he listened to her ramble. There was no filter when it came to Kareena Mann. As brash as she may be on a normal day, apparently she showed unfiltered joy as well.

"Don't forget," the woman who looked like Ms. Frizzle shouted. "The first group back here gets a coupon to the Met cafeteria!"

When the moderator began directing people to form lines, Kareena turned to Prem, her eyes bright. "Why would you go out of your way to plan something like this? I thought we were just supposed to get to know each other so we don't look like idiots if we have to use Plan B."

"I want to prove to you that we're a team, Rina," he said. He tilted his head toward the scavenger hunt organizer. "That if you agree to do this with me, we could both get what we want because we can win together. We're not on opposite sides of a table anymore."

Understanding dawned on her face and she nodded. "Smooth," she said. "This was really smooth, Dr. Dil."

"I thought so." He slung an arm over her shoulders, enjoying the feel of her close to him. "Now come on."

They made their way to the front of the line where people were grabbing different colored pamphlets and pencils. Before they could take theirs, a group of kids, both South and East Asian, cut in front of them.

"We're so going to win," one of the children said to them. "You may want to cut your losses now."

Prem and Kareena looked at each other and when their eyes met, they nodded in unison. There must've been some unspoken children of immigrants' message that passed between them.

Their competition grabbed their supplies and left, their heads held high.

"Are you thinking what I'm thinking?" Prem said quietly.

"I don't know what you're thinking but I'm thinking these kids have nothing on us."

Prem handed her a pencil and pamphlet. "Here. Where do you want to start?"

"With the instructions," Kareena said.

"You have five minutes!" the organizer shouted. "Then we'll unblock the entrance, and the hunt begins!"

Kareena led Prem over to an empty bench in the corner. She began reading through the bio of all the suspects and circled clues as she went.

Prem read quickly, cross-referencing Kareena's notes that he was able to see from over her shoulder. "What do you think about matching the clues with the rooms, so we're not going back and forth across the museum?" he asked.

"Good idea. Can you check the map?"

He was already pulling up the museum map on his phone to look up the room numbers on the pamphlet.

"Um, why are you still here? We told you we were going to win. Aren't you two a little old to do this?" The interruption came from one of the South Asian girls who had forced her way in line ahead of them.

The comment was callous considering there were other grown couples participating in the hunt.

"Aren't you too young to not have a chaperone?" Kareena replied.

"Whatever," one of the petite girls with pink hair said. "You probably will know all the answers because you *lived* through the time period."

"Yeah, with your dad. Tell him I said hi."

Prem muffled a laugh this time when every single one of the teenagers stared back at them with traumatized expressions on their faces.

"Whatever. Just stay out of our way. We're the only Asians who are going to win this."

They stormed away.

"That's internalized colonialism that's making you competitive! We Asians are supposed to support each other!" Kareena called after them.

Prem brushed a wavy lock of hair that had come out of her ponytail and tucked it behind her ear. "Rina, honey? I think, technically, we all have internalized colonialism."

Kareena scrunched up her nose. "Whatever. Let's win this." She folded her instructions in half and tucked the pencil in her ponytail in a way that was so efficient and sexy that he had to shift in his seat.

"Thoughts on what to do first?" he asked, praying that she would say something that would cool him off.

"It's the janitor. We have to figure out how he did it, write down all the clues to get the points, and then find the murder weapon."

Prem looked at his paper and then back at her. Well, that certainly cooled him off. "What do you mean it's the janitor? How do you know that so fast?"

She pointed to her notes, confidence written in every line of her body. "He's the least likely to do it. The instructions use persuasive language along with random cleaning product references. If you trust me on this one, I can lead us to cafeteria coupon victory."

Prem must've looked skeptical because she added, "Tick tock, Dr. Phil."

He wanted to convince her that they'd be a good team. That meant trusting her. And if she was right, then she was an even more spectacular partner than he'd realized. "You know what? Fuck it. Yeah, lead the way."

The organizer stood up on one of the benches again, her red hair a beacon in the otherwise gray, black, and chrome room. "And your time starts now!" she shouted.

For the first time since they met, Kareena reached for Prem first, grabbed his hand, looped her tote bag over her shoulders, and ran out the door.

The first clue directed them to a massive room with two-story ceilings, wall-size canvases framed in ornate gold, and the impressionist painters from France.

"We have to find a painting that has a purple aphrodisiac flower in it," she said.

Prem scanned the room. "There are thirty paintings in here. It looks like half of them have flowers."

"You take the left side, and I take the right?" she asked.

"Yeah, let's do it." They split up and looked for the portrait. Prem was the first to spot it and called Kareena over to read the plaque. The next clue led them to the Egyptian tombs.

"Keep up, Mann," Prem said when they jogged up to the second floor.

"Shut up," she mumbled from behind him.

The Met had arranged the giant slabs of rock in the same shape they'd found it, ensuring all the carvings in the slabs were lighted appropriately.

"We have to find the shape of a penis now," Kareena said.

"*Excuse* me?"

Kareena drew a symbol that looked like an eight, and an elongated D.

"That's the smallest damn penis I've ever seen," he mumbled. He turned to her just as she glanced down at his crotch, and away.

"*Kareena Mann*," he said, faking scandal.

"What?" she jumped, scampering back.

He didn't let her get that far, snatching her ponytail to bring her back to his side. She gasped when he tugged gently and brought her close so he could whisper in her ear. "If you want to know, you can just ask."

Kareena flushed even as she pulled away and crossed her arms over her chest. "Excuse me, but you're the one who didn't put out when it was time to shine."

Prem burst out laughing, then leaned in to kiss her on her temple. "I guess we're stuck with prehistoric dick then. Let's just find the penis and get out of here."

It took them ten minutes before they found the carving, which led them to their next clue.

"How did you know about the symbol?" he asked as they hustled to another wing in the museum. "I mean, that was pretty specific."

"*Jeopardy!*," she responded. "My grandmother is obsessed with *Wheel of Fortune* and *Jeopardy!* That's how she improved her English."

"Mine too! Watched it until the day she died almost ten years ago."

"I'm sorry she's gone," Kareena said, pausing to touch his arm.

"Yeah, me too."

They ended up in the Japanese art atrium where they found the jewelry chest with the same floral design as the French impressionist painter.

They worked together like a well-oiled machine going from clue to clue.

Prem never trusted someone else's instincts more than his own when it came to achieving a goal, but it was hard not to immediately rely on Rina. Because they were moving so quickly through the museum, an hour and a half flew by, and when they found the last clue, they were sweating.

"Here it is!" Kareena shouted. The second-floor patrons hushed her, but Prem jogged across the room and sidled up next to her to read the inscription on the plaque.

"I'll be damned. It was the janitor!"

"Told you. Now we just have to make it to the rooftop . . ."

"Not so fast."

They turned to face the group of teenage bullies standing at the other end of the corridor. They were in a V-shape with the pink-haired jerk right up front. "That final clue is ours, losers."

"Losers?" Kareena gasped. "You're the ones who couldn't figure it out on your own."

"But no one else has to know that," one of the other kids said.

"Rina?" Prem whispered so only she could hear.

"Yeah?"

"Run."

Without a second's hesitation, Rina shoved her tote at him to carry, and in her three-inch heels, sprinted toward the exit. They slid across slippery marble floors and ran through one of the largest museums in New York City side by side. They didn't know how far behind their competition was, but Prem couldn't lose time by looking back.

Two security officers told them to slow down before they reached the rooftop. Breathless, they pushed open the double doors, weaving through groups of people, families, and strollers before they spotted Ms. Frizzle at one of the lookout points in front of the city skyline. New York was painted in a wash of orange and dark blues with hints of violet tracing steel skyscrapers.

Prem grabbed Kareena's hand, and they raced to their scavenger hunt moderator.

Kareena slapped her answer sheet in front of Ms. Frizzle. "It's the janitor!"

Mrs. Frizzle looked down at her paper and then back at her. "You got *all* the clues? In an hour and thirty-nine minutes?"

Prem pressed a hand at the small of Kareena's back. "Yes," he said. "Are we first?"

Ms. Frizzle smiled, then scanned their answer sheet. "Yes, you are. Congratulations. You've won the scavenger hunt and found our murderer."

"Yes!" Kareena's victorious howl echoed above the sound of the city below and the rooftop patrons. She jumped in his arms, and he twirled her around twice. Her face glowed when she slid back to her feet. "We won the coupons!"

"We did," he said, settling his hands on her waist. "See? We make a killer team, Rina."

Her expression turned rueful as he put her down. "Okay, I give you that much. We do make a pretty good team. I'm not ready to give up finding what my parents had just yet, but if I do switch to Plan B, I'm . . . grateful that you're it."

"Excuse me, winning power team!" Ms. Frizzle called. She held up her phone and gestured for them to face her. "I'd love to take your picture for our social media accounts. You two make such a striking couple."

"Oh, we're not—"

"Thank you," Prem said cheerfully.

He dropped her tote bag and pulled Kareena against him until she fit against the planes of his chest and thighs. The past melded with the present, and the familiar curves under his hands gave him a high that he'd been craving for weeks.

Prem's gaze dropped to her lips. "I didn't think we'd be in this position again, Rina, honey."

Kareena's eyes widened even as she gripped his shoulders. "Wh-what are you doing?" Her pink tongue darting out to lick her bottom lip.

"It's customary for first dates to end with a kiss. We jumped the gun a little bit, but consider this a do-over."

"This is not a date—"

Before she could say anything more, Prem leaned in under the Manhattan sunset and pressed his lips against hers. Time slowed, and the noise faded into the background.

Kareena's lips parted under his, and the impact was electric. They fit together. Not just bodies, but lips, tongue, touch. His hands streaked up her back, and her fingers dove into his hair. Prem felt the current shoot through the roots of his hair as Kareena gripped him hard enough for him to swallow a surprised groan. He wanted another chance with her alone. No, he wanted all of her for as long as possible.

He pressed against her chest to breast, tongues tangled, while all thoughts of an audience completely slipped their minds.

Then she bit his lower lip, and in an instant, Prem knew that his midbrain and myocardium were hooked on the stimulus, and he was in deep, deep trouble.

Indians Abroad News

It appears as if a relationship has developed between Jersey City's South Asians News Network host Dr. Prem Verma, or Dr. Dil, and Ms. Kareena Mann, the woman who interrupted his show a few weeks ago. What started as an explosive, hostile argument between two American-born desis has turned into something more. Dr. Verma reshared a post on Instagram from a local scavenger hunt company of the couple inappropriately touching in a public location. What appears to be even more scandalous is Dr. Verma's lack of concern for the image. When asked on his last talk show about the topic, he responded to an audience question with the following:

> Kareena and I have more in common than we realized. What started off with a public argument allowed us to connect and meet on common ground. Getting to know her more personally has been a special experience. But I'm not here today to talk about Rina and myself. Let's go back to discussing recovery stages after heart surgery.

We'll stay tuned for more details on the viral couple's relationship.

CHAPTER THIRTEEN

Kareena

PREM: You've been avoiding me.

KAREENA: I've been busy. My sister is planning an engagement party.

PREM: And? The search for Mr. Right in all those dating profiles?

KAREENA: Why are you an asshole?

PREM: Could be because the last time we were together, you ran away like someone lit your stilettos on fire.

KAREENA: Hey, you can't hold that against me. You've run away before, too.

PREM: Fine, we're even. But just remember that your Mr. Right will never kiss you like that.

KAREENA: My true love will be BETTER at it.

PREM: Well, until he comes along, buy yourself some time with me. The aunties invited me to Sonali Aunty's husband's birthday party next Saturday. I'll see you then.

KAREENA: WHAT.

PREM: Sonali Aunty told me that her husband had a few questions about my community center, so she invited me over.

KAREENA: You could've said no.

PREM: Not until you say yes, Rina, honey.

If there was one thing Kareena hated more than anything in the world, it was obligation. She hated feeling obligated to keep her mouth shut or dress or act a certain way.

"Bas," her grandmother used to say. "Bas. Enough, Kareena. You are taking your independence too far." Like independence was something that was only allowed in small doses. In reality, her grandmother was blaming Kareena's independent spirit when she was just mad that Kareena disagreed with her.

After her grandmother and father saw the picture of her smooching Prem, they'd read her the riot act about acting appropriately.

What would her job think?

What would potential matches think?

What would their community think?

Thankfully, the aunties were the ones who stepped in to protect her. This wasn't 1950s India, after all, and Kareena's parents apparently did their fair share of smooching before marriage.

But because she could only fight so many battles at the same time, Kareena let her grandmother have her way about the way she dressed for Dinesh Uncle's birthday. She had to leave her hair down, put in contacts, and dress in a lehenga for a party that was supposedly to be a themed birthday get-together.

Themed Indian parties almost always meant some variation of Indian clothes to her grandmother. Even if the party was in their living room, they had to dress up like they were going to a three-hundred-person wedding.

What's worse, because Dinesh Uncle was one of her dad's good friends, the party was at their house.

Kareena affixed a single payal with a trio of chiming bells around her ankle. It was the one piece of jewelry that she enjoyed wearing when she was dressed in Indian clothes. The lehenga skirt that started as light pink at her waist and faded into orange, red, and then gold at the hem was a little too much for her, but at least the blouse was a tasteful peach with a row of eyelet hooks down the front.

She would've preferred pants.

Then again, what would Prem think seeing her in traditional Indian clothes? Would he notice the jhumka earrings glittering at her lobes or hear the subtle chime of her anklet?

"I DON'T KNOW what it is about sweater vests, but they make me feel like I'm in work mode. I'm comfortable in them."

Prem leaned closer until their breath mingled and she could see the gold flecks in the deep brown of his eyes. "I bet you look stunning in Indian clothes."

Kareena shook her head, snapping out of the memory. She couldn't think about Prem right now. He'd robbed her of her concentration all week since their date at the Met, and since that kiss that fried her available brain cells. This was no corner-mouth kiss. This was a full-frontal assault on her senses. With the absence of alcohol, it was one of the best she'd ever had in her life.

There would be other men to kiss. Specifically, the one she planned on spending her entire life with. Here's hoping he'd be just as skilled as Prem with commanding strokes of his tongue, and an iron grip around her body that made her feel like she was the sole source of water in the desert.

She could barely look at herself in the mirror after she realized that she'd masturbated more times in the shower that week remembering that kiss than she cared to admit.

"He isn't the one," Kareena whispered. "He isn't the one."

Her front door swung open, and her best friends burst in.

"Hey, where's the fire—"

They shoved past her, their salwar kameezes glittering as they moved.

"You have got to see this," Veera said as she and Bobbi rushed to Kareena's window that faced the front of the house.

"The car pulled up right as we got to the front door," Bobbi said. "They're wearing *Indian clothes*."

The words were said with such reverence that Kareena bolted after her friends and squeezed between them so she could get a clear line of sight through her bedroom window to the front walkway.

Then it happened.

Three desi men got out of the low-slung Audi at the curb with grace and power in every movement. They all wore black or slate-gray sherwani kurtas and dress pants. All of them carried flowers or bottles of alcohol.

Like a goddamn slow-motion movie scene, they either ran their fingers through their perfectly styled hair, or over their trim cut beards as their long, powerful strides ate up the concrete. Each one of them walked with swagger-and-plunder vibes.

Kareena's heart caught in her throat when Prem, front and center, glanced up at her window, then did a double take. He slowed, and his friends, both taking their cue from Prem, came to a stop at his side.

His eyes locked with hers, and her pulse pounded in her throat.

"Holy shit," Bobbi said with a whisper. "That man came to slay you, Kareena. With that fitted black kurta? He's playing *dirty*."

"And damn, does it look good on him," Veera added.

They weren't lying. The kurta opened at Prem's throat and cut at midthigh. It fit snug across his wide chest and accented his muscled arms. He passed over the bottle he was holding to the man on his right, and slowly folded up his sleeves.

Bobbi gasped and Veera muffled a squeal behind her hand.

"The *audacity*," Bobbi said with a whisper. "He wants to kiss you again. Guaranteed."

Damn if Kareena didn't want that, too, especially when he was looking like such a snack. "I should've never told you what happened."

"Honey, everyone knew what happened after that Instagram post," Veera said.

Prem's friends looked amused when Dr. Dil himself pointed an index and middle finger at his eyes then at her.

I'm watching you. I want you. I'm going to win.

She wasn't sure if that was exactly what he was thinking, but it didn't matter. The bastard was not going to have the upper hand here. Not in her home. Kareena pulled away from the window and straightened her lehenga. "I have absolutely no idea why his friends are with him."

"Probably because you told the aunties you were inviting us as decoys so that the attention wasn't going to be on you," Bobbi said.

"And what, they told Prem to bring his friends? To distract you both?"

"It could work, too," Veera mumbled.

"Hey!"

"I'm just saying!" She shrugged. "By the way, you look great."

"At least that's something," Kareena said, smoothing a hand over her long skirt. "It's the first time I'm going to see the aunties after they found that picture of Prem and me kissing. I need to have my armor shiny and secure. And with Prem here, the pressure is going to be even worse."

Bobbi was still glued to the window. She flipped her long parandi over one shoulder. The end of her braid had a shiny jeweled tie. "The taller dude looks superfamiliar."

"That might be his friend Benjamin Padda."

Bobbi turned slowly until she looked coolly at Kareena. "*The* Benjamin Padda? Chef and owner of Phataka Grill? The guy I've been trying to get in touch with for months?"

Kareena nodded. "I told you they were close. Hell, we made out in the guy's office."

"This dinner party just got a lot more entertaining," Bobbi said. She strode across the room, pausing only for a second at the door to say, "I don't know what game you both are playing, babe, but I would unbutton the top button of your blouse. If he's trying to seduce you into whatever plan he has, you should seduce him right back."

Kareena waited until her friends left before she looked at the row of tiny metal clasps down the center of her blouse. "No, that's . . . you know what? Fuck it." She unhooked the top one and hoped that Dadi or her father wouldn't say anything in public to embarrass her.

She tossed a chunni over her shoulder and waited for the long stretch of sheer fabric to settle across her back before she raced out of her room, her voluminous lehenga skirt billowing around her. Kareena reached the bottom step in time to hear Benjamin Padda and Bobbi confront each other.

"I have left numerous messages with your office."

"I have a serious disdain for catering, so I ignored your messages."

"Disdain? Who even uses that word anymore? And ignoring messages is unprofessional."

Benjamin looked like a large, overwhelmingly handsome Punjabi model with sharp features, impeccable grooming, and a silver kada around one thick wrist. He shoved the bouquet of flowers at Bobbi. "I hope the food is better than the conversation."

"Probably better than anything you could come up with," Bobbi snapped and followed on Benjamin's heels as he strode out of the room.

There was a beat of silence before Veera adjusted her own chunni drape across her ample chest. "Hi," she said and held her hand out to Prem's friend to shake. "Veera. Friend of the family."

"Deepak," the man said, shaking Veera's hand. "Friend of Prem."

"Beer or whiskey?"

Deepak looked at the red wine in his hand, then back at Veera. "Whiskey if you have it."

"It is a Punjabi party. If I know Kareena's father like I do, there is Johnnie Black Label, Chivas, Jameson, Glenlivet, Crown

Royal, Jim Beam, Jack Daniel's, and Laphroaig for those under the age of fifty. Pick your poison."

"Laphroaig," he said, and followed Veera out of the foyer.

Kareena and Prem stood two feet apart in silence. Prem still had that all-knowing smirk on his face.

"You look stunning, Rina."

"Thanks. I have pockets," she said and shoved her hands into the discreet pocket inserts in her skirt where she'd hidden her phone.

Prem grinned.

"Why are you here, Dr. Dil?"

He motioned to her house. "I was invited. I was also asked to bring along Deepak and Bunty, since apparently, your aunties wanted to make sure there were enough single men for the single marriageable ladies around."

Kareena didn't laugh. Prem may have found this whole situation hysterical, but she doubted that he dealt with the backlash like she'd had to. And yet, he still caused a flutter of butterflies in her stomach in his presence. "You didn't have to come. You know this is not going to make me change my mind about our little deal."

His expression grew pensive. "Rina, I know I can't be the guy that you want. But I can help you buy time. After we get the money, I'll do everything in my power to help you."

"And the kissing?" she blurted out, desperate to know the answer. It had been plaguing her. "Why did you kiss me again? Why did you kiss me like that?"

"To make all this believable," he said with such precision, as if he'd prepared his statement.

His words cut her deeply, slicing the small part of her that had found his touch, his kiss, utterly romantic. The flame of hope that burned deep in the shadows of her heart since their very first conversation snuffed out.

In the short amount of time that they'd texted and talked and spent time together, she'd thought that Prem was braver than that.

Kareena backed away from him with her chin tilted up and her shoulders back. "For a moment you had me second-guessing myself, Dr. Prem Verma, but I was right all along. You are a liar."

She whirled, ignoring his shocked expression as she marched down the short hallway into the open kitchen and living room. The aunties and uncles were already there, having arrived while she finished getting dressed. Her father was pouring drinks, and her grandmother was ordering her friends around in the kitchen.

The most out of place things in her house were the clusters of balloons in each corner featuring a famous Bollywood actor. As Kareena scanned the two rooms, she realized that Shah Rukh Khan's face was not only on the balloons, but he also graced the table napkins and the cardboard cutouts angled in each corner.

People could get anything Bollywood related in Edison, New Jersey, these days.

As she stepped into the kitchen, she saw Shah Rukh Khan from his earlier movies and from later movies where he sported a full beard. When the balloons swayed from people walking past them, or from the ceiling fan, it was as if the movie star was judging her with a shake of his head.

"Screw you, Shah Rukh," she muttered. "You had a script."

Kareena spotted Dinesh Uncle right away. His brightly bald, shining head was a beacon to anyone searching for him.

She squeezed through the small group of people until she

reached his side. "Happy birthday, Uncle," she said, and gave him a quick hug.

He patted her shoulder. "Thank you, beta. Thank you, thank you. How are you doing?"

"Living the life," she said with a grin.

"Ahh yes, we heard." An echo of laughter surrounded her. She glanced at her father who was pouring a drink at the bar cart, and his expression was mutinous. Damn it, as progressive as some Indian families had become, there were certain moments that reminded Kareena why there was truth to stereotypes.

"How are the twins?" she continued.

Dinesh Uncle scoffed. "Too busy for their dad. One is at MIT and the other at Harvard. Between school and sports, they couldn't make it home."

She should start her tally. How many times would an uncle or aunty name-drop? Kareena knew that the twins were at MIT and Harvard, but Uncle's comment was just a subtle reminder that she went to Rutgers instead so she could stay close to home.

"Well, we're here to celebrate with you," Kareena said, smiling as brightly as she could.

She greeted all the rest of the uncles before moving toward the kitchen and meeting her aunties. She was very aware of Prem exiting the foyer and joining the group of men. Veera and Deepak appeared to be deep in conversation next to the whiskey bottles, while Benjamin and Bobbi were nowhere to be found.

Prem continued to watch her from a distance as she kissed Sonali Aunty, Falguni Aunty, Farah Aunty, and Mona Aunty on their cheeks.

"I hope you don't mind that I invited your match and some of his friends," Sonali Aunty said, tongue in cheek. "I'm so glad that we found someone for you!"

Kareena couldn't help but roll her eyes. "That Instagram post was, er . . . staged, and you know it, Aunty."

"I wish we had staged photos like that in my youth," Mona Aunty said, her eyes sparkling. "If anyone had caught me like that, my mother would never let me hear the end of it. But yours? She would've probably loved it."

Sometimes Mona Aunty knew exactly what to say. "Mama would be so happy I have all of you to take care of me," Kareena replied, ignoring the ache in her chest.

Farah Aunty draped an arm around her shoulder. "Beta, you have to tell us the truth. You two are dating now, nah?"

"No, Aunty," Kareena said. She knew someone was going to eventually ask the question. "But if you're so set on helping me, then why don't you look at that huge network you all are always bragging about to find me the love of my life? I think the harassment all these years was just for show."

Falguni Aunty picked up a pakora from a serving tray and dipped it in mint and coriander chutney. "Nonsense, beta," she said. "It's just hard to find someone for a woman who has such high standards. Which you should! But being as educated and outspoken as you are, men have sensitive egos."

"Then I would rather not have a man," she said.

"Quiet, both of you," Mona Aunty said. Her rows of bangles chimed as she waved a hand in dismissal. "Kareena, if you're asking us for help, then we will deliver the same wonderful human that your father was to your mother, darling. It's the least we can do. If Prem is not for you, then we accept that. No more meddling with your Dr. Dil. Achha?"

"Achha, Aunty," Kareena said.

"All of you keep talking nonsense," Dadi said from the stove. "I've already started packing for India." She tucked the end of her sari into her waist, so it didn't get in the way of food prep. "This girl is not going to be engaged by the time we leave, and we'll just have to sell this house to someone else."

"Dadi," Kareena interrupted. "I don't think this is the time to—"

"You know Bindu got Kareena a massager for her neck for tension?" Dadi continued. "It's a good gift! Maybe if she relaxes, she'd smile more, and people will see how beautiful she is. This girl doesn't want it, which is good for me, because I think I need the massager now more than she does! I have all this tension. I'm old now, ready to die, and this massager is the only thing that helps me."

She pulled open the kitchen drawer filled with spatulas and ladles to pull out the Asian Sensation clit stimulator vibrator.

"Oh my god," Kareena gasped. She glanced around, hoping none of the uncles or her father could see this. Where was Bindu?

Kareena had no idea what she did in her past life to deserve this.

"Dadi, I don't think you should—"

Dadi placed it on her neck and pressed a button. "See? I keep it in the kitchen so I can relax while cooking. It has twelve different speeds and patterns."

Farah Aunty laughed. "I have that, too! Except I use it to massage other things."

Kareena knew her grandmother was going to ask a follow-up, and the aunties weren't going to hold back. "Something's burning," she blurted out.

It was like she dropped an atomic bomb in the kitchen. Everyone hustled to the stove, the oven, and the microwave.

"It's not the daal, is it?" Sonali Aunty asked. "Something smells."

"Maybe it's your frozen samosas," Farah Aunty replied.

"They aren't frozen, they're fresh!"

"Ha," Falguni Aunty said. "You've never made a fresh samosa in your life, Sonali."

In the midst of their distraction, Kareena rushed her grandmother, snatched the vibrator out of her hand, and tossed it into the drawer before slamming it closed.

"Kareena, what is this bakawaas you say?" Dadi hissed. "That's my vibrator!"

"Exactly," Kareena whispered back. "It's a *vibrator*. You can't use it in public!"

"I'm here!" Bindu's voice boomed from the front entrance. She walked in decked out from head to toe in jewelry and sparkling clothes. Loken, an expression of exhaustion on his face, followed closely behind. "Happy birthday, Dinesh Uncle!" she shouted.

For the first time in her life, Bindu's entrance was right on time. Everyone gravitated toward her like moths to a flame.

And when she heard a buzz coming from the drawer she'd just slammed, Kareena knew she'd reached the end of her rope. Scanning the kitchen, then the living room, she spotted Veera first and tried to catch her attention. Her bestie was still engrossed in a conversation. Bobbi was still nowhere to be found, and Prem was speaking with Mona Aunty's husband in a corner.

No one would care if she left, Kareena realized.

She backed out of the sliding doors leading onto the deck and closed it behind her. She needed a moment with her car, with her memories, away from everyone. Especially Dr. Dil.

CHAPTER FOURTEEN

Prem

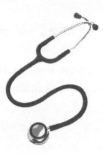

MOM: You're kissing a woman in public, Prem.

PREM: Yes, I've heard from the family WhatsApp chat this week.

MOM: Now you have to marry her.

PREM: Please tell me you're joking.

MOM: You ruin all my fun.

PREM: If my life is your only source of entertainment, you need better hobbies.

MOM: I do, but your father doesn't like anything I want to do.

PREM: Your hobbies shouldn't be attached to Dad's.

MOM: He gets sad if I do things on my own.

MOM: Is there something between you two?

PREM: No, Mom. I'm leaving.

MOM: Fine. But just know that if you don't visit soon, your father and I will.

PREM: Noted.

DEEPAK: Hey, have you seen Bunty?

PREM: What? No. Why do you ask?

DEEPAK: I haven't seen him, that's all.

PREM: Is Rina's friend boring you?

DEEPAK: No, she's awesome. But if Bunty makes this uncomfortable for all of us by doing something stupid, then we're going to be SOL. He has the car keys.

Prem knew that the party was going to be a setup. He was willing to chance it because he was desperate to see Rina again. He hadn't been all-consumed like this with a woman ever.

Their second kiss changed everything. It meant that the first time he tasted her wasn't a dream, because he could replicate the feeling of being with her. Now he was hooked. Her mouth was the only thing that he could think about since their Met Museum date. Between patients, late nights while he was lying in bed, during his workouts in his building's gym.

When Sonali Aunty asked him to bring a few friends to a

dinner party, he figured Bunty and Deepak could help distract everyone so that he could have a talk with Rina.

What he didn't expect was for her to punch him in the mouth by standing in the window like a queen, and then calling him a liar. She practically glowed with fire when she told him off.

Their kiss at the Met *was* for show. That was the whole point of their date, wasn't it?

Dinesh Uncle clapped him on the shoulder. He'd been going on for twenty minutes about his kids at MIT and Harvard. "Hopefully my son goes to medical school and does something as important as you. It's a hard road, but I salute you for doing this for our community. Not enough physicians in America understand our health needs are different. Increasing numbers of my patients have heart disease and diabetes. It would be good to refer them to a safe place."

"Thanks, Uncle," he said. Prem wasn't expecting people to be open and accepting of his plan at an aunty party, but he'd been pleasantly surprised. Now if only he could get away to find Kareena.

"Your center should bring you some money, too," a voice said from behind him.

Prem turned and came face-to-face with an older man with Kareena's eyes. His mouth was set in a thin line, and he was the only one who didn't introduce himself, or welcome him, even though it was obviously his home. Prem didn't blame the guy. Prem was smooching his daughter in public after he'd said some very choice words to her on video.

"Hopefully," Prem said slowly. "But that's not the objective. If I wanted money, I would've gone to Einstein."

His brow twitched at the name-drop. "You sound like my daughter."

"It's one of the things we've found that we have in common."

The man hummed. "You know, she has it in her head that she wants a love marriage."

"She told me. Kareena said that you and your wife had a love marriage."

Sadness and exhaustion painted the older man's face at the mention of his wife. "What Kareena continues to ignore is that marriage, either for love or for economy, can be hard. I'm afraid my practical daughter is being very impractical here, and you're going to take advantage of her."

"Kareena and I have our differences, but we aren't lying to each other."

Lying. The word echoed in his head from Kareena's earlier accusation. Were they lying to each other? Or better yet, was he lying to her about what he felt? No, feelings had nothing to do with it. Science, chemistry, a physical attraction to pheromones.

For fuck's sake, he was spending a lot of time justifying something that was already consuming him whole.

And that's what freaked him out the most. Being with her was becoming his biggest priority, and Rina deserved to know the truth.

He had to talk to her. He scanned the crowd, and when he didn't see her, Kareena's father cuffed his shoulder. "You'll find her in the shed sitting in her mother's car."

"Oh. Uh, thank you," Prem said.

"And Prem?"

"Yes, sir?"

"Kareena has her own mind, but she's softer than people think."

Well, that was unexpected. It sounded like Rina's father was giving him his blessings. "Thank you, sir."

The man held up his empty whiskey glass and moved to the

makeshift bar in the corner of the room, officially dismissing Prem.

With all thoughts on Kareena, Prem scanned the room for his friends. Bunty had finally returned, and both he and Deepak were eating together, surrounded by aunties. Bobbi was scowling in Bunty's direction, and Veera was playing chess in the corner with one of the other uncles.

Now was his chance. He kept his head down and stayed close to the wall until he slipped out the sliding door and into the back-yard.

Two seconds later, he was crossing the deck. It was muggy and humid outside. The sound of insects buzzing and crickets singing echoed in the night as he stepped into the grass. The lights were on in the shed, and the doors appeared to be open.

Anticipation curled up inside Prem with the realization that he'd be alone with Kareena for the first time since he'd arrived. He paused a few feet from the doors when he saw a glint of silver at his feet. He reached down to pick up a single payal with three bells at the end.

He'd wondered about the chiming sound coming from Kareena's outfit. He pocketed the anklet and continued his way to the shed.

"Kareena?" he called out, and pushed the double doors open wider.

She lay on the hood of the Beamer, resting against the wind-shield. Her brightly colored lehenga skirt fanned across the hood, and her bare feet with painted pink toes peeked out at the hem. He could see the curve of her thighs, her belly, and the swell of her breasts like an outline that he desperately wanted to trace.

With his mouth.

Prem cleared his throat. "You escaped early."

Kareena's head rolled to the side so she could look at him. "I reached my quota of bullshit. And also, my grandmother traumatized me by pulling out a vibrator from a kitchen drawer and using it as a neck massager."

"Holy shit, where was I?" He would've paid money to see Kareena handle that mess.

"You were in the living room, talking to Dinesh Uncle, I think."

He turned to look at the house across the yard. It was a beautiful home and lit up like Diwali.

"It's nice of your dad to offer the house up for the party. All the Shah Rukh Khan stuff is weird as hell, but I get it. Themed party."

Kareena hummed. "My mother used to do that, too. Themed parties. She was a lot better at it though. She loved having people over. That's one of the reasons why she wanted a big house."

"Is that why you love it, too?"

"Over the years, decorating the home for company became something my mother and I shared. We'd also do these renovation projects together, like painting rooms or adding shelving. When she died, I continued that legacy. I've also redone the bathrooms myself, wallpapered the laundry room, and redesigned the landscaping."

"What's your favorite room?" he asked.

"This shed," she said. "This is an add-on, and it feels uniquely mine, but it's part of what my mother started here."

Prem motioned to the car. It was all making sense and coming together now. "You're a fixer. The car, the house, the job, everything."

"Except my love life, apparently," she muttered. She shifted, and her chest rose and fell. That undone button at the top captured his attention.

"That Instagram post is more trouble than you can imagine," Kareena continued, unaware of his fragmenting concentration. "I had this dumb fantasy when I was growing up. I'd pull into the driveway in my E30, walk in through the front door, and embrace my family. The home that my mother built would be the home that I'd create. But I'm thirty now, and I'm asking a bunch of gossiping desi women to help me because I'm that desperate."

Prem pulled at his kurta collar that began to stick to his skin from the heat. Despite the weather, he pushed the shed doors closed so that only a sliver of light peeked through. "I may not believe in love marriages, Rina, honey, but if you believe in them, then you should have it. Wait as long as you want for the right person to come along."

She lifted her head to look at him. "Even if you think it's stupid?"

"Even then."

"That's a lie that I can get behind."

Ouch. He moved to the front of the car and pulled the payal from his pocket. "You dropped something," he said.

She raised an eyebrow, and after hesitating, she fisted her lehenga fabric in one hand and pulled it up slowly to expose her ankles. Then her calf and finally her knee.

Desire shot straight to Prem's groin as he watched Kareena expose inch by golden brown inch. Charlie threatened to poke a hole through his pants, he was so turned on. If that's how she wanted to play this, he was game.

Tracing a fingertip over the top of her foot, he touched the delicate lines of her ankle and enjoyed her shiver. "I didn't get to touch this yet," he murmured.

Prem urged her to bend her knee so the sole of her foot rested against the car hood before he wrapped the payal in place and fastened the ends together. The bells fell against her ankle joint, and he flicked them once to hear the sweet chime. Then, without warning, he ran a hand up the length of her leg under her skirt, gripped her thigh, and pulled.

Kareena gasped and slid down the length of the hood, until she was straddling his waist. Prem hooked two fingers in the front of her blouse, right over the unfastened clasp, and tugged until she was sitting up. Her head fell back, exposing the lines of her throat.

"What are you doing?" Her voice was breathy and indignant all at the same time.

Prem rested a finger against her lips. "I'm sorry," he said.

Her eyes widened, and they were so soft, so beautiful in the dim light of the shed. "Wh-what?"

"I said I'm sorry. You were right to call me a liar. I shouldn't have said that the kiss was just for show."

"Then . . . wh-what was it?"

"I don't know, Kareena," he said softly, exposing himself. "I don't know, but ever since I saw you standing at the bar, I knew that you were going to change me. I wasn't wrong, because even now, even after knowing that we want different things, I plan on kissing you again." They were close now, and his heart was beating at an erratic rate. He touched her face, tracing the line of her jaw, and watched as desire filmed over her gaze.

"This was only Plan B," Kareena whispered. She shook her head so that her hair fell in a sleek black waterfall down her back.

Prem leaned in kissed the curve of her collarbone. "Now who's lying," he whispered. She tasted deliciously soft, and the heady scent of sandalwood and vanilla haunted him the same way the memory of it haunted his dreams.

He cupped her face, his mouth hovering over hers for a moment in frozen time. Then Kareena's hands streaked up his chest to tangle in his hair. He groaned as her mouth claimed his.

The rush of lust was just as potent as the first time. Prem pressed a thumb to her chin, and when she parted her lips, he slid his tongue against hers, fitting against her. He hadn't imagined it. She was perfect.

His hands fell from her face and gripped the top of her thighs that bracketed his hips. The skirt bunched, and even as their lips locked, sliding over each other with a cresting hunger, Prem moved the fabric aside so that he could grip the bare skin of her inner thighs.

She jerked at the first touch but didn't pull back. Lost in the feel of her kiss, Prem slid his hands farther under the lehenga until he could brush the top of her mound.

Kareena whimpered and pulled away, even as her hands fisted at his shoulders. "Prem, there are people," she whispered.

"Fuck them," he replied, his voice heavy and harsh before his mouth crashed against hers. She shifted closer and tilted her hips forward enough for him to slide two fingers under the fabric of her panties.

God, she was soaked. He'd sell his soul to get a taste of her, but because there was a chance, as small as it may be, that they'd get caught, he stayed standing, hiding her pleasure with his body. She shivered as he parted her and found her clit.

They were breathing heavy now, tongues tangled as he began rubbing slow, maddening circles over her swollen clitoris. It felt perfect under his fingers, and he pressed harder just as she began to quiver in his arms. She tightened like a bow, back arching, hips gyrating in slow, even movements, until he prodded at her entrance with two fingers.

She tore her mouth from his and wrapped her arms around his neck. "Prem," she whispered shakily.

"Do you want to come," he whispered back. "Or should I leave you like this, aching for me?"

She groaned, gyrating hard against him. "Would you run upstairs and get yourself off with the thought of my dick pumping inside you until you're screaming?"

She bit his jaw, her teeth nipping just hard enough for his cock to jerk in his pants. "Make me come," she whispered back. "Please."

"Good little Indian girls don't get finger fucked in the shed," he said roughly as he pushed his fingers inside her. The sound of her gasp was like music to his ears. He let her adjust to his intrusion, then slowly retracted and pushed back inside her with a little more force. "But you're a dirty girl, aren't you? I knew you were different the moment we met."

"Prem," she gasped when his thumb brushed against her clitoris.

"I want you to remember me whenever you touch yourself," he whispered, and began pistoning into her hard.

Her arms wrapped around his shoulders, and she shuddered, her hips rolling forward, silently begging him for more. He was hard now, his erection pressing against his zipper, but this was for Rina. This was for her to feel him so deep that she'd be thinking about him as long as he'd been thinking of her.

She rocked in his arms, harder, faster, her hips moving in a way that had him dreaming of her on top. He buried his face in her neck as her body tensed and she grew closer to orgasm. The sound of the party continuing across the lawn was a reminder that they had to be quick, or they could be discovered any second, as he touched her, her lehenga skirt at her hips, the chime of her payal ringing against the back of his thigh as she fucked his hand.

"Kiss me while you come," he groaned, and her mouth found his, fastening together like a key finding a lock.

Her body tensed impossibly harder in his arms before she let out a muffled shriek into his kiss. Then her pussy tightened around him as she came.

She was magnificent, he thought as he held her through the shudders and after quakes of her orgasm. He stroked one hand down her back as he removed the other from her deliciously soft pussy.

Rina gasped for air, and in the shadows of her shed, watched him lift his fingers to his lips and suck off her juices.

She tasted just as sweet as a gulab jamun that dripped with sticky decadence. He couldn't wait to taste her again, but this time in a bed where he could take his time and she rode his face.

And they would end up in a bed together soon.

"I—you—"

A sound interrupted them, slicing through the moment like a utility knife.

"Kareena! They're about to cut the cake, and your grandmother wants you to be there!"

Prem dropped his forehead to hers. "Damn," he said quietly.

"I didn't . . . we didn't . . ."

"Later," he said. "You can touch me later, Rina, honey. Right now, I need to calm down."

He pulled back, letting her lehenga fall to her knees. They were both still breathing heavy, drunk on lust.

"I hope they don't know," she whispered, adjusting her hair and clothes as she slid off the hood of the car. "Just by looking at us."

He stepped back and admired her in the starlight. "Your father already has an idea that we're out here alone," he said. "But if it makes you feel better, I'll walk around to the front of the house. I'll need another moment anyway."

She nodded, then straightened her shoulders. Before she could move past him, he touched her arm. "Before you go, tell me what you want to do."

His stomach twisted when she shook her head, then pulled back. "I-I don't know," she said. "I just need more time."

Prem slid a hand over her bare arm until it reached her shoulder. Then, he adjusted her chunni and dropped a quick kiss against her mouth one last time.

"Fine," he said. "Then I'll give you time." He hooked his fingers in her cleavage, feeling a surge of power when she shuddered, and quickly fastened the top clasp. "But you don't have a lot of it, Rina, honey."

"You'll wait for me," she replied, her voice stronger now, her eyes cool as she looked straight at him. "You'll wait for me as long as I ask, because now, Dr. Prem Verma, you're invested."

CHAPTER FIFTEEN

Kareena

JERICHO: Hey, what's up.

KAREENA: Hey, how's it going.

JERICHO: Pretty good now! Tell me three things you like to do.

KAREENA: Um . . . I like hanging out with my friends, Taylor Swift, and reading romance novels. What about you?

JERICHO: Nice. I like hunting, fishing, and kayaking.

KAREENA: Oh, gotcha. Um . . . what do you hunt? Is that a question ppl ask?

JERICHO: It is!! And I'm glad you asked. I LIKE HUNTING FOR PUSSY.

KAREENA: *BLOCKED*

XI: Hey.

KAREENA: Hey.

XI: Wow, I can't believe there are still attorneys that WORK as attorneys.

KAREENA: ?

XI: I mean, why would I need you, when I have Legal Zoom? Anyone can argue their own case.

KAREENA: *BLOCKED*

FRANK: Hey! You're that viral girl who went berserk on TV! I can't believe you're even online after that incident.

KAREENA: *BLOCKED*

RAHUL: Hey.

KAREENA: Hey.

RAHUL: How's it going?

KAREENA: Ha, it could be better.

RAHUL: Yeah, online dating is always emotionally draining.

KAREENA: Exactly!

RAHUL: Your profile is cute. Would you be interested in talking on the phone sometime instead of messaging through this app? Maybe going out for a drink?

KAREENA: Yeah, sure. Here's my number.

BINDU: Where did you go? I need you here this weekend. I have a to-do list for you. You need to fold all the invitations and programs for the engagement party, stamp them, and mail them for me. Then you need to drop my clothes off to the tailor. I am going to the spa. Daddy is treating me because he knows I've been so stressed out.

KAREENA: No.

BINDU: WHAT? WHAT DO YOU MEAN NO????

BINDU: KAREENA??? KAREENA!!! YOU'RE BEING SELFISH AGAIN.

PREM: Hey, so I realized that I don't have a problem with taking off your clothes. Just your sweater vests.

KAREENA: PREM!

PREM: Sorry, I couldn't help it. Listen, I'm going to be in Edison on Friday for a few hours before I go back to Jersey City. Interested in having dinner?

KAREENA: Sorry, I can't.

PREM: Oh yeah? Working late.

KAREENA: Not exactly. Uh, I have a date.

PREM: Seriously?

KAREENA: Please don't make this even more awkward than it already is.

PREM: Too late. But this is what you want, so I'll respect your wishes.

PREM: . . . I don't have to like it though.

Kareena spent all day thinking about different ways to cancel her date for that night. She didn't want to go out. It didn't feel right anymore. Not when she was kissing Prem. Or when he was giving her explosive orgasms by just touching her. God, that was a first.

After they'd gone back into the house, she could barely concentrate. It was a good thing that everyone was so focused on Bindu and her wedding plans.

But she knew that she couldn't give up yet. Prem was her Plan B. She just had to keep telling herself that.

The car service pulled up at the restaurant in Woodbridge seconds after she checked her texts for the hundredth time that day.

Still nothing else from Prem.

Kareena thanked the driver, and within seconds of approaching the front door of Harvest Grill, someone called her name.

"Excuse me, Kareena?"

She turned to face a tall, slender man with curly hair, scruff, and thick black-framed glasses. He carried a backpack and wore Chucks with whitewashed jeans, a T-shirt featuring some Star Wars spaceship, and a baggy suit coat.

She pushed her matching glasses up her nose. "Hi, yes, that's me. Are you Rahul?"

"I am, yeah." He held out his hand for a shake. She took it and appreciated the firm grip. "Do you want to go in?"

"Sure."

Rahul held open the door for her and then approached the hostess desk. "Hi, can we have a table for two?"

"Do you have a reservation?"

"Yes, under the name Rahul Dasa."

Kareena's mouth dropped. The dude was on time, held open the door, and made a reservation for their date? Okay, that was something that hadn't happened to her yet. She hadn't been superattracted to him based on his profile and their initial conversation, but he seemed nice, and she knew that she had to give him a chance. Maybe this was going to lead to something pleasantly surprising.

"Follow me." The woman grabbed two menus and led the way to the dining area. They maneuvered through tables until they reached a corner booth.

"Your server will be right with you," their hostess said as she dropped the menus on the edge of the table and left.

Kareena noticed that Rahul's backpack was roughly the same size as her tote, and he threw it onto the booth bench just like she'd tossed in her tote first. When they sat down, their knees bumped.

This is way too strange, she thought.

Then there was a loud clatter under their table.

"Oh, did you drop something?" Kareena bent to the side to see what had fallen and spotted three twenty-sided dice. Before she could comment on them, Rahul had snatched them off the floor, then shoved them back in his pocket.

"It's nothing. Sorry about that."

He sounded a little flustered, so instead of commenting, she grabbed a menu and opened the drinks page.

"Thanks for coming out to Hoboken to meet me," he started. "I know it's a pain for you to get home because of the trains, but I appreciate it."

"No problem," she said. "I wrapped up work a bit earlier today, so I had the transit time."

He smiled as they scanned the drink menu.

"What are you in the mood for?" she asked.

"I think I'll have an IPA. Is that okay with you?"

She nodded. "I drink. I might have a mojito, though."

"Go for it," he said. Rahul glanced at her over the top of his menu, then adjusted his glasses. "Can I tell you something without judgment?"

Oh no, Kareena thought. Here it was. The moment when he'd share something truly disastrous, and she'd have to plan her exit. "Uh, sure."

"My mother put me on the site. It's a weird thing to admit to, but since you're South Asian, too, I figured I could tell you the truth."

She let out a deep breath. "I appreciate that," Kareena said with a smile.

"Would it be okay if we, I don't know, acted like friends meeting up instead of a date? It feels weird to be set up online by my mother, and I'd rather ease into this."

Kareena laughed. "Yeah, that works for me." She wasn't feeling any electricity between them, anyway. Like with Prem. The memory of his fingertips along the curves of her anklebone had her shivering despite the warm temperature in the restaurant.

Their server stepped up to the table. "Hi, folks. What can I get you to drink?"

Rahul motioned to her, and she smiled.

After their server jotted down their drinks, he left without another word.

"Is this the part where we talk about ourselves?" Rahul asked, folding his arms on the table.

"I guess so. What do you want to know?"

"Well, I think one of the most important questions for me is, what is your favorite color?"

What in the world? "My favorite . . . color."

He nodded. "Your favorite color. Preferably choosing between black, white, red, green, and blue. It's important."

How was it important? It sounded superficial to her. With superspecific choices. She had to wonder if he was searching for a particular answer.

"I know it may sound strange, but black is probably my favorite out of all those," she finally replied. Kareena pointed to her black slim-fit pants, and her brand-new black sweater vest that she'd purchased to replace the one that was ruined in the hospital. "It goes with everything, and I think it looks pretty good on me . . . What? What did I say?"

He'd balked, and some of the melanin in his skin faded. "Life drains," he whispered.

"Um, excuse me?"

He shook his head. "Nothing, nothing. I didn't mean anything."

"No, I'd really like to know."

He looked at his backpack, and then back at her. "You know how I'm a gamer, right? I build video games? That was in my profile."

"Yes, I do remember seeing that."

"Well, in one of the . . . er, games that I play, colors often represent personality. If you had told me that your favorite color was green, I would've thought that you were open and welcoming as a person. If you told me that your favorite color was white, then I would've assumed that you were pretentious and shallow."

"Oh! Like *The Great Gatsby*."

It was his turn to look confused. "Excuse me?"

"Color is symbolic in *The Great Gatsby*. I was an English major. I had to read *The Great Gatsby*. Hated the book. However, I loved that white meant shallow and pretentiousness."

Rahul raised an eyebrow. His face lit up. "That's so interesting how white means the same thing in the game. Okay, cool. Well, you chose black, and with black . . . well, it represents a life drain."

"Like vampires? Into the dark of the night kind of thing? I read *Dracula*, too."

He grinned. "Yes! Exactly like vampires."

Kareena knew that when she'd first read about Rahul's interest in gaming, she judged pretty hard. But hearing him talk about what he loved was relatable. She had interests she could go on and on about for hours. Like her car, or redoing kitchen cabinets.

Their server delivered their drinks, then left with a "Call me if you need me."

"Tell me more about the gaming," Kareena said after taking a sip of her drink.

His eyebrows nearly reached his hairline. "Yeah? Huh. That's pretty cool of you."

"It's early yet," she said with a laugh. "Why do you like it?"

"I was picked on in school, you know? But gaming gave me a place where I felt safe."

She nodded. She could understand that. She found her people on the debate team. "Your color code thing was interesting. What game is that from?"

"Ah . . ." He ran his fingers through his hair. "It's from Magic: The Gathering, which is usually a four-player game. I play Commander."

"What do you do?"

"The cards and the colors that I mentioned? Each colored card has a purpose and a theme."

"Wow, that's a lot."

"We haven't even gotten into Dungeons and Dragons. I can go on and on about that. I'm one of the best dungeon masters on the East Coast."

She could not stop smiling. "Wait, wait. Isn't that the board game the hot actors in Hollywood started playing?"

"Kareena," Rahul said with a sigh. "I never thought you'd be one of those people. They aren't even that good!"

Kareena laughed at the dismayed expression on his face.

"What? I'm just asking. The board game you're talking about is like Harry Potter, right?"

"Oh my god, you poor child. You have no idea, do you?" Rahul asked. "Harry Potter is for children. It's only a small portion of mythological possibilities. In Dungeons and Dragons, you can literally be any sort of creature."

Kareena took another slurp from her drink as she tried to make sense of his game references. "I'd still be a witch because *Practical Magic* is one of my favorite movies. Or a vampire."

"Please don't say it," Rahul said, covering his face with his hands.

"Because of *Twilight*!"

"You are a horrible human," he said.

He looked so miserable, but there was also humor in his face. Kareena had to admit that this had to be one of the better dates she'd been on. She motioned to his open backpack at his side that was filled with gaming paraphernalia. "Do you bring that on every Indian marriage dot-com outing in case you meet someone who is as interested in gaming as you?"

"No, not really," he said. His cheeks deepened in color. "I sort of assumed this date wasn't going to go well, so I double-booked a Dungeons and Dragons game with a few people who came in from L.A. They're at a friend's house, and I was going to join them after drinks with you. My dice and cards are pretty valuable so I couldn't leave them in the car, which is why . . . well, I'm sorry about that."

Kareena knew exactly why he'd done it, but for the first time, she was sad to see a date end early. "Don't apologize. Since gaming means that much to you, I'm totally okay with calling it an early night."

There was a beat of silence. Rahul looked at his watch, and then back at her. "I don't want to sound creepy, but I have an idea if you're really interested in learning more about Dungeons and Dragons."

Kareena cringed. Whenever someone started off a sentence like that, it was usually because they were about to say something creepy. "What is it?"

"Would you be interested in coming to play a game with us? There will be a few women there. The guy who is hosting the event is married, so it's not like a bunch of dudes. You can be a witch character. I can drive you there and drop you home whenever you want. The only caveat is that the friends from L.A. are pretty high-profile, so you have to swear no social media or anything like that."

Kareena was . . . intrigued. She weighed her options, then looked at the rest of her drink. What the hell? As long as she was safe, right? Social media wasn't an issue for her anyway, since her viral video made it impossible to have an online presence right now.

She opened her text chat with her friends. "What is the address of where we are going? And I need your license so I can take a picture of it."

Rahul lifted his hip to take out his back pocket wallet. "Absolutely." She took a picture of the license and sent all the info to Bobbi and Veera.

That's when she remembered that Bobbi was at an event so she wouldn't have her phone on her, and Veera was out with her twin.

After running through her contacts, she forwarded the text to Bindu, and after waiting for a thumbs-up emoji, she finished her wine and put her empty glass on the table. "I'm ready to go play some dungeon masters! This is not like the *Fifty Shades* dungeon, is it?"

Rahul balked. "Please don't say that in front of my friends." He pulled out a credit card and paid the bill that was discreetly left at the edge of their table. "First, it's Dungeons and Dragons, and the person who is the storyteller is the dungeon master. And if you're going to be a witch, you have to pick your powers, like fire, ice, or both. And you have to pick your personality. For example, are you lawful, neutral, and chaotic? I'm sorry, there is a lot to learn."

Kareena scooted out of the booth. "I'm a pretty quick study."

Rahul grabbed his things and led her out of the restaurant. For the first time since she started dating, she was having a good time, in a comfortable, friendly kind of way. This wasn't exactly the same as running through a museum or receiving corner-of-the-mouth kisses after food-eating competitions or having mind-blowing orgasms on the hood of her car. But it was a start.

Because as wonderful as her connection with Prem had been, he still couldn't give her what she wanted. She'd have to accept second best.

CHAPTER SIXTEEN

Prem

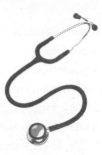

> **BINDU:** Hi! My sister is at a strange man's house. She just met him tonight. I thought you should know.

> **PREM:** WHAT??

> **BINDU:** Here is what she texted me.

> **PREM:** Kareena, where are you?

> **PREM:** I just tried calling and you didn't pick up. What the hell, Kareena?

> **PREM:** Is everything okay??

> **PREM:** That's it, I'm coming to get you.

Prem came to a screeching stop in front of a town house on a hilly street in Hoboken. He didn't even take a second to appreciate the fact that he was able to find parking. His only concern was Kareena. In seconds, he'd jumped out of his car and practically run up the walkway. He had his phone ready in case he had to call 911, since he had no idea what he was getting into. His nerves were frayed the entire drive over, even as he called Kareena a dozen more times.

With a deep breath, he pounded on the door, and then rang the doorbell three times.

A few short barks greeted him.

These were probably attack dogs. Dogs that were trained to kill intruders. Dogs that were going to tear him apart. He braced his feet. He'd worked out that morning and was a little sore, but he'd take on some dogs to bust Kareena out of there if he had to.

A woman's voice followed. "Luke, stop! Luke, down."

The front porch lights came on, and he had to squint under the glow. A Korean woman with bright blue hair opened the door a crack.

"Can I help you?"

That was unexpected.

"Hi, I'm looking for Kareena Mann? I'm her friend. Her ride. Her . . . I'm here to take her."

She scanned his scrubs, squinting at the ID tag still attached to his breast pocket. "You're a doctor?"

"Yes."

"Which hospital?"

"Excuse me?"

"Where do you practice?" she asked.

"I'm at a private practice. I'm sorry, I'm just looking for my friend."

The woman opened the door wider, and the dog that had been barking bolted out. A Pomeranian the width of a beach ball wobbled out and circled Prem's feet. It barked three more times in quick succession.

Okay, maybe not an attack dog.

"Luke, in the house. Your father is going to be very upset with you if you run away again. Come on, let's go!"

Prem waited for the dog to go back in. Damn, the tiny little furball had sounded just like a scary, bloodthirsty wolf with sharp teeth. It had probably been the adrenaline pumping through his bloodstream that made him think the sound came from a larger animal. Totally normal reaction.

"I should go," Prem said. "I'm just looking for my friend. Thank you for your time."

"Come on in," she said. "Kareena's here."

"Uh, excuse me?"

The woman motioned for him to step inside the tiny tiled foyer. "Kareena is here. She came with one of my husband's friends, Rahul. They're all playing downstairs. What private practice are you with?"

"Jersey City Cardiology Center."

The woman held her hand out. "Dr. Su-jin Kim. I'm with Hoboken Dermatology."

"Oh. Uh, nice to meet you." He took the woman's hand and shook. *Why the hell was Kareena here?*

"Come on. Follow me. I'm sorry if you were worried, but Kareena's fine. They should be wrapping up soon."

Prem followed the woman down a hallway, through a basement door, and down a narrow flight of stairs toward loud cheers and conversation, most of it male.

When he peered over the stair railing and first saw the group of people in the basement, he realized he would've been less surprised at an orgy.

A large poker table covered in black felt sat in the middle of a group of six men and two women. Most of the men were ripped and covered in tattoos. The other woman in the group looked like she was a rockabilly model. Then there was Kareena. His sexy librarian/lawyer with her black sweater vest, her black framed glasses, and her hair in a ponytail. She was also wearing a large red cape.

"I can't believe my witch died!" she shouted.

There was a mix of groans and laughs from the group.

"Hey, Kareena?" Su-jin called from the base of the stairs.

Kareena turned around, her mouth dropping when she saw Prem. "What in the world are you doing here?"

He answered in Hindi. "Your sister told me you were at a strange man's house. I texted you a dozen times and you didn't answer."

"Uh, excuse me," a desi dude said from the spot next to her. "Even though I can understand Hindi, not everyone here does. That's super rude."

Prem was ready to snap back when Kareena rested a hand on the dude's arm.

What the hell? Knots twisted in the pit of his stomach.

"It's okay. Prem, sorry, I got caught up in the game."

"I was . . . worried."

Prem hated that so many people were staring at him, judging him for wanting to make sure that Kareena was safe. How was he supposed to know that she wasn't in trouble? It's not like she was answering her phone. He crossed his arms over his chest, ready to take all of them on. Even the one who looked like he was in the HBO vampire show.

"Are you ready to go home?" he asked, turning back to Kareena.

She looked at the game board and then back at him with a raised brow. He shook his head in response. He did not want to stay, and he had every intention of driving her ass all the way back to Edison where it belonged.

"Yeah, I should be heading home now," she said out loud.

The group protested with various degrees of sadness. "How are you going to learn what happens if you leave now?" the movie star doppelganger said from the other side of the table. "I'm only in Jersey for twenty-four hours before I have to head back to L.A. Last chance."

"Hey, I swear you look like the guy from—"

"Time to go!" Kareena interjected. "Joe, you're brilliant, and I hope I'll have another opportunity to play Dungeons with you soon. Frankie, thanks for letting me come to your home. And, Gina? I'm going to come and visit you for Mexican pizzas!"

"Don't forget," the guy Kareena called Frankie said. "We're playing again in a few weeks. Do you have our number?"

"I do," she said. She motioned to the Indian dude next to her. "Rahul texted it to me earlier."

"Do you want me to walk you out?" Rahul said. "I mean, this was a date."

Kareena snorted. "Your character is about to take control! Stay. But let's go to your sister's restaurant for pancakes soon."

"You got it."

They hugged, and Prem had to hold himself back from lunging across the room and tearing them apart. Before he could make a move, Kareena took off her cape and tossed it over her recently vacated chair.

"This was awesome."

"Glad you had fun," Rahul said. The dude turned to Prem and glared.

What the hell was that about?

Prem stepped aside and let Kareena pass him. He brushed his fingers against hers, and they tangled for a moment before she moved by. The room had already turned back to their game. "Now that our witch is gone, who's going to be brave enough to open the chest?"

He thanked Su-jin again when he reached the kitchen, petted Luke, the Pomeranian, and left with Kareena at his side. They got into his Audi, and he punched in her address.

"I can't believe you drove here because you thought I was in trouble," she said after they got onto the main road. "I mean, I know you're not that far, but still. Also, you don't have to drive me all the way home. That's forty-five minutes each way at this time of night."

Prem just grunted at her as he followed the directions on the screen. He watched out of the corner of his eye as she pulled her phone out of her bag and scrolled through text messages in the dark console of his car. She let out a laugh. "With the way you were panicking, it's like you think I found my soul mate already. I know getting the money means a lot to you, but I promise you I'll give you the heads-up before I get that far."

He couldn't blame her for automatically thinking that his only vested interest was the money, but it still hurt. "Kareena, that guy wanted to go down to brown-town."

"Go down to . . . oh my god. Prem, Rahul was into Dungeons and Dragons. I was intrigued. He asked me to play with him and his friends. And just because we—"

She bit her lip, cutting off the rest of her sentence.

Prem shifted in his seat. "No, I think you need to finish that thought," he said evenly. "Just because we what?"

Kareena waved a hand in dismissal. "Rahul hates eggs, North Indian food, and has a pumpkin spice latte obsession. We're better off as friends, Prem."

"Perfect brunch date," he asked, and tucked her hair behind her ear. *"What would you want in the morning? When you're not having birthday paranthas from your grandmother."*

The corner of her mouth quirked. "I love eggs, too. My mom used to make them for me when I was a kid, and now there is a sense of nostalgia attached to them."

"Scrambled? Fried? Over easy? Hard-boiled?"

She laughed. "Scrambled. The delicious soft way that looks all bright and yellow. There is nothing like scrambled eggs with coffee."

"Cream and sugar?" he asked.

"Cream. Peppermint, regardless of the time of year. Why all the questions?"

"Now I know what I'm making you in the morning."

PREM NAVIGATED DOWN the single-lane street toward 1-9. The sun was already setting behind the mismatch of row homes crowded together on sidewalk streets. Groups of people were out walking pets, or on their way to restaurants. In the dimming light of Hoboken, Prem cursed at how much he wanted to say, and how little he knew how to say it.

Rina adjusted her ponytail in the visor mirror and settled deeper into her seat. "Prem, if you're insistent on taking me all the way to Edison, the least you can do is talk to me."

"About what," he ground out. About how he hated having to pick her up on a date with a different guy?

She shrugged. "I don't know. The one thing we've always been good at is talking. Hell, the first time we met we talked for three hours. Distract me from thinking about how I'm losing at this dating thing. Just don't mention your antilove theory."

"I don't know why you're going through all the trouble," he burst out, "when we could—"

"Oh god, not again—"

"I'm just telling you the truth—"

"No, you're telling me your version of the truth," she shot back. Kareena's voice had an edge to it now. It was an octave higher since she'd started talking. "You always forget that my stakes are a lot higher, so I'm not going to shake hands with you when I know that you'll walk away whistling, and I'll be left picking up pieces. Relationships and love are not a game to me."

Prem swallowed hard, his hands gripped tightly on the steering wheel. He began to sweat. "Rina, I may have a reason for pushing hard, but I'm not playing games. That night in the bar? Last weekend in your shed? Those moments were real to me. What we have together may be short-lived, but it's real. I'm sorry it's taken me so long to admit that, but I'm putting all my cards on the table here."

Kareena let out a frustrated growl that had his back going ramrod straight. "You don't get to do that, Prem. You don't get to send me flirty texts, take me out on dates, then tell me that our almost hookups were real to you," she said, her voice raising with each word. "Not when I know that your plan is to lie about us getting married then break things off once you get your community center. That still leaves me at square one. No, square *zero*. Because our very public fight means we'll have a very public breakup. So many Indian men are infected with misogyny, casteism, colorism, and internalized colonialism. And the ones left may not want the baggage!"

"Then focus on finding a stronger guy who can carry the weight," he murmured.

"What, and that's easy? Prem, damn it, I'm trying here. Being with you can *ruin* me."

The very thought of hurting her was appalling. That was the last thing Prem wanted to do. Rina deserved to be happy, but he knew without a shadow of a doubt that there was no way she'd find it by going on a wild goose chase searching for love. And if she was being honest with herself, then she'd admit she knew that, too.

Prem turned at the next traffic light and tapped the horn when a delivery truck pulled out of a parking spot in front of him. "Rina, if you really want to find your true love, your mythical happily ever after, then why did you wait so damn long for it? Why is it all of a sudden so important to you?"

"Because I wanted to achieve my career goals first, and—"

"Bullshit," he said, jerking the Audi around a double-parked car and easing into traffic. "I'm calling bullshit. If someone you really connected with had walked up to you in law school, would you have turned him away?"

"No, of course not, but—"

"And I bet if you had a connection with any of the people that you've dated since law school, you would've straight up eloped."

Rina crossed her hands over her chest. "What are you getting at, Dr. Dil?"

"I'm trying to tell you that maybe love doesn't exist! Maybe what you're really looking for is connection. And you have that with me. You have a connection with *me*."

"I don't believe that," she said, vehemently shaking her head. "I don't believe that for a minute. I know better than you what I need, Prem."

Prem let out a humorless laugh, and before he could stop himself, words kept tumbling out of his mouth. "Or maybe you don't know what you need at all?"

She gasped like he'd just scandalized her in the worst way. "I know exactly what I need, Dr. Dil. I also know that connection does *not* make a relationship work, fake or otherwise."

"Fine. If you're so convinced that you and I don't have a connection, then come home with me."

"*What?*"

"Come home with me," he repeated. Lust, frustration, and desperation fisted in his gut. He felt like he was fighting for his life here. "If we don't have a connection, we'll figure it out really quick. I can prove to you that we can be together, and love doesn't have anything to do with it."

Kareena shifted in her seat so she could face him. "Why?" she blurted out.

"Why come home with me? Other than this . . . this thing between us?"

He came to a stop at the traffic light in front of the Holland Tunnel that separated Hoboken from Jersey City.

"I'm attracted to you," he finally said, shifting in his seat so he could look her in the eye. "And despite our history, the times we've laughed together have been amazing. We'll both regret never knowing what it's like to be with each other. If that's not what you want, then I'll live with it. But if you want me, too, I think we should— You know what? Fuck this."

Prem threw the car in park, then slipped her glasses off her face and tossed them on his dashboard.

"My glasses!"

"Eyes here, Rina."

He leaned across the console and pressed his mouth against hers.

His craving for her was only getting worse as his heartbeat altered rhythm. Her hands came up to cup his face, and her fingertips singed his skin as they scraped through his stubble.

Kareena tasted like coming home. She was sweet, and wet, and fit him like the other half of his puzzle. Their tongues collided, and Prem was desperate to touch skin.

He cursed when the sound of a horn honking interrupted them. He shifted his car in gear and inched forward with traffic. It took him a few more seconds until he'd merged into the right lane and positioned himself for a left turn.

"Well?" he asked shifting so that his knees bracketed the steering wheel, and he could grip the back of her headrest. They were both still breathing heavy. "Are you willing to find out whether I'm right or you are?"

She plucked at the fabric of her pants, and despite the dark, Prem could see that she didn't have anything on her pants. "Prem," she said softly. "This is only going to make things more complicated."

"I'm always going to wonder. Aren't you?"

When Kareena didn't respond, he flipped on his signal so he could exit onto the highway.

"No," she said, gripping his arm. "L-let's go to your place. One night. Just one night to get it out of our system. Just so I can prove to you that . . . that I'm right."

"Are you fucking serious?"

Kareena nodded in quick jerky moves.

Prem didn't waste another moment. He turned the wheel, cut off a honking semi, and sped toward his apartment.

Dear Readers,

If your matches have taken a liking to each other, it's important to keep them apart. Yes, this may seem counterintuitive to building a strong relationship, but oftentimes it's best if couples do not have an opportunity to spend quality time together alone.

Accidents do happen.

Mrs. W. S. Gupta
Columnist
Avon, NJ

CHAPTER SEVENTEEN

Kareena

"I'm not really a bar person," Kareena said. "Even before I sort of stopped dating to focus on my career."

"Me neither," Prem said. "I'm usually working."

There was a pause that kick-started Kareena's heartbeat. "So . . . the real version of Netflix and chill?"

His smile was beautiful. "You mean Jeopardy! *and jalebis? Yes. Absolutely. That is my speed, too. And Rina? I may be a desi boy, but I do really well with jalebis."*

KAREENA LOOKED OVER at Prem's profile, then back to her interlocked fingers in her lap. She was a healthy, independent (sort of) woman at thirty. She had every right to have sex whenever she wanted, and however she wanted.

But this was Prem Verma. This was Dr. Dil, the man who vehemently denied that love could sustain a lifelong partnership. He was her polar opposite. She had to wonder if sleeping with him was the smartest idea she'd ever had, or the dumbest.

As they turned down narrow side streets, Kareena knew Prem was right on the money, that bastard. She had been avoiding dating not just because of her busy schedule, but also because failing at intimacy truly scared her. Intimacy was supposed to be the easy part, but for some reason it was always the hardest for her.

The older she got, the harder it became to open up to someone else.

Until Prem.

Kareena's heartbeat quickened. Normally, if she was about to take her clothes off, or do anything sexy with a man, she would think of a hundred reasons why she shouldn't go through with it, right before she took the plunge. But for the first time in . . . well, forever, she couldn't think of a single reason why not.

Other than the fear of getting attached to someone who couldn't love her back.

No, that wouldn't happen. It couldn't.

Prem pulled into a parking lot underneath a high-rise. She watched as his palms slid over the soft dimpled steering wheel.

"One day, after my clinic is set up, I plan on moving to the suburbs."

"Oh yeah? You strike me as a city guy."

Prem rolled his eyes before sliding into a numbered spot and shutting off the car. "I grew up in a neighborhood with yards and picket fences in California. I want the same when I'm done with my community center. Come on."

They got out of the car and walked to a bank of elevators across from the lot. He motioned for her to enter the elevator first, then scanned a tiny key fob against a sensor.

"I just realized something," Kareena said, praying that the nerves would stay at bay. "This is the first time I'm going to see your place. Did you ever think a month ago that this is where we'd be?"

"A month ago, I was thinking of ways to hide your body," he said. "But I like this result a lot better."

The way he looked at her had her blushing. And then, the elevator doors opened and Prem motioned for her to step out before he followed. "Last door at the end of the hall," he said. They walked the short distance, a foot between them, to a black door with brass fixtures. He keyed in.

"Welcome to my home," he said, and the door swung open. She slipped past him, brushing against his chest and trying to focus on his apartment instead of his ridiculous body.

When he flipped on the lights, Kareena's jaw dropped. Exposed ductwork in the ceiling. A brick wall to the left. Modern appliances in the kitchen. Floor-to-ceiling windows with a tiny balcony. He had a large living space, with what looked like a soft leather sectional facing a massive flat-screen.

Oh my god.

"This is what I want to do with the house," she blurted out. "I always thought the open kitchen and living space we had would be *perfect* for this. All we have to do is take down some more walls, freshen the paint, and put in modern furniture." She could see it crystal clear, and it surprised her that she and Prem shared the same vision for comfort.

Prem toed off his shoes near a discreetly positioned closet, and she quickly followed suit. "Between my parents helping me out, and scholarships to keep student loans down, I was able to afford this place by the skin of my teeth," he said behind her as she crossed to the windows. "I want to move into a house, but it makes sense to be here right now until my community center is established."

"Don't apologize for what you have," Kareena replied. She thought about her car, the house, both symbols of so much more than money. "You should never be ashamed of the sacrifices our parents made for us, and the work you've done on top of that."

"I don't know why, but I *always* feel the need to apologize. My father used to tell me how if he didn't come over to the States for medical school, then we would've never left Delhi. He has that whole 'fifty dollars in his pocket' story that I always think about when I spend my cash on big expenses. Are your stories the same as mine?"

"My father doesn't like to talk about it a lot," Kareena said. "But I know that despite the little cash they had at first, they celebrated their love every day. And that's what makes what they had so much more special."

She enjoyed the feel of bare feet on his plush area rugs and leaned against the glass pane of the sliding door. The apartment was so high above the noise on the streets, it brought her a sense of peace she'd been chasing for so long she forgot what it even felt like. Bobbi was on a second floor, and Veera was a little higher up. Neither of their places felt like this.

She heard Prem moving around the apartment behind her while she watched the city lights.

"Here," he said a moment later.

He approached her with two highball whiskey glasses pinched together with his fingertips in one hand, and a bottle in the other.

"I don't know. Remember the first time I drank with you?"

"We're not going overboard this time."

Kareena grabbed the glasses so that he could pour a little whiskey in each. He then set the bottle down and toasted her, his body close to hers. "The first is for courage."

She tossed it back. The warm liquid burned as it slid down her throat. She took the bottle from the table, then poured another half inch into both their glasses. "The second is for honesty."

They drank in unison, clearing their throats.

Prem poured a third finger. "And the last is for friendship that includes pani puri competitions, scavenger hunts, and your search to find you your true love."

"I'll drink to that," Kareena said with a laugh. She tilted the glass back, and this time the burn wasn't nearly as abrasive in her throat. Her head felt a little lighter, her skin warmer.

Prem took the glass from her when she finished and set the bottle and discarded tumblers on the coffee table. He returned to her side and brushed his fingers against the back of her hands at her sides. "Okay. Make your first move, Rina, honey."

"What? What do you mean?"

Prem grinned in the dim glow of his overhead lighting. "I've known you long enough to understand that you like things a certain way. I'm not going to screw it up by taking control and letting you be a passenger on this ride. You have to ask for what you want."

She wanted to just tell him to take the lead. Judging by the look on his face, he knew exactly what to do. But then again, when would she ever have an opportunity like this to play doctor?

Her mind raced even as her thighs clenched and panties dampened with anticipation. Kareena said the first words that came to mind. "Do you have condoms?"

He was leaning in, his eyes fixed on her mouth. When his eyebrows jumped, she had to wonder if she was killing the mood.

"I do."

Kareena nodded. "Okay, good. I mean, I'm clean, and it's been a long time, but I still prefer a condom."

"Of course." Prem ran his index finger over the curve of her jaw. Their height difference was more pronounced now that she wasn't in heels, and it felt like he was surrounding her, with his wideset shoulders and thick arms that seemed to capture her even though they were barely touching.

"Prem?"

"Mm-hmm?"

"I've read romance novels since I was in high school, and so many of the heroines are ashamed when they don't have sex after four months, and I'm, like, is that the scale I have to go by? It's been a lot longer than four months for me, so by romance standards, I'm screwed."

"You will be," he said. She jumped when his fingertips scraped down the side of her neck, and his calloused rough skin raised goose bumps.

Holy cow.

She shoved her glasses up her nose. "Wh-what do we do now?" she whispered.

"Tell me what you want, Rina, honey. I promise I'll make it good."

His mouth was inches from hers, and her face felt warm. The base of her spine tingled. It was now or never. "Kiss me then. The way that you did in my shed. The way you kissed me at the bar. And the promise of what you made me in the car before we started driving here."

Prem stepped closer, his body inches from hers. Her breath caught. The soft pad of his thumb traced over her cheek and touched the corner of her mouth.

"No corner kisses," Kareena whispered. "Kiss me, mouth to mouth."

She froze. "Wait, that came out wrong. Like mouth to mouth, but not as if you were doing CPR, because you're a doctor and I'm sure that's the first thing that popped into your mind when I said that—"

He swooped in, wrapping his arms around her waist, tugging her against his hard chest, and kissed her. Her brain completely melted just like it had the last two times.

It always feels like magic.

Kareena wrapped her arms around his neck and hesitantly

opened her lips. He did the same, giving her just enough space to slip her tongue over his.

This was Prem, and he smelled delicious. He felt delicious.

He groaned, and ran his hands over her back, until he was cupping her butt. It was her turn to groan.

She didn't know how long they stood there, in front of the windows, sipping from each other's mouths, but the more they kissed, slowly, deeply, the more Kareena eased closer to Prem, enjoying the feel of him, burning under the slow exploration of his tongue and lips.

Then he pulled away.

"Wh-at?" she said with a gasp. She was breathing fast. "What happened?"

Prem took Kareena's glasses again and tossed them on the coffee table.

"My glasses . . . gah!"

He tossed her over his shoulder in a firefighter's grip and carried her through his apartment.

In her life she had *never* been tossed over someone's shoulder. She didn't think anyone could do something like that. But Prem kept walking like he was on a stroll with a handful of daises instead a hand full of—

"Ass!" she shouted, as the sting on her left cheek sent shock waves straight to her groin. "Prem, you just smacked my ass."

"That I did." She swore she could hear him chuckle.

He dropped her onto a soft king bed with a gray spread.

If the kiss didn't do it, the bed tossing sure as hell made her wet.

Kareena sat up, resting on her elbows, then homed in on the bulge in his pants. "Prem . . ."

He whipped off his top and his pants, leaving on a pair of boxer briefs and a white fitted T-shirt.

"Anything else?" he said. His voice was hoarse, and he watched her in a way that made her so aware and tingly all at the same time. Damn it, he was teasing her. He definitely left on the boxer briefs because it drove her mad, but maybe that was a good thing. This way they could undress in stages.

"I-I could use some more kissing."

"On the mouth?"

She glanced at her pants, and then back at him. No way. She was not brave enough to flat out tell a dude that he should—

"Fucking ask me, Rina," he snapped.

"Okay, yes, I want you to go down on me." Holy shit, had that even come out of her mouth?

"No, use your words," Prem said as he leaned forward and unbuttoned her waistband. Her stomach quivered. "What do you want?"

"I-I want you to kiss my . . . my—"

"You are a fucking strong, capable woman," he said. His voice was hard now, and the lines of his shoulders stiff from tension. He was unrelenting. "Come on. Ask for what you want, Rina. I promise you, I want the same thing, too."

"I want you to eat me," she said with a rush. "I mean, maybe I should shower first, and then shave my legs. But in the end, that's what I want."

"No time for either of those things," Prem said. He nudged her flat on her back, and pressed small kisses down the front of her body over her clothes, as if leaving little promises for later.

Finally, he reached her waistband, and with a few quick tugs, her pants were around her ankles, then off. Before she could focus on the insecurity of being almost naked in front of a man who looked as fine as Dr. Dil, he hooked a finger across the crotch of her panties and ripped them off her. Then his hands were on the inside of her thighs, and he was separating her lips with his thumbs. Finally, finally, his mouth caressed her delicate, soaking pussy, and Kareena practically came off the bed in pleasure.

"More," she gasped.

"More?" Prem replied. "Where?" He started by kissing one labia, then the other. There was a hint of tongue when he caressed the crown of her pussy. "Where?"

Damn it, why was he purposely driving her crazy like that?

"I want you to lick me deep," she said in gasping breaths.

The rough feel of his five o'clock shadow scraped against her sensitive inner thighs before he settled against her, and he licked her firm and strong, his tongue igniting her entire body. "More!"

"Where?" he asked. Stroking to the left. "Here?"

"No, over, over more, oh my god!"

Bingo.

Prem savored her, tasted her in a way that she never experienced before. Then, he added a finger, two fingers while he focused on her clit.

She rode her pleasure until it peaked, and every muscle in her body tensed, desperate for relief. When it came, her orgasm crashed through her like a tidal wave, consuming every last molecule of air in her lungs.

Kareena leaned up on her elbows, expecting Prem to strip the last of his clothes and get to work, but all he did was look up, meet her eyes, and wipe his wet lips with the back of his hands. He then pressed down on her inner thighs again, and still meeting her eyes, he licked her pussy with one long stroke of his tongue.

She collapsed back on the bed, oversensitized from orgasming already. "I can't," she gasped. But he didn't hear her and continued to drive her wild until she was shrieking and pulling the blanket from under her, trying to gain purchase.

Her voice was robbed when she came a second time.

"You doing okay?" he asked gruffly.

She nodded, stars flashing in front of her eyes.

"Good. Time to level up." He gripped her hands and pulled her into a sitting position. "No earrings this time, right? I'm not going to fuck this up again." He gripped the hem of her sweater vest, and with more care than necessary, he pulled it over her head and tossed it aside. Then, he worked on the long row of buttons down the front of her collared shirt, his fingers moving swiftly and competently. She let out a sigh of relief when Prem saw her sheer black bra and let out an expletive.

"I will forever think of this under your sweater vests now," he said.

She reached behind her back and unhooked the bra, too eager now to pay attention to the insecurity yammering in the back of her brain. "My boobs are great, but I love the sweater vests," she said, breathlessly. "Are you going to take off the rest of your clothes, too?"

"Do you want me to?"

When she nodded and watched in the shadows of the room as Prem stripped off his shirt, Kareena nearly orgasmed again at the sight of firm, ridged muscles and pecs covered in the perfect amount of chest hair. And then, when he pushed down his boxer briefs, his penis practically popped out and whacked her in the eyeballs. This South Asian man was obviously proof that stereotypes could be lies. How was it supposed to fit inside her?

"It'll fit," he said.

"How did you know—"

"You looked intimidated." He kneeled on the bed and pushed her on her back. And then Kareena couldn't think at all again. They were skin to skin, touching and stroking now.

"I want to take everything from you," he said into her mouth before consuming her with long, drugging kisses. "And you can take all of me."

She pulled back, and under the weight of his body, in the dim lights of the room with the New York skyline outside the windows, she met Prem's eyes and whispered, "Take everything. I want you to have it."

Their mouths met again in a tangle of tongues as they rolled across the bed. He kept asking her what she wanted, and she was too lost in him to do anything but answer with truth.

DO YOU LIKE this?
    What about this?
    I'm going to slap your ass, Rina, honey.

AT ONE POINT, she knelt in front of him, taking his cock in her hands, and took him in her mouth. He tasted salty and warm as she ran her tongue over his mushroom head and down the thick vein.

"Suck it," he said hoarsely. "Hard. Squeeze your nipples."

She almost orgasmed again as she took as much as she could in her mouth and pulled at her nipples. He gripped her hair and with a sharp tug that had her juices flowing, guided her up and down his dick.

"No more," he said breathlessly, and pulled away.

They were covered in a sheen of sweat when he finally slipped on the condom he pulled from the bedside table and pushed into her, slowly with a firm, hard stroke. She was so full that she couldn't breathe. She was lost in the pleasure of holding him close as his thrusts became long, hard strokes.

The sound of his sac slapping against her ass and the near painful pleasure had her screaming his name. Tears welled in her eyes and slipped through her lashes.

Seconds, minutes, hours after Prem rode her hard, guiding her where she'd never gone before, she came again. With her last orgasm, Prem joined her, collapsing in her arms.

In the wild roaring thoughts inside her mind, one fact became crystal clear to Kareena. Dr. Prem Verma set the bar so high that she may never find a man who could ever make her feel this way again.

Dear Readers,

The best way your sons can romance a young match is by complimenting her virtues. Commenting on her beautiful hair, her beautiful skin, her lovely singing voice, even if she does not sing. This will allow the heroine to feel trusted and appreciated.

Silence is not a good option.

Mrs. W. S. Gupta
Columnist
Avon, NJ

CHAPTER EIGHTEEN

Prem

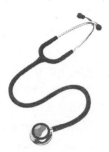

Prem hated leaving Kareena naked and sprawled on his bed like a shipwreck survivor, but he had to get rid of the condom.

And he was freaking out.

Truly freaking the fuck out.

He felt like he was experiencing cardiac arrhythmia as he pulled away from Kareena's body in a completely pleasured and sated state.

"I'll be right back," he said, dropping a quick peck on her smiling lips. He didn't want her to know that he was about to check himself into a hospital for an ECG.

Kareena hummed, her arms thrown over her head, her hair a tangled mess around her face. Her relaxed, mush-for-brains state was only going to last so long. If he knew her as well as he thought he did, she was going to be doing her own mental gymnastics soon.

He slid off the end of the bed and closed himself in the adjoining bathroom. After discarding the condom, he washed his hands, and then splashed cold water on his face.

"Oh my god, oh my god, oh my god," he whispered as he dried his hot skin, then pounded a fist against his chest. "Get it together."

Sex had always been fun and a great release for him. But it had never been like this. Even when he was with Gori, his sex life paled in comparison.

He wasn't sure when the mood changed, or how it happened. One minute, he was throwing back shots and kissing Kareena at Bunty's office, the next he was thinking about how long he could keep this woman in his bed.

And in his life.

He was already ready to go again. Normally Charlie needed a moment to catch its breath, but nope. Not this time. His adrenaline pumped through his body like he'd just ingested narcotics and his dick was at a half chub.

Prem wasn't a stupid man, and as much as he wanted to say it was all body chemistry, what he just experienced with Kareena felt so much deeper than that, and the deeper business was what frightened the shit out of him.

But despite his fear, he was in no way going to give up a chance to be with her for as long as possible.

Not wanting Rina to come out of her daze alone, Prem shoved his own racing thoughts in a compartment to examine later. He shook out his hands, rolled his shoulders, and strode back into the bedroom.

She had shifted from the prone position Prem had left her in. Now, Kareena's arm flung across the cover, and one knee was lifted, as if that was enough to hide her delicious plump pussy from him.

He moved to get on the bed, to hold her close, to caress her tits and spend more attention on them before he tried to convince her to stay the night with him, when he heard the distinct buzzing of the doorbell.

The lazy dreamlike expression on Kareena's face was gone in the blink of an eye. She vaulted to a sitting position, and her eyes widened in shock. "Oh my god, I'm naked."

"It's probably a delivery person who has the wrong apartment number," Prem said quickly. He grabbed his briefs off the floor and pulled them on. "Stay right here. Seriously, don't move. I'm just going to tell them to go away."

She'd brought her knees up to her chest and remained on the bed, but she hadn't agreed with him. *Shit*, he thought. It was going to be much harder, significantly harder for him to get her to stay the night now that they've been interrupted.

He marched down the hallway to the front door. He yanked it open, and before he could tell his intruders to fuck off, Bunty and Deepak were already talking.

"We brought Chinese," Deepak said. He held up a brown bag inside a plastic bag with a yellow smiley face on it.

"I was back in town and decided to do dudes' night in person," Bunty added, and lifted the two six-packs of beer.

"Oh shit," Prem said. He glanced over his shoulder then stepped outside and quickly pulled the door closed behind him. "You two cannot be here right now. You need to leave."

Bunty and Deepak glanced at each other and back to him. Prem watched his idiot friends realize what was happening.

"You dumb son of a bitch," Deepak hissed.

"Dude, I can't believe you slept with her!" Bunty whispered. "You're seriously Doctor *Dick*!"

Prem shoved his fingers through his hair. "Shh! She's still in bed, and she's a flight risk."

"That's because she's smart," Deepak whispered back. "What the hell are you doing with her? Seriously low of you to try to sex her into your plan. That really is a Doctor Dick move."

Prem shoved him back a full stop. "You're the dumb son of a bitch if you ever think I'd do something like that to Kareena. It's not like that."

"How the hell did this happen?" Bunty asked. He put the beer on the hallway floor, took one out, and popped the top with his cuff link in a move his father had taught both of them. Prem went to take it from him, but instead Bunty passed it to Deepak.

Prem, still itching for a beer, responded. "I-I honestly don't know. One minute we're fighting, and the next we're at my apartment. Bunty, this is all your fucking fault."

"Me? How the hell is this my fault?"

"Because I saw her at your bar! Because it was supposed to be one night where we hooked up in your office, but no. She had to come to my show, and we had to learn how different we both are when it comes to relationships, and then her aunties got involved and she's the best kiss I've ever had. And I thought I was lucky with Gori in my life, but now there is Rina!"

"Did you get that?" Bunty asked Deepak, taking a beer for himself.

Deepak shook his head. "That makes no fucking sense to me."

"You two aren't helping," Prem hissed.

"Well, you need to help yourself first!" Deepak said. "Being with Kareena is only supposed to get you your investor back. You want to prove to Gregory at LTD Financial that you're a solid family kind of guy. That you're trustworthy with his money and you'll make a *family* community health center a success. This! This is not going to work if she bails on you before you can get the money for the down payment!"

Prem spun in a circle and scrubbed his hands over his face. "Okay," he said, not believing the words that were about to come out of his mouth. "Okay, I hear what you're saying, but I have a little bit of a problem with that."

His friends waited patiently, drinking their beers in his hallway.

"What if," he said, and then glanced at the door. "What if I kept her?" He immediately covered his mouth with a fist.

"What the fuck do you mean by that?" Bunty said in his normal voice, then quieted after both Deepak and Prem hushed him into a whisper. "Prem, she's not fucking chattel!"

"No, I know that, you idiot. It's just that maybe I want our fake engagement to, to be more . . . real."

Both Bunty's and Deepak's mouths dropped in unison.

"I know! I know," Prem said, and pounded a fist to his chest again. God, he really needed to get one of coworkers to run some tests. He had some tightness in his chest whenever Kareena was in his head, and that had to be some glitch in his system. It wasn't normal.

"Dude, you slept with her once and now you want to marry her?" Deepak asked. "Does she have a magic—"

"Don't even think about finishing that sentence."

Bunty held up his free hand like a stop sign. "You can't blame the guy for asking. After Gori died, you wouldn't even consider dating a woman more than two times. It's been three years since your fiancée died, and—"

"And I've been busy!"

"You're *still* busy," Deepak said. "Nothing has changed from a year ago to now. If anything, you're even busier now."

Prem closed his eyes again. Deepak and Bunty were right. That wasn't an excuse he could use here. Hadn't he just had the same conversation with Kareena? "This is different."

"Different, but you two want completely different things," Bunty said. "Hello! You're Dr. Dil. The cardiologist whose first name means love and who actually thinks love is an illusion. And she's Kareena! The smart-mouthed babe who isn't afraid to fight anyone who doesn't believe in love. She wants Prince Charming and happily ever after and a Bollywood-style romance!"

"And that's something you won't give her," Deepak added.

They were right again. About everything. And Prem hated that.

"God damn it," Deepak burst out. "Why can't you just admit it? Admit that you have feelings for—"

The door opened to a fully dressed Kareena with tousled hair and glasses.

"Hey!"

"Kareena! How's it going."

"Fancy seeing you here."

Prem rolled his eyes as his friends looped arms over each other's shoulder and talked over each other as they saluted her with beer.

"You look great," Bunty said. "Love the sweater vest."

"Uh, thanks," she finally said. She turned to Prem, a confused expression on her face over the beautiful glow. "It looks like you have company. I should probably get going. I'll catch an Uber."

"No!" All three of them shouted at the same time.

"No, we were just leaving," Deepak said. He shoved the Chinese food bag in her hand. "We just brought this over for you."

"And beer," Bunty said, and handed over one of the six-packs to Prem. "Just your friendly neighborhood delivery service. We're heading out now. Have fun, you crazy kids!"

"We'll catch up with you later," Deepak said, giving Prem a pointed look.

Then both of his friends rushed down the hall toward the elevator bank.

Prem watched them stumble inside one of the cars and heard the soft swish of the doors closing.

He had to admit, even though they were idiots, Prem was lucky to have people like Deepak and Bunty in his life. They may not agree with him right now, but they still had his back.

"I still think I should go," Kareena said at his side.

She held the bag against her chest, and deliberately put space between them, but Prem wasn't ready for that yet. Space meant he'd have to process his thoughts about her, and she'd make even more excuses for them to stay away from each other.

"We just got Chinese," he said, motioning to the bag. "And beer."

She looked up and down the quiet hallway. "Prem, I don't know if this—"

He opened his apartment door and ushered her inside before she could finish that sentence. Then, without hesitation, he pressed a hard, firm kiss against her mouth.

"Do you want to go?"

"Prem . . ."

"Do you *want* to go?" he said when she finally opened her eyes.

"No," she whispered back.

"Then don't do that just yet. Spend the night with me. You can sleep in one of my shirts. We'll Netflix and chill."

Kareena's lips twitched. "You mean *Jeopardy!* and jalebis?"

He ran a hand over her hair. "Exactly. You can pick what we watch. Then sleep over."

She was already shaking her head. "I am a *terrible* sleeper. I need all sorts of things just to get to bed, none of which you have here."

"I have blackout curtains. The sun can be out, and I swear you'd think it was the moon instead." He knew he sounded desperate, but this was important. She was important. "If you can't sleep, I promise I'll drive you home in the middle of the night myself."

Kareena chewed on her bottom lip, and a small line appeared between her brows. "I don't know, Prem."

He kissed her again, and this time, her mouth relaxed under his. Some of the tightness in his stomach eased. "At least stay to eat with me?"

"Okay," she replied, and this time her free hand touched his bare chest. "Maybe just for dinner."

CHAPTER NINETEEN

Kareena

BOBBI: How was it? Tell us everything.

KAREENA: I just left.

VEERA: Whoa. You spent the night?

KAREENA: I SLEPT LIKE A FUCKING BABY. I can never sleep anywhere but in my bed! He woke me up with coffee at like seven! And only because he had to go to work and wanted to drive me home!

BOBBI: That's shockingly sweet coming from someone who I expect to act like a desi fuckboy.

KAREENA: I KNOW! What do I do???

VEERA: Honey, I think this is a moment where you have to ask yourself, what do you WANT to do? Did he ask you out again?

KAREENA: No, but it's not like we're really dating. This is not real!

PREM: Hey. Want to try a Turkish restaurant with me? I have surgeries this week, but I'm off on Saturday.

KAREENA: *copies Prem's text and sends to friends*

KAREENA: WHAT DO I SAY??

BOBBI: Say yes, you fool.

VEERA: Ooh, I wonder where he's taking you?

KAREENA: Okay.

PREM: Pick you up at 6:30 from the train or your house?

KAREENA: From my house. I'll drop my work stuff off.

PREM: And pack an overnight bag?

KAREENA: *copies Prem's text and sends to friends*

KAREENA: He wants me to spend the night again!!

BOBBI: Men.

VEERA: Aww!

KAREENA: Anything more helpful than that?

BOBBI: Fuckboys are tricky, but they have their uses.

VEERA: Do what your heart desires!

KAREENA: If I pack an overnight bag, then I'm going to have to go back to the train station. I can't be seen with my bag getting into your car, otherwise Dadi and my dad will have a field day.

PREM: I think at 30 they encourage this kind of behavior.

KAREENA: Ugh, probably, but I'm not taking chances.

Kareena didn't know what she was doing with Prem, but she wasn't exactly sure she was ready to stop, either.

She stood in her closet, examining the rows of sweater vests. She knew that Prem liked them, but it was over ninety that day. It felt weird for her to wear one even though that was her preferred date outfit. Prem had seen her naked. And if she was spending the night, she was probably going to get naked again. There was no point in wearing something uncomfortable.

Sweater vests had never been uncomfortable to her before. "That's a first," she mumbled.

It freaked her out that for the first time in a long while she didn't want to cancel her plans to stay home and read. That she felt sexy and turned on and *excited* to be with a man. Even though there was a time limit.

No, she wasn't going to think about that right now.

After scanning the row of hangers, Kareena stopped when a

piece of fabric caught her eye from the back of her closet. It was an emerald-green sundress that she'd bought on a whim one day. It reminded her of the one her mother wore in a picture taken on the front stoop when she'd finished renovating the house.

No. She couldn't wear that.

Kareena kept pushing aside clothes until finally she found a simple black maxi dress. She could pair it with the payal that she'd worn at Sonali Aunty's party for Dinesh Uncle since she knew that Prem liked that so much. Good lord, now she was dressing for him.

She pulled it off the hanger and slipped it over her head. It fell around her ankles in a soft waterfall of fabric just as a knock came from her bedroom door.

"Kareena?" her grandmother called out. Before Kareena could respond, Dadi was already opening the door. She took one look at Kareena and her lips pursed.

"Beta, if you're wearing a dress for the first time in years, could you put on something with a little more color? Black invites negative energy." Dadi's Hindi, Punjabi, and English mixed together like language soup.

And the criticism hit her just as Kareena was feeling herself, too. She stood in front of her floor-length mirror and turned side to side. Damn. She should've just worn her sweater vest. "Dadi, I'm going to meet up with Bobbi and Veena." The lies came easily to her, just like when she was young and first started dating.

Dadi shook her head. "You can't tonight. You have to help your sister with her sagai party decorations. She wants some flower wall. She has dinner with some work people she has to go to and needs this done."

"And I have plans," Kareena said. The fact that she was automatically the person everyone expected to pick up the slack was so irritating. They never tried to help her when she had a problem but had no qualms about asking her for assistance in return.

Kareena slung her giant tote and overnight bag over her shoulders. "I'm going downstairs to get a car to the train station."

"Kareena, I said your sister needs *help*," her grandmother called out, hustling behind her. Dadi twisted the hem of her faded floral kurta between her fingers. "You're the older sister and your mother isn't here. You should be focusing on the engagement party and the wedding."

Kareena checked her phone and thanked the lords that there was a car service nearby. She only had to wait a minute or so in front of her house, which meant less time listening to Dadi. After confirming her location and the car service pickup, she hurried down the stairs. "Where is Dad?" she asked. "Why isn't he helping?"

Her grandmother paused. "He's meeting with the real estate agent."

Kareena stumbled over the bottom step. "He's *what*?"

"You know that he's planning on listing the house right after your sister's engagement party," Dadi said. "The agent needed him to sign some paperwork."

Kareena wheezed like she'd just been sucker punched. "Why am I always left out of the loop?"

Her father was meeting with *real estate agents*. Her time was already so limited, and now it was speeding up at an exponential rate.

Dadi motioned to the wallpapered walls in the foyer. "Beta, it's just a house. Once you're married, you can find another home and decorate it however you want. And this is good for you. It'll force you to be more independent."

"I thought I was *too* independent already?" Kareena said, yanking open the front door. "My mother built this house. She dug the first hole and decorated every corner. And before she died, she'd made plans to do so much more. Then she said that it would go to me. *I've* done so much more with this house to carry on her legacy."

Her grandmother's lips puckered, accentuating the deep wrinkles around her mouth. "Oh, don't be such a drama queen. Why can't you do what we ask of you and just help your sister, and be a good girl?"

Kareena hated that every time they had this conversation, a piece of her heart cracked. "Because I'm not the hired help here."

"Watch your tone with me," Dadi snapped. She looked so much older than the last time Kareena really looked at her. She had deep-set lines in her face, bracketing her permanent frown. "I may be old, but I haven't lost my senses yet. You're being disrespectful now."

And that was how almost all their arguments went, Kareena thought. Dadi would call her disrespectful just because Kareena didn't agree with her. As much as she loved her grandmother, there was something fundamentally wrong with their relationship, too.

She remembered her conversation with Prem the weekend before. He'd mentioned how difficult a relationship he had with his mother, and Kareena had to wonder why it was so much harder for South Asians to break ties with those who loved yet caused the most hurt.

Kareena strode through the house as she checked the location of her driver. She couldn't do anything about her relationship with her grandmother right now. She had too many other things on her mind that she had to sort out. She needed some space, some time to just think.

Prem's offer lingered over her head like a dark cloud. If she saw him now, then he'd definitely convince her to accept.

Dadi continued to ramble on in her mix of languages before Kareena cut her off.

"I'm leaving," Kareena said to Dadi when she reached the front door. "Please tell Bindu to handle her own wedding. And please remind Dad that he has two kids." She shut the door behind her and ran to the curb where a black Volkswagen was waiting for her. She verified the license plate, then slid in the back seat. After rubbing the heel of her hand against her aching chest, Kareena knew that there was no way that she could meet Prem now. She was running out of time. She just needed a little more time to save her home.

Kareena squeezed her eyes shut and took two deep breaths before she scrolled through her phone to find Prem's number.

"I THINK WITH the careers we've chosen, and some of the pressures we feel in our community, burnout is a real problem. But burned out or not, I'll still fight for my patients."

"I'd fight for my clients, too," Kareena said. "And my family and friends. I'd even fight for the things that mattered to my mother. Her memories."

"That's a lot of fighting, Rina. Do you ever get tired of doing it alone?"

"Yes, but some people are worth the burnout."

KAREENA TAPPED ON Prem's name in her phone and closed her eyes as she pressed her phone to her ear.

"Hey," he said, his voice warm and intimate. "I'm a few minutes from the train station. Are you there yet?"

She shook her head, then tried to swallow the lump in her throat. Why was this hard? This shouldn't be difficult. They were just messing around. Getting to know each other. Exploring a, what was it? A connection.

"Prem," she said, her voice croaking. "I-I'm not coming tonight." She desperately wanted to be with him, to talk to him, to tell him how fucked-up it was that she was doing all this. And that desperation for Prem was exactly why she couldn't go.

There was a pause. "What is it? Is everything okay?"

"Yeah, it's just that—"

She'd cut herself off right before she could tell him that she was supposed to help her sister with wedding planning. No. No, she wasn't going to lie to him.

"Rina, honey? What is it?"

"I . . . I can't tonight," she said. "My father met with the real estate agent, and I realized how little time we have. I need to at least try—"

"You don't have to!" he burst out. "You don't have to date anybody. That's the whole point! Just be practical for once, Kareena." His voice was taking on an edge. The sound of a car horn echoed in the background.

She could feel her own anger beginning to surface. "I don't think it's fair for you to judge me when you're obviously biased."

"I'm not judging you for saying no," he said.

She had to pause at his strange choice of words. "But you're still judging?"

"Kareena, maybe you haven't found love yet because your understanding of love *doesn't exist*. Your mother died when you were really young. Are you sure what you remember is love between your parents, or just a few choice memories of happiness because your mom had *you*?"

The question was like a knife digging below her rib cage. "Just because your parents have a shitty love marriage doesn't mean that love marriages can't happen, Prem. That they can't sustain a relationship."

"And just because your parents had a great love marriage doesn't mean that love kept them together for so long, Kareena."

She pinched the bridge of her nose and leaned against the seat back. "Look, I'm calling to cancel because I need to figure out what to do. I've told you this before, and I'll say it again. If I agree with your plan, it'll make it a hundred times harder for me when we're done. You know what desi men can be like. Hell, men in general! And the desi community? They don't forget anything, and they'll remember that not only did I publicly humiliate myself on YouTube, but Dr. Dil and I didn't work."

"Who cares what people think, Rina? None of them matter!"

"No, none of them matter, but that doesn't mean I'm going to subject myself to more ridicule when I'm already so tired from fighting."

The line went quiet.

"I'm going to Veera's. It'll give us some time to cool off, too."

"I don't need to cool off," Prem replied. His voice was calmer now. "Not when I know exactly what I want, and you want the same thing, but you're too stubborn to see it. Call me when you're ready."

With those final words, he hung up the phone.

Kareena had to stop herself from calling him right back. Instead, she sent a text message to Veera letting her know that she was heading her way.

As the car raced down the Jersey Turnpike, Kareena's argument with Prem circled her mind. Damn it. She was going to miss him.

CHAPTER TWENTY

Prem

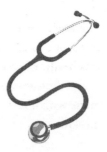

Prem had never been the type to reach for his phone, but he kept checking his messages in hopes of getting something from Kareena. He'd scrolled through his notifications before his show and then again whenever he had a commercial break. His producer shot him a funny look halfway through his newest segment, but Prem didn't care. This woman made him irrational, and there was nothing he could do about it.

He stood at his marker and waited for the signal that the playback reel was over, while the heavy weight of his cell sat snugly in his breast pocket. "As you can see, takotsubo cardiomyopathy, or broken heart syndrome, is really an extreme stress response. This is prevalent in women, especially South Asian women, who are often younger when they get broken heart syndrome than other races and ethnicities, which means that we as a community need to do better in providing the support women need to thrive."

His producer, Varsha, began counting down, and Prem closed out his show, rattling off his script as quickly as it appeared on the teleprompter. "Tune in next week, when we discuss how communication can lead to positive health benefits. Thanks again for watching."

The fake applause machine echoed through the studio, the camera panned out, and someone yelled "Cut!" Prem's fake smile fell like a Jenga tower. God, his face hurt sometimes from holding it for so long.

"Great job, Prem," Varsha said. She pulled her headphones down to rest on her collarbone, then came over to him to remove his mic. "That was definitely different."

"Oh yeah? How so?"

She ran a hand over her cropped magenta hair. "Darling, we asked you to talk about stress and how it affects the heart for today's topic of conversation. You go into broken heart syndrome. That seems a bit more . . . personal than usual."

Prem rolled his eyes. "Stress effects on heart health is a huge topic. I had to narrow it down somewhere." And he'd been thinking about Rina's health. She took on too much sometimes. Was she taking care of herself? Was she eating or sleeping? She'd sleep fine if she stayed with him.

Nope, he had to stop thinking about her. About being with her. In all sorts of ways.

"Look, I'm just saying that I really like the way the show is going," Varsha said as she wrapped the mic wire around her fingers. He'd watched her do the same movement a hundred times. "Our viewers are liking the change in content this season, too."

"Are you sure it's not just a residual following from that insane video of me and Rina?"

"I'm pretty sure," Varsha replied. "I've known you for three years, and something's different. In a good way."

"I hope you're right," Prem said. He adjusted his collar and ran a hand over the crease where the microphone had been clipped. "Maybe my old investor will also see a difference and reconsider pulling out. I need him if I'm getting the space I need for the center."

Varsha shrugged even as she motioned to someone about the

lights. "I mean, I can always send him the video files for the last few episodes. We still have his contact information for when he asked to see back episodes a few months ago."

Prem vaguely recalled Varsha handling everything behind the scenes. It was good for Jersey City, for the South Asians who lived there, and for the TV show, she'd said. He wasn't so sure if it would help the network that much, but he'd been appreciative of her. Appreciative of all the help that she'd given.

"I hate to ask you to help again when you've already done so much," he said.

"Not a problem at all. You're doing something good. And you've done a lot with this show. That's why I've been here for so long."

"Thanks, Varsha," he said. "That means a lot."

"You got it," she replied. "See you next week!"

He waved, and just as he turned to go back to his dressing room to grab his bag, Yash, one of the camerapersons, called his name from across the studio over the sound of rolling light boxes and retracting cables.

"Prem, you have visitors. They said they're family. The Randhawas? Want me to have them come up to your dressing room?"

Prem stilled. What in the world were Gori's parents doing in New York? How did they know he'd be recording?

Before the thought finished forming in his head, he knew the answer. His mother. God, how long had it been?

Prem pressed a palm against his beating heart. Most days he was okay with just the lingering reminder of his former fiancée, but sometimes, the pain was so sharp, so real, that he felt incapacitated.

But there was no way out of this.

"Prem?" Yash called again.

He shook his head and braced himself with the same resolve

that he'd had to use for years after Gori's death. "Uh, yeah. I'll go down to the lobby to meet them," he finally said. "Can you let them know I'll be right there?"

"Sure thing." Yash left the studio through the narrow exit.

Prem paced back and forth across the floor for a minute before he stepped off the stage and left through the back hallway. After grabbing his bag, he took the long way through the building, down the cement gray stairwell and into the brightly lit studio's lobby level. The time helped him repackage all those raw feelings back into the boxes he'd put them in after Gori's death.

After pushing through the lobby double doors, he spotted Gori's parents in the center of the expansive space, wearing visors and fanny packs. They were about the same age as his parents, with gray streaks in their hair and lines around their mouth. However, these two had Gori's eyes and her laugh.

There was that pang in his chest. It was so familiar, but so distant all at the same time.

"Look at those two handsome people," Prem called from across the room. Uncle and Aunty turned at the same time. Their faces lit up when they saw him. "What a great surprise!"

"Prem!" Aunty was the first to approach him. Her white sandals had a gold paisley design at the buckle. "Darling, it's so good to see you."

"You look as gorgeous as ever," he replied and returned the hug.

"Hey now, don't make me look bad," Uncle said in Punjabi.

"I could never," Prem replied and turned to give Gori's father a hug as well. The old man slapped him hard on the shoulder, a reminder of all the hugs they'd shared after he and Gori agreed to getting married.

"We were both playing tourist in New York City," Gori's father said. "We haven't been in years, and we had some extra vacation time, so decided to come out and see for ourselves. And of course, while we're here, we had to see you."

Prem stepped back and motioned to both of them. "I'm so glad. You look like locals."

Aunty's face lit up with joy, and she nudged her husband in the arm. "See? We look like locals! Beta, why don't we take you out to dinner? We can go into the city."

Prem shook his head. "I'd love to, but I'm on call. I can't leave Jersey City until tomorrow."

Uncle clapped a hand on his shoulder. "Of course, beta. We know you're busy. We sort of sprung this on you."

"I'm glad that you did," Prem said, trying his best to sound . . . happy. But he didn't want to leave them standing in the studio when they'd come all the way out just to see him. It didn't feel right after so much shared history. So many memories. "There is a coffee shop around the corner if you'd like to take a break and sit with me for a bit?"

They both nodded, a look of excitement crossing both of their faces.

"We'd love that, beta," Aunty said softly.

"Then let's get going. I would love to hear all about your New York City adventure."

He hooked an arm around her shoulders and led the way outside and down the street to a cute little shop that had large murals on brick walls and a soft instrumental track playing in the background. Prem found a table for all of them toward the back of the restaurant. Then they got in line to order. Uncle continued to chatter about stocks, and traveling, and the weather, while Aunty took pictures to send to Prem's mother.

Once they all ordered cups of iced coffee and had their customary argument over who was paying, they sat down at the table.

"So?" Prem started. "How are things back home?"

"Oh, you know," Aunty said, stirring two packets of Splenda into her cup. "Always busy. I saw your mother the other day. She's worried about you, but I told her that you were always so capable of handling everything on your own. Prakash, why don't you tell your son-in-law what you've been up to?"

No. Never son-in-law.

Every moment with them was suffocating.

Prakash Uncle looked at his wife, then at Prem. "We decided to move, actually. We're leaving California."

"What? Really?" When Gori was alive, she was so sure that her parents would never abandon their home. They built such a robust life there. "Where are you going?"

"My sisters have all bought houses on the water in Naples. Very affordable retirement community. We're going to live there for half the year and travel back and forth to India. Six months here, six months there."

"That's really nice. I heard they have a temple down there."

"They do!" Uncle beamed as if Prem had given the million-dollar answer. "We'll have to do another Diwali party when we get settled. You must come and visit. Remember the one we had a few years ago? Gori was so happy."

Prem smiled, cupping his hands around the mug. "Yeah, that was a good day."

Aunty's eyes looked a little wet. An instant faucet. Gori had been the same.

This was going to hurt, he thought, but it was like a Band-Aid. He just had to rip it off and tell them.

"You know, ah, Gori was the perfect match."

"When we matched your star charts, it was like magic!" Aunty said. Her whole expression brightened. "We were so happy that you two connected so well."

"Ah. Yeah." Prem rubbed the back of his neck. "I never thought I'd find someone who would complement me, and who I would complement, as well as Gori."

It took a few moments of awkward silence before Uncle's eyes widened. Understanding dampened his happiness. "Oh. You found someone."

"As you should," Aunty burst out after an awkward pause. She patted her husband on the shoulder, then motioned at Prem as if it were the most natural thing in the world for Prem to share the news that he was dating other women.

"You're a single man. A single man needs a woman in his life. Pr-Prakash, I was just telling you the other day, no? That Prem is such a handsome boy. It's been years since our Gori has left us. It's time for him to find a suitable wife."

"You did!" Uncle burst out. Prem could see the corners of his mouth tightening with disapproval. "I agree. Beta, it's time for you to move on. Our Gori would've wanted it."

"Gori is such an important part of my past—"

"For all of us," Aunty interjected. "Don't you worry, Prem. It's very kind of you to tell us, but it's okay. I wish your mother would've told me. I would've loved to celebrate with her."

"Oh, my parents don't . . . it's complicated. I'm glad I had a chance to talk to you first. I cared for Gori even though we only had a little bit of time together, and—"

Uncle held up his hand. "No, no need to discuss. We understand. No words needed."

"But—"

"We understand, beta." The couple at the table next to them

turned to stare for a moment because of the cutting tone in the old man's voice. "Losing Gori wasn't easy for any of us. We're happy that you're moving on. As you should. Your parents must be so happy. That you're finally dating again. Hopefully you'll be married soon, and they'll have grandchildren. That's what Gori would've wanted, too."

Aunty's hands shook as she brushed hair out of her face. "Prem, we'll always be happy for your joy. You'll be family for the rest of our lives."

She didn't believe that, though, Prem realized. Before his very eyes, Gori's parents seemed to age. Part of the happy veneer cracked, and bursts of pain seeped out like darkness and shadows sneaking between their lips. They were two older Indian parents, still mourning the loss of their child, the one they'd uprooted their lives for in India, and now, they were mourning the loss of their son-in-law, too, in a way.

Prem thought of losing Gori all over again, and then spiraled into something worse. What would happen if he lost Rina? No, he couldn't even begin to think like that. Because Rina and he were always going to be on different wavelengths. But sitting here with Gori's parents, he realized something that he hadn't been prepared to face.

If Kareena wasn't going to accept him for who and what he is, without the fanciful daydreams she wanted, then that meant he only had a short amount of time with her. The joy they'd felt together was finite even though he wanted so much more.

But did she realize that he was playing for keeps now?

She was putting space between them when they'd come so far . . . it meant he'd have to go to her, hell, drag her out of her home if she was being completely stubborn.

Because one thing was for certain. He didn't know how much

time he had with Kareena, and he'd never recover if he lost her before they could have their life together.

While Gori's parents talked about their trip, desperate to forget the past, Prem plotted his future with a woman who had called the shots for way too long.

Dear Readers,

Now, more and more matches are being made across states and countries. This requires virtual dating. Virtual dating is when the candidates meet on their own through one of the online platforms. Remember, there is no harm in listening in. Providing valid critiques to matches is a part of the process. That is how they become better candidates.

Mrs. W. S. Gupta
Columnist
Avon, NJ

CHAPTER TWENTY-ONE

Kareena

Aunty WhatsApp Group

SONALI AUNTY: Hello, darling! Your grandmother said you've been down the last few days.

KAREENA: Not down, just stressed. Dating on a deadline is not easy.

SONALI AUNTY: I have some good news that may be able to help. My cousin's brother-in-law's son is single and we think he'd be the perfect match for you.

SONALI AUNTY: If it's okay, I'll give you his number and you can text him to set up a get-together. He's in Atlanta right now, but he may be able to meet in person. But you can do the FaceTime.

KAREENA: Thanks, Aunty. Yes, feel free to share my number. Thank you!

PREM: Did you find your true soul mate yet? Your sister's engagement party is a little over a month away.

> **KAREENA:** Prem . . .

> **PREM:** I'll take that as a no. Pack an overnight bag.

> **KAREENA:** Uh, what?

> **PREM:** I'll type it in Hindi if you want. I may have to google the Punjabi phrase to get it right, but I can do that, too.

Kareena sat at her desk in her bedroom, staring at Prem's text. It was the first conversation between them since she'd bailed on their date. What was this man up to? And why did her heart jump when she saw his text come in?

"Dangerous feelings, Mann," she said to herself as she put down her phone. "Dangerous feelings only lead to bigger feelings."

She didn't have time to dissect his cryptic message right now. She had to focus on herself. On her miserable dating life. Damn, it was like the Sahara out there for her. Dry and lifeless. It was as if she was standing on the top of a sand dune, begging someone to love her the same way she wanted to love back, and the only response back was a caw from a vulture.

Which was why she'd accepted Sonali Aunty's matchmaking attempt.

She yawned, then checked the time, and realized that she had to open the link for her virtual date. She adjusted her laptop on her desk, fixed her ring light, and navigated into her personal calendar. Apparently Sonali Aunty's contact had to work late and couldn't touch base before ten that night. She should've just said no, but again. Sahara. Lifeless. Zero hits on dating apps, or pretty much anything.

Her mother's house stood in the balance, and even though she desperately wanted to say yes to Prem, her future hung in the balance, too.

She logged on to her video conferencing app, and after checking her makeup one last time, adjusted her lighting, and then taking the water that she'd put in a mug, she joined the meeting.

Vikram's face on-screen was identical to his picture that Sonali Aunty had shared with her. He had a green screen backdrop of what looked like a Restoration Hardware showroom.

Finance bro. That's what Bobbi and Veera had thought of him when she'd shared the deets. Veera had gone so far as to recommend canceling, but Kareena couldn't judge just yet.

"Hi, Kareena?"

"Hi, Vikram. Nice to virtually meet you."

"Same," he said.

Okay, his shirt was ironed. That had to be a good thing.

Vikram flashed her his hundred-watt smile and held up a tumbler with amber liquid in it. "I appreciate you accommodating my work schedule. Do you mind if I drink?"

"Not at all," Kareena said and motioned to her mug. "My family drinks, too."

"Great. Hey, your biodata document they sent me didn't have a lot of information about your interests. Just your basics, and like your job title. What do you do up in New York? Nonprofit work?"

"Start-up work, actually," she said. "I'm the general counsel of a start-up that helps women establish businesses and generate economic wealth."

"Wow, a GC at your age? Well, it *is* a start-up, so you must be like the only attorney on staff anyway."

She sat up straighter. "Uh, no, I have a team."

He looked impressed, which only irritated her more. "How did you end up in your field?"

"It's what I've always wanted to do."

He cringed. "Work for a start-up focused on helping women? Sounds like . . . a lot."

Red flag. Kareena could see it from a mile away and they'd just started talking. God, what was she going to tell Sonali Aunty? More importantly, how was she going to get out of this?

"It's a challenge, if that's what you mean. What do *you* do down in Atlanta?"

He grinned, and a dimple winked in his cheek. "I'm a VP. It's a lot of work, but I have to make time for dating, you know? Like tonight. My parents have been on my case about getting married for years. But I told them, guys, my worth is more than my relationship status."

Kareena nodded. "Yeah, I believe that. We should be on our own timelines."

"Exactly! And for me, I think it's finally time."

She'd been searching for a man for a few months now, and it irritated her—no, it burned her ass—to think that this man could probably find his soul mate faster than she could.

Shaking herself out of a downward spiral, Kareena asked, "You're looking for an arranged match?"

"Oh yeah. A love match is great and all, but it's not necessary for me."

What the hell? Was she the only person who believed in love anymore? Since this was already feeling not-so-great to her, she figured that she had nothing to lose if she went all in.

"Vikram, can I ask why love isn't important to you?"

He shrugged and swirled his liquid in front of the camera as if demonstrating a proper technique. "Because I come from a pretty conservative family, and we believe that when people marry, they marry the family, not just the person." He let out a short laugh. "Also, dating is hella hard. I mean, I have so many time commitments. It's just less stressful this way."

They had a point, Kareena thought. "Dating is hard for me, too. That's mostly because everyone is in my business since I still live at home."

There must have been something she said, or how she said it, that had him freezing. "At home? Like, together?"

She nodded and motioned to her bedroom behind her. "Yes, I still live at home." And she planned to for as long as possible.

"You're . . . serious." His eyes widened almost comically.

"You sound surprised."

"I am." He looked around and sat up in his chair, hands up in surrender. "Not judging. Do you live in a separate apartment or something in your parents' house?"

Kareena shook her head even as her back stiffened at the judgment in his tone. "My mother designed this house. It was her dream home when my parents could finally afford a place. After she died, I started renovating it myself because I knew that's what she would've wanted. It's a labor of love."

"Wait, wait, wait." He let out a humorless laugh. "Kareena. Sonali Aunty said you were interested in dating someone long-term. He has to be ambitious, and a bunch of other requirements you'd shared with them."

"That sounds about right. Why?"

His table lamp cast a shadow of harsh light across his face that made his sneer look ugly. "I'm not telling you anything you probably haven't heard before, but maybe you should manage your expectations."

"*Excuse* me? Manage my— Okay . . . I'm a sucker for punishment. Why?"

He gave her the once-over and shrugged. "Let's start with the sweater vests. You're not exactly opening yourself up for connection."

She ran a hand over the soft fabric that covered her from shoulder to waist. "You're judging me because of my sweater vest?"

"Hey, no need to shout." Then he shushed her. He looked over his shoulder, and the green screen background shifted. "It's late. Kareena, you just admitted that you live at home. I mean, women like you have to find solace in their job, because I doubt you'll find a man to support you financially."

"I'm hoping you're not implying what I think you are, because that's fucking obnoxious."

His mouth fell open at the curse word, but like she could care.

His hands came up in a defensive gesture. "All I'm saying is that maybe you're single because the things you're looking for in a guy are what you're really lacking in yourself? I mean, how can anyone take you seriously? Living at home as an attorney tells me that you have zero ambition to start your life. And let's not even get into how you chose to wear a sweater vest to our virtual date. It's *summer*." He motioned to her maroon sweater vest. "It's like a uniform or something."

"Those are big words for a man with a pea brain."

"I'm just trying to help you here!" he said. "If you ever want to find someone, you have to listen to advice, even if it's painful to hear. Maybe do some introspection, you know? Maybe reevaluate your standards. Lower them to . . . well, your level. Get your life in order, move out of your house, be more independent so that you're more marketable on the dating scene. Oh, and you could probably use a better skin care routine. With some makeup."

He had to be the ugliest man she'd met. "A woman's worth isn't only to be a wife," Kareena said. "And I don't give a *fuck* what you think. I'd rather be alone than lower my standards for any man who doesn't deserve me."

"Oh, honey. You could never—"

"See you never, Vikram," she said, and she slammed her laptop shut.

Fuck Vikram and his bullshit assessment of her wants and needs. Of her sweater vest and her home life. Fuck her aunties for setting her up, and her father and grandmother for putting her in this situation in the first place. And fuck Prem for making her doubt love in the first place.

Kareena paced the length of her room, fuming and cursing men for a full fifteen minutes before she was able to calm down. Damn it, she deserved everything she wanted in life, and no one was going to tell her differently.

After another minute, she debated going downstairs and getting a glass of water, but the TV was still on in the living room. She could hear the barely-there hum of late-night Indian soap operas. If Dadi saw her in her current state, then she'd be grilled and berated until every last hope for peace was out the window.

"I just have to separate myself from shitty men," Kareena murmured as she took her sweater vest off and changed into a pair of leggings, a T-shirt, and zip-up hoodie. There was no way she was going to sleep now. Hell, she hadn't had a good night's sleep since the last time she'd been with Prem. It was as if he was the secret to getting a solid eight hours for her.

Grabbing her Kindle, she rolled onto her bed and prepared for a night of drowning herself in paranormal romances. At least shape-shifters and vampires understood the meaning of fated mates.

"Fuck you, Vikram," she said, her hands steadying as she tapped on the icon of her current read.

KAREENA WAS ABOUT a page and a half into the newest Nalini Singh book when her phone pinged with a new text message. It was probably one of the aunties texting about the date. No doubt Vikram went and tattled right away. Kareena ignored it, but when it started ringing from an incoming call, she got up to check the screen.

Her chest constricted when she saw Prem's name. He was probably the last person to talk to in her current state, but a part of her missed him and wanted to hear his voice.

Okay, it was a big part of her.

"Hello?" she said, answering after the third ring.

"Hi, you need to come out to your shed," Prem whispered.

"What? Why? And why are you whispering?"

"Shh!" he whispered. "Just come out to your shed."

"Are you . . . are you here?"

Her bedroom faced the front of the house, so she wasn't able to check, but the idea of Prem being so close by was simultaneously thrilling and shocking. He came for her. Was that . . . romantic? She pressed a palm to her chest. "Prem, tell me what's going on."

"I came to kidnap you," he whispered.

"*What?*"

"Shh!" he hushed her again.

She held her breath, waiting to make sure that her father, two rooms over, hadn't heard her and that her grandmother downstairs was still occupied with her serials. When no one came calling for her, she cleared her voice.

"You can't kidnap a person, Prem. That's not a thing."

"It is," he hissed. "But I forgot that you have an alarm system, and then the fear of getting caught by your grandmother is pretty paralyzing. Now I'm stuck in your backyard, and I have no idea what to do next. I'd appreciate it if you cooperated and came outside so I can kidnap you down here versus trying to break into your house."

"Prem . . ."

"Unless you *want* me to talk to your grandmother? I mean, I don't mind—"

"Fine," she said. "But I'm not being kidnapped. I'll come down to talk to you. That's it."

"We'll start somewhere," he replied and hung up the phone.

"He is out of his mind," Kareena mumbled after hanging up. Anticipation and adrenaline at perhaps being caught began pumping through her bloodstream as she paused in front of the mirror long enough to make sure she had nothing in her teeth and her hair wasn't too frizzy.

She tucked her phone in her back pocket and opened her bedroom door. After listening for a moment, Kareena managed to sneak past her father's room, waiting to hear his snoring through the door before she crept downstairs. She had tiptoed past the living room entrance and through the kitchen to the back sliding doors when she heard the very noticeable creak of the leather sofa as her grandmother got off the couch.

Oh shit, Kareena thought, and she quickly grabbed her flip-flops and slipped out the back sliding door. She pressed up against the side of the house when the kitchen light came on a moment later and waited as she heard her grandmother puttering around inside.

The fridge water dispenser sound was barely audible over the beat of her heart. She waited a moment longer for the light to go out before she was able to take a deep breath. Kareena crossed the deck and stepped onto the grass. Using the moonbeams as her guiding light, she cut across the yard dampened by midnight dew until she reached the shed platform.

Just as she got to the double doors, she saw a figure step out from the side of the shed.

She bit back a scream and was about to kick the intruder in the nuts, when shadows from the moonlight helped her identify Prem.

Kareena pressed a hand against her chest. "Holy Vishnu, you almost gave me a heart attack," she hissed.

"It's a good thing I'm a cardiologist then," he said.

Kareena squinted until she could make out his form in the dark. "What are the black smudges under your eyes? Why are you wearing black? That's not your normal look, Dr. Dil."

"I'm on a mission," he whispered back. "Now come on. We have to sneak around the side of the house before your grandmother decides to look out the window."

He grabbed her hand, but Kareena dug in her heels. "Do you know how ridiculous this is?" she said in a hushed tone. "It's a work night!"

"A *work* night? What are you, twelve? Do you have a curfew?"

"No, I'm a desi woman living at home, you idiot. Why couldn't you have just texted me like a normal person?"

He stepped closer, and his familiar clean, earthy scent had her breathing in deep.

Wow. How long had it been? How long since she'd seen his

beautiful face? The dangerous feelings were growing inside her, and she didn't know how much longer she could hold off the avalanche.

"Rina," he said, leaning in closer, the familiar lines of his jaw highlighted by night shadows. "You wouldn't have answered my texts. We both know that. And if I had showed up at your house, your grandmother and father would start talking, and I know you aren't ready for them to know about us—"

"Technically, there is no 'us.'"

"And because you're clearly the reason for me losing my mind, here I am wearing black, with gunk on my face so that no one can identify me because I can't stop thinking about you."

"You . . . you can't?"

He leaned forward until his breath mixed with hers. "No," he said again, and lightly brushed his lips against hers.

She returned the kiss, and followed his mouth when he began to pull back. Prem's arms banded around her waist, and for the first time in way too long, she was able to relax in the pleasure of his closeness.

The flicker of the deck light turning on had both of them jumping apart, then scrambling around the side of the shed. Seconds later, the sliding door opened.

"Hello?" Dadi called out. "Is anyone out there?"

Neither of them answered. They stayed completely still, trying to control their breathing. Damn it, why were they breathing so loud?

A few seconds later, Kareena heard her grandmother grumble something. Then the screen door closed and the deck light flickered off.

"Hang on to your glasses, Rina, honey," Prem whispered, then bent down, and lifted her off her feet, tossing her clear over his shoulder. She bit back her yelp and hung on to his shirt as she flopped like a fish against his back. He stayed in dark shadows along the fence until he reached the street in front of the house. Then, putting her down on her feet, he linked his fingers with hers and tugged her to the end of the block where his car was parked.

She should just go back home, back to her room, and get in her bed where she'd planned on spending the rest of her sleepless night dreaming about fictitious men.

But Prem was here, and he was real.

And that scared her the most.

She climbed into his passenger seat and waited for him to start the car.

"I'm taking you to my place," he said.

"Okay."

Dear Readers,

If your matches are eager to leave any sort of social gathering that you've designed for them without food and dressed as if they are in a hurry, then please note that they might be engaging in coitus. It's important to encourage marriage right away.

Mrs. W. S. Gupta
Columnist
Avon, NJ

CHAPTER TWENTY-TWO

Prem

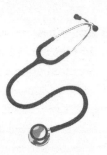

Prem hadn't thought too far past the kidnapping. He wanted to see her, wanted to make his intentions clear, but then they'd kissed outside her shed, and he lost his ever-loving mind. He needed more time with her. He needed her in his car, in his bed, in his life.

They sat in silence for most of the drive, the awkwardness almost suffocating as they cruised down the Turnpike.

What were they supposed to talk about that wouldn't start an argument?

Kareena seemed to be content with leaning back against the passenger seat, the window open to let the summer night air in. Her fingers cut through the wind as she made waves all the way down the turnpike.

Ten minutes from his apartment, her phone went off. She checked the name on the screen and let out a miserable groan. "I have to take this," she said. "It's Sonali Aunty."

"Sure."

She answered then closed her eyes and rested her head against the palm of her hand. "Hi, Sonali Aunty."

Prem couldn't hear what the woman was saying on the other end of the call, but he heard Kareena's sighs loud and clear.

"Aunty, he was so rude. He told me that I needed to lower my standards. That I was the type of woman who looked like I'd always have to work because a man wouldn't want me enough to support me. I know! I'm so stupid for getting mad about that, because I always plan on working. But it's still insulting."

Prem's fingers tightened on the steering wheel. What the hell? She'd been on a date today? Had she had any good ones since they'd last been together? Had anyone kissed her, held her like he had? No, he had no right to ask those questions, even though jealousy was like a sore. At least the last guy she'd been with sounded like a complete douche.

"No, it's fine," Kareena said. "But if you could avoid telling Dadi and the Aunty WhatsApp chat until tomorrow, I'd appreciate it. I escaped to, uh, Bobbi's house, and Dadi doesn't know I left. No, Aunty, I am not reading the W. S. Gupta advice column. I don't think it applies to me. Okay, thanks, Aunty. Love you, too. Bye."

The sound of that word, *love*, coming from her mouth grated against his skin, but he ignored it and put it aside. When she hung up, he said, "Fuck the douchebag who said those things to you. He doesn't deserve you."

Kareena rubbed her fingertips against her temples. "Yeah, but I'm hoping that someone does."

"Doubtful," Prem replied.

"Seriously?"

Prem shrugged. "It's true. It's doubtful anyone deserves you. But you'll inspire someone to be the best person they can for you. I know you inspire me."

"Prem," she said with a shaky breath.

They descended into silence again as he maneuvered his car toward his building. The ride was short, and a few minutes later, he was parking in his underground garage.

"What are your plans for when we reach your place?" Kareena asked, breaking the peace between them.

"Are you hungry? I can order some food."

"Not really," she said.

"Okay, then we'll shower first. And then decide what to do."

"Shower?" Kareen asked.

Prem turned into the underground parking garage entrance and slowed as he descended to his level before parking the car. When he turned off the vehicle, he finally looked at her. "I have to take a shower," he said. "Because I have war paint on, and I would like for you to join me."

He could see the interest in her eyes, but all she did was pull the door handle and step out of the car. They walked side by side, less than a foot between them, to the elevator and stepped into the small box. Prem could practically feel the tension crackling like a live current between them as they took the elevator to his floor.

Kareena was with him, and they were finally alone again. Memories of the last time they were at his place cascaded in his mind, mixing with their hours of conversation, their text messages, and the argument that still sat between them like a ghost.

He made sure to give her plenty of space as they stepped out of the elevator and into his hallway. They walked in silence until they reached his condo. He then let her step inside first. He took off his shoes, his jacket, and then watched her as she cut toward his windows to take in the skyline view.

She did that the first time she'd come over, too. There was something about watching her in his place that made him feel comforted. Not because of the space itself, but just knowing that she felt at home with his things.

Prem went to her now, taking slow, easy strides across the room to meet her. He brushed her ponytail over her shoulder and then kissed the back of her neck, enjoying her shudder. When she turned around, he traced her lower lip with the pad of his thumb and brushed his lips against hers. Their kiss at the house was intense and frenzied. This one was perfection.

He felt her soften under him, just a little, just enough for her to kiss him back.

"Missed you . . . friend," Prem whispered against her mouth, hoping to God that didn't scare her away that he admitted it.

"Missed you, too . . . friend."

"I THINK FAMILY is important, but sometimes, found family understands us more," Prem said, clinking his water glass with her drink.

"I get that," Rina replied. "I have a few close friends that are my ride-or-die."

"Are we friends yet, Rina?"

She smiled, and her eyes brightened behind her glasses. "I'd like to be."

KAREENA RESTED HER cheek against Prem's chest and wrapped her arms around his waist in a gesture that had his chest constricting in the oddest of ways. He hugged her back.

"Today really sucked," she said.

"How can I make it better?"

She pulled back just enough to brush at the smudges on his cheeks. Her giggle was delightful. "You look ridiculous. That's helping."

"Bunty's idea. He said that I had to look the part."

"Your first problem was that you took advice from Bunty."

"It made you laugh," he said.

When she relaxed against him again, he knew it was time. Prem led her into his bedroom where he opened the automatic blinds. In the darkness of his room, lit only by the city view, he pulled her close and unzipped her sweatshirt. It fell in a soft hush to the hardwood floor.

"More," she said with a sigh. She gripped the hem of his shirt and pulled it over his head. One after another, they began removing their clothes until they were naked, and wanting. He was erect and had been since her sweatshirt came off. His cock pulsed between them.

"Come on. Let's take that shower now." He pulled her into the adjoining bath, where he finally removed her glasses and set them on the counter.

After turning on the shower, and setting it to warm, Prem took Rina back into his arms, their sticky skin pressing against each other until breast and chest were fused. He ran a hand over her frizzy hair and traced the flare of her hips and softness of her ass. He felt her fingertips against his chest tracing his collarbone.

He wanted so much more of this, Prem admitted to himself before he nudged her under the spray.

"Do you know how long it takes to wash Punjabi hair?" Kareena grumbled as her thick dark waves began to soak. "We're going to be in here forever now."

"I don't mind," Prem said. He helped her tug off her hair tie and watched her roll it onto her wrist. Then he pumped face wash into his palm and began massaging it into his cheeks. She laughed and helped him until the smudges were completely gone.

"Your turn," he said, and squeezed out some shampoo to massage into her scalp. She let out a sigh and tipped her hair back. Water cascaded over her face, her neck, down her collarbone, and rolled off the tip of her breasts. His cock tightened impossibly harder as he tried to concentrate on her and her needs.

"Are you getting enough water?" she said after he turned her so she could rinse off. "I never had a shower with someone, but always assumed one person didn't get enough water."

"I'm fine," he said hoarsely as he stroked her butt. "Let's finish washing your hair."

"Listen . . . I shed. Maybe I can just dry it and—"

"Relax," he said and dropped a kiss on the curve of her neck. "It's okay." He gently scrubbed her scalp, taking time to make sure all the suds were rinsed through.

Then, because he wanted to touch her, he cupped the sides of her neck, then ran his hands over her collarbone, the slope of her wet breasts, and down her belly before pulling her close against him.

"Nice?"

"Nice," she said in a barely audible whisper.

When he reached for the soap, she brushed his hand away and took the bottle. She'd been ignoring his erection that poked her all this time. But now, she squeezed a healthy glob of soap into her palm and began sudsing him up starting with his shoulders and moving over his chest down toward Charlie.

"Feeling better?" he murmured as he cupped the back of her neck and watched her wash his body through the rising steam.

"Much," she said, her voice slow and husky. Droplets clung to her lashes now. Her skin glistened and her hair had a healthy shine to it as it hung down her back to her shoulder blades. Her hands roamed farther down until they wrapped around his penis. He hissed at the contact.

"Rina, honey."

"Kiss me."

He could do nothing more than oblige her every wish. As their mouths came together, Kareena slid her hand up and down his penis in long, firm strokes.

Prem was dangerously close to coming, and that wasn't allowed. He shuddered when Kareena applied pressure to his tip, and he pulled away; she needed to come first. She would always come first.

"Prem, what are you—"

She gasped as he got to his knees on the shower floor, then lifted one leg to drape over his shoulder. Kareena went completely silent as he gently parted her folds, admiring as the rivulets of water traced over her belly and dripped like a rain shower in front of her pussy. He blew gently on her clit, and as she shifted from the sensation, his grip became iron hard.

Leaning forward, Prem licked Rina in one hard stroke. She jerked, gasping at his touch. Rina leaned against the tiled wall, her mouth falling open in a silent prayer.

"Aha. This is how I can keep you quiet," he said with a chuckle, before he licked her again. This time, he buried deep, sucking and tasting her, drowning in the pleasure of her feast. Her pussy was delicious, and he wanted all of it.

She dove her fingers into his hair, and pushed against him, rolling her hips forward so that he could eat more of her, devour more of her as she grew wetter against his mouth.

When Kareena's knees began to weaken, he turned her so that her cheek rested against the shower wall, her hips out, her legs spread.

"Hold," he said, his voice hoarse.

"W-what?"

"Hold," he said again, gripping her hands and pulling them back so that she could part her ass cheeks.

"W-what are you—"

"Like this," he said, and pulled her cheeks apart.

"Prem, are you going to—"

"Yes, is that okay?"

"Y-yes, god yes, but are you okay doing—"

He pulled her cheeks even wider, slid a finger into her delicious heat, then buried his face between her ass cheeks. Rina let out a breathless scream, and as he rimmed and ate her, satiating the hunger that he couldn't fill without her, she came against his fingers, her legs shaking so hard that he was surprised she was able to hold herself up.

Before she could even stop shuddering, Prem stood and, with the strength he had left, hoisted her up against the wall. He positioned himself and paused with the tip of his penis inside her opening.

"Do you want me to get a condom?" he said breathlessly.

"No," she gasped in his ear. "No, I want all of you. I have an IUD. And there is no one but you."

"Then take me." He adjusted his hold on her and thrust into her in one full long stroke.

He shouted and Kareena screamed, the sound echoing in the steamy chamber of the bathroom. Then, Prem adjusted his hold and pounded into her in slow, steady strokes. She gripped him hard, her fingers in his hair, against his back, desperate to find purchase. Her teeth grazed his neck as she gasped his name.

"More," she sobbed.

"Harder or softer?"

"Harder, Prem. I want . . . all of you."

He thrust into her with force now, feeling the slap of skin against skin. She tensed under him, and when she was as tight as a bow string, straining against him with the same madness that possessed him, Prem pressed down on her clit until Kareena's orgasm seized her. She screamed his name, and he barely lasted a moment longer before he came deep inside her. Their shouts, then panting, mixed as he held on to her through the most intense orgasm he'd ever had. They collapsed against the tiled wall with the water going cold.

Had it ever been like this with anyone else? No. Only with Kareena. Only with her. And even though they had so many differences between them, there was a connection he'd be a fool to ignore.

As they came down from their high, Prem held her close, skin to skin, wet and slick, chest to chest. He'd claimed her, just as she'd claimed him, and he didn't know if things were ever going to be the same for him again.

CHAPTER TWENTY-THREE

Kareena

Kareena woke to a blasting alarm that sounded like a herd of fire trucks roaring through Prem's bedroom.

"What the hell?" she grumbled and pulled a pillow over her head. She was having the best sleep ever, and she did not want it to end this early.

She felt Prem shift behind her. One naked arm reached across her body for the phone on the side table. His hip nudged hers, and morning wood automatically had her wiggling her butt against it. Prem clamped a hand over her hip to make her stop.

"Yeah?" She heard his sleep-rough voice say. "Yeah, okay . . . I'll be there . . . No, don't bother. He's my patient. I'll take care of him. Send me the chart, and I'll meet Dr. Villasante at the hospital."

She pulled the pillow off her head but couldn't get the energy to open her eyes yet. "You have to go?" she whispered sleepily.

"Yeah," he said. "I have a patient in surgery right now."

"Mm."

She couldn't help but smile when she felt the firm kiss on the corner of her mouth before he hopped off the bed. "Stay," he called out. "Sleep." She didn't have to be told twice.

The next time Kareena opened her eyes, the room was brighter, and there was a familiar smell of coffee and eggs. She sat up and rubbed the sleep out of her eyes. What time was it?

She reached out and felt the cool spot on the bed next to her. How was it that she always had trouble sleeping elsewhere, but the minute she was with Prem, sleep was the easiest thing in the world?

She grabbed her glasses from the bedside table and slipped them on. Her vision cleared, and she was able to focus on her phone screen. Eight a.m.

"Holy shit!" She bolted into an upright position. How the hell was that even possible? She never woke up that late. After Prem and Kareena had showered, or what other people may loosely consider a shower, she had put on one of his shirts and went to bed at a respectable time.

Kareena grabbed Prem's sweatshirt, then found her cotton panties and managed to pile her hair on top of her head as she walked into the kitchen. The New York City skyline was shining brightly, gleaming with steel and glass, which meant that she was going to be late for work. Very late. And she'd have to justify to her grandmother, if Dadi was home, how she ended up coming in the house with the same clothes she wore the night before. That was going to be a fun adventure.

She turned the corner and found Prem in a pair of scrubs standing in front of the kitchen stove with a frying pan. He flashed her one of his cocky smiles over his shoulder. "I'm sorry I woke you."

"I should've been up a long time ago. Didn't you have to go to see your patient?"

"The patient's still in surgery. I have more time than I'd thought," Prem said. He kept glancing at an iPad propped on the counter to his left, while simultaneously wielding a spatula.

"You know," Kareena said as she slipped onto one of the barstools. "This is pretty sexy."

"What is?"

"You having people depend on you. It's very adult. Grown-up. And I guess that's sexy."

Prem grinned, and the familiar dent in his chin deepened. "You're into competence porn, huh? I guess that suits you."

Before Kareena could ask if there was coffee, he slid a cup in front of her. Instead of the black tar that she knew he preferred to drink, this one smelled like peppermint creamer.

"You hate creamer," she said as she cupped her hands around the mug.

"Yeah, but you don't," he said. "I have to say, it was hard getting peppermint this time of year. No wonder you freeze it."

It was a jolt to the system to realize that he'd bought something just for her. The coffee, the breakfast. It was all more than she could've ever imagined.

Fuck, how the hell did she get this deep?

Prem slid the soft scrambled eggs out of the skillet onto a plate and put the plate in front of her. They were light and fluffy, just like she preferred.

"You made me eggs," she blurted out, not knowing what else to say. Her heart practically stopped at the sight of them.

"Yeah," he said as he turned off the range and dropped dishes into his sink. "I remember you said that's your preferred breakfast food."

"I LOVE EGGS, too. My mom used to make them for me when I was a kid, and now there is a sense of nostalgia attached to them."

"Scrambled? Fried? Over easy? Hard-boiled?"

She laughed. "Scrambled. The delicious soft way that looks all bright and yellow. There is nothing like scrambled eggs with coffee."

HE WASN'T EVEN looking at her as he rushed through his kitchen, grabbing his tablet, his bag that he'd left on the other barstool, and his car keys.

"You're not going to have any?"

"I had some before you woke up. You never told me how you liked them, so I had to make an educated guess."

Kareena stared at her fork like it was a snake.

"So?" Prem prompted. He walked over to the front door and slipped into his sneakers. "How are they?"

She tried to smile at him, even as her stomach knotted, and her head pounded in rhythm with her heart. She forked a tiny piece at the edge of her plate and slipped it in her mouth.

Butter. Just a little wet. Scrambled. With . . . chaat masala?

She dropped her fork with a clatter. "How did you know to put chaat masala on my eggs?" she blurted out.

Prem snorted. "Seriously? We had a food eating competition. Half the time you mumble to yourself over your plate. You season everything you eat, and you think I wouldn't notice?"

Kareena nodded. She had no words. Prem Verma, Dr. Dil, had just produced the perfect scrambled eggs.

"They're . . . great," she said.

"Awesome." Prem strode to her side, grabbed her chin, and pressed a hard kiss against her mouth. "If you want to stay, feel free to hang out until I get back. I don't know when that'll be, but definitely by dinner."

"I have to work," she said. "This week, I have a client case that I'm working on."

"Damn, and I'm in back-to-back procedures. I have to pick up a weekend shift, then prep for my show." He pressed another quick kiss to her mouth. "Then next weekend. You want to get away with me?"

"Get away? Like where?"

"I don't know. I'm not on call, and they're doing a rerun of one of my old episodes because there is supposed to be a special broadcast conflicting with the time slot. We can go to the beach if you want?"

"You mean the shore," Kareena replied. "You're in Jersey. It's the shore."

Prem kissed her again, this time longer, and with a small lick of his tongue. "Fine. The shore. Come with me."

"I'm helping with my sister's engagement party," she said.

"Fuck it."

These bubble moments with him were . . . amazing. She felt like she didn't have to worry so much when it was just the two of them. "Fine," she said before she could change her mind. "Let's do it."

"Great. Front door code is my birthday. Let yourself out whenever." He started walking backward, juggling his bag, files, coffee mug, and keys. "We need to talk, but I have to go. I'll text you later."

Kareena nodded and waited for him to close the door behind him before she picked up her fork again. She'd just agreed to go with him on vacation to a place that would be especially hard for her to leave.

Her mind turned back to focusing on the eggs. The last time anyone made her eggs with chaat masala was when her mother was still alive. It was so special. Those Sunday morning breakfasts with eggs, and hot milk with just enough tea in it to make her feel special.

Kareena took another bite, and then a third.

Prem took her out on the most fun dates she'd ever been on. She'd never had mind-blowing sex the way she'd experienced with him. And most importantly, he listened to her. She could sleep when she was with him, and he was constantly feeding her.

She took her time finishing the eggs, and when her plate was clean she sat back in her chair and crossed her arms over her chest.

She'd been prepared for almost every scenario: losing her mother's house, living alone in some rental property, and having to sell her car. Or worse, settling for someone she didn't love at all.

The one thing that Kareena hadn't prepared herself for was falling in love with a man who could never love her back.

CHAPTER TWENTY-FOUR

Prem

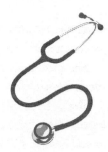

> **PREM:** Mom, don't freak out, but I met someone.

> **MOM:** Oh my goodness, really?? My beta, I'm so proud!!

> **MOM:** ::religious meme::

> **MOM:** ::religious meme::

> **MOM:** ::party meme::

> **PREM:** It's Kareena. The woman who interrupted my show.

> **PREM:** . . . Mom?

> **PREM:** Mom, did your phone die?

> **MOM:** No, but you killed a part of my heart. That woman?? The woman who practically ruined your reputation?? Why her?

PREM: Would you rather I stop talking to her and go back to being single?

MOM: Is she from a good family at least?

PREM: Mom.

MOM: Whatever, you're thirty-five, she'll do.

PREM: MOM. Can you at least PRETEND not to be a mess?

MOM: What's the fun in that?

Prem knew that Kareena had never gone away for a weekend with a man. With her friends, sure, but alone with another human being for an extended period of time?

She was going to put up walls.

Or at least he expected her to put up walls.

Instead, she'd relaxed in his passenger seat, trading in her sweater vest for a V-cut strappy ankle-length dress made out of gauzy cotton that had a row of buttons from the center of her breasts down to her knees. When she'd changed at his apartment, he almost dragged her back into his bedroom, but she had a wild, excited energy around her. Prem never thought a night away at the beach would make her so happy.

They'd spent almost two hours stuck in traffic with the windows down and a Taylor Swift playlist blasting through his speakers. They barely paid attention to the music, though. They were so busy talking. Podcasts, college, favorite restaurants, movies, bucket lists, travel plans.

And Kareena made Prem laugh. Really, truly laugh.

The first time they'd slept together, he knew that he'd wanted to keep her. To be with her. It was a gut reaction that didn't go away.

But now, he didn't know what would happen if she didn't want to keep him right back. Because she still wanted something that he couldn't give her.

"Come on," he said after parking in the assigned spot for their rental condo. "Let's dump the bags and get some food."

"You read my mind."

It felt like the easiest thing in the world to be with her in that moment. After putting their bags inside the master bedroom, he linked fingers with her and walked down to the boardwalk toward the small Mexican restaurant.

Unfortunately, there was a horde of people standing outside. Prem hadn't gone down to the shore as much as she apparently had, because it took Kareena two seconds to pivot and submit a takeout order.

"Let's go eat on the beach," she said as they grabbed the white plastic takeout bag from the hostess up front. "It's dark, but the weather is great."

Prem didn't argue and led the way down into the sand and toward the water. They found a quiet dune illuminated by the boardwalk lights behind them, but dark enough for privacy.

"I bet you get this kind of weather in California all the time," Kareena said as she set up their takeout containers.

"Better sometimes. I used to go to the beach after school when I didn't have any homework. I'd just sit on the sand and read."

"Anatomy and biology books?"

"More like sci-fi fantasy. I didn't trade those in for nonfiction until I hit college."

Kareena passed him a foil-wrapped burrito. "That's when my fiction reading habit kicked in. I would rather stay at home and read than go out."

Prem watched as she unwrapped the foil from around her burrito, inspected the bulging contents, and took a quick bite. She let out a moan that went right through him.

"Wow," Kareena said with her mouth full. "This has got to be the best burrito that I've ever eaten in forever."

He shifted, drawing up his knees to hide the fact that Charlie wanted to come out and play. Clearing his throat, praying that his erection went away, he said, "Did you date the book nerd in college, too?"

She shook her head. "I started working on the Beamer my junior year and needed help fixing it by myself because I didn't want to ask Dad for money for repairs. I began seeing this guy who worked at his dad's garage. He had a motorcycle."

"Wow, look at you," Prem said, leaning back to eye her up and down. "Did you ever go for a ride?"

"*Fuck* no," Kareena said with a snort. "I couldn't stop thinking what would happen to me if my father, my grandmother, or my aunties ever found out. We broke up when we both realized we were too different. As sweet as he was, whenever I talked about my family, he didn't understand why I still lived at home when it got so toxic."

"Mm-hmm," Prem said as he bit into his burrito. "It's hard to communicate the immigrant experience with those who don't understand. We want to support and be with our families, and sometimes we sacrifice our mental health and our emotional well-being to do it."

"I can't give them up, though," Kareena said softly. "They

make me happier than they make me sad. Even though lately, with Bindu's wedding planning, it's more sadness."

"Now you can stay with me if they hurt you."

Kareena smiled, burrito in hand. "I'll hold you to that."

They ate in silence, enjoying the weather and the sea breeze. The breeze grew colder, and the beach patrons started to dwindle. Prem moved closer to Kareena and enjoyed the feel of her ponytail sliding against his bare arm.

He shifted on the sand, so he was facing her as she continued to watch the water. "Can you tell me?" he blurted out. "Tell me how a beautiful, vibrant person like you believes in a house filled with memories? Why do you think love is more than an illusion? That love can sustain a relationship for years?"

Her eyes widened, and she put her wrapper away before brushing her hands of sand. "Well, uh, okay. I guess it's because I've seen how love has sustained my father for years. And I've felt those same memories keep me going for just as long. And I read romance novels. Romance novels sell an idealized fantasy that we all want to experience. They may be fiction, but there is a reason why so many people connect to love stories. Because that's the type of feeling we want to give, and want to receive."

"You're so sure about that."

"I am."

Prem thought about Kareena's past, her relationship to her parents, and then his relationship with his own parents. The arranged marriage. "I don't think I've ever heard my parents tell each other that they love each other. Maybe when I was younger they showed each other affection, but they never even held hands. It's like whatever fleeting emotions they had for each other dried up before I could witness it."

Kareena smiled at him. "And that's why you believe in partnership over love. Despite all the science about long-term love, or whatever. Prem, maybe it's not one or the other. Maybe you have to have both for partnership to last forever. That's what will sustain forever."

"Forever is a long time," he said, softly. He looked down at their linked fingers. "Did I ever tell you I was engaged?"

Her jaw dropped, and her eyes widened. "No. W-what happened?"

Prem nodded, thinking of Gori and the memories he had with her. They were hazy now, like he was watching them through a fog. "It was an arranged marriage. Our parents knew each other. We had a lot in common. We believed in the same life philosophies. She was in business; I was in medicine. We also were pretty good in bed together. Three months after we met, and dated casually, we announced our engagement."

"Wow," Kareena said. She let out a deep breath. "That's . . . that's fast."

"Our parents were already celebrating after our first meeting. They found a venue and set the wedding date for a year or so after our engagement. Gori's headaches started soon after that." He could remember the first one so vividly. He'd stayed over at her apartment, closed the blinds for her, tucked her in. Everything he could possibly think of doing to make her comfortable as she curled in the fetal position under a blanket.

"She went to her general physician who told her she just had some headaches. I convinced my attending to give her a checkup, too. As a favor they scheduled an MRI and CT, but it was too late."

"Oh no. Prem . . ." Kareena whispered.

"She had a brain aneurysm that ruptured and caused a hemor-rhagic stroke the day I was accepted at Einstein Medical in their cardiothoracic surgery fellowship. I got the call right as I was about to accept."

Kareena scooted closer to him until their legs were tangled, and they were chest to chest, with Kareena's head on his shoulder. "I'm so, so sorry."

It was easier to talk about Gori when Kareena held on to him this way, he thought. He combed his fingers through her unravel-ing hair. "After Gori died, I was lost for months. I should've done something more. I could've done something more. Health care for women, specifically women of color, is terrible, and if Gori had a place to go, with doctors who understood what she needed, then maybe she would be alive today."

Awareness dawned on Kareena's face. "Your community health center."

"Yeah." Prem scanned the now empty beach as he held Kareena close to his chest. It was dark, and a few couples walked hand in hand along the surf. The distant sound of music and chatter from the boardwalk intermingled with the soothing, consistent crash of surf.

"You are a good person, Prem Verma. Our parents view our success as a sign of whether or not their sacrifices in coming to this country were worth it. And you giving back, by making sure that their health and well-being is taken care of? That's amazing."

If only I can get the funding for it, he thought. But that wasn't her problem anymore. He wouldn't burden her with that right now.

They stayed intertwined, listening to the water for a few mo-ments before Kareena spoke again. "You know what I find funny?"

"What?"

"That we believe in a fundamental difference in how people connect, but in the end, neither of us have found peace. We both are alone."

Prem snorted. She had a point, but he hated to hear that she still considered herself alone when they were together, holding each other. "That's true. But at least I'm out here trying to make it work so we don't have to be. When are you going to try, Kareena Mann?"

"I'm dating. I'm going out. If anything, I'm trying harder than you."

"You know what I mean," he said.

She looked away from him, as if their connection was something that she could avoid when it was already too late. He pressed a kiss to her cheek. "Will you tell me why the house is so important to you?"

She let out a deep shaky breath, and then, almost in a quiet whisper, she said, "I'm like her, you know. My father still says that some of the things I do remind him of her."

"Your mom?"

Kareena nodded. "Her house is the one place I know I can be me. I don't think I'll ever find a place that I can be as connected with someone who accepts me for who I am." She scrunched up her nose, as if to move her glasses. He did it for her and pressed a kiss at the corner of her mouth just the way he knew she liked.

"You are a wildflower, Rina. You will plant and grow wherever you land."

"And with whoever?"

There was that strange twisting feeling in his gut again. "Yes. With whoever."

They sat holding each other for a bit longer, their faces close and the sea breeze cooling their warming skin. The sound of joyful laughter and boardwalk games mixed with the echo of crashing waves.

"You know what this reminds me of?" Kareena asked. She had a little note of amusement in her voice that had him smiling. "A song."

"Oh god, really?"

She dug into her bag and pulled out her cell phone and a pair of earbuds. "Will you listen with me?"

He couldn't deny her anything. Prem held out a hand and took one of the earbuds. He put it in his right ear as she did the same with the other earbud in her left ear.

They stretched out their legs and lay back on the cool sand. Prem tangled his fingers with hers again and closed his eyes as they listened side by side. The soft strains of guitar and piano filtered through the earbud.

He felt Rina squeeze his hand.

Prem listened to the lyrics, the words that Kareena always resonated with, and he realized that the longer the song went on, the more attuned he was to the woman next to him.

His heart pounded as he slowly opened his eyes and turned to watch her in her meditative state for the rest of the song. Her mouth was relaxed, her chest rose and fell with easy breaths, and she'd pushed her glasses up on top of her head so he could see her lashes fan over her cheeks.

Never in a million years did Prem think his brain chemistry would betray him and make him doubt for the first time in his life that maybe, just maybe, love could be real.

Dear Readers,

One of the hardest things for us to come to terms with as parents is when things don't work out the way we hope.

Remember your youth. Religion and reputation should never be used as weapons to incite fear.

Now, that doesn't mean you can't use blackmail and bribery.

Mrs. W. S. Gupta
Columnist
Avon, NJ

CHAPTER TWENTY-FIVE

Kareena

"I feel like I'm the obnoxious friend who can't stop talking about the guy they're sleeping with. I don't know how I became obsessed!" Kareena folded another tent card and passed it to Veera. "How many more do we have to go before we can leave?"

Bobbi checked her printed spreadsheet and the tablet in front of her. "About fourteen," she said. "The Ramkumaran family. Adults, kids, and grandkids all confirmed for the engagement party. We have to split them between two tables. I think you're obsessed because you're getting laid. Hell, I'd be obsessed, too, if I was getting dick."

"I don't understand why I have to be here," Veera mumbled. She looked at the small portable printer, along with the cardstock pages in front of her that she'd been feeding into the machine. "I'm not planning the engagement party. Why is my Friday night shot with you two talking about penis? It makes me feel FOMO."

"If you want dinner and drinks, it'll have to cost you something," Kareena said. "After this is over, let's leave before my sister and Dadi come back. The tailor they went to is in North Brunswick, and they've already been gone for two hours. They should be home soon."

"I'm surprised you're here, too," Bobbi said. She wiggled her eyebrows. "Didn't your boy toy say something about meeting up again this weekend?"

"He did," Kareena said. And she couldn't stop thinking about it. The elephant in their room was getting bigger and bigger as her sister's engagement party closed in on them.

"Are you going to tell him how you feel?" Bobbi asked.

Kareena shook her head. Damn her best friend for knowing exactly what was on her mind. "I don't think he'll react . . . positively. Prem has been nothing but honest about what he thinks of romance from the very beginning."

Bobbi and Veera looked at each other, then busied themselves with the tent cards.

"Oh my god, I hate when you two do that. It drives me insane."

"Honey, if you don't tell him how you feel, then are you two really being honest with each other at the start of your relationship?" Bobbi asked.

"He doesn't think love sustains a relationship. I think it's partially to do with his past, but also, I don't know, maybe his parents? How am I supposed to argue against that?"

"You can only blame your parents for so long before you start making decisions on your own and using them as an excuse," Bobbi said.

"Bobbi!"

"What?" she said with a shrug. "I learned that from therapy, girl. And we're talking about Prem's view on love. If he's sleeping with you now and asking you to put your future reputation on the line for him, then it's only fair that he's honest, too."

"Which means you have to be honest with him, too," Veera added.

Kareena folded her arms and leaned against the table. "You know how some South Asian families aren't that expressive? They just bring you a bowl of fruit when they want to say 'sorry' or 'I love you'? Maybe Prem's kidnapping attempt was just that. An act of service."

Bobbi threw her hands in the air and got out of her chair. Veera groaned and dropped her forehead to the desk.

"What? What did I say?"

"Kareena," Bobbi said as she leaned across the table. "The biggest mistake you can make is trying to interpret someone's actions in a way that fits your definition for love! If he doesn't tell you, then he doesn't love you. That simple!"

"And trust me," Veera said. "We've met him and his friends. They're all the 'say what you mean' type."

"You're telling me," Bobbi muttered.

Their words circled in Kareena's head as her dark thoughts bubbled and spread like rain clouds. At the shore, he'd thrown her with the news about his fiancée, and why he started his community center. It wasn't until later when he dropped her off at home that she was able to dissect all their conversations over the weekend.

Damn it, her friends were right. She was interpreting something in a way to make herself feel better.

The front door opened, and a flurry of voices came through the entrance.

"We're too late," Veera whispered.

"And there is more than one," Bobbi added.

Before Kareena could dive under the table and hide, the aunties poured into the room with Bindu and her grandmother behind them.

"Hi, aunties," Bobbi, Veera, and Kareena said in unison.

"Hello, beautiful betas," Mona Aunty said. She put her small purse on the kitchen counter and held open her arms and accepted a brief hug from each of them.

"Are you done yet?" Bindu said when she looked at the cards on the table. She held two shopping bags in each hand. "This was supposed to be finished by now."

"Honey pie, I'd be careful the way you talk to me," Bobbi said to her, crossing her arms over her chest. "You pay me just enough to plan your events, not to take disrespect."

Bindi stepped back, and even though she had a look of irritation on her face, she didn't respond. Damn, Kareena really needed to learn that trick.

"Are you here to help with the planning?" Veera asked the aunties.

"Bindu called us to see her final outfit selections," Sonali Aunty said. "Loken should be here soon to try on his clothes so we can give the final approval for the sagai."

"Beta, what are you going to wear?" Farah Aunty asked Kareena. "Not something black, I hope."

"I'm not sure yet," Kareena said. Usually, her grandmother and sister put her in whatever outfit they expected her to wear for events like this, so she didn't have to hear them complain for weeks on end about her choice of style or color.

"Well, you're less than a month away," Sonali Aunty replied. "You really need to select something soon; otherwise, you won't be able to get it tailored and pressed in time."

"Forget her clothes; who is she going with?" Dadi called from the kitchen. "Bobbi, Veera, are you two helping Kareena find someone for her sister's engagement party? Even though not that many people care anymore in the community, I still think it looks bad for Kareena that she's the oldest sister and still single."

"I thought you all were looking for her?" Bobbi asked.

"We tried, but she wanted nothing to do with the match we

found," Mona Aunty said. She rounded the kitchen to help Dadi take food out of the fridge and to set the water for chai.

"I think it's because you all realized that it's not as easy to find a man as it once was," Veera said bemused.

"She's right," Falguni Aunty said.

All the aunties and Dadi turned to her, calling her name in unison.

"What?" Falguni Aunty said. "They're smart girls. They know if we're bullshitting them. Kareena, don't you worry. When you find someone, he'll be wonderful."

"She's already found someone," Bobbi mumbled.

The entire kitchen went quiet.

"I'm sorry, beta," Farah Aunty said calmly. "What did you say?"

"I'm going to kill you," Kareena whispered at Bobbi.

Her friend shrugged and continued to fold the remaining tent cards. "Now you can't back out tonight."

She wasn't going to back out. She'd planned on telling Prem she was willing to do the relationship thing and she'd made up her mind about it. But telling the aunties? That was a whole different experience.

Kareena stood, straightened her shoulders, took a deep breath, and faced the five women who stood around the kitchen like statues.

"Aunties," she said slowly. "Dadi. I met someone a few months ago. On my birthday. We hit it off really well, then when we met the second time . . . we realized we had huge, fundamental differences. But slowly we, sort of, came to terms with our differences. And now, we're . . . we're . . ."

"Dating," Bobbi and Veera said at the same time.

A series of gasps sounded throughout the kitchen.

"Who?"

"Is he desi?"

"Does he come from a good family?"

"Does he live in New Jersey?"

"Is he real?" Bindu added. She'd been leaning against the back wall checking her cell phone and playing with the curls at the end of her braid.

"Shut up, Bindu," Kareena said. "He's real. And you've actually all met him. It's Prem. Prem Verma."

Kareena waited, counting the seconds of the total silence. Then the entire room exploded with shrieks. The aunties swarmed her, surrounding her with hugs and heavy perfume. Everyone was talking at once, and Kareena had no idea where to turn and who to respond to first.

"We knew he was the perfect person. See? Your aunties know."

"How could you not tell us right away? We should've known earlier, beta."

"This is so wonderful. I hope that your father is just as happy."

What the hell was this insanity? She didn't event receive this kind of joy when she'd achieved her perfect career goals or graduated from law school. The thought that people were happier for her that she found a partner than she found happiness on her own was so cliché it made her nauseous.

But then again, this was something that these women who were like family understood. This was something that they knew well, and finding happiness in home meant something so much to them. Kareena hated that she wasn't telling them the whole truth, but if she did, they'd never accept her decision to work with Prem.

Dadi squeezed through the masses and gripped Kareena's face

between her hands so that the only person she could focus on was her grandmother. "Beta, do you love him?"

Everyone quieted again, and Kareena felt the back of her neck prickly when all eyes zeroed in on her facial expressions.

"I— I, ah . . ."

"Of course she does!" Veera burst out. "This is the start of her love story!"

The cheering started all over again, and Dadi wrapped Kareena in a hug that squeezed her heart.

Falguni Aunty hustled over to her tote bag and pulled out a large three-inch-wide binder brimming with tabs and hole-punched sheets. "Beta, I've already started putting together information for your wedding. Now that we know the groom's name, we can start planning better."

"What in the world? I'm dating Prem, not engaged to him!" *Not yet.*

Sonali Aunty squeezed her shoulder. "You know, I have a standing appointment with the pandit at the Bridgewater temple to review your star charts. Do you think you can have Prem's family send over his janampatri? That way when you are engaged, we can speed up the process a bit by making sure your charts align."

"Oh, the roka!" Mona Aunty said. "I have to order your necklace. Unless you want to wear Dadi's?"

"I'm proud of you," Dadi said. "Your mother would be so proud of you, too."

Kareena's eyes immediately began to burn, and she could feel the tears climbing her throat. No, her mother wouldn't be proud of her. She wanted to shout it, to tell everyone to stop celebrating. There was nothing to celebrate.

"Okay, move out of the way. My turn," Bindu called out as she squeezed between the aunties and enveloped Kareena in a hug.

Kareena let go, ready to step back, but Bindu's arms tightened around her. "Do you need an escape?" she whispered.

God, how long had it been since they'd done that for each other?

Kareena nodded before letting Bindu go.

Bindu burst out, "Bobbi, I want to change the menu. No Indian food. Just Italian food. And we're limiting the wedding guest list to a hundred people."

"Leh," Dadi said. "This one is talking nonsense."

"Yeah, I'll call the venue and make those changes now," Bobbi said. "Aunties, it's totally doable and even makes sense in this situation."

This time the aunties went absolutely ballistic. With their backs turned, and their attention on Bindu, Kareena, Bobbi, and Veera managed to sneak their stuff out of the kitchen and to the car at the end of the block.

When they were seated and strapped in, Kareena took her glasses off and rubbed at her eyes. "Bobbi, you shouldn't have said anything."

Bobbi squeezed her shoulder. "I'm sorry, friend. Why don't we get you to Prem? Maybe being with him will remind you that you don't have to say the words to love someone."

For those of you who have watched *The Dr. Dil Show* on the Jersey City South Asians News Network since its inception, you may find that the content as of late has taken an interesting turn. Our very own Dr. Dil, Prem Verma, has been bringing more and more relationship advice experts onto the show. Part of his reasoning has been to showcase the vast array of concerns that affect the South Asian community that he hopes to address in the Jersey City health community center he's developing. But some viewers have begun to speculate if the content has been influenced by a change in his personal relationship status.

CHAPTER TWENTY-SIX

Prem

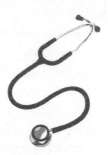

Prem put away his notes for the next *Dr. Dil* episode and ordered takeout. One day he'd make dinner for Kareena, but he was too amped up to focus on anything else but her arrival. There were candles and her favorite playlist as background music.

He was going to ask her today for permanence. For something more than what they had now. He believed in loyalty and commitment and hard work. He'd take care of her, and hopefully that would convince her that they could have a lifetime together.

Before he rearranged the cheese board and the wineglasses for a third time, the front door rang. Prem was surprised to find Kareena on the other side with her overnight bag and purse.

"I was going to have the front desk call you to let me up, but they said I was on a list."

Prem nodded. "You're preapproved. Is that okay?"

Her shoulders lifted and dropped with an exaggerated sigh. "I suppose so," she said.

"Good," he said, and leaned in for a quick peck before taking her bag and leading the way inside his apartment.

He watched her kick off her shoes and drop her purse on the kitchen island.

"Do you want some wine?" he asked. "I figured we can talk, and—"

"You know what? I have a better idea."

He dropped her bag when she launched herself at him and affixed her mouth to his. His hands were full of hair and hips, and when her tongue stroked over his, he lost all ability to concentrate.

Homecoming.

He curled his fingers behind her neck, his stomach tightening when he felt her shudder. They were chest to chest, breath to breath, and when her arms wrapped around him, demanding that he give her everything he had, Prem kissed her with all the pent-up frustration he'd been holding on to since he dropped her off at the train station the Sunday before.

Her tongue slipped between his lips, and he groaned against the wet brush in his mouth. Heat pooled in his groin, and he grew thick with need for her. He sucked her tongue now, and then nipped her lip, demanding more.

He'd been away from this woman for a week. He missed her touch, her smell, her laugh. Every time he was out of his apartment, he swore he could smell sandalwood and vanilla, or see a flash of sweater vest. He didn't know why she was so hungry for him right this instant, but if Kareena needed him, he'd ask questions later and provide.

Prem ran his hands underneath her sweater vest and squeezed her breast. She let out a throaty moan. He pulled back, just enough to speak, his lips still moving against hers. "What do you—"

"No," she whispered, and pulled at his hair. "No talking."

"Rina?"

"You know me, Prem," she said. "I don't need to tell you what I want."

If love existed, this woman would have his heart, and he'd willingly take his scalpel to carve it out and give it to her.

Her hands found his butt and squeezed, interrupting his train of thought.

Charlie bounced up like a spring, immediately at full staff.

Without thinking twice, Prem bent at the knees, picked Kareena up, and carried her down the narrow hallway to his bedroom. Seconds later, he was tossing her on the bed.

"No talking still?" he said.

She shook her head.

The twinkling city lights cast a glow over Kareena's prone form. She leaned up on her elbows, then slipped off her glasses to hand them to him.

Together, they undressed. The easy exploration of familiar skin and curves was both comforting and arousing. From the undercurve of her breasts to the sensitive spot behind her knees and the inside of her wrists. Kareena was like a feast, and Prem took pleasure in every bite.

When she was naked, all golden brown against his white comforter, with dusky brown nipples and heavy round breasts, wide hips, and a trim triangle at the apex of her thighs, his hunger for her, his need for her surged.

"Prem," she said, holding her arms open for him.

"Not yet." He slid off the bed, then gripped her ankles and flipped her over onto her stomach before smacking the soft curve of her ass. She let out a choked gasp but pushed her butt out against his hand so that he could do it again.

This, he thought. This was how he knew that even in bed, they'd be perfect together.

Dropping a soft kiss on the red handprint mark he'd made, Prem shed his briefs, then slowly crawled onto the bed until his chest pressed against her back, and his dick nestled between her ass cheeks.

She shuddered at the contact.

Rina, honey, we're just getting started.

Prem gripped her hips to position her. "On your knees."

There was that gasp again. He could see from her profile that her eyes were closed, and she swallowed hard, but she shifted under him until she was on all fours with Prem positioned behind her. His fingers immediately dived between her thighs and began stroking her clit, first softly until she settled against his touch, then with firm strokes.

"Prem," she whispered as she rolled her hips back.

When Kareena whimpered, Prem curled one hand around the front of her throat and pulled her up so that they were back to chest. She gasped, and her breasts rose with each labored breath.

"Let me finger fuck you," he whispered and pushed two digits into her tight pussy. He could come watching her enjoy the pleasure he was giving her. When she relaxed, he pulled out and rubbed her flowing juices over her clit.

"Prem," she sobbed.

He began to rub her clit alternating between firm and hard strokes. When he felt her reach a precipice point right before an orgasm, he inserted his fingers inside her, and waited for her to calm before driving her slowly mad all over again.

"I can't," Kareena cried out, her head rolling against his shoulder as he brought her to the tipping point a third time. "I can't, Prem." She tugged on her nipple with one hand and reached back to pull his hair with the other. "Oh *god.*"

He moved faster, their hips undulating as she begged him for more without words, without anything but the growing dampness.

Prem felt the tension coiled tighter and tighter into her body until she pushed against his unyielding hold. Her scream of ecstasy was like music to his ears. He held her as she came in his arms. His fingers dampened and he continued to gently run his fingertips in circles over her clit, stroking her lips as her body shook against his chest.

Kareena whispered his name, and her head rolled against his shoulder.

"Not yet," he whispered.

Just as she took her first breath, Prem pushed her down until her cheek was pressed against his mattress. She shuddered but remained in position.

"Condom?"

"No condom," she whispered.

Prem pressed a kiss to her spine, spread her knees wider, positioned her hips, and then slid his painfully erect cock into her.

She gasped, and he groaned at the contact.

He pulled out a little, and then pushed back in, hard and firm. Because her ass demanded it, Prem slapped her cheek again, and she bowed against his touch.

He had to fuck her, had to bring her pleasure again. With a ruthless grip on her hips, he began thrusting into her in long, steady strokes, until she was silently screaming into the blanket. Her fingertips squeezed and clenched the comforter, and she pushed back against him, seeking every thrust.

"That's it, Rina. Take me." He didn't know if she could hear his words, but he said them, asking for more. Whispering endearments. Demanding that they claim each other.

Prem felt Charlie tighten, but he wasn't ready. Not yet. He wanted to come when they were together, looking at each other eye to eye.

"No!" she gasped when he pulled out all the way. But he was already rolling her onto her back and shoving one of his pillows under her hips.

"Yes," he gasped. He towered over her, as he positioned her hips and plunged deeper into her than he ever had before. He was taking her, all of her, and finding all the hidden parts of her body that he knew no one else could ever fill like he could.

Kareena tensed under him, gasping his name. She tightened around him, almost painfully, and he tried to remember every second of this moment together with her.

"Rina," he growled, as he fucked her harder and faster. "Say yes."

"Wh-what?" Her eyes widened as she held on to him, legs in the air, on the cusp of an orgasm. "Wh-what?"

"Say yes!" he demanded. "You know what!" his voice was hoarse, desperate for her.

He leaned in close, pressing his lips to hers, savaging her mouth the way that she'd savaged his life.

She tensed, her mouth open wide in a silent scream as the orgasm tore through her. "Y-yes!" she whispered.

"What was that?" he demanded, as he pushed into her so hard that the bed frame pounded against the wall. "Tell me, damn it."

"Yes!" she screamed. "Yes!"

Prem came harder than he'd ever come before. When he let go in that moment, releasing inside of her, he'd gripped her hips and held her flush against his, saying her name like a prayer before collapsing on top of her.

She'd said yes.

LATER, WHETHER IT was minutes or hours, he wasn't sure, Prem rolled to the side, then pulled a blanket over both of them. Kareena's skin was starting to feel cool from the air-conditioning, and he didn't want her to be uncomfortable.

When she rolled over to look at him, eyes sleepy, she said, "I hope I didn't answer the wrong question."

"Do you want to make this a real thing?" He swallowed hard, hoping that her answer remained the same.

The hazy look in her eyes cleared. "Yeah. I guess I did answer the right question."

"Does your answer still stand?" he asked. He'd already begun envisioning their future together. Working together. Traveling together. Long nights where they talked until the sun set and made love until sunrise. He may not be able to give her the words that she needed, but he'd stay committed to her if she were willing to make this real. If she was as invested in a . . . a partnership as he was.

She looked pensive for a moment, and he could swear he saw a glimmer of regret in her eyes.

Regret?

"Yes," she said in a rush. "Yes, let's do this."

"Okay," he whispered and pulled her close. "Rina?"

"Yeah?"

"Just to be clear, I want more than a fake engagement with you," he whispered.

She lay eyes closed, her lips quivering. "Okay."

They lay like that, lost in their individual thoughts. He was happy. Truly happy.

He looked down at her face with that one line of tension between her brows and ran a thumb over it.

"Rina, honey?"

"Hmm?" she said, her eyes remaining closed.

And because he couldn't think of what he was *supposed* to say to find out why she didn't sound as content, as happy as he did, he said the only thing that came to mind.

"I don't deserve you, but I'm going to try every day to be someone who does. Is that enough?"

The line between her brows smoothed out, and for the first time since she walked in his door, a smile curved her full mouth. She pressed a hand against his cheek.

"Okay," she whispered in response.

CHAPTER TWENTY-SEVEN
Prem

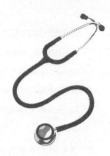

PREM: I feel like I need to give you a real proposal. You know, before we announce it at your sister's engagement party that we're together.

KAREENA: Uh, sure. I mean, I don't need one, but okay?

PREM: Really? For such a romantic, I thought you'd like the idea. You know. Rings and things.

KAREENA: Well, if you're interested in proposing, just for you and me, I'd prefer if it was a surprise. You know, because texting me that we're announcing an engagement is not really something that sparks romance.

PREM: Ahh. Yeah, okay. That makes sense. Hey Rina, honey?

PREM: Are you happy?

KAREENA: ☺

GREGORY LTD FINANCIAL: Hey Prem, do you have time for a quick meeting in NYC tomorrow? I saw your last few shows. Your producer sent me the tapes and a pretty compelling note. I'm reconsidering my investment into your community center.

PREM: That's great! I'd be happy to meet you tomorrow. I have patients, but I'll see what I can do to move my nonurgent appointments. I'll keep you posted on my availability.

GREGORY LTD FINANCIAL: Great. I let my assistant know you'll be putting time on my calendar. Talk to you soon.

Prem walked into the chrome and glass building on Park Avenue and checked in at the wide security desk. After they took his picture, verified his ID, and called up to the top floor, he took the designated elevator up to floors twenty-five through thirty-five.

The thirty-fifth floor had sweeping views of the river, with the Statue of Liberty in the distance.

"Dr. Verma?" a woman said. Her perfectly styled black hair was coiled on top of her head. She held a tablet in one hand.

"Yes, that's me."

"Deepak is waiting for you. Please follow me."

Prem trailed behind the woman, keeping up with her clipped pace down wide corridors with large glass offices along the walls and spacious open desks. In the center of the floor were couches, espresso machines, and gathering tables.

The woman stopped in front of the corner office and motioned through the open door. "Right this way, please."

Prem stepped inside, and the last thing he expected to see was a familiar face seated across from Deepak with her feet propped up on the adjoining seat, or his best friend in his office chair casually trying to solve a Rubik's Cube, as if the woman's presence was completely normal.

"Veera? What are you doing here?"

Veera's feet dropped to the floor. "Oh. Uh, sorry. I thought I'd be out of here before you arrived."

Deepak continued to fidget with the Rubik's Cube at his desk. "We had a business lunch, Prem. Don't make a bigger deal out of it than it is."

Veera nodded like a bobblehead. "And please keep this to yourself so my friends also don't make a bigger deal out of it."

"Oh," Prem said. "Are you asking me to keep a secret from Kareena?"

Veera nodded again. "If she finds out about this, she and Bobbi will jump to conclusions. And there is nothing to conclude. Obviously."

"Right," Deepak added.

"Oh . . . kay," Prem said. "Deepak, you want to meet up with me later?"

"Nope, we're finished," Veera responded before Deepak. She grabbed her purse and looped it over her shoulder. "I have another meeting with a client one building over. Bharat, Inc. The tech company."

"The Singh brothers are good people," Deepak said and nodded at her. "Just tell them straight, and they'll be receptive."

"Thanks," she said as she picked up her bag that she'd left next to her chair. "Prem, it's good seeing you."

"Uh, you too?"

She zipped past him, her billowing top brushing his arm as he passed. Before Veera could reach the door, Prem called her name. "Yes?"

He thought about Kareena, about how quiet she'd been the night they'd talked, and then decided it was best to trust her to tell him how she felt directly. "Never mind. I'll see you around."

Veera shot him a wary look, then wiggled her fingers at Deepak before leaving the office and disappearing down the hallway.

"Trouble in paradise?" Deepak asked from his chair.

Prem zeroed in on his friend's smug expression. "Oh no. No, you don't. Don't turn this on me. What about you? Lucy, you have some esplain'in to do. What was Veera doing here?"

Deepak put the Rubik's Cube down on his sparsely decorated desk. "We started talking at that dinner you dragged Bunty and me to. She's smart. Intuitive. More importantly, she can be an asset on this project I'm working on that requires a lot of number-crunching foresight skills. She's also looking to diversify her clientele. It's a perfect fit."

That sounded reasonable, but it definitely wasn't the whole story. Of course, Deepak never revealed his cards until he was ready, so harassing him for details wasn't going to work in this situation.

"Now your turn," Deepak said. "What's up with Kareena?"

Prem thought about his girlfriend.

His *girlfriend*. The word made him unreasonably delirious. He had enjoyed Gori, respected her and appreciated her in his life, but this feeling was new. A little odd, but he could work with it. "I woke up next to her for two nights in a row. Between our trip to the shore, and the hours we spent in the park on Saturday, I really think this can work."

"After four months? Good for you. Have you figured out your community center issues yet? Is your engagement to Kareena Mann going to help you get the cash you need?"

Prem shook his head. "It has, in the most surprising of ways. Apparently all this love talk with Kareena has influenced some of my segments on the show, and Gregory at LTD Financial had a change of heart. I had a meeting with him today, and he said he loved the new content."

Deepak's head jerked up. "LTD Financial is investing again?"

"Yup, Gregory changed his mind about pulling out of the community center project. This time he's willing to commit more money." Prem was still buzzing from the news. He texted Kareena, but she was in client meetings until four. The next best thing was his friends. With the larger investment, Prem could not only secure his dream location and start building out his center according to his plans, but he could also hire a larger staff to start.

In honor of Gori's memory, and for the South Asian community.

"I'm happy for you, brother," Deepak said. "You're finally doing it."

Prem picked up the Slinky that Deepak left next to his monitor on his otherwise pristine desk. "Finally. We're pulling out the original contracts, tweaking the numbers, and by next Friday, I should be able to sign the lease with the center location."

Deepak tossed the Rubik's Cube in the air and caught it in one hand. "Does this mean that you and Kareena no longer have to do the engagement thing? I know you're officially dating and all, but the engagement part was fake, wasn't it?"

"Well, no. We still need to do the engagement thing so she can get the money for her mom's house. She's determined to save it, and I'm sure as hell not going to stop her. It's a great house." Prem had seen the inside twice, and both times he could see imprints of Kareena in the design, in the decor. It was as if it always belonged to her.

"And you *want* to be engaged, too."

"Well, yeah," Prem replied. "We make sense together. We have similar likes and dislikes. We have physical chemistry and want the same things out of our future."

Deepak's thick black brows shot straight to his hairline. "And love? That's a big thing for her, right? Is she just going to accept that you can't love her? That you *don't* love her?"

Prem felt an odd pang in his chest. "I think she's accepted that I don't believe an emotion that I have literally referred to as an illusion is the foundation of a relationship."

"Mm-hmm. Prem, you seem pretty lovesick to me."

"No way," Prem said. His pulse jumped at the thought. "Love isn't what makes a relationship. That's not what makes Kareena's and my relationship . . . fit. We're based on compatibility. Like an arranged marriage, except we found each other first and needed a bit of inspiration from her aunties."

Deepak tossed the Rubik's Cube one more time. "Not gonna lie, brother. That surprises me she's cool with you never saying how you feel about her. I mean, you guys went viral because of how adamant she was about love marriages. But hey, as long as you're sure."

"I'm sure. I mean, of course I'm sure." They hadn't talked about it, but why did they have to? Kareena would've mentioned it, or she would've told him to take a hike otherwise.

Deepak's feet hit the floor with a thud. He stood and straightened his coat. "Whatever, man. Don't worry about it then. Fixating will make you nuts. Melancholy is the nurse of frenzy and all that jazz."

Prem rubbed a hand over his stubble. "Maybe I'll talk to her after Bindu's party," he said.

"Suit yourself. Now thanks for visiting, but I have to do some work around here."

"I thought we were going to grab something to eat?"

Deepak turned to his computer. "I don't want to spend the next hour talking about how you're not in love with Kareena."

"I'm not, damn it," Prem said. He wasn't. The idea that people thought he potentially could be seemed unfathomable "Love is not *real*. It's just our need for attachment and building partnerships to create community."

"And you aren't your parents, Prem," Deepak replied. "You could get away with that shit with Gori, but this is your life partner. Your . . . what is it again? Jeevansathi. Now go be grumpy pants somewhere else. I'm happy for you, but come talk to me when you're happy, too."

CHAPTER TWENTY-EIGHT

Kareena

"Hey, Dave's Restoration. This is Dave, how can I help you?" The voice had a sharp South Jersey accent to it that was somehow endearing and amusing.

"Dave, it's Kareena Mann. I have the BMW 1988 E30 in Henna Red with tan seats?"

He let out a low whistle into the phone. "The E30 M3! Yeah, of course. Kareena. How can I help you?"

She looked out the kitchen window to the open shed doors. The front taillights were visible from where she stood. "I've restored as much as I could on my own. I think it's time to bring her in."

Dave let out a whoop and a holler. "Johnny! *Johnny!* I got the E30 M3 restoration on the phone! She's ready for us!"

Kareena couldn't help but smile. She found Dave's shop by happenstance, and she kept going back to him for parts because he loved cars like they were his children.

She waited for him to come back on the phone before she said, "The car isn't road ready. She's going to need a tow to your shop. Can you arrange that for me?"

"Hell, I'll tow that beaut myself," Dave said. "Don't you worry, doll. I'll take care of her. I can be there tonight if you want."

"Wow, um. Yeah, sure." She was supposed to see Prem tonight. It was the only time they had together before Bindu's engagement party next weekend, but she could cancel. This was important.

And she honestly could use the weekend to think.

Oblivious to her train of thought, Dave started rattling off information. "This is what I need from ya. Tell me when you're ready."

"Go for it."

"Maintenance records?"

"I'll email them to you."

"List of restored, replaced, and original components to the vehicle?"

"I'll send you the spreadsheet."

"The list of products that you need to buy from us, along with what you want us to leave, and what you want us to take care of."

"No problem," Kareena said. "I'll attach that to the same email. I still have your contact information, so as soon as we hang up, I'll send it off. Also, the car is in the back shed, so if you have tracks you can put down so my grass doesn't get completely wrecked, I'll thank you forever."

"Psh, you know I'll come just as prepared as you are," Dave drawled. A sound of an air compressor whirred in the background. "I'll be there in an hour or so. Thanks for trusting us with this car, M3. We promise we'll do your mama right by it."

"Thanks, Dave," she whispered in kind. "I appreciate it."

"Hey, M3. One more thing."

"Yes?"

Dave let out a deep breath. "Why now? You've been working on this thing forever."

Kareena held out her left hand and looked at her bare ring finger. Would it be strange to feel a piece of jewelry there?

Getting engaged didn't scare her. But getting engaged to someone who didn't love her back? That was terrifying.

"M3?"

"Yeah, Dave," she said, and cleared her throat. "I've been working on it myself a long time, and I'm finally ready."

"Well, we'll be there soon."

After hanging up the phone Kareena scrolled through her recent call log and tapped Prem's name. "Hey," she said when he answered.

"You're canceling," he replied, his voice deadpan.

"Wait, how did you know?"

"Because the last time you called me, you canceled. Please tell me you're not going to play Dungeons and Dragons with gamer dude tonight. Or FaceTime with a douchebag. Or drink cinnamon to go to the hospital."

Kareena snorted. "No more bad dates. Hopefully. I have to stay at the house. Dave is coming to pick up my car. I'm finally done with it, and now the rest of the work has to be done by a garage."

He let out a low whistle. "Wow. Congratulations. I know you said you were close, but I didn't realize you were *this* close. How does it feel?"

Exhilarating. Terrifying. Sad. Giddy. Like she'd lost her purpose.

"I'm . . . okay," she replied. "I know you're on call next week and I have to help Bindu. Her fiancé's family is coming in today. You okay meeting at Bindu's engagement party?"

There was a long pause. "Are you okay with us telling your family about our future plans at your sister's party?"

No. Definitely no. "Yes," she said.

"Okay, well, if you're sure . . . then we'll talk every night? I'll call you later, okay?"

"Okay," she said. The words *I love you* were on the tip of her tongue, but she bit them back. "Later."

"Later."

She heard pounding down the stairs just as she hung up the phone. She turned, clutching her cell to her chest, just as Bindu's wild expression greeted her.

"What's wrong?" Kareena said, taking in Bindu's hair piled on top of her head and the stained T-shirt that said MATHLETE CHAMPION—NORTHEAST REGIONALS on the front.

Bindu's eyes glittered with unshed tears. "There is so much going on, and I completely forgot that I'm supposed to take over halwa tonight to meet Loken's family! Dadi said I'm supposed to make it for the prayer service they're having? There isn't any time! Loken just picked them up from the airport, and he's driving them to his house right now. I have to get ready and Dadi is out at her kitty party with the aunties, Dad decided to work this weekend, and now I have to cook and wear a stupid sari! We're Punjabi! Why can't I wear a suit instead? But *no*. Loken said his mother would be more impressed if I wore a sari Gujarati style. Now she's going to hate my halwa and my outfit!"

Kareena held up her hands to stop the tirade. "Did you iron the sari yet?"

"Oh my god, no!" Bindu's voice screeched. "I was filming videos and editing and working on grading a stupid quiz I assigned my students last week. What am I supposed to do?"

Before the first sob could break through her lips, Kareena shushed her.

"First things first. Go iron the sari. Second, I'll ask Bobbi if anyone on her wedding planning team is nearby and knows how to tie a Gujarati-style sari. And while you get dressed, I'll make the halwa."

"Okay," Bindu said, letting out a deep breath. "Really? Really you'll do that for me?"

Kareena nodded. "Now get out of here. I'll start cooking."

"Thanks," Bindu said with a sniffle. She turned toward the hallway and looked back over one shoulder. "Didi." She rushed back upstairs.

Kareena shook her head. Damn it, she was always a sucker when her sister needed her.

She sent Bobbi a text first, then Dave all the information for her car, before she put the phone down and walked into the kitchen.

"Halwa," she said to herself. "You and I haven't met since I was forced to make you for the last pooja. Let's do this."

She started by pulling out all the main ingredients. Chickpea flour, ghee, sugar, raisins, and slivered almonds. Kareena then set a small pot to boil.

Now she had to find the wok. Her grandmother preferred to make halwa in a saucepan, but Kareena liked to use the same wok her mother had used. It was good luck. Unfortunately, that meant digging through all of Dadi's stainless-steel crap.

She began opening base cabinets and drawers. There were so many stainless-steel bowls, pots, and pans. Her grandmother kept buying new stuff and shoving the old ones in the back.

I really have to clean this up, she thought. She made it to the corner cabinet that barely got any use since it was harder for Dadi to bend at the knees. She had to get down on the floor to search the bottom shelf.

When she saw the handle of the wok, she cheered. "Gotcha!" Kareena reached inside to feel the back of the cabinet when her hand brushed the corner of some paper. "What the hell?"

Pulling her hand out of the cabinet, she grabbed her phone, then shined some light into the back. There, stuck between the base and the wall was a folded yellow piece of paper. It must have dropped back there when she took out all the drawers to reface the cabinets a couple years ago. And since it was stuck in the edges, unless someone cleaned the cabinets with a flashlight, it would've been impossible to spot.

Contorting her body, she pulled out the stuck piece of paper. She sat on the kitchen floor, then carefully unfolded it.

"Oh my god," Kareena whispered, letting out a heartfelt breath. "Mama."

Her mother's neat handwriting had long sweeping curves that crowded together. On the top of the note, she'd written:

10-year plan for kitchen renovation.

The list was extensive, starting with taking down the wall between the kitchen and living room. That was exactly what Kareena had wanted to do for years, but her father wouldn't let her. She wondered if the plans were too close to what Kareena's mother wanted.

The second task was to reface the cabinets, which Kareena had done a few years ago.

The third had Kareena chuckling.

Replace the appliances when my cheap-ass husband finally comes to his senses.

Kareena looked around and nodded. "He's still a cheap ass," she muttered.

Number four had to do with the fixtures, and number five was . . .

Number five.

Kareena's chest tightened, and her throat began to burn.

Fill the kitchen, and the rest of the house, with love. The love I share with my husband and my children.

Love.

The house had been filled with love at one time. Now, there was some love that remained out of obligation. But if Kareena was able to keep her home, and Prem was sincere about making what they had between them a real thing, then the only love remaining would be hers.

Was it enough?

"I wish you were here, Mama," she whispered to the note. "Then you could tell me if I was doing the right thing."

With a sniffle, Kareena got up off the floor, tucked the piece of paper in her back pocket, grabbed the wok, and started to make halwa for her sister.

PREM: Ready for tonight?

KAREENA: Yeah.

PREM: Rina, honey, are you *sure*?

KAREENA: I mean, this is good for both of us, right? This is my only chance to get my mom's house.

PREM: And because we'll be happy. Together.

KAREENA: Right.

PREM: Let's talk when I get there. I'll see you soon.

Kareena walked into the ballroom at the Marriott off Route 1 wearing the payal and her mother's earrings. Bobbi and Veera helped her pick out a black-and-silver lehenga from one of her sister's favorite shops in downtown Edison.

She'd gotten dressed by herself since her father had to run errands before the event, and her grandmother was with Bindu at the hotel helping her get ready.

Even though it felt like people forgot about her, the short bout of solitude was nice. The feeling of nausea in her gut grew stronger the closer she got to seeing Prem again. They didn't practice or talk at all about what they were going to say, how they were going to say it, and to whom they'd spill the news of their relationship first.

"This is going to be a disaster," she whispered.

Kareena strode through the double doors marked with a heart-shaped sign with her sister's and Loken's name on it, and took in the beautiful work that Bobbi and her team had done with the hall. Flowers hung from tall crystal vases, and the chairs were draped in cream coverings with gold tassels.

She had to hand it to Bobbi. The woman knew how to make parties happen, even if they were for a two-hundred-person engagement celebration planned in four months.

"Kareena!"

Kareena turned to face her grandmother's voice. Dadi wore a deep-emerald-green sari with silver embroidery draped across the front and through her pleats. She wove through the table settings with cream-colored plates and red, orange, and yellow napkins. "Dadi, I thought you were supposed to be upstairs with Bindu?"

"I came to tell you that you have to stand by the door to greet those coming in," Dadi said, adjusting the front of her sari. "Loken's family should be here first, and we want our family to be the first faces they see. Now let me look at you."

She stepped back and tilted her head back and forth in the bobblehead yes gesture she often used. "Hahn," she said, with satisfaction in her tone, and reached out to touch the gray-to-black balayage skirt covered in a smattering of silver crystals. "Is your chunni pinned?"

Kareena touched the pleated shawl she'd draped over one

shoulder with heavy embroidered gems along the trim. "No, but I'll find Bobbi and ask her to do it for me."

"Yes, otherwise it'll come off and you'll look like a stage dancer. What will Prem think?"

"Ah, I knew it was coming. The warning to not remove the *sheer shawl draped on one shoulder* otherwise I'd look like a Bollywood prostitute. I think Prem would enjoy that actually."

Her grandmother shook her head.

"Don't be such a besharam," she said. "Shameless." She reached up and touched Kareena's cheeks. "The contacts suit you, though."

"I knew you'd yell at me about pictures," Kareena muttered. The contacts were already dry, and every time she tried to push her glasses up her nose, she ended up poking herself in the face.

"Dadi, I'm going to go get a drink and then find Bobbi." Kareena needed liquid courage if she was going to do this thing with Prem.

"You can't leave! I just told you have to stay here and greet our guests."

"First of all, this is a party for family and friends. It's not that big of a deal."

"There are two hundred people coming tonight," her grandmother said, deadpan. "You and the aunties are meeting Loken's parents for the first time. We have to put on a good impression."

"Indian Standard Time, Dadi. That means people won't show up for another two hours."

"We still have to do a run-through of events tonight," Bobbi said from behind her.

Kareena stepped back to take in Bobbi's pink-and-silver Patiala salwar. She even braided her hair in a choti with a paranda hanging from the end. Her jutti shoes matched the outfit, and her winged liner was on point.

"Excuse me, but have you seen my friend? I seemed to have lost her in a mustard field in Punjab."

"Up yours," Bobbi said. "Sorry, Aunty."

"I don't know what that means, but, Bobbi, you look so beautiful," Dadi said in Punjabi. She reached out to fuss with her chunni that draped from one shoulder, across the front and pinned to the other. It was low enough to expose a tiny diamond necklace that matched the jhumka earrings, those pretty little umbrella-shaped drops that hung from Bobbi's ears.

"Am I late?" Veera called out from the doors. She strolled in wearing a deep-teal-colored gown with a strip of belly showing. Her simple black fitted velvet blouse was elegant and sexy.

"You're just on time," Dadi said, and opened her arms for a hug. "Beta, you look lovely as well. Now you and Bobbi have to find someone just like my Kareena."

The DJ, a sixteen-year-old music genius that Bindu had found on Instagram, began testing his speakers in the corner under a canopy of fake marigolds. The soft strains of sad Bollywood music filtered through the speakers.

Kareena's father walked out of the back room holding a box that had a whiskey brand on the side. He wore a tux that was a little loose at the shoulders and a little snug at the waist. "I brought more for the bar," he called out. "If we run out, I can get the alcohol from our basement that I started collecting for the wedding."

"Daddy, you know we have to use the alcohol that the hall provides," Kareena said.

He walked right past her toward the bar on the other side of the room. "They're not going to have enough."

"Keep up the good work, Uncle!" Bobbi called out. "And don't worry about the extra alcohol. I already cleared it with the owners."

She grabbed Kareena's and Veera's hands and dragged them across the hall. "Sorry, Dadi, I need a moment with these two."

"Take your time. I'm going back into the dressing room to check on Bindu."

"What is it?" Kareena asked when they huddled in the corner together.

"*What is it?*" Bobbi mimicked Kareena's voice. "Hey, asshole, you are supposed to announce an *engagement* tonight. Is that seriously happening? You've been AWOL for the last week and wouldn't answer our texts!"

Kareena's stomach pitched again. "This is all very surreal."

Veera squeezed her hand. "Oh my god, that means it's happening! Wow, one of us is getting *engaged*. You manifested it into existence at your birthday and look at you now!"

Bobbi touched Kareena's and Veera's shoulders. "Unless you don't *want* to be engaged."

"I can't stop thinking about my mom," Kareena whispered shakily. "I wish she was here to give me some advice. I mean, I'm stupid, right? I love Prem."

Just saying the word gave her stomach cramps. She pressed a palm to her stomach.

"I love Prem," she repeated, "but I want to be loved, too. Am I getting caught up in semantics? If so, why can't I accept the fact that I'll never hear him say how he feels about me?"

Veera rubbed the small of her back. "He *loves* you. Even if he's a dummy and hasn't said it. He has to! I mean, look at the way he tries to take care of you."

"But if the words are important to you, then take the time you need to get them," Bobbi said.

"That's why I'm remembering Mom," Kareena whispered. "I

feel like if she was here, this would never be an issue, and she'd know exactly what to say about Prem. And then she'd freak out at Dad and Dadi for putting me in this stupid position of fighting for something that means a lot to me."

Bobbi and Veera looped their arms over Kareena's shoulders and waist. They put their heads close together and stood in a triangle, close together, borrowing strength from one another. "I'm scared that this is all I deserve," Kareena said, in a shaky breath.

"That's not true," Bobbi said. "Never think that."

"You deserve whatever you want," Veera added softly. "What can we do to help fix this? Do you want us to take you home? Pretend you're sick?"

"No, I have to figure this out myself," Kareena said. They pulled apart, and even though Kareena still felt shaky, it was comforting to know that her friends were right behind her.

Bobbi's phone buzzed, making all three of them jump. After she pulled it out of her bra and checked the screen, she let out a screech. "Oh my god! Why didn't anyone tell the Indian Italians that Indian IST is later than Italian IST? Loken's family is all here!" She rushed out of the ballroom.

Dadi yelped from the front entrance. "The aunties are coming, and the caterers are still setting up in the next room over! Kareena, I'm going to check the food, you stay here and tell the aunties where their table is."

Veera was still holding her hand. "I'll wait with you."

Kareena shook her head. "No, you go. I'll be fine. I'm going to be happy."

"I'm so sorry," she whispered, her eyes sparkling. "But I love you. Bobbi loves you. And your mom *loves* you. No matter what you decide for the house, you're going to be okay."

"I hope so," she whispered back.

Kareena swallowed her tears, her warring thoughts, as she stood in position.

The DJ changed the music to a basic Punjabi dhol beat and like slow motion, Kareena watched her four aunties enter side by side. Farah Aunty flipped her hair, Sonali Aunty checked the little mirror in the flap of her purse, Falguni Aunty adjusted her chunni on her shoulder, and Mona Aunty straightened the bracelets on her wrist.

Farah Aunty approached her first. "Beta! Don't you look stunning. Just like your mother."

"Well, isn't that just the nicest compliment," Kareena said as she hugged Farah Aunty back. Sonali Aunty was next, who did the customary *hello, hi, how are you.* Then Mona Aunty, who gave Kareena air kisses.

"Darling, you've gotten so good at eyeliner!" Mona Aunty said. "And to think when I taught you all those years ago, you would poke yourself in the eyeball."

"Practice does make perfect, Aunty."

Falguni Aunty squeezed her hand, her smile fading. "Are you okay, beta?"

"Of course, why wouldn't I be?"

Her smile didn't reach her eyes, but she patted Kareena's arm. "It's just something that I heard. I wanted to make sure that it was just a rumor."

"Excuse me?"

"Falguni, what rumor?" Farah Aunty asked. Her red lips pursed. "We rode here together, and you didn't say a thing."

"Mind your business, Farah. It's just a little something between me and Kareena."

Kareena had no idea what Falguni Aunty was talking about, so she just nodded her head.

Dadi came waddling back into the hall, gripping her sari pleats in one hand and her dupatta end in the other. "Oye! They're coming. Be on your best behavior!"

The front doors opened with a rush of wind. Kareena's hair flitted around her face like she was the heroine of a damn Bollywood movie, and in walked Loken's entire family led by Prem, Deepak, and Bunty all wearing custom-fit three-piece suits. Their hair was groomed, and their beards were trimmed and styled. Each of them had shoes that shone, and the crowd of Gujarati Italians behind them drooled.

Loken's entire family was beautifully dressed, and their traditional clothes glittered as everyone entered the ballroom and dispersed.

"The groom's side is here!" Farah Aunty said. She clapped her hands together.

Holy hell, Kareena was going to throw up. The aunties huddled around her as they all waited for the introductions and the greetings to begin.

Seconds before Prem and his friends reached them, Falguni Aunty spun Kareena around to face her and blurted out, "You're going to make a lovely bride and groom."

The other aunties gasped in horror.

"Beta?" Sonali Aunty said gently.

Before Kareena could respond, Dadi gripped her shoulders and pulled her close. "Beta? Are you engaged?"

"I knew I should've kept that appointment with the pandit," Sonali Aunty said. "Now you'll have to wait until after his vacation to get your janampatris reviewed!"

"Is this true?" Dadi asked quietly. She had tears in her eyes as she pressed closer to Kareena. "Is this . . . is this true?"

"Ah, we were supposed to announce it together—"

"Tell me, it's not because of the house, is it?"

Kareena's jaw dropped. Holy shit, her grandmother went in for the kill. "I mean, it would've been nicer to have time, but since the house is so important to me—"

"Chalo, no matter. As long as you're engaged."

The way her grandmother said those words had Kareena's back going rigid. "Dadi, you know better than to say something that ridiculous."

Dadi patted her hair and smiled at the guests. "I worried about you. That you'd be all alone, beta. Because you think it's easier to be alone. Your wedding is going to be lovely with Prem. Look how handsome he is."

"My wedding with Prem won't be for a while."

"What?" The aunties gasped as well.

This time Dadi spun around to face her. "This is too much, Kareena. This is too much, you're giving me a tension headache and we haven't even started yet!" She unzipped the clutch she'd tucked under one arm and pulled out the Asian Sensation vibrator, turning it to a high speed and resting the writhing sex toy against her neck. "So much tension!"

"A group of beautiful women shouldn't look so distressed . . . oh my god, is that a—"

"Dude, Grandma has a vibrator," Bunty whispered loudly.

At that moment, Kareena's father walked over with two glasses of whiskey. "Prem! Here, have a drink." He looked over at Dadi, his eyes bulging. "Ma! I told you to leave that at home!"

"It's the only thing that relieves my tension," she snapped back. "Your daughter is at fault for giving it to me in the first place!"

Kareena couldn't handle this anymore. Loken's family was staring. Her father was greeting Prem with joy. The aunties looked so unhappy for her as they waited for her reaction.

And Prem. He had a hesitant expression on his face. Bobbi and Veera had the same.

Kareena couldn't stand there anymore, faking nice, pretending everything was going to be part of a happily ever after. That wasn't real. None of this was real. It would break her heart to lose the house, but it would hurt even more to know that she'd settled for something less than she deserved. Prem couldn't love her, and even if they got engaged, they got married, and they spent the rest of their lives together, she'd be constantly wishing he did.

"I have to go," she blurted out. Then before anyone could stop her, she bolted out of the ballroom and through the double doors.

CHAPTER THIRTY

Prem

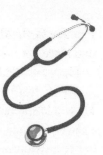

Prem barely stepped out of the way in time for Kareena to come rushing through the crowd to the lobby. She looked like a stunning goddess, the queen dressed in black, come to slay. But instead, she was trying to escape.

"Runaway dulhan," Deepak muttered. "Uncle? I'll take that whiskey."

Prem knew that something was bothering Kareena, that maybe she was having second thoughts about him, but her grand exit was definitely unexpected. He spun on his heels and strode after her. Behind him, he heard Bunty tell Kareena's father, "I think she's changed her mind."

"About what?" Kareena's father replied.

Prem caught up with Kareena just as she reached the parking lot. His hands brushed her arm, and he called her name again. "Rina, will you just stop and tell me what happened?"

She spun around, her lehenga billowing at her ankles, and the distinct sound of her payal punctuating her turn. Her eyes glittered with unshed tears.

"Do you love me?" she said.

His heart seized, and he couldn't catch his breath. His mouth moved to form her name, but nothing came out. *Yes*, he thought. *Yes, absolutely. Without question.* From the moment he saw her at

Phataka Grill. Through every conversation, every fight, every second since her birthday.

Her eyes filled with tears. "Oh god . . ."

Prem's heart pounded, thudding like a stampede in his ears. He was losing her. He could tell that he was losing her. "I'm sorry, I can't . . ."

"No, you *won't*." She wiped the tears off her cheeks, ignoring the burning and blurriness from her contacts. "I know you have the capacity to love. You loved Gori, so is it just me?"

He jerked back like she'd slapped him. "Gori and I were arranged to be married. We were compatible."

"You changed your entire life for her!" Kareena shouted. "You changed your entire life for that woman, and you think you didn't love her? That community center is in her memory!"

No. No, he didn't. She didn't understand. What he felt for Gori was special, but for Kareena? It was so much more. "Gori needed me, and I wasn't there for her—"

"Bullshit," Kareena said. "People don't spend three years raising money for a community center and dedicating their entire future to a person's memory because of guilt."

"Kareena, you can't decide how I feel about a person." If he could just take her away, whisk her far from the crowd that was forming behind them in front of the banquet hall doors. Then they could talk in private.

"I'm asking you to tell me yourself," she cried. Tears spilled down her cheeks now. She looked so beautiful, but unlike the Kareena that he . . . that he wanted. Without her glasses, and with a full face of makeup, she was ethereal, and that was unnerving on its own.

"Why can't I just show you how I feel about you?" he burst out.

His heart pounded hard and fast, and this time, he couldn't fix it. "That means so much more, doesn't it?" He gripped her shoulders, then ran his hands over her arms. "Every day. I promise you, I'll be here for you. Isn't that better than words? So many arranged marriages are built on—"

"Stop it!" Kareena pulled away from him. "You said it yourself, this has *nothing* to do with arranged marriages. Even if we were arranged, I'd expect the words. I *need* the words, because sometimes, the words are more powerful than anything you can give me or do for me. Come on, Dr. Dil. You're smart enough to know that."

"Kareena, I can't give you what you want."

The sound of her sob almost brought him to his knees.

"What the hell is going on?" A Barbie princess voice roared from behind the crowd. Kareena's family and friends parted like the Ganges to reveal a fuming Bindu. She stood frothing at the mouth. "Why isn't everyone inside for my big entrance?" she shrieked.

When she spotted Kareena, her eyes widened. "You!"

"Okay, time to go," Bobbi called out. Like a football player making his way to the goalpost, she weaved through Loken's family and rushed across the lot to Kareena. Prem was still so stunned, so scared that she'd go, he didn't realize that her friends had already planned her getaway before he could intercept.

Kareena took the small black bag from Bobbi, spun on her heels, and ran toward a Subaru crossover vehicle at the corner of the lot.

"Wait!" Prem called out, ready to run after her, when a viselike grip on his arm pulled him to a stop.

"Not so fast there, Dr. *Dick*," Bobbi said. "You know the magic words you need to say to see her again."

What the hell did this woman think he was going to do? Sit around while one of the most important people in his life got away? "She's upset."

"And you're not going to help her. Trust me when I say that you should let her have her room before you grovel."

"She ruined everything!" Bindu shrieked, interrupting their conversation.

Kareena's grandmother and father appeared to be trying to console Bindu, but nothing looked like it was working.

"Looks like Bridezilla is blaming her sister again. Excuse me, I have to fix this."

"I'm in the mood to fight," Prem muttered. He was sick and tired of this pipsqueak running rampant on Kareena's family. If he had to take care of her first before going after Kareena, he'd do that. "Bobbi, move."

"Oh boy."

Prem stormed over to where Bindu was yelling at her fiancé for not intervening.

When Bindu turned to face Prem, her expression became murderous. "*You*. You're to blame for this, too!"

"Nope, you're the only one to blame, honey. You're the one who recorded the video, who tried to monetize off your sister's pain, and then guilt-tripped her into helping with your engagement party for the last four months."

The entire crowd hushed.

"What, you think because you're spoiled, you can treat people like garbage? Your sister is twice as beautiful as you'll ever be, and she isn't a bitch."

There were gasps and *ooh*s from the crowd. Someone muttered, "That's the truth."

Bindu propped her fists on her hips. Her all-sequined outfit from bralette to lehenga skirt glittered. "If she's so great, why aren't you with her? Oh, that's right, because she tossed *you* out on your ass."

"I'm going to ask her to forgive me," Prem said. "And honestly you should, too. She's always tried to take care of you, and it's easy to use her for a punching bag because you know she's always there, but one day she may not be."

"Prem, beta, let it go," Dadi said, stepping between them. Her Hindi was soft and apologetic. "Bindu has every right to be upset. You know how Kareena is. She just can't keep her mouth closed. A trait from her mother."

"A trait I'm thankful for," Prem interjected. He threw up his hands. Were these people really that dense? "Do you still honestly believe that Kareena should always stay quiet to keep the peace, even though she's telling the truth? One of the best things about Kareena is that she doesn't let people get away with anything! Other than you three, apparently."

He whirled to face Kareena's father. "I don't get why *you* treat your daughter like shit, either. Seriously? You decide to sell the house and talk to your youngest brat and your mom, but leave out the one sensible person in your family?"

Kareena's father turned thunderous. His accent thickened as if he'd just come from India the day before instead of thirty-three years ago. "Get out! You bloody rascal, get out of this place!" He pointed a finger at the parking lot. "You can go to hell!"

Bindu started crying at that moment, and Loken looked like he had no idea what to do. The guy was a well-groomed idiot with absolutely no personality.

"Mommy?" he whispered.

Before Prem could go off on the spineless fool, Veera tugged on his sleeve.

"Time to go," she said. "Seriously, Kareena's father is Punjabi. He will punch you if you egg him on."

Prem shrugged her off. "One last thing," he said. He turned to Loken. "I hope you know what you're getting into, because when Kareena and I get married—"

Before Prem could finish the sentence, Kareena's father roared. He charged forward, and the older man swung a fist and connected with Prem's face.

> **PREM:** Kareena, I am so sorry I hurt you. You're it for me. You KNOW that.

> **KAREENA:** That's not enough. I need to know you love me.

> **PREM:** I don't want to lie to you.

> **KAREENA:** Sometimes I wish you did. Please don't text me right now. I need some time.

Thank god for her friends, Kareena thought. She sipped her venti hot chocolate in the empty shed as she looked up at her mother's house. It was awash in a soft glow from the outside lights.

Some of her tension was finally slipping away, but that could be because her best friends helped her take off all her jewelry and remove the hairpins while she sobbed in their arms. Then they waited for her while she showered and tossed the contacts, and took her to a late-night Starbucks.

Her eyes were still gritty from crying, but Kareena felt better now that she was wearing one of Prem's old sweatshirts she'd taken the last time she was over his place, paired with leggings.

It had to be one or two in the morning. She didn't know. She left her phone in the house.

"I'm so sorry, Mama," Kareena whispered. She tried so hard to hold on to the house, and she was so desperate to find love, that she forgot to protect her heart. And she'd fallen harder than she thought. If she took a deep breath, the fissures in her chest burned.

Kareena closed her eyes to the gentle summer breeze that blew through the open doors. The sound of crickets made a beautiful melody. She lay back on the seat creeper and must've dozed off, because the next minute, she heard the sound of a chair scraping against the concrete slab floor.

Kareena bolted up, barely juggling her half-empty hot chocolate cup at the same time. A dim light cast a shadow over her father's face as he lowered himself onto the chair. He still wore the suit pants and the button-down shirt from the party, except his tie was gone and his collar was unbuttoned.

"Kareena," he said running his fingers through his thinning salt-and-pepper hair. "It's late. Why aren't you sleeping inside?"

"I feel better out here," she said.

He looked around at the empty garage, taking in her tools and the discarded parts barely visible in the dim lighting. "Where is the car?"

"Body work," she mumbled. "Last weekend."

He looked startled. "Last *weekend*? Why didn't you tell me?"

Kareena took a sip from her cooling hot chocolate. "Maybe because I haven't spoken to you since before last weekend. You're always at work avoiding wedding planning, and you and I aren't exactly seeing eye to eye right now. But don't worry, once I have my car back, I'll drive right on out of here."

He watched her, flexing one hand as if he'd hurt it. "Where will you go when you can finally drive that old clunker?" he asked, completely disregarding her comment.

"I'm not sure. Probably to get some food."

The corner of his mouth curved. "Sometimes, in the summer, we'd take a drive to Taco Bell. You and your mother loved the Mexican pizzas. Bindu and I preferred the quesadillas."

Kareena didn't think she had any tears left in her, but her eyes began to water again. "Are you rubbing salt in the wound? That I'm like her and she's not here?"

"No," he said. He let out a short laugh. "The last time we went for Taco Bell, it was after we had a big fight. Your mother and I. She was so mad at me that she wanted to go back to India for a while. Just to get a break."

Kareena's jaw dropped. Her parents *never* fought. At least she didn't think they did. "I don't understand why you're telling me this."

Her father rubbed the back of his neck, then slouched back in his seat. "I think because you're old enough now to know that your mother and I didn't argue in front of you girls. We loved each other, but even we had our differences."

Kareena put the pieces together of his cryptic message. She took a sip of her Starbucks and leaned back in her chair. "Things with Prem are complicated, if that's what you're asking."

"Life is complicated," he said. He rubbed his knuckles. "He said you were getting married."

"I-I can't go through with it."

"Is it because he didn't come and meet me formally? Or because I haven't been introduced to his parents properly?"

She rolled her eyes. "And you wonder why I'm such a smart-ass," she said. "No, it's because Prem doesn't love me. Doesn't think that love is anything more than an illusion."

"But you love him?"

Kareena nodded, swallowing hard. "Enough to almost go through with the engagement."

Her father made a humming noise, as if to say *han, samajh gaya. Yes, I understand.* "This didn't have anything to do with your mother's house, did it?"

"Dadi asked that question, too." Kareena debated telling him the truth and figured there was no harm in it now. He was going to list it regardless. "At first, Prem and I talked about a fake engagement. He needed to repair his reputation to get his community center, and I needed you to give me the down payment money for the house."

Instead of an angry retort, her father chuckled. "That son of a bitch. Smart idea."

"Daddy," Kareena chided.

"What? It is. Better than what that Loken can come up with. At least your sister scares him. I never have to worry about her."

She snorted. "I wonder what they thought of me after I left?"

"That there's one in every family," her father replied. "They were fine. The party was cut short because no one was in the mood to be there. We all decided to give you space, so we stayed until everyone left, but your grandmother wouldn't let me drink any more after you left so I could drive. Bindu's mad at you for 'killing the vibe.' Those are her words."

Kareena cringed. "I'll make it up to her. When she moves out, I can help her clean her room and get the house ready to put on the market." The process would be so heartbreaking, but she was already hurting.

"If that's what you want."

"It's not, but like you've reminded me repeatedly, it's your house."

"Only if you don't want it."

Kareena sat up. "What?"

She could make out her father's crooked smile in the dark. "I've decided to hold off selling the house for another six months. It gives you time to save money to buy it from me. And if you still fall short, I'll lower the sale cost."

Kareena didn't know what to say for a full minute. She put her hot chocolate down on the shed floor because her hands began shaking.

"Why?" she whispered. "Why would you do that?"

"It's what your mother would've wanted. And what's six more months?"

Kareena looked up at the house with glowing lights accented by moonlight. She could feel the tears burning in her throat again. Oh my god. She could stay here, stay in her home like she'd always wanted. If she worked hard, she could save more than enough money for the down payment. And then it would be hers.

"You mean it?"

Her father rested a hand on her shoulder. "I loved your mother," he said quietly. "But I love you, too. I'm sorry I'm so hard on you. Take the six months, Kareena."

"Thank you, Daddy," she said with a sniffle. "I really appreciate it. I'm going to make Mom proud."

He grunted. "You already have, beta. You already have."

They sat in silence for a moment longer, with the midnight breeze rushing through the grass and the surrounding trees.

Her father finally got to his feet. He cleared his throat. "So. When am I going to meet this man's parents? Do you know his birth date, and the time he was born?"

"I appreciate the questions, Dad, but I think that ship has sailed."

"Nonsense," he said, flexing his hand again. "If he has as thick of a skull as I know he has, then he'll come around."

"I'm going to focus on other important things," Kareena said. "Like getting ready for home ownership."

Kareena stood and looped an arm through her father's. Her heart still felt broken, but at least she knew that she was handy and could work on fixing it herself. She didn't need a cardiologist after all.

CHAPTER THIRTY-TWO

Prem

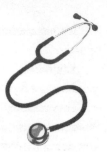

The last time someone dumped a bucket of ice-cold water on his nuts was when he was a junior in high school and about to be late for the SATs. This time, it was much, much worse.

He woke with a startling gasp and bolted off the couch. Then, because he was still in shock, he missed the empty pizza boxes, jabbed his toe against the coffee table, and fell flat on his ass in front of the TV.

"Fu—"

"Prem Verma!"

The sharp, high-pitched tone was enough for him to stop mid-expletive and jump to his feet. "Mom!"

Prem looked up to see his primly dressed mother in tan slacks and a cream-colored blouse with a small rolling suitcase at her side. In one hand was the mop bucket from his utility closet. The other hand was propped on her hip.

Her mouth thinned. "I let you come to the East Coast so you could study and be a contributing member to society. And this! This is the son I raised?"

He looked down at his soaked, stained shirt and boxers. The living room was filled with empty cartons and boxes, half-drunk beer cans and bottles. Of course, it had to be the one time that he didn't clean his condo that his mother showed up.

"It's been a long . . . er, weekend," he said. "What's with the shower?"

"You needed it," she snapped. Then dropped the bucket. "Don't you have a TV show today? Aren't you going to be late?"

"They're doing a rerun today." He rubbed his eyes, then winced when he touched the bruise on his cheekbone. "Mom, what are you doing here?"

"I came to talk to my son! And here I am, seeing that I've failed as a mother." She motioned to the living room. "What kind of a woman would want to marry a man who doesn't know how to take care of himself?"

"I can take care of myself just fine."

"I have yet to see proof," she said. "Go shower, brush your teeth, and get dressed. I'll make some breakfast."

Prem was soaked to the skin, still slightly hungover, and his head was full of thoughts of Kareena. He glanced at his disaster of a kitchen and back to his mother. "Aloo paranthas?" he asked.

She sighed, then reached into her bag and pulled out an unmarked jar of pickled mango achar. "This was hell getting through TSA. I'm assuming you have potatoes. I sent your friends to buy ginger, but if they need to get potatoes, too, tell me now."

"I have a few potatoes."

"Fine. I'll boil them. Shower. Then we'll talk."

Prem didn't need to be told twice. He hobbled across the room and into the bath. When he saw the bright purple bruise on his cheek, he winced. He was surprised that his mother didn't ask him about that first.

He got in the shower and remembered holding Kareena under the spray. He leaned against the tiled wall and let out a sigh as the memory and the scalding hot water coursed over him. God, he missed her.

He picked up his body wash and began scrubbing the sticky sweat and alcohol smell off his skin. After showering and brushing his teeth, Prem moved through his bedroom, past the bed he couldn't sleep in anymore, and walked into his closet. He put on fresh clothes, thinking how his very shirt smelled of the woman who asked for more time apart.

When he reentered the living space, his mother had rolled up her sleeves and was kneading dough at the island. What was even more surprising was that the entire place sparkled. The pizza boxes and beer bottles had been transferred to the trash. The rug looked like it was vacuumed, and all the dust and crumbs were swept off every surface in the house. The hallway closet rumbled with the sound of the washer in the background.

Prem pulled out one of the stools at the island and sat. "Thanks, Mom."

"Thanks, ka bachcha," she muttered before slamming the dough down onto the counter. "You go to an engagement party with the intention of announcing your engagement, but don't invite your parents to be there."

He winced. "You know it's complicated, Mom."

"Only idiot sons make it complicated," she said. The microwave dinged, and she pulled out a steaming container of giant potatoes. It must've been burning hot, but since his mother hasn't felt anything in her fingertips after singeing them while flipping rotis for years, she didn't blink an eye as she leisurely moved it to the sink to rinse in cold water. "If your father and I were there, you wouldn't have gotten yourself punched in the face."

"Did Bunty and Deepak tell you all this?" Prem asked.

"No, Falguni Kaushal did."

"*Who?*"

His mother made a smacking sound of impatience. "Falguni! You know, my bahu's aunty?"

"Bahu . . . wait what? Are you talking about Kareena? My Rina?"

"Do I have any other daughters-in-law?"

Prem cradled his head in his hands. His mother spoke a different language sometimes. "Mom, you have *no* daughters-in-law."

"Semantics," she said, and made quick work in peeling the hot potatoes. She dumped them in a bowl and began pulling out the Indian seasoning he kept in the back of one of the cabinets for when she visited. "Kareena has four aunties. One of them is Falguni Kaushal. That's who I talked to. She's a lovely woman."

"How did you meet one of Rina's aunties?"

"Do you remember Namrita Aunty? She had the failed Botox in her upper lip. Now she looks like she's snarling all the time. Namrita's brother-in-law has a cousin in New Jersey. I asked if he knew anyone in the Edison area who was friends with the Mann family. His sister is a Hindi teacher who taught Falguni Kaushal's kids when they were young. After speaking with his sister, and confirming the connection, I immediately called Falguni when I got her number, and we connected the dots."

Prem didn't know whether to be mortified or impressed. "You are scary women," he said.

"I'm resourceful." She seasoned the potatoes while Prem watched in silence. Garam masala. Salt. Dried mango powder. "Falguni told me everything. She even told me about Kareena's house, and how concerned they were for your engagement. Because Kareena Mann is looking for a love marriage, and my idiotic son can't see past his own big brain. You get that from your father, you know."

"Mom, I—"

She held up a hand sticky with potato chunks. "You deserve it."

"Wait, what?" That was the last thing he expected his mother to say.

She wiped her cheek with the back of her wrist and let out a huff when she transferred a smudge of flour. "You're my only baby, but you hurt my poor bahu."

"She's not your daughter-in- . . . you know what? Never mind." Prem sat in silence for a few minutes, watching his mother move around his kitchen like it was her own. She grabbed a rolling pin and began pinching golf-ball-size pieces from the dough ball she'd created. Like a pro, she stuffed the dough with potato mixture.

Kareena would love these, he thought. She would probably love his mother, too.

The problem was that she also loved him.

She loved him, past tense. How could she possibly feel something for him after the engagement party?

Prem leaned against the countertop, arms folded. "Can I ask you something?"

"What is it, my beta," she said as she put a flat tava on the front burner and added some ghee from a small container that he'd left in the back of his fridge.

His heart began pounding like when he was a kid, and he was about to have a serious discussion with his parents. "How come we don't say 'I love you'?"

She stopped flipping the parantha back and forth between her palms and stood blinking wide-eyed. "What in the world is this bakawas garbage, Prem? Why would you ask that?"

This conversation is going well, he mused. He stood from the island and went over to the corner cabinet to pull out some ibuprofen. After popping two pills and swallowing them dry, Prem leaned against his counter and faced his mother.

"Rina wants a love marriage. Bells, whistles, all of it. We have rising divorce rates, and mounting studies out there that talk about how love can actually cause heart damage. That it can be a fleeting emotion, and it's not enough to sustain a long-term relationship."

"Prem?" She said his name as if expecting him to continue, to go on.

The sticky, raw conversations were always hard to talk about with his parents even though he was lucky enough to always have their support. "You and Dad had a love marriage, didn't you?"

"Of course. We told you that. Your father's witch of a mother didn't like me. But now she's finally *dead*."

"Mom!"

She flicked a hand at him again like he was a gnat, and a small puff of flour clouded the air at the end of her fingertips. "Everyone hated her. It's fine."

"You and Dad are like polar opposites, and I don't think I've ever heard you say 'I love you' to each other. What makes you stay together? Convenience? Me? The community?"

This time, his mother flipped off the stovetop and turned a full ninety degrees to look at him. "Love! And I do say it. Every day."

Prem snorted. "No, you do not. I've never heard those words from you before. Not to Dad, not to me, not even to the extended family."

"That's because I don't say them with my mouth. I feed you your favorites, I put your Superman socks in the dryer so when you get out of the shower they're toasty warm—"

"No," he said, cutting her off for a second time. "Not actions. The words. Why haven't you ever said them?"

His mother turned back to her parantha and began rolling

out the stuffed dough. He waited, watching as her hands moved quickly, but she took the time to gather her thoughts. "Sometimes," she started quietly, "the words are hard to say, because you're so scared that something will happen to the person you care about if you say them. And the longer you go without saying them, the easier it is. Our parents never said the words, and honestly, we never did either because it was more comfortable for us to just show you."

Her words rocked Prem to his core. He moved to the closest counter stool and sat.

That was *exactly* it. His heart, bruised and sore, ached as he first thought of Gori, and how hard it was for him to survive her death. How could he possibly survive losing Kareena?

"Words are important to her," Prem finally said.

"Do you love her, my beta?" His mother added oil to the pan.

It took a moment for Prem to respond, even though he didn't have to look her in the eye to say it since she was busy at his stove. "Rina's what's been missing, what I've been waiting for. From the moment I saw her at Bunty's restaurant. It's as if my center of gravity shifted."

His mother flipped the parantha onto the skillet and wiped her hands on a dish towel she'd pulled from his drawer. "Darling, there are no guarantees in life, but if you feel love for her, don't you think she deserves to hear the truth? Communication. You're always talking about how important communication and honesty are for healthy relationships. Think of this as communicating and being honest."

Prem rubbed at his still aching head. "The words won't come out. At the engagement party, I just stood there while she cried, and I felt like the biggest asshole, Mom. All because I was so worried that if I told her, maybe it'll stop. And maybe she'd leave when it's over. Maybe all the things I've always thought were true would happen to me again. After Gori—"

"Darling, your circumstances with Gori were different. You can't compare your past with your future."

"I know, but Rina could get sick or bored and I'd be left with these words that I've said, and old memories."

"Hai bhagawan," his mother called out as she tilted her head back to look at the ceiling. "How did I raise such a scared child?"

"Gee, thanks. I'll send you my next therapy bill."

His mother ignored him. "Saying what you feel out loud doesn't stop those feelings. If anything, your love will only grow." She filled the beautifully made parantha and smiled. Her happy lines around her mouth winked at him. "I have so much love now after years of marriage. I may not say it, but I wake up every day grateful for it."

Prem sat in silence and watched as she grabbed a plate from his cabinet, put a chunk of mango pickle on the edge, a blob of butter, and then a second blob on top of the parantha still on the tava.

"You know," she started as she put the parantha on his plate, "I can't wait to meet Kareena. She must be something special. She was ready to sacrifice her feelings just to be with my son!"

"She's definitely something special." But Prem had no idea if she still felt the same way now after what he'd put her through. It was as if his mother had flipped on a light switch, and the idea of loving someone felt so much more comfortable than it did before.

Prem's mother slid the plate in front of him, and he smelled the delicious spiced potatoes, the tart mango pickle, and the richness of the butter.

"Hey, Mom?"

"Hmm?"

"I love you."

He saw her flush. "I love you, too. Now what are you going to do with my bahu?"

"If you keep calling her daughter-in-law, you're going to jinx me. Right now, I have to convince her to hear me out."

"Are you ready to plan a wedding and move to the suburbs?" his mother asked.

"Yes." The word was out of his mouth before he could stop and think about it. Yes. There was no one else who made him feel, that made him want that kind of future, like Kareena.

The front door burst open, and Deepak and Bunty barreled in carrying paper bags filled with what looked like vegetables. "We found a farmers' market," Bunty said, shaking one of the bags. He had the biggest grin on his face. "The veggies in season were *superb*."

"Ooh, is that parantha?" Deepak asked. He crossed the room and pulled out the stool next to Prem. "Aunty, can I have one?"

"Of course, beta. Bunty? Do you want one?"

"Yes, Aunty. Thank you. I'll start the chai."

"What a good boy," Prem's mother said to Prem's six-foot-five friend who towered over everyone in the room.

"How's the head?" Deepak asked Prem.

"Better. I love Kareena."

Both Deepak and Bunty paused.

"What did you just say?" Bunty asked. He held a hunk of ginger in one hand.

Prem grinned at his friends. "I love Kareena. I mean, I've always loved her, but now I'm okay with saying the words. I can even say them in front of my mother. Wow. It gets a lot easier now that I've repeated it a few times. Like all I had to do was— Ouch!"

Deepak slapped him upside the head. "That's for ignoring your two best friends," he said. "You seriously waited for your mom to give you permission to love a woman?"

"What? No, of course not."

"Dude, we're trying to break the desi mama's boy stereotype," Bunty said, shaking his head. "You're not helping us out."

"He'll learn," Prem's mother said with a smile. She held a plate stacked with three paranthas ready to go. "Now, who's first?"

CHAPTER THIRTY-THREE

Kareena

NOTIFICATIONS:

Your subscription for Indian Dating has been canceled.

Your subscription for American Desi Matrimony has been canceled.

Your subscription to Desi Seniors Dating for 25 and Older Singles has been cancelled.

Kareena tucked her phone back in her pocket when her rental car pulled onto her street.

"Just park right in front?"

"Yes, please," she said.

Her house. Well, almost. She'd woken up every day that week, still bruised from her interaction with Prem, but acknowledging the silver lining.

She'd have her home, even though it would be devoid of the love she'd always wanted there. But she could survive. She would survive.

"Whoa," she heard her driver say reverently. "Is that a BMW E30 M3?"

"What did you say?" Kareena jerked forward until she was practically in the front of the car with him. There, through the front windshield, was her beautiful shiny new baby with a fantastic paint job, new tires, rims, the works. "Oh my god!"

She bolted out of the car and ran in her heels, her feet sliding from being so sweaty in the late summer heat. "It's my Beamer!" Kareena shrieked. She vaguely heard the car service vehicle peel away from the curb behind her. Her entire focus was on the classic BMW parked in front of her home.

Dave, her crusty, middle-aged mechanic, climbed out of the driver's seat. He had clean clothes on for the first time since she'd met him years ago, and held up a set of keys. "She's done!" he proclaimed proudly.

Kareena ran her hands over the rear of the small sedan, tears pouring down her cheeks in earnest now. It was finally here. The vehicle she'd been working on for years. "I thought I was supposed to come to you! I have to pay for all the work." She'd been worried about that, because the bill was going to take a huge chunk out of what she was hoping to use as a down payment to her father.

"The bill has been taken care of," he said, grinning.

"Oh, Dave. You can't comp me—"

He snorted then let out a wheezing laugh. "Girl, I love this car, but I ain't stupid. Rims, custom paint, all that body work was a fortune!" He named a figure that was thousands higher than what she anticipated paying. "Your boyfriend paid for it."

Her brain stopped and stuttered like a Microsoft application. She brushed away her tears under her glasses. "I'm sorry, what?"

"Your boyfriend!" He reached in the driver's seat and pulled out an envelope with a stack of papers inside. "Here is your repair and restoration records. On the top is the invoice. A man named Dr. Prem Verma called. Said that you'd mentioned that you gave us your car to work on. He paid for everything, including a rush fee and a delivery fee."

Kareena took the envelope, then opened it to see the invoice on top.

Oh my god, Prem paid thousands for her car.

Was this a way to apologize to appease his guilty conscience? She had no idea what it meant, and she wasn't even sure she wanted to text him to ask.

"Thanks, Dave. I really appreciate it."

"Thank *you*. If you need a repair job, let us know. But I think you can handle most of it yourself. You did a bang-up job on restoring what you did."

"Really?"

He nodded. "I can always tell when beauties like this are going to be in good hands." He patted the hood of the car. "You're going to be okay."

She smiled. "Yeah," she said. "I'm going to be okay."

A massive Tacoma roared down the road toward them and stopped right in front of Kareena and Dave.

"That's my ride," Dave said, and pulled open the passenger-side door.

"Thank you again. Seriously, this is the best present ever." She had her car now. She felt like her possibilities had to be endless.

"No problem," Dave replied. He hauled himself up into the truck. "Oh! I forgot. Your boyfriend asked me to include a document in the back of that folder. You may want to check it out when you get a chance."

"Oh, okay. Thanks."

Dave waved, and Kareena turned back to her car. In the bright light of the early evening sun, it sparkled. The interior leather looked polished and new. It even had the new car smell again.

The simple dashboard was clean, and the only upgrade was a music system that allowed her to connect to Bluetooth on her phone.

Kareena looked up at the house, at her grandmother's car in the driveway, then down at her car. She then opened the envelope and flipped to the back where there was a journal article from the *Cardiology Journal of America* called "The Illusions of the Heart and Misconceptions of Love."

"Prem," she said with a sigh. She was about to toss the article when a highlighted line drew her attention to the second page.

"The physical pain we feel from loss, the damaging effects on the heart, may be linked to an illusion that we call love, but that doesn't make love any less real. Regardless of how the subjects find each other, whether through a cultural practice such as arranged marriages, or through childhood friendship turned life partners, studies show that feelings of love can grow stronger and affect other parts of the brain as well."

She stared at the line for a long moment, rereading it a dozen times over.

"Damn," she whispered. This man played dirty.

She began to tuck the documents back in the envelope when a small slip of paper fell out. She turned it over to read the simple block letters on the front.

I'm sorry I couldn't say the words. But I'll tell you them as often as you want to hear them if you'll let me be in your life. This is my grand gesture. Does it work for you?

Kareena began to sniffle. She took the note and tucked it into her bag next to her mother's note she'd found in the kitchen. After inspecting her beautiful pride and joy, she got in behind the wheel. She'd have to examine the buttery leather seats, the beautiful trim, and the finishing work under the hood some other time. Right now, she had to come up with a game plan. Prem could've brought the note to her himself, but he'd always made the first move. He was letting her decide now, and she had to respect him for that.

She had to go see Bobbi and Veera. Her besties would know exactly what to do.

And maybe she'd pick up some Taco Bell along the way.

Kareena turned the keys in the ignition, and the purr of the engine boosted her spirits. It was time to secure her happily ever after.

CHAPTER THIRTY-FOUR

Prem

Prem checked his phone again for missed messages. Nothing. Dave at the mechanic's shop said that she'd gotten her car, but Kareena still hadn't reached out.

Was he too late?

"Prem?" his producer said from the other side of his dressing room door. "You have a full audience today. You ready?"

"Yeah, coming."

He straightened his jacket, glanced in the mirror to smooth his hair, and went to do his last *Dr. Dil Show*. The set was decorated with marigolds and twinkle lights like an Indian wedding. Sometimes Prem forgot that his channel was on a South Asian TV network, and they would do things like hang garlands and lights on the stage backdrop.

His producer gave him the one-minute warning, and he positioned himself at stage left, mentally running through his notes.

"I hope you're watching, Rina," he murmured.

The lights went up, his producer called his name, and he stepped out into the spotlight. He straightened his cuff link and took a deep breath.

"Hello everyone, and welcome to *The Dr. Dil Show!*"

There were cheers, and clapping, and most importantly, there were a lot of people. The entire studio seemed to be so packed that Prem was barely able to make out individual faces in the crowd.

And they were all here to see the series finale. Or watch him eat his words.

He started with his tagline. *Holistic health of the heart, my ass*, he thought.

"Now before we begin, I wanted to start with some bittersweet news. I have been doing *The Dr. Dil Show* for a few years now, and it has been absolutely incredible. I started it after the death of my fiancée as a way to raise awareness—and frankly, attention—from investors for a community health center I wanted to build right here in Jersey City. Well, that dream is finally coming to fruition. Thanks to a few amazing investors, we have secured a location downtown that will be dedicated to supporting the South Asian immigrant populations in the tristate area."

The crowd cheered and clapped appropriately.

"Unfortunately, that also means that today is my last show."

Pin-drop silence.

"Going forward, I will be focusing on patients and building my community health practice. I appreciate all of you who have followed along over the years, and who have written to the show about parents, family members, and your own health. It makes every moment I'm here on the stage worthwhile."

The studio audience cheered. This time the noise was a roar, and as the sound washed over him, Prem looked up and smiled.

Thanks, Gori.

When the clapping slowed, Prem continued. "As my final show, I wanted it to be special, but I didn't know how much. I have my boss, the chief of the Jersey City Cardiology Center, here to talk about how you can finish the year taking care of your most important body part. I have Swami Talish here to discuss how we can stay focused in the present through meditation."

He looked out at all the expectant faces, all the aunties at the edge of their seat so invested in his love life, as if the key to his happiness was a key to their joy, too.

"But now, an update on my personal life."

The sound guys rolled the music, the lights flashed, and the audience laughed.

"Four months ago, Kareena Mann, a successful attorney and member of the South Asian community here in New Jersey, came on my show and, quite frankly, put me in my place. She, like so many South Asian women, was faced with a daily reminder of her single status. Although we've progressed as a community, there are still so many families that set a ridiculous level of importance on single women getting married and starting a family."

He pressed a hand to his heart.

"I was part of that problem. By invalidating the feelings of women in our society, by removing the emotional connection aspect from matchmaking as a consideration, I was hurting rather than helping people like Kareena."

He took a deep breath. "We began spending time together, and four months later, I asked her to marry me. Kareena taught me that all the science, the studies, the facts about heart health are only part of the story. Relationships and South Asian marriages are so much more complicated. The communication aspect, the trust and honesty that couples need to share with each other. That's all true, but that's not all. And that's when I realized that I love her. And love may be terrible for heart health sometimes, but the absence of it can be just as bad."

The audience gasped. An aunty in the front row whispered, "Ae kii kenda eh?" *What did he say?*

Prem's palms began sweating.

"I can't believe that after all these months, you still can't just come out and say that you're wrong and I was right," a voice said.

People gasped in the audience, and Prem whirled to see Kareena step out from behind the stage backdrop. She looked . . . perfect. She wore her lucky black sweater vest with a puffy capped sleeve shirt underneath. Her hair hung around her shoulders in loose waves. He immediately focused in on her shoes, though. Her heels were a vibrant magenta with peonies painted along the slides. And she was wearing his favorite payal.

"Why is it always about trying to make a point, Dr. Dil?" Kareena said. The corner of her mouth twitched.

At the signal from his producer, Prem cleared his throat and motioned for Kareena to join him at center stage. "Ladies and gentlemen, Kareena Mann."

When the audience clapped and cheered, he leaned in to whisper, "What are you doing?"

"I wanted to tell you that . . . I, ah . . ."

"She loves you!" The crowd yelled in unison.

Hell. She was miked.

"You love me?" he said.

She blushed, her cheeks deepening in a golden glow. "I love you. You're the one, Prem Verma. Did you honestly think you'd be able to pull off this grand gesture without me?"

"I never doubted you for a moment," he said.

They stood staring at each other, the audience straining forward in their seats to listen.

"Well, that was fun. Now that it's over, I should probably sit down." Her fingers trembled in his, and she kept glancing over at the nameless faces watching them intently.

"Kareena, wait." He squeezed her hands. "I'm so sorry I was an ass."

"It happens."

He laughed, then blurted out before he could stop himself. "Marry me. For real, for real."

"Wait, what?"

Riding the high of seeing her for the first time in a week, from knowing that she still loved him, and they still had a chance at her Taylor Swift happily-ever-after love story, Prem dropped to his knee, and blood rushed to his head, drowning out the sound of his beating heart. All he could see was Kareena's face. "Kareena Mann, will you marry me?"

"I mean, we were going to for the house and stuff—"

"Kareena—"

"Four months isn't that long, you know. We could—"

"Will you just answer the damn question?"

"Fine, yes!"

It was like someone had counted down to New Year's. The entire studio exploded with cheers, whistling, and applause again. The audio technician played music, and Prem's producers tossed files in the air like graduation hats. Everyone was on their feet applauding.

Prem stood and covered his lapel mic. "Do you mean it?"

Kareena did the same to hers. "I . . . I do."

"I swear, I just wanted to be with you, and Rina, I totally screwed it up—"

"Just a warning, your penance is coming. You still have to ask my dad for permission and we have to compare our star charts, apparently."

"Noted," he said. He linked his fingers with hers and leaned close to her mouth. "Hey."

"Yeah?"

"I'm going to love you for as long as I live. That sounds cheesy as hell, but I promise you, it's going to happen."

"I'm going to love you, too," she said.

Prem stepped back when his producer rushed onstage with a microphone and shoved it in Kareena's hands.

"Oh, uh. Okay," she said. "I mean, people usually buy me dinner first."

The teleprompter flashed "QUESTIONS FROM THE AUDIENCE."

Prem glanced at Kareena who gave an imperceptible nod. "We have time for a couple questions before we break and bring on our first guest. Our film crew will come around to raised hands and pass the mic."

Prem's jaw dropped when the entire studio audience raised their hands.

What's worse, the mic went to a familiar woman in the front first.

"Is that your—"

"My aunties?" Kareena whispered back. "Yup."

There, in the front row sat Kareena's grandmother, Farah Aunty, Mona Aunty, Sonali Aunty, and Falguni Aunty. Falguni Aunty was the one on her feet motioning to the mic in her hands.

"Hi, Prem. Falguni Aunty," she said. "I would like to know, where are you having your wedding?"

"Aunty," Kareena hissed. "You promised you'd *behave* if I brought you."

"I'm not sure," Prem responded, then reached out and squeezed Kareena's hand. "But it won't be in four months. I think we're done working with deadlines. We'll take another question. Yes, you in the back."

A woman wearing a bright orange sari, and a long braid draped over one shoulder practically shouted in the mike. "Hello, yes, Chitra from Jackson Heights. I also would like to know when you are getting married and if you will be filming it? And Kareena, is it? Darling, wearing black is a bad omen for someone of your age. In Mrs. W. S. Gupta's last article, she even said so. You should read it."

"Oh boy," Prem murmured.

"Hi, Aunty," Kareena said sweetly. "How about we take a moment to unpack that? Starting with how Mrs. W. S. Gupta is a troublemaking creeper."

CHAPTER THIRTY-FIVE

Kareena

Aunty WhatsApp Group

FARAH AUNTY: Darling, thank you so much for taking us today. We had such a good time. Congratulations!

FALGUNI AUNTY: You really put that Chitra in her place. Good for you.

MONA AUNTY: Prem looked so happy. We found you the best match.

SONALI AUNTY: And thank you for taking us to Taco Bell! Your mother loved that car, and some of our favorite memories with her are going to Taco Bell.

BINDU: Hey.

BINDU: I'm sorry I've been a bitch.

BINDU: I saw the show. I hope you guys are happy. Prem is a good person.

DADDY: Beta, I'm glad you finally saw things my way and you're back together with Prem. I received a call from his parents. We're talking about the house.

DADDY: Your mother would be happy for you.

DADI: THIS IS YOUR DADI.

DADI: BRING PREM FOR DINNER.

"I can't believe you brought all the aunties," Prem said. "Seriously, you knew they were going to ask questions."

Kareena slurped her soda and then shoved it back into the makeshift cup holder that was definitely not designed for Taco Bell drinks.

"They wanted to go for a ride in the car," Kareena said. "I forgot how they had memories with it, too. My mother would drive them all around, packed in this tiny thing. I was getting ready to leave for your show when they arrived at the house for a wedding-planning-related thing. They all got in my car instead."

"Do you want me to hold that for you again?" Prem asked when he saw her struggling with the cup holder.

"No, you held it the entire drive up here."

The man had been a trooper. He didn't complain when she asked to go to Taco Bell and handled her drink to Washington State Park, where they stopped at a lookout point.

Kareena sighed as she admired the newly restored interior of her BMW again. The drink holder situation wasn't ideal, but man, did her car look good.

The night sky was clear, and the air was warm enough to roll the windows down. Prem crushed his chalupa wrapper and tucked it back into the bag at his feet. He turned to her, his knees hitting the glove compartment in front of him. "You know? I didn't think this car would be so . . . tiny."

"It's built for speed, and it's perfect," Kareena said. She scowled at him. "Have some respect for my vehicle."

Prem took her empty box as well, and after she finished wiping her hands on the napkin, he took it from her and linked her fingers with his.

Prem squeezed her hand. "Can I ask you something?"

Kareena nodded.

"Has it sunk in yet for you that I dropped to one knee and proposed on live television?"

She snorted. "No, not at all." They were planning on going ring shopping in a few days. Even though they'd only known each other for four months, Prem knew that she'd want to pick something out on her own. Maybe when they found the right ring, it would seem more real. The idea of having a real symbol of their commitment together was more and more exciting the longer Kareena thought about it.

"It hasn't sunk in for me, either." Prem cleared his throat. "I know we haven't talked about a wedding date, but I'm assuming your sister is going to kill you if you set the wedding any time close to her event. Which means we're not getting married for a while. I want to be with you, though. In your space. Is your dad still postponing his retirement until you buy the house from him?"

"I think so. But don't worry, the time will be here before you know it."

"Not nearly fast enough," Prem said. "I'm ready. I want more.

With you. With us. More dates. More trips to the shore. More scrambled eggs with chaat masala in the mornings. The sooner the better."

He pressed a kiss against the corner of Kareena's mouth. She shifted until their lips met. She tasted hot sauce and Prem and cupped his stubbly cheek. *This is perfect*, she thought. *This was worth waiting for.*

When they pulled apart, Kareena swiped a thumb over her bottom lip and enjoyed watching Prem's eyes narrow on the gesture.

"For now, are you coming home with me?" he asked.

"I'd like that."

He leaned in to kiss her again, but Kareena's phone buzzed in the car mount. Her sister's name flashed across the screen.

"I'll get it later," she said. "She is probably calling to make sure I got her apology text."

Kareena pulled Prem back in for another kiss, but her phone began ringing again.

Prem sighed. "You might as well pick it up."

She groaned but answered the phone. "Bindu? What's up?"

"Kareena? Listen, I need a favor." She sounded like she was in the middle of a crowd. The dull echo of an overhead speaker buzzed faintly in the background.

"Where are you?"

"The airport."

"What? Where are you going?"

Bindu let out a giggle. "Loken and I are eloping! We're headed to Vegas. We don't have classes until next week, so we're just going to go, get married, and be done with it!"

"Oh my god, Dadi is going to kill you." Just the thought of her grandmother finding out that one of her granddaughters got married without family around was like envisioning a bomb deto-nating. And that bomb was dangerous.

"About that," Bindu said. "Can you cover?"

"Bindu, how the hell am I supposed to cover your *elopement*? Dadi is going to be on the first plane out, where she'll find you and drag you by your hair down the Las Vegas strip back to the airport, and back to New Jersey!" The very thought of Bindu for-going the entire wedding that she'd been planning for months was the most outrageous thing that her sister could do.

"Just make something up, okay? Oh! They started boarding. Love you, Didi."

"Bindu, wait—"

Kareena heard the click of her sister hanging up the phone and pulled her cell away from her ear to look at the blank screen. "Damn it. She put me in a position, again."

"Who says you have to help her out?" Prem asked. He was sip-ping from her drink. "You can always just tell Dadi where your sister is when she asks. Let Bindu figure it out later."

Her gut reaction was to disagree with him. Of course, she'd cover for her sister. But then again, even though they'd made up after her engagement party, Bindu didn't seem like she had changed all that much.

"You know what?" Kareena said. "You're right. Why am I wor-ried about it? Bindu's life, Bindu's problem."

Prem leaned across the center console and began nibbling on her jaw. "We'll deal with it in the morning."

"We?"

Prem cupped the back of her neck and squeezed ever so gently. "We're a team, Rina, honey. We have been from the start, but it just took us a bit of time to figure things out. Now we have a lifetime together."

EPILOGUE

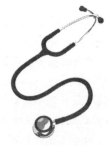

Indians Abroad News

Dear Readers,

I, as I'm sure all of you are, am keeping up with the fascinating love story between Dr. Dil, or Dr. Prem Verma, and Ms. Kareena Mann that began on the South Asians News Network during *The Dr. Dil Show*. The couple has announced their engagement, and I for one am incredibly happy for them. Their story teaches an important lesson. It's better to take a chance on a match once in your life than never experience partnership at all. Because never can be too late.

Mrs. W. S. Gupta
Columnist
Avon, NJ

PREM & RINA'S TAYLOR SWIFT PLAYLIST

1. 22
2. Look What You Made Me Do
3. Blank Space
4. Delicate
5. I Knew You Were Trouble
6. New Romantics
7. Don't Blame Me
8. I Know Places
9. Willow
10. Call It What You Want
11. Wildest Dreams
12. Cruel Summer
13. State of Grace
14. Cardigan
15. You Belong With Me

ACKNOWLEDGMENTS

When I first conceived of the idea to write Shakespeare-inspired romances, I wanted to use Shakespeare's plays as a vehicle to focus on the nuance in my American desi culture. What does arranged marriage mean to desis versus non-desis? Why are people my age embarrassed to talk about successful arranged marriages? And why is dating as an educated older South Asian woman STILL so difficult? As you can see, this is a tall order, and I honestly don't know if I tackled it all in this one book, but I did learn something about myself.

That we all deserve the love we want.

This revelation would not have happened without the support I received from my agent, Joy Tutela at David Black Literary. I also have to thank the woman who has my back even though I'm a hot mess when she has to support me, Elle Keck. Your friendship means the world. Thank you also to the production team who worked so hard to get this book out on time! You have my eternal gratitude, Shelby Peak, Rachel Meyers, and Robin Barletta!

Thank you to my family, specifically to my sister Shikha Sharma, who always fights for me, even when I struggle to fight for myself. To my baby brother, Shiv Sharma, for buying my books even though the idea of his oldest sister writing romance weirds him out. To my friends Tracey Sumler and Smita Kurrumchand, who are always my hype girls. Thank you for literally listening to me reading this out loud to you and telling me that it's not boring.

Thank you to my early readers, Tracey Livesey, Joanna Shupe, Dee Ernst, Megan Bannen, Nam Patel, and Andie Christopher. You all helped me get to the finish line! Thank you to my early morning writers crew that held me accountable, including Adriana Herrera and Alexis Daria. Thank you to Sierra Simone, whose advice about Shakespeare pulling punches was my guiding light throughout this entire novel.

I'm so glad I found my South Asian romance writers group. I love all of you so much, but I need to mention the ones that helped get me through this book. To Alisha Rai, Sona Charaipotra, and Falguni Kothari, thank you for letting me rant, or cry, or just sit in silence. More importantly, thank you for understanding me in ways that so few people have been able to.

And thanks to girl gang behind the *Fated Mates* podcast, Jen Prokop and Sarah MacLean, for releasing an episode (S03.27, 33:33) when I was a month into writing this book. I'm humbled that you had so much faith in me to say the words, "[*The Taming of the Shrew*] is not a great model for a modern romance, right? And I want to call out Nisha Sharma's doing it right now. Her book *Dating Dr. Dil* is coming out . . . and I trust Nisha implicitly to pull this off, but I think it takes chops." Jen and Sarah, you inspired me to write the best I could, and I'm forever grateful.

ABOUT THE AUTHOR

NISHA SHARMA is the award-winning author of YA and contemporary romance. She grew up immersed in Bollywood movies, eighties pop culture, and romance novels, so it comes as no surprise that her work features all three. She lives in Pennsylvania with her Alaskan-born husband; her cat, Lizzie Bennett; and her dog, Nancey Drew.

The aunties will return when Bobbi and Benjamin
discover there is too much ado about love

Winter 2023